I0778467

WONDERS IN THE DEEP
by
Columba Booth

Christian Fiction
Women's Contemporary

ISBN: 978-1-962168-32-8

Dedication

To Paul. Without your love, encouragement, and beef stroganoff, I could never have written this book. I love you!

Acknowledgements

Writing my first novel would not have happened without support.

Thank you, Cynthia, owner of Winged Publications, for taking a chance on a new writer and for the beautiful cover design. And thanks, Diane Tatum, for saving my author reputation before it began, with your pristine edits!

The amount of research a novel demands astonished me. Thank you, Dr. Richard Cherlin, for taking the time to help me understand the complexities of type 1 diabetes, healthcare software, and the challenges and rewards of a career in endocrinology. And thank you for answering the call to serve patients in their lifelong struggle with type 1 diabetes. You and your colleagues are heroes.

Thank you, John Tracy, for sharing the dramatic details of how law enforcement might handle a kidnapping in Henry Cowell State Park—and for encouraging me to write!

Greg Ayotte, your input about traumatic brain injuries was sobering, allowing me to grasp a little of what patients must endure. In the tragedy of brain injury, people like you are a bright light. I hope some of your light is reflected in these pages. Thank you!

Bob and Christine, it can't have been easy to relive your TBI journey as you shared it with me. I am indebted to you for what I hope is a realistic portrayal of my brain-injured character's challenges. Thank you!

Thank you, David Akers, for your insights about medical products that make life with type 1 diabetes easier. Your positive focus and strength provided inspiration that I hope comes through in my story.

Jim Brown, thank you for your knowledgeable answers to my questions about personal injury law in California. Meeting you at the American Christian Fiction Writers Conference was a godsend!

Thanks, Mom and Dad, for all your love and support through the years. The grace evident through your lives is a solid foundation for our family.

Elliot and Danielle, Caleb, and Rosie: Parents can't express all their love for their children. It's just too big. You are my inspiration and my precious gems. When type 1 diabetes crashed into our family, your courage and love amazed me. I'm so proud to be your mom.

To Jen and Cody, Andrew and Denielle, Daniel, Melissa and Ryan, and Emily and Kama: Thank you for sharing your amazing father/father-in-law with me, and for accepting me so graciously into your lives.

Paul, my hero and the love of my life, I could not have written this book without your support and encouragement. You changed the whole picture for me, and you still rock my world, every day.

Most of all, I am grateful to the Lord Jesus Christ for paying for my sins, and to God the Father, for adopting me into His eternal Kingdom. I could never thank You enough for forgiveness of sins, redemption, and the free, undeserved gift of salvation.

CHAPTER ONE

Dodging traffic and crossing Plaza de Cesar Chavez to Legally Fit Gym took two minutes and thirty-eight seconds—twenty seconds if Audrey jogged. She jogged, gym bag swinging, eyes fixed on the gym doors. She had to get her bench presses in before one o'clock.

Yesterday was legs day. Today was upper body—which, if omitted, would mess everything up. She had upheld her fitness goals all year. She was not deviating in September. Today's short workout would allow time for a quick shower and a protein shake. Back at her desk, she would prepare for her two o'clock expert witness meeting.

San Jose's residential towers gleamed in the afternoon sun, shadowing the downtown's historic buildings. Audrey glanced at her phone as she closed the last feet to the gym. There was no margin. She slammed through the doors and rushed to the locker room. Soon, a buddy serving as spotter gripped the barbell she held above her head.

"Ready?" CJ had paused his workout to assist her with a milestone bench press. Sweat spiked his hair.

She nodded, the padded bench secure under her back. *Please don't drip sweat on my face.*

CJ released the bar, stepping back from her sightline. Audrey began the descent, her muscles holding the weight like ocean waters supporting a ship.

Think through the move. She stopped the bar just above

her chest, then pushed up, exhaling. The weight ascended. *It's on a pulley. I've got this.* She flattened her lower back into the bench, curled her toes, and kept pressing. Her arms straightened. One rep.

Keep it moving. Again, she lowered the bar to her chest. Down, slow, steady—until she stopped at chest level and pressed up again. Two reps.

Three.

Four—slower, but still in control.

Ending her fifth rep, she locked her elbows.

"Take!" she gasped.

CJ grabbed the bar and helped her reload it onto the rack.

Audrey whooped and sprang up, standing tall to match CJ's compact height. Success, in what she privately called the gym's Club of Brothers, thrilled her.

CJ slapped her on the back. "A hundred pounds!"

She steadied herself—CJ had almost knocked her off-balance—and turned, swiping her short hair with a small towel. Other gym members chimed in.

"Great job!" Steve was general counsel at a big tech firm.

"Congrats, Audrey!" That was Kevin, a tax attorney.

Roger Pine, estate planner, nodded approval.

She high-fived CJ. "Leg day tomorrow, guys!" Her dad would have been proud—if he'd stayed around.

Legally Fit Gym attracted legal professionals from around the Bay Area. It was perfect for networking. The predominantly male clientele minimized female drama, and Audrey had even met Frank Spade of Spade, Lau, & Coleman, LLP, California's biggest personal injury firm. She kept Spade's card in her desk. Maybe someday she'd apply.

Quickly, she finished her workout, showered, and dressed. Her phone rang.

"Hey, Patrick." She slung her gym bag onto the counter and stuffed her sweaty clothes inside. Patrick was the sole non-equity partner at Tate Personal Injury. Suzanne, the receptionist, was at lunch.

"Your expert witness is here. Name's McKenzie."

"He's an hour early!"

"Well, you better get back here." Patrick laughed.

"I'll be right there. Thanks." Heart pounding, she hoisted her bag over her shoulder, lurched through the front door, and hurried back to the office tower. "Who shows up an hour early?" she muttered, punching the elevator button. "Rude!"

The law firm door clicked shut behind Audrey, and Dr. McKenzie turned from the window to face her. In his early forties, he stood tall, hands in pockets. He was casually dressed, with pleasantly weathered skin. His wideset eyes, friendly and creased at the edges, invited trust.

"Audrey, so nice to meet you at last!" His powerful handshake slightly crushed Audrey's small hand.

"You, too!" Audrey pumped his hand, enthusiastically.

He smiled, showing white, even teeth. "My apologies for being early. Traffic from the airport was lighter than I expected."

"Oh, no worries, Dr. McKenzie!" She stuffed her irritation because it was important to start this relationship on a positive note. "Let's chat in my office."

She led the way past Patrick's office. Her colleague swiveled comfortably in his chair. A pen from his expensive collection flashed in his fingers as he waved.

They passed the corner suite, which belonged to the firm's founder, Alex Tate. While she waited to make partner, she was handling the suits Patrick and Tate didn't want, alongside Meghan's med mal case. She opened the door to her cramped room, which was jammed between the reception area and the small legal library. At least it had a window.

Above the worn credenza hung her California Bar Association admission certificate and JD degree. The documents were seven years old, but she still got a jolt when she looked at them. Chairs and a nineteen eighties-era desk completed the room's furnishings. On the desk sat a framed photo of her brother with his wife and children.

Ex-wife. Wherever she was.

"Have a seat." She indicated the guest chair across her desk.

Dr. McKenzie sat and leaned back, resting his elbows on the chair's arms.

"I appreciate you stopping by. I know it's out of your way." Audrey turned to her credenza and poured chilled water into a glass.

"Nah." Dr. McKenzie waved a hand. "I'm here for other business. I like to meet the attorneys I work for in person." He took the glass from Audrey. "It's warm today."

She poured herself a glass and sat.

"You sound like you're from the south," observed McKenzie. "Been here long?"

"Texas. I came out for school. How's the case review going?"

McKenzie sipped the water. He put the glass on Audrey's desk and leaned onto one arm of the chair. "Dr. Taylor is guilty of negligence, in my opinion. And we can prove it."

"Even though the software—"

"The medical records software is problematic, yes." Dr. McKenzie put on reading glasses and swiped his phone. "Let's review your initial email." He began to read.

"'The patient, Meghan Patel, suffered a low blood glucose when she was hospitalized with a stomach bug, in April of this year. The defendant, Dr. Eric Taylor, endocrinologist, made an insulin dosage error. Dr. Taylor ordered an NPO, indicating no food. Patel was throwing up.

"'Dr. Taylor neglected to verify her food and insulin intake. Before arriving at the hospital, she had taken insulin for a meal she never ate. The doctor entered into the software the carbs she should have eaten to use up that insulin. But it looks like he never verified with the patient whether or not she actually consumed those carbs. We know that she did not. She was too nauseous.

"'The NewDay medical records software includes a verification warning to check carb consumption and insulin doses, but Dr. Taylor just checked the box. Therefore, the software didn't calculate that Meghan had eaten no carbs to use up the earlier dose. Presumably, Dr. Taylor was in a hurry.'" He looked up. "Presumably, he's arrogant," he added, snidely.

Audrey nodded.

"'During her resulting episode of hypoglycemia, she fell and sustained a subdural hematoma (basically, a traumatic brain injury). She required a craniectomy and three months of inpatient rehabilitation, followed by outpatient rehab. Her prognosis is positive, but everyone responds differently to a brain injury. We're suing Dr. Taylor for pain and suffering, as well as medical expenses.'" Dr. McKenzie removed his glasses. "Straightforward enough."

"Yes, but opposing counsel will blame NewDay's health records software for the doctor's carelessness. How will you address that?"

"She'll blame the software." He dipped his head. "The doctor did everything right, it was a system weakness, blah, blah, blah." He scrunched his brow and dangled the glasses. "That software is notoriously confusing. But doctors can't make that excuse. And they must always double check their doses." He raised one palm and tilted his head, as if they'd already won the case.

Dr. McKenzie's demeanor boosted Audrey's confidence—a factor that had compelled her to hire him in April, before filing the suit. Even via Facetime, it was clear he could influence a jury's opinion, should the case go to trial.

He studied his phone. "Ah! Meghan's records." He scanned for a few moments, then glanced at Audrey. "An

NPO, she's throwing up, and her regular background insulin via IV, with a full meal's dose on board and no carbs." He laughed. "You can't make this up!"

Audrey frowned. It wasn't funny.

Dr. McKenzie polished his glasses on his pant leg. He drew a deep breath and blew it out slowly, reviewing the document. "Patient could have died. Taylor should have slowed down and checked his notes."

~

After Dr. McKenzie left, Audrey stuffed Meghan's file into her briefcase and left to visit her client. She checked her calendar and texted her brother as she closed her office door. "Hey Luke, I'm coming for dinner Friday. Did you remember? It's been a while."

Minutes later, she got into her Tesla and read his reply.

"Looking 4ward get takeout i'm pay u bak"

She smiled. Luke never had been a fan of grammar. She steered the Tesla through the downtown area and took Interstate 280 towards Highway 17. In her rearview mirror, Silicon Valley's eastern foothills lay in baking curves, seamed with California oaks and edged by residential neighborhoods. Ahead loomed the forested Los Gatos mountains—dovetailed ridges, bristling with redwoods and firs.

Meghan's mom, Beverly, had served with Audrey in a church ministry fourteen years prior, when Audrey and her brother had arrived at the University of California, Santa Cruz. Audrey hadn't heard from Beverly since Audrey had graduated—until the lawsuit.

She navigated the winding mountain roads and pulled onto the dirt driveway that fronted the Patels' white farmhouse. The wide, level property stood in a clearing among towering trees. The bushy branches of several California oaks clustered around the home's roof and window dormers.

Beverly opened the front door and welcomed her in. The

home was cozy, and photographs on the walls showed a happy family—seventeen-year-old Meghan, Beverly, and tech VP Anish Patel, the square-jawed Indian man who was now Meghan's father figure. Audrey shoved down a burst of sadness. She had always wanted a stepdad.

"Meghan's out back. We can talk there." Beverly led Audrey through the kitchen.

Audrey reminded herself to speak slowly to Meghan. When she'd visited the family at the hospital five months prior, the injured teen had been unconscious. An oxygen mask covered her mouth and nose, a wide, white bandage gripped her bald head, and a line, threaded between the bed's guardrails, connected her listless arm to an IV pole. Audrey braced herself, shutting down memories of Meghan as a lively girl. But when Beverly opened the door to the back deck, Audrey gasped.

Meghan held a lunge, one leg stretched behind her, the other bent at the knee. Her arms were spread like an eagle in flight, her chin lifted. Her blond hair curled close around her head, reaching her neck. She smiled as Audrey and her mother joined her on the deck.

"Watch my stork stand." She exited the lunge. Frowning in concentration, she extended her arms, turned her right knee outwards, and drew her right foot up to her left knee.

Audrey noticed her standing leg trembled. "Is that hard?"

"Very." Meghan wobbled and stumbled sideways, catching herself on the patio table beside her. "Easier than it used to be, though!"

"The rehab helped a lot." Beverly drew her daughter into her full arms for a quick hug. "She just finished up the out-patient program. We're still doing memory exercises, cognitive stuff, things like that."

"You look very well, Meghan. Your progress is amazing."

"And you never look a day older." Beverly looked at Audrey. "How old are you now, anyway?"

"Thirty-two." Audrey had forgotten about Beverly's bluntness.

"*Thirty-two?* I was younger than that when we met!" Beverly gestured to the low Adirondack chairs that faced the property's corral and barn. "Have a seat."

Audrey sat, ignoring Beverly's observation—and her pointed glance at Audrey's left hand.

"I do Pilates and weights," Meghan blurted, sitting next to Audrey.

"Great! Weights are excellent." Audrey glanced at a small device taped to Meghan's upper arm.

"That's my, my…" Meghan stopped, pointed at the device, and looked at Beverly. "Mom?"

"Your insulin pump."

Meghan slapped her forehead. "Yeah—that! It helps keep my blood sugar in range."

Audrey opened the case file she'd brought. "You like horses, right? Are you working with them again?"

"Not yet. I forget things, so it's dangerous." She sighed and looked down at her hands.

"She should be riding in a year, maybe sooner." Beverly nudged Meghan cheerfully.

Meghan remained silent and stared at the corral. A grey horse stood in the shade, swishing its tail against the flies.

Beverly gently squeezed Meghan's hand. "Honey, I told Audrey you'll be riding again in a year."

"Right! Sorry—I still space out." Meghan's smile faded. "I missed running the camp horse program over the summer."

"What camp was that?"

"She was the horse program lead for Strong 'n Free camp, for kids with type 1 diabetes," Beverly said. "Obviously, she couldn't do the job over the summer. The camp directors replaced her for the spring camp, too."

"Which is stupid, because I'll be fine by spring." Meghan scowled.

"They'll prioritize you next summer," Beverly reminded her daughter.

Audrey lifted some papers from the file. "Let's review the case. I met with the expert witness today. Your deposition is upcoming, too." She showed Beverly her documents and explained the case's timeline. After ten minutes, Meghan's attention began to drift.

Beverly stood. "We should wrap this up. Meghan's getting tired."

On the porch, Audrey pushed the button on her key fob, promising to email the rest of the information. She pursed her lips as she descended Highway 17 to Los Gatos. Dr. Taylor must be held accountable.

CHAPTER TWO

Sunshine blazed through the blinds of Audrey's bedroom window. She pulled her pillow over her head and tried to sleep. Her dinner with Luke, the night before, had not gone well. She'd looked forward to a fun visit, but Luke's cabin was a mess. The kids were agitated and whiney. When she'd tried to engage ten-year-old Easton, he went to play video games. Nine-year-old Lillie retreated to her room, and Audrey had no idea how to relate to Warwick, who was only four. She'd had trouble staying civil.

After the children were in bed, she'd stood with her twin beneath a grove of redwoods by his cabin's driveway. Deep shadows slanted across Luke's hollow cheeks and the weary sag of his mouth. Beyond the glare of his flashlight, the forest was black. Late summer crickets chirped.

"Move to Sunnyvale. The kids could take all kinds of lessons. And Great America's right there." As far as she knew, the kids had never visited the iconic amusement park.

"I like the solitude. I'd go nuts in the city." He sounded surprised she didn't know. "Besides, the kids are in school, and my job is here."

"You could find a new job. The kids could adapt."

"Why should they?"

She gave up. "Have you heard from Dad?"

"I emailed him when Nancy left."

Luke's wife had left ten months prior. Their father, no

doubt, had not replied. Audrey and Luke hadn't seen him since they were teenagers.

"Mom giving you advice?"

"Every weekend." Luke's brief smile dropped, as if his face couldn't handle the strain.

"I wish she was closer." Their mom, in Corpus Christi, had never recovered financially from the divorce. Audrey sent money when she could. Support didn't work the other way around.

Audrey hugged her brother, shocked by the slimness of his shoulders, and slid into the driver seat of her white Tesla. She watched Luke walk heavily back to the cabin, the flashlight bobbing beside him. Driving back to Sunnyvale, she hadn't been able to remember a positive thing about Nancy.

In the kitchen, the coffeemaker hissed, finishing the brew Audrey had set before going to bed. She got up and poured herself a mug. Flopping onto her worn loveseat, she gazed at the fireplace.

Working and raising three kids couldn't be easy. Maybe the kids' whining was partly about divorce issues. God knew, her own parents' divorce had put her in a tailspin, at ten years old.

She sipped the coffee. Luke was stressed. The kids were struggling. Audrey was family. Although kids with issues stressed her out, and country life was dull, she decided to visit more—weekly, if she could. She grabbed her phone and searched for child development and divorce information. She should educate herself since she planned to be around.

~

Next Friday, she tried again. Luke's cabin was an hour's drive from her condo. Rush-hour traffic ascended the curves of Highway 17, snarling and squeaking in the heat. Audrey moved to the fast lane, passing a sputtering pickup. Rays of late sun slanted between tall, shaggy redwoods, brightening patches of the forest floor.

The traffic's speed increased, and Audrey breached the Summit. Grey-green ranges stretched down to Monterey Bay. Above the ocean, the sun tinged feathery clouds to reds and golds. She tapped the Tesla's screen and listened to a legal podcast as she descended to Scotts Valley, where she picked up Chinese food. Twenty minutes later, she parked on Luke's dirt driveway.

The cabin sat on a quiet road in Ben Lomond—a cluster of old homes and quaint neighborhoods in the forested San Lorenzo Valley. It was dusk, and Luke had turned on the porch light.

"Easton, get off the computer! It's my turn." Lillie was yelling.

Audrey closed her eyes and took a deep breath. Grabbing a bag of educational toys she'd bought, along with the dinner, she walked to the front steps.

"Dad! Easton won't let me do my homework!" Lillie was crying now.

"Get off the computer." Luke's voice came from the living room.

Audrey wished Luke would teach the kids to get along. He could use some information about discipline. She lowered the bags onto the stoop and knocked on the red door to Luke's kitchen. No one answered, so she went in and set the food on the kitchen table, trying to avoid smears and a puddle of water. Dishes filled the sink, and dog food had spilled near the stove. She put the toys and her purse on an old ladderback chair and closed the door, swatting at whirling moths.

Warwick ran in from the living room. His t-shirt was filthy, and his little legs, below the line of his shorts, were smeared with dirt. A twig nestled in his curly brown hair. He halted shyly and looked at Audrey. "I climbed that tree." He pointed out the kitchen window.

Audrey chuckled. It was impossible to know which tree he meant. She ruffled his hair and tried to pull the twig free.

"Hi, Warwick! How was your day?"

He squirmed away and sloshed filtered water from a pitcher into a plastic cup. Ignoring Audrey, he guzzled the water and ran back to the living room. The twig dropped to the floor.

"Daddy! Auntie Audrey's here."

Lillie skipped into the kitchen. She wrapped her slim arms around Audrey. "Tell Easton to let me use the computer!"

"Um…" Audrey had read about redirecting emotional children. She grabbed the bag of toys. "Want to see what I brought you?"

"Sure!" Lillie brushed back her blond hair and leaned into Audrey, looking at the bag. Still wearing her gymnastics clothes, she smelled like forest air and garden dirt.

"This is for you." Audrey grinned enthusiastically and handed Lillie a box of math flash cards.

"That's nice." Lillie glanced at the box and put it on the counter. She skipped back to Easton, in the hallway. "NOW, Easton!"

Audrey tuned them out as Luke came into the kitchen. Warwick followed, carrying Bella, the old Chihuahua his mother had left behind.

~

Audrey reached up and embraced her twin. "Your jeans are baggy. Don't you ever eat?"

"Sure!" He grabbed a bag of chips from the counter.

"Not chips, Luke. Protein. And some veggies once in a while." She playfully yanked the dark locks that hung in his eyes. "I'll bring you a green smoothie next time."

"No, thanks. I prefer food."

They laughed, and Luke began loading the dishwasher. Warwick set Bella down. She snuffled at the scattered dog food. Audrey grabbed a paper towel, dampened it, and wiped the smears off the kitchen table. She sat down. Warwick cuddled next to her. She put her arm lightly around his shoulders, trying to keep her shirt clean. She'd forgotten to bring a change of clothes.

"How are you, Warwick?"

"I miss my mom. Is she coming home soon?"

Audrey's scalp prickled. "Um, I'm not sure. Luke, what do you think?"

"About what?" Luke pushed a mug into a tight space on the top rack of the dishwasher, oblivious.

Her heart pounded. "Warwick wants to know when his mom's coming home."

Luke turned and blinked, a dripping dinner plate in his hand. The florescent light cast harsh shadows around his eyes. His lips parted, then closed. Audrey wished she could force a few parenting books into his head, right there.

"Warwick," he said, "I don't know. Please set the table."

Warwick sighed. He yanked open a once-white drawer and put knives and forks on the table, his small shoulders drooping. Luke's dark eyes glistened. Audrey walked to him and put her hands on his shoulders.

"Luke, you're doing a good job," she whispered. "But you could use some books about getting kids through divorce. Do you want me to look?"

Luke shrugged. "Sure."

"It's important." She released his shoulders. "I read that children need at least one parent who provides security and stability."

"I get that, Audrey. I'm just so freakin' busy."

She nodded and walked to the living room doorway. Papers, notebooks, and computer cords covered Luke's desk. Family pictures were taped around the edges of his monitor. It looked like a lot of work, even with Luke's mental bandwidth. And the kids' needs were always present.

She turned back to her twin. "I was thinking I could come by on weekends. Help out with cleaning and stuff. What do you think?"

Luke started the dishwasher, then straightened to look at

Audrey. "That would be great, Audrey."

Warwick tapped his dad's arm. "I finished the table."

Luke inspected the table and rubbed his son's back. His silver wedding band shone on his finger. "Good, Warwick. Could you take Bella out to go potty, please?"

He led Warwick through the living room and forced open the slider that led to a fenced-in yard. Warwick set Bella on the patchy grass. She sniffed around.

Luke called towards the hallway. "Dinner!"

Easton came, carrying a paper with school problems. He wore Bermuda shorts and a t-shirt from a kids' camp. Like Warwick's, his straight, dark hair needed a trim, but he had brushed it. Lillie hopped next to him, pulling on his arm.

Easton watched his sister's face, holding the paper out of reach. "What's an antonym for healthy? An... Tow... Nim..."

"Sick!" Lillie jumped to grab the paper.

"Good." Easton swooped the page into her raised hand. "Write that in for number three. You can do the rest later." He patted her head, which wasn't much below his own.

Easton was lean and strong, and his head reached Audrey's shoulders. He looked closely at people when they spoke, listening attentively. He was smart and responsible for a kid. During Audrey's last visit, he had reminded Luke to pay the water bill.

Audrey unpacked the warm dinner bags and the kids sat up for dinner.

Luke looked around the table. "Who wants to say grace?"

"I do!" Lillie folded her hands and glanced around the table. "For what we are about to receive, may the Lord make us truly thankful."

Well, that was one thing: The kids knew how to say grace.

~

On Monday, Audrey arrived at Tate Personal Injury

eager for the satisfaction of work. She started up her laptop and began an interrogatory. The muffled sound of Patrick Rogers laughing with Suzanne came through her office wall. Patrick hummed a tune as he walked the hallway. Soon, he tapped on Audrey's door.

"How was your weekend?" He sauntered to her guest chair, clearing his throat and smoothing his hair.

"Packed. Yours?"

"Always busy, yeah. Got a few minutes?"

"Six. And I will be billing you!" she half-joked. She had planned her day to the minute.

He sat and rested his foot on his opposite knee. "I had a great dinner with Tate." He rocked slightly. The chair squeaked. "Good conversation, too."

She tapped a report into a neat stack and leaned forward. "What did you talk about?"

"He's impressed with my winning streak. You're looking at an equity partner!" Patrick slapped Audrey's desk, his signet ring clicking on impact.

"Congratulations!" Audrey punched the air, but insecurities clawed her mind. Why hadn't Tate made her a non-equity partner? She won her cases. She'd worked long hours for years.

She listened while Patrick told how he and his fiancée had celebrated in San Francisco, visiting Fisherman's Wharf and going to a show. Patrick was a good lawyer. He won often, and he studied and learned. He was honest, too—not conniving. He'd earned his promotion.

Trouble was, so had she.

"Well, my six minutes are up." Patrick stood, grinning. "Thanks for letting me rave!" He practically skipped past her desk in his well-tailored suit.

Audrey sighed as he closed her door. She looked at her bar admission certificate. The frame looked grubby.

~

Driving home that evening, she scrutinized past cases.

She had drawn clients to the firm, she was scrupulous about her casework, she worked hard to be a team player. *What the heck, Tate?*

A migraine threatened. She dug ibuprofen from her purse and swallowed it with a gulp of water. An old car, spewing fumes, cut in front of her and crept along, slower than the rest of the traffic. Sensing pollutants, the Tesla sealed its vents. Audrey blew out a short breath, then merged left, glancing at the driver as she passed. The man hunched over his wheel, oblivious.

She massaged the back of her neck, remembering a rare meeting in the conference room. It was a Friday afternoon, late, and Tate had called a team-building session to get her and Patrick's ideas. Audrey knew the firm needed more collaboration to benefit from their shared expertise. She'd researched carefully and prepared charts and links to articles to prove her point.

But Tate had been dismissive. "Good ideas, Audrey. I'll consider this going forward." Nothing had materialized from her input.

More memories emerged. Tate, rolling his eyes when she raved about an early deposition. Questioning her commitment. "We'll be doing overtime if Audrey gets married, Patrick."

"That's not going to happen!" she'd assured them, laughing. She'd been on exactly three dates, ever. Two were with fellow law students. She had discussed her law classes, until both men politely paid the tab and said goodbye. The third date led to an unpleasant stalking drama. She'd sworn off dating after that.

She parked at an EV charging space in the condo parking lot. Tate didn't take her seriously. Being dismissed was the story of her life. She rested her head on the steering wheel, remembering.

Waves crashed and fizzed up a slope of sand.

"Daddy, I can throw it further than Luke!"

"Nah! You're just a girl."

"No—watch!"

The beachball had landed far from the ocean's edge. Pushed by a little breeze, it wobbled along the sand, proving her wrong.

"Mommy's little girl!" She could still hear her father's derisive laugh. He had knelt to her level, his eyes cold. "You'll never be a man, Audrey."

It was probably why she still avoided friendships with women. Luke was her closest friend. Despite their dad's favoritism, he had always stood by Audrey. Their parents' divorce had only deepened their understanding.

She plugged in the Tesla and walked through the condo grounds to her unit, her head pounding. Inside, she heard the muffled sounds of her upstairs neighbors talking and preparing dinner. She hung her purse in the closet and cried, despising the tears.

~

After a few minutes, she threw a wadded tissue into the trash and replaced her stiff professional shirt with a comfortable t-shirt and sweats. She assembled a power bowl and ate at the breakfast bar, considering her options.

She didn't trust Tate. Challenging him might lock her out of partnership. Should she just keep quiet? The thought rankled her. Perhaps a transfer was in order—to a firm with a clear path to partnership. It would both accelerate her career and relieve her of Tate's toxic attitude.

Did Frank Spade remember meeting her? She scooped up a last bite of quinoa and onions, and tapped open the website of Spade, Lau, & Coleman, LLP. Setting her bowl in the sink, she browsed the Careers page. The firm had several associate positions open.

She went to the table and opened her laptop. "Frank Spade encouraged me to apply…" she typed into the introduction field, praying he remembered her. The application process was easy—she kept her resume up to date—and after an hour, she hit Submit and prayed for success.

CHAPTER THREE

Eric Taylor typed notes into an exam room's computer. He frowned and rotated his pneumatic stool, facing the family behind him. A teenaged male patient sat on the examination table, legs dangling. His parents perched on the side chairs, their faces anxious, like most parents of newly diagnosed juveniles.

"Josh, you need to check your blood glucose more frequently."

Josh grunted.

Eric looked at Josh's parents. "Do you check in with him?"

"Yes." Josh's mother glanced at her son. "But he's busy and doesn't want us interfering."

He'd heard that before. "It's challenging, but better communication helps pediatric patients take charge of their blood glucose. Josh, do you tell your parents how you're doing?"

Josh shrugged.

Eric scooted out of the family's sightline and pointed to a chart on the computer screen. "This is from Josh's meter. You're only checking once or twice a day, Josh. I'd like to see at least five times, and you should tell your parents what your levels are every night. Think you can manage that?"

Josh gave him a sideways look. "Yeah."

His parents leaned in to view the chart.

"I read cinnamon helps regulate blood sugar," said Josh's mom. "Should I add it to his diet?"

Eric laughed, shortly. "If he likes cinnamon." Where did people pick up these notions?

Someone tapped on the door.

"Come in!"

Nurse Jenny bustled into the room. "Hi, guys! How are you doing, Josh? It's great to see you."

Josh straightened. His mother smiled. His dad leaned back in his chair.

"Hey," said Josh.

"Nice to see you, Jenny." Josh's mom loosened her grip on her grey purse. "Josh isn't checking his blood sugar enough."

"Oh, he'll learn." Jenny flapped her hand dismissively. "Josh is only a couple months in. New patients have their ups and downs, but they catch on."

Eric tensed. His nurse was too good at putting people at ease. Early habits after diagnosis were foundational to a healthy life. Jenny thrust a printout at him. He stood his ground. "It's important to develop good habits early. I'll let you know when we're done, and you can review Josh's options with the diabetes educators." He grabbed the printout.

"See you in a few minutes!" Jenny swept out, closing the door behind her.

He flipped through the printout and showed the family a graph. "Josh's A1C is 8.9. That's too high. The problem blood sugar levels occur after dinner and overnight. I'll increase his long-acting dose and adjust his evening ratios." He input the new doses and stood. "I can't emphasize enough that Josh must check his blood sugar throughout the day, and that Mom and Dad tune in daily. Some of my patients find an evening review helpful to stay on track." He shook hands with the family and left.

In the hallway, Jenny was labeling insulin pumps and

chatting with a technician. When she saw him approaching, her chatting stopped.

"Josh and his parents are ready for you." Eric strode past the tech station. "You might mention further training on his ratios and dosing frequency. I'm not comfortable with his fluency."

"You bet."

~

In his office at the end of the hall, he switched on his computer and updated the teen's records. His partner, the senior Dr. Fisk, had suggested the heavy antique desk and comfortable chairs around a glass coffee table. A couple of family photos stood on the desk—an elderly couple holding hands in a garden (his parents), and a boy, laughing in sunshine and backyard sprinklers (his brother, when they were kids).

He clicked *Save* and turned his chair to face the window. His phone rang, and his lawyer's name and number showed on the screen. "Elizabeth, hi." He stared out the window, rigid in his desk chair. The lawsuit had become a constant source of stress.

"Good afternoon, Dr. Taylor." The muffled swoosh of traffic backed her voice. "Opposing counsel, Audrey Beach, sent me an interrogatory we need to respond to. When can you meet to go over that?"

He opened the calendar on his phone. "Friday at one?"

"That works. Audrey also wants to schedule her expert witness's deposition. You don't have to do anything. I'm just keeping you updated."

"Am I allowed to know who this individual is?"

"Dr. Harrison McKenzie is based in Arizona. He's an endocrinologist, obviously. Have you heard of him?"

"No." He glanced at his phone. His next appointment was imminent. "Anything else?"

"Audrey will schedule your deposition soon, too. Look carefully at everything I send you, ahead of time. You want to go in prepared."

He clenched his jaw. He had not signed up for time-consuming distractions from his practice.

Elizabeth was waiting.

"Got it."

"Excellent! Just remember, you cannot let the opposing counsel rattle you. How are you doing, stress-wise?"

Eric swatted at a fly. He strolled to the window and watched Josh and his parents cross the parking lot. Josh's mom tried to put her arm around her son. Josh pulled away.

He returned to his desk, eyes low and mouth downturned. "Fine."

"So, stress is something you take in stride. That's very helpful. Many of my clients go into this process on edge. It gives the opposition an advantage."

"Of course."

"See you on Friday."

"Thank you, Elizabeth." He put his phone into his pocket and went to his next appointment. He would just have to push through the lawsuit.

CHAPTER FOUR

In late October, Elizabeth announced a milestone. "Your deposition is scheduled for November 8, two weeks away." Setting her purse on her conference table, she handed Eric a folder. She sat and tucked grey whisps into her loosely confined hair.

Eric thumbed through neatly stapled documents. He'd seen most of them before. He took a seat and glanced at the clock on the conference room wall.

"The outline of our strategy is what I'd like to focus on." Elizabeth perched a pair of unframed glasses on her narrow nose.

"Fine." He perused the outline. Elizabeth had listed topics she anticipated Audrey would use to attack his competence.

"Our defense will center on the NewDay software." Elizabeth fetched water bottles from her credenza and handed one to the doctor. "Are you familiar with the software's weaknesses?"

"Of course." All healthcare software caused problems.

"How about you explain what happened, as practice. I have no doubt Audrey will dig deep on that."

Eric sat still and straight, his back muscles tight. "After I planned the patient's care, I filled out the verification checklist and submitted my notes and instructions. The software glitched somewhere and prescribed too much insulin. There's no other explanation. What more does she need to know?"

"Oh, plenty." Elizabeth laughed tightly. She gripped her copy of the deposition outline with cigarette-stained fingers. "First, she'll ask why you didn't verify the patient's food intake and insulin status. Then, she'll want to know how often you use the software, if you're familiar with its glitches, whether you've been trained on it."

"I always verify everything. The software won't allow me to progress until I do."

"Let's review NewDay. You pulled in the patient's doses from her blood sugar meter and insulin pump, to the software."

"No. The intake nurse does that."

"You ordered an NPO." Elizabeth peered at the page, wrinkling the edges. "What is that?"

"Nothing to be given by mouth. She was too nauseous, so I hydrated her and provided background insulin via IV."

Elizabeth perused the document. "Then, somehow she arrived in a state of dangerously low blood sugar, fell, and got the head injury, right?"

"Yes." He frowned. "It was clearly a system error. This is a waste of time. Beach should be going after the software manufacturer, not me."

Elizabeth set down the papers and looked straight at him. "Dr. Taylor, I know you're certain you didn't cause the error, and that's what we're going to prove. But if you come across defensive, a jury will develop a bias against you. You absolutely must remain calm. Relax! It's my job to defend you. Besides—" She paused.

He waited, eyebrows raised.

"We can file a cross-complaint against NewDay, if you're interested."

He couldn't help rolling his eyes. There were so many on-ramps to the legal swamp. "Not today."

"Alright." She picked up the papers again briskly, her

mouth bent down in disapproval. "Now, could you have missed something with the software? Maybe a warning popup about the dose? I'm only asking to make sure we're prepared for anything."

"Of course not. I'm scrupulous about dosing." When would she let it go?

"And on the off chance that you missed something, we can blame the software's design flaws."

Perhaps he should hire a different attorney. "I didn't miss anything."

"I understand," Elizabeth snapped.

He folded his arms. "Ms. Weaver, if we're going to work together, I'll need a basic level of respect."

She was polite for the rest of the session.

~

Audrey's discovery process indicated Dr. Taylor had no other lawsuits on his record. He was in good standing on medical boards. He was respected for his participation in research, having contributed to several cutting-edge diabetes treatments.

She had to admit, his error with Meghan seemed an anomaly, not habitual carelessness. But he should have caught it, and she would hold him accountable.

Meghan performed well at her brief deposition. Audrey was proud of her coaching. The teen was not rattled by Elizabeth Warren's badgering, even while struggling with the cognitive impacts of her brain injury. And Audrey was confident Dr. McKenzie would verify Dr. Taylor's negligence.

She gazed out her office window, daydreaming. "Did you verify the patient's carb intake, Dr. Taylor?" she imagined asking.

Dr. Taylor, sweating and anxious, stammered for an appropriate comeback. Meghan and her parents hugged and celebrated their victory.

She checked her emails and drew a quick breath. Spade,

Lau, & Coleman had received her resume. "Dear Ms. Beach, we are impressed with your competencies and qualifications. We would like to schedule an interview at your convenience. Please respond with your availability."

Audrey jumped from her chair and pumped the air with her fists. Weeks had passed since she applied, and she'd given up. Quickly, she wrote back, asking to schedule the interview for the following Monday evening. She tapped her fingers on her desk, nervously waiting for a reply. Ten minutes later, she received a confirmation. The interview was scheduled for Monday evening at seven.

She couldn't wait to see Tate's face.

~

On Friday, she drove to Luke's for her weekly visit. She'd kept her September commitment, bringing take-out dinners every weekend and helping with chores and the kids' homework.

Lillie threw open the kitchen door. A rectangle of light extended into the dark yard. "Auntie Audrey! Can you watch my handsprings?" She ran to Audrey and skipped beside her, hanging on her arm.

"I'm busy." Audrey pulled her arm free to avoid dropping a bag of dinner. All day, she'd looked forward to preparing for her interview.

"Look at my handstand then." Blocking Audrey's path, Lillie extended her arms down and forwards, pointed a toe, and flipped onto her hands. Her slim form, silhouetted against the doorway, was perfectly straight. She stood, and they walked into the kitchen.

"How'd I do?"

"I can't evaluate handstands. That looked alright, though." Audrey closed the door. Lillie skipped across the kitchen.

"Luke, I'm here!" Audrey called. "Lillie, wash your hands."

Lillie ran to the sink. Audrey went to the living room,

where Luke bent over his desk. Warwick lay on the couch playing with a toy phone. Its lights blinked. *"Call your friend!"* the phone instructed. Warwick pretended to talk to someone.

Luke glanced over his shoulder. "I'll be right there. Warwick, set the table, please."

Warwick ignored him.

Easton came from his room. "Smells good. Thank you, Auntie Audrey!"

"You're welcome, Easton."

"I'll put the food out in a minute." Luke typed something.

"Watch my handspring! We've got time." Lillie skipped past Audrey to the sliding door. She flipped on the light, flooding the backyard with a white glare. Audrey followed her.

Standing at the edge of the grass, Lillie glanced at Audrey. She hurtled forward, then leaped onto one foot with her hands raised, sprang upside down, landed on her hands, and flipped onto her feet, wobbling as she finished.

Audrey's jaw dropped. "I don't know much about gymnastics, but that was impressive!"

Lillie grinned, showing her oversized permanent teeth, and ran back to Audrey. "Coach Minnie says I'm doing well. I'm Level 5."

"What's Level 5?"

"It's compulsory. I have to pass Level 5 to get to Level 6." She ran inside and snuggled onto the floor with Bella.

Audrey closed the slider and went into the kitchen. The food was still bagged. "Luke? Dinner?"

"Right!" Luke stood, not taking his eyes from the screen, and closed a document. He went to the kitchen and tossed the wrapped packages onto the table, ignoring their contents.

Easton and Lillie came to the table. Audrey divided the burritos, tacos, and Spanish rice onto plates. She set out napkins and cutlery.

"Warwick!" Luke sat down. Audrey heard Warwick's phone thump onto the floor. Warwick joined them and crawled onto his chair, next to Luke.

"Did you forget to set the table, Warwick?" asked Luke.

"Aw, yeah." Warwick stretched his arms onto the table, pushed his plate aside, and leaned his head onto his dad's arm.

"I'll remind you next time."

"Ok, Dad." He rubbed his eyes.

"Did you work hard at school today?"

"Yeah."

"Is he sick?" asked Audrey.

"It's just allergies. He doesn't sleep well." Luke went to the bathroom and brought back a bottle of pediatric antihistamines. He gave one to Warwick.

"You're getting skinny, Warwick," Easton observed. "Eat."

"I brought pie." Audrey tried to tempt him. Like Luke, Warwick didn't have weight to lose.

"He's ramping up for a growth spurt, I bet." Luke rubbed Warwick's back. He touched his finger to his chin, thinking. "Are you going to be as tall as me, Warwick?"

Warwick snuggled close to his dad. "I'm gonna be taller!" He nibbled his taco.

~

In the morning, Audrey filled a bucket with hot water and started scrubbing the kitchen cabinets and organizing the countertops. Luke worked on his car and the kids played outside.

Lillie came in, wanting to help.

"This is a grown-up job." Audrey still hadn't had time to prepare for her interview.

"Please, Auntie Audrey!"

Audrey found another sponge and bucket and gave them to Lillie. "You start at this end of the cabinets, and I'll meet you in the middle."

Lillie lifted her dripping sponge from her bucket directly onto the cabinet door. Water sloshed onto the counter and splashed into the toaster.

"Stop!"

"Oops!" Lillie went to the sink, dripping water from the soaked sponge on the countertop as she went. She squeezed the sponge into the sink.

"You can squeeze it into the bucket next time." Audrey wiped up the water and showed Lillie how to spray cleaner onto the cabinets and scrub them clean.

"Cool!" Lillie gave the next cabinet a couple swipes, then moved on.

"You're not done."

Audrey demonstrated how to clean around corners, avoid spills, and scrub away dirt and splatters. They finished at lunchtime. After lunch, she tried to help Easton with his math, amazed she'd forgotten so much.

Easton thanked her. "I'll just look online."

Audrey helped Warwick pick up his clothes, started a load of laundry, and vacuumed the kids' rooms. She said goodbye and left at five, much later than she'd planned, still unprepared for the interview.

~

The drive home was perfect for mentally reviewing work tasks. She needed to wrap up a slip-and-fall case. Winning it would be a good start to the holidays. Maybe she'd get the kids something special—if she could figure that what they liked.

Her phone rang as she ascended Highway 17, and she recognized Luke's number. She pulled onto the broad Sugarloaf Road turnout. "Hey!"

"I need to talk to you. Is now good?" Luke sounded tense.

"Fire away."

Luke spoke quietly, and she pressed the phone to her ear.

Clearly, he didn't want the kids to overhear this conversation. "I've been sentenced to a year in jail."

CHAPTER FIVE

Audrey got out of the Tesla and walked down Sugarloaf Road, away from the traffic. "What's going on? You could have told me before disaster stage!"

"I was hoping nothing would come of it." Luke kept his voice low. "I embezzled from Cabrillo College."

Audrey stared at her phone, stunned. "You embezzled? Why? How much?"

"A couple years ago, when Nancy took the kids to Mexico on vacation, she said she had an emergency and needed five grand. She wouldn't tell me why, but she sounded panicked. I was going to return it, but I got caught."

Audrey remembered Luke had been unable to accompany Nancy and the kids, because of work obligations. She had wondered why Nancy couldn't opt for a "staycation." But Nancy got what she wanted, and she wanted a Mexico trip. "Why did she need it?"

Luke laughed, sharply. "She never told me. Probably for a better hotel or some fancy excursion."

"Why didn't you tell me?"

"I figured you wouldn't need to know. I thought I'd be acquitted."

Luke had always tried to cover his mistakes, but she'd never dreamed he would do something illegal. Nancy was a convincing actress. Audrey walked briskly towards the car, scaring up a blue Steller's jay. It flew, screeching, to the safety of a redwood tree. "I'm coming back. We have to figure out what to do."

"I can't talk with the kids around. They don't know anything yet."

"Maybe we can appeal."

"There's too much evidence. It's really cut and dried, Audrey. The jury found me guilty. The judge was lenient. It's usually a felony."

Stealing anything valued above $950 was a felony in California. But Luke had no criminal record, and the judge had no doubt designated the charge a misdemeanor, punishable by jail time rather than prison. Anyway, the sentence was passed, and the case sounded straightforward. She doubted an appeal would be successful. She reached the car and sat behind the wheel, closing the door to block the traffic noise. "When can you talk? And why aren't you in jail yet?"

"The judge gave me a report date, so I could get my affairs in order. Let's talk on Monday, when the kids are in school. I won't be going to work." Luke paused. She heard the kids asking him about dinner. Finding out his commitment date could wait.

"What time shall I call?"

Luke sighed. "How about nine Monday morning?"

"OK. Do you want me to come over tomorrow?"

"That won't change anything. I have to go. Thanks, Audrey."

"Alright, talk to you Monday."

They hung up and Audrey pulled onto Highway 17, her mind racing.

~

She parked the Tesla and hurried through the common area to her condo. Inside, she tossed her overnight bag into the coat closet. Jittery and anxious, she fussed around the place, trying to order her mind by organizing her surroundings. Finally, she grabbed her Bible and a notepad and curled up on the loveseat.

As a civil attorney, she didn't know much about criminal law. A quick search on her phone convinced her that unless Luke had pled not guilty, there was no hope for a reduced sentence. She texted Luke. "Did you plead guilty?"

"yes"

Filing an appeal would not help. She researched the sentencing for grand theft and found the judge had been lenient, as Luke had said. Technically, he could have faced up to three years in prison and a hefty fine.

"Did you present any evidence that you thought the money was for an emergency?" Although it was too late to retry the case, if she could prove it was an emergency perhaps the judge would revisit the sentence.

"The email from nancy"

That was all the evidence there was, since an emergency had never materialized. She gave up. It was simple: Luke had embezzled. The judge had sentenced him accordingly.

"Luke, we can't get your sentence changed," she texted.

"Yes told you that"

"Goodnight." She set down her phone, then picked it up again. "If you'd asked for help, I would have given it."

"im sorry audrey"

She closed her eyes, wrestling with anger. *Luke, what were you thinking?* But it was hard to be angry with him. He had always stood by her. Besides, the whole thing boiled down to Nancy's selfishness. She swiped her phone open again. "Love you."

"same"

She poured herself ice water and tore a page from the notepad. She brainstormed, scribbling categories. "Income Sources, Education for Kids, Lillie's Gymnastics."

She could have strangled Nancy. Who did the woman expect to replace her? Luke hadn't heard from his wife since she'd left, apart from one email instructing him not to contact her. Then too, Nancy's instability couldn't be good for kids. Audrey had heard her scream at Luke, furious about having to take the kids to school. Luke had had a dental appointment and couldn't do it.

Her mom couldn't help. Audrey could think all she wanted, but she was the logical caregiver for the kids. She stood and paced the room. Weekly visits were one thing. Becoming a de facto mom was another. She stomped to her bedroom and flopped onto her bed.

The med mal suit and a myriad work tasks flooded her thoughts. Suddenly, she remembered the interview with Spade. She couldn't take a new position now. She went back to the loveseat and canceled the appointment, hot tears streaking her cheeks.

She wiped her eyes and took a deep breath, strong-arming her emotions. Caring for the kids with her long work hours seemed impossible. She was in the office from six or seven in the morning until late. The commute from Luke's cabin to the law office was an hour or more, depending on traffic. Luke took the kids to school at around seven forty-five.

Could the kids get themselves up and off to school without her help? She had no idea. School was only a ten-minute walk away. Ideally, she could leave the cabin at around five-thirty. The children would need to get up, make their breakfasts and lunches, and walk to school, arriving there by eight o'clock.

She stared at the fireplace. If the kids couldn't do that, she'd have to be there, as Luke had been, until they were ready to go. She couldn't realistically leave the cabin until seven thirty. After-school hours posed still more challenges. Lillie had gymnastics practice every afternoon.

If Tate allowed her to work remotely, she could continue. Hopefully, she could reduce her caseload, too. Briefly, she considered moving the kids to the condo. But even she knew children needed their home and friends, for stability.

Her anger rushed back. She stood again, clenched her

fists, and let out a loud moan. She wasn't cut out to be a mom. She couldn't even pick a toy the kids liked.

She needed an action list. She paced the floor, counting tasks on her fingers. "Lease the condo, write financial plan, buy appropriate clothes…" (She would have to dress like a mom, for the kids' sake.) "Get sexist Tate to reduce my hours and keep my position open…"

She sat down and rested her head on the loveseat's soft headrest. *Everything will be OK. I'll get through this.* She opened her Bible and browsed through the Psalms. "Serve the Lord with gladness." She pressed her hand against the thin paper, the page cool beneath her palm.

This situation was impossible. But it was also God's.

~

Piles of documents loaded her desk on Monday morning. She shoved them aside, closed her office door, and called Luke.

"Hi." His voice was faint and low.

"So, when do you turn yourself in?"

"Friday."

"Do the kids know yet?"

"I'll tell them tonight. Can you be here?"

She looked at her desk. "Not really, but I will. I'm going to the Santa Cruz courthouse to file a motion for temporary guardianship. I assume that's what you want?"

"Yes, Audrey. Thank you."

"Can you contact Nancy?"

"I've been trying. She changed her contact information."

"Keep copies of all your attempts. I'll file an affidavit." She waited. "Are you there?"

"Yeah, sorry."

She closed her eyes, frustrated. "Get it together, Lukey. We need to figure out how I'm going to fit my new mommy career in with my real career. I'll need a document listing the kids' teachers, their doctors, stuff like that."

"Yeah."

"Have you told the school what's going on?"

"Not yet."

"Well, I'm not going to."

"I'll tell them."

"When?"

"Tomorrow. After we tell the kids." Luke sighed. A long pause followed.

"Look, I've got a lot to do before I head over. I'll meet you at the courthouse at four thirty."

"Yeah, thanks, Audrey."

"Keep your chin up, Luke."

~

After filing the guardianship paperwork and scheduling a hearing, Audrey followed Luke's car up Highway 9. The evening sunlight streamed through trees and over fields, lighting pines, redwoods, and dry grasses to glowing tans and greens.

They stopped for groceries and picked Lillie up from gymnastics. They reached the flowery, tree-lined neighborhoods of Ben Lomond and parked in Luke's driveway. Easton and Warwick had walked home from their after-school care program.

Audrey walked to the cabin. *Gorgeous setting to break the kids' hearts in.*

After dinner, Luke stopped the kids from running off to play. He stood tall, his thin shoulders pressed back, his hands restless at his sides. "Auntie Audrey and I have something to tell you."

The children stared at their dad.

"Is Mommy coming home?" Warwick balled his hands into fists and jumped.

"Not yet. Let's sit in the living room."

The kids scrunched next to each other on the frayed couch. Warwick leaned against Easton's slender arm. Lillie sprawled on the couch arm, weaving her hairband through her fingers. Easton kicked his feet on the worn carpet.

They look so small.

Luke and Audrey sat in the two armchairs across from the couch. Bella curled up on her ancient blanket.

"Kids, I made a mistake a couple years ago. I was worried about you, so I borrowed some money from Cabrillo, without asking."

"Did you give it back?" asked Lillie.

"I was going to, but people found out first. They knew I hadn't asked, so they told the police."

"Everything's going to be fine." Audrey hated to see the kids' worried faces.

The children kept their eyes on their father.

"What did the police say?" Lillie leaned forward, resting her skinny elbows on her legs.

"Well, Daddy has to go to jail for a while," said Luke. His mouth curved down and quivered. He forced a smile.

Lillie ran to her dad, wailing and throwing herself into his arms. Easton cried where he sat, hiding his face in his hands.

"No, Daddy! Stay with me!" Warwick blurted, between sobs.

"Daddy, you can't go! We'll be all by ourselves." Lillie clung to her dad.

"I'm not leaving you alone." Luke took a deep breath and rubbed his palms on his jeans.

Easton rubbed his eyes and looked up. "Who will take care of us?"

"Auntie Audrey. She'll take good care of you and bring you to see me every week."

The kids were quiet.

Audrey leaned forward. "Kids, it'll be fun! Daddy will be home before you know it."

"It won't be fun for Daddy." Easton sniffed, noisily.

Lillie cried again, clinging to Luke's neck.

Warwick pounded the couch cushions with his fists. "No, Daddy!"

Luke's head hung over Lillie's. His thin hand stroked her hair, and his shoulders shook.

Well, that helped. Audrey held her breath. She had no idea what to do. She went out to the backyard, giving Luke and the kids time alone. A California quail's flute-like notes floated through the trees. A car door closed. Children laughed. She rested her arms on Luke's drooping wood fence and stared at the short bank, which dropped down to Love Creek. A couple of ducks floated on the dark water, upending to search for food. Ferns arched down, reflected on the glassy surface.

Her stomach was tight. The evening air grew cool, and she returned to the cabin, shivering. Luke sat in his armchair, head in hands, staring at the carpet. The heavy sag of his jeans outlined his knees. He hadn't changed his style since they were kids. He straightened wearily.

"The kids are getting ready for bed. Thanks for being here."

"No problem. You did a great job."

"They're traumatized." Luke looked at her, red-eyed, then went into the kitchen. "I gotta make their lunches."

Audrey followed him. "I better get going. Should I say goodnight to them?"

"Sure." Luke rummaged through the refrigerator.

In the boys' room, Warwick sat on the floor in his pajamas, rocking and crying. He had torn up a coloring book. Scraps of crayon-marked paper littered the floor. His clothes were tossed, rumpled, on his unmade bed.

Easton's oboe was half-buried in a pile of clothes. Its worn case lay sideways in the closet, atop a few pages of scrunched music. To Audrey's knowledge, her nephew hadn't practiced in weeks. Easton lay on his bed beneath the window, still in his clothes. His hands were folded on his tummy, and he looked out the window, ignoring Audrey.

Audrey blinked, hard. "I have to go home. I came to say goodnight."

"'Night." Easton's voice was flat.

"Daddy's bad." Warwick was crying still.

Audrey crouched beside him. "He just made a mistake. Daddy's a good man. Everyone makes mistakes sometimes."

Warwick looked at her. She couldn't read his expression. "I think you should go to bed, Warwick. Would you like me to help you?" She stood.

Warwick got up and crawled onto his bed. Audrey tossed his clothes into a laundry basket by the closet and sat next to him.

"Goodnight." She bent to kiss his cheek.

"You're not my mom!" Warwick wiggled away and began crying again.

Easton kept his gaze out the window. "Don't worry, he likes you. He just misses our mom."

"OK. Goodnight." No other words came to Audrey. She went to Lillie's room.

Lillie lay curled on her stained pink rug. Her eyes were swollen, and she was shaking. She paid no attention to Audrey.

"I came to say goodnight."

Silence.

"How about I put you to bed?" Audrey took an awkward step towards Lillie. She stopped when Lille looked up at her.

"It's alright. I can put myself to bed." Her voice was low. She got up and trudged to her bed. Her grubby pink sheets were twisted and wrinkled. She didn't bother to pull them up. She just lay down and pulled her faded mermaid comforter to her chin.

"Lillie, I'm so sorry about your dad. I feel so bad for you kids—"

"Please leave me alone." Lillie turned over and faced the wall.

"Goodnight." Defeated, Audrey rejoined Luke in the kitchen.

~

Nancy stretched. Her arms and back scratched comfortably against the stone edge of the Secret Lagoon pool, in the hamlet of Fludir, Iceland. She ignored other guests, who chatted around her. The geothermal water steamed and sloshed against her skin, relaxing her tired muscles. She turned and drifted out to the middle of the pool. She lay back, swirling her arms and legs in slow, vine-like motions to stay afloat.

It was the end of a bucket-list day she'd dreamed of—watching geysers shoot up from rocks, strong winds toss the manes of Icelandic horses, and the green-and-white crash of glacier waters, tumbling down Gullfoss Waterfall.

She'd walked bravely up the path to the falls, feeling the freezing spray on her face. At the top, she stretched out her hands and braced herself against the cold blast of wind that roared up the canyon. Below her, the water cascaded in a violent, rushing torrent.

Dusk was falling—signaling the end of twenty-four-hour sunlit days. The air was a chill forty degrees and dropping. Nancy returned to the pool's edge and gazed up. Pinpricks of starlight emerged. Soon, darkness followed. She glanced towards the changing area. Jasmine, her friend since high school, walked towards her, carrying towels. They'd been dreaming of this trip since tenth grade.

"The tour guide says the Aurora forecast is showing high activity. We'll probably see Northern Lights tonight." Jasmine slipped into the water and sighed. "Feels amazing."

Nancy pressed her wet hair back. "I'm so excited to see the lights!"

"Oooh, look!" Jasmine pointed to whirling columns of green stretched across the dark sky. The columns twisted and swirled, like curtains closing across a stage.

Nancy gaped. Other tourists stopped their chatter and watched the sky, murmuring admiration. When the light activity dwindled, the tour guide directed Nancy and the others back to their bus. Nancy snuggled in her parka at a window seat. The bus chugged back to the Reykjavik vacation rental. Jasmine dozed.

Nancy opened the camera on her phone and scrolled through her pictures. She swiped too far, and Warwick looked at her through his thick, dark curls, head cocked to the side. His wide blue eyes were quizzical. A grin showed his baby teeth. She had snapped the picture moments after he had asked for ice cream.

Quickly, she closed the camera and started up a game.

CHAPTER SIX

Alex Tate strode across his office and closed the door. Audrey sat in the chair opposite his desk. She gazed at the room's elegant furnishings and the view of San Jose, through huge windows that met in a corner. She'd been in Tate's office fewer than a dozen times.

She had insisted on the meeting, telling Tate she had an emergency and wanted to discuss continuing to contribute to the firm's success. That got his attention.

Alex returned to his seat and clasped his hands on his desk. At fifty, he was model-level handsome—confident, wearing an expensive suit that complemented his symmetrical features.

He smiled, disarmingly. "So, family's kicking you around lately?"

"I need to reduce my caseload for a while." She didn't trust the smile. She didn't trust Tate.

"What type of cut are you suggesting?"

"Forty percent. I can work in the office from eight thirty to four fifteen and remotely for the rest. I need a personal leave this week and next Monday."

Tate raised his eyebrows and rubbed his stubble beard. "For how long?"

She swallowed. "A year."

Tate leaned back and briefly raised his hands. "A *year?!*" He threw the word at her like a spit wad.

She placed a printout on his desk, showing the firm's revenue growth and her contributions. "I win my cases. I work fast, and I've increased your revenue thirty percent since I came on board. I will make this work." She leaned back and folded her arms.

He glanced at the printout, pursed his lips, and raised an eyebrow. "Yeah, you're a great asset."

"And...?"

He rolled his eyes and flapped a hand. "Ah, come on, Audrey! You know how legal work is. No flex time, no do-overs. I'll pay you for the rest of the week, like you asked. Then clear out your stuff and hand your cases over to Patrick." He began working on some project Audrey couldn't see.

"Will you hold my position?"

Tate looked up. "Uh, no." He said it like a question, as if it was ridiculous for Audrey to ask. "Things move too fast around here, honey."

Her anger rose, so she stood quickly. "I understand, Alex." Exploding wouldn't help.

~

In her office, Audrey stomped to the window, fuming. Tate was unbelievable. No concern whatsoever for her future, despite all her contributions. She went to her desk and crossed the first item off her action list: "Get Tate to let me reduce caseload."

Oh, well. She scheduled an afternoon meeting with Patrick, then stopped and balanced her forehead on her fingertips, squeezing her eyes shut. She had nurtured her reputation like a delicate houseplant, and her five-star reviews would help her land a position at a new firm. She would have to go part-time. It wasn't impossible, but she doubted Tate would provide the glowing reference she needed. And would she have time to apply for new work, while taking on the kids' care?

Career disaster aside, in just three days she'd be a

substitute parent. She pulled her thoughts together and read the next item on her list: "Make financial plan."

She'd done well this year. Despite Tate's faults, she could count on a healthy bonus at New Year's. That, along with her savings, part-time work, and her credit cards would get her and the kids through the year—barely.

The school needed to know she was the children's new guardian. She called and scheduled an appointment for her and Luke. Next, she drafted quick plans to provide the kids a healthy diet and teach them to help with the cleaning. After that, she relaxed a little. Stepping in for Luke was really just doing housework, cooking, and supporting the kids' education. How hard could it be?

~

Still flushed from her workout, she knocked on Patrick's door. Patrick had recently won a challenging case. His soft face beamed at Audrey as he swung the door open. He gestured to his guest chair.

"I need to take some time off, and I could use your help with my cases." She sat down.

Patrick's smile faded. He sat comfortably in his cushy leather chair and pulled out a notepad and pen—this one engraved with his initials.

"Everything OK?"

"Yeah, fine. Can you take my caseload until Tate replaces me?"

Patrick's eyes were round. "So, it's not just a vacation, obviously."

She shook her head. "My brother is going to jail for a year. I'm taking care of his kids. Tate won't cut me any slack." Patrick might as well know.

"Shoot! I'd be happy to take your cases, Audrey."

"Thanks."

Patrick tapped his pen on the notepad and squinted at the ceiling. "Do you mind if I offer a suggestion?"

"Fire away."

"Have you considered a nanny?"

"Nannies are a thing!?" She gaped, astonished. "I thought those went out with Peter Pan!"

"I know someone who has one." Patrick leaned onto his desk, suit jacket tightening around his full shoulders. "They live with you, take the kids to school, make dinner, clean the house—basically everything a parent would do. Working parents use them all the time."

Audrey was already typing a search into her phone. She tapped on the first entry—Goodnight Moon Nanny Services—and saw a picture of a well-dressed young woman, playing with a little boy. In the background, a girl sat at a table. Their home looked immaculate.

Audrey stifled a whoop of excitement. "Could I wait on forwarding my cases, while I look into that?"

Patrick smiled, tipping his head understandingly. "Of course. Let me know how it goes."

"I will. Thanks, Patrick." She walked out of the room, staring at her phone and almost bumping into the potted bamboo by Patrick's door.

~

Goodnight Moon's nannies were screened and Red Cross-certified. They worked with kids of all ages. They could travel. They were perfect.

Audrey completed the new-client profile and scheduled a Facetime call with Rosemary Finch, Director. She told Tate her plans had changed. She could continue full time in the office, after taking the week off to make some arrangements.

Tate gave her a thumbs-up. "See you next week."

She went to her office and sank into her desk chair, closing her eyes and exhaling slowly. Her career was saved. She dialed Luke's number.

"Tate wouldn't let me cut my hours. I'm hiring a nanny."

"Oh, boy!"

"What's wrong? The service I found is perfect. Their

nannies are highly trained. I scheduled a time for us to meet our nanny." The last thing she needed was Luke pushing back.

"Can you send the information? I want to be sure they'll be safe."

"Of course." Audrey texted the link. "Luke, it's the only way I can keep my career going."

"I know."

~

Children's drawings and thank-you notes covered the walls of Goodnight Moon's spacious meeting room. Director Rosemary Finch handed Audrey and Luke glasses of ice water.

"I have just the nanny for you." Rosemary opened a photo of a smiling woman with friendly blue eyes. She wore a boho floral headband in her wavy blond hair. "Claire Owens is from Santa Cruz. She's only twenty-two, but she's very capable, and she loves kids. She's new to our agency. She came highly recommended by local families."

Audrey scanned the girl's references. Parents raved about the fun activities she did with their children. She was energetic and playful, and she had cared for children from infancy through twelve years old.

"Does she drive?"

"She does. She can use her car, or yours. Now, I understand you need an immediate placement, and your nanny will live in during the work week."

"Yes. I'll leave for work at five-thirty and get back around bedtime, Mondays through Fridays. I want the nanny only during the week."

They discussed the cost. With savings withdrawals and Tate's bonus, Audrey would about break even. Moments later, a tall figure breezed past the frosted glass window that overlooked the hall. Following a sharp tap on the door, Claire entered. She was all flowing clothes and freshness, exuding laid-back beach charm. A pink Hawaiian shell necklace hung around her neck.

She greeted Audrey and Luke, squeezing their hands warmly, a little breathless. "I'm so excited to hear about your kids!" She sat quickly, accepting the water Rosemary handed her.

Rosemary explained the situation.

"Oh, that's perfect! I just finished a contract with my little boy's family in Aptos. They're moving to D.C. They wanted me to go with them, but I can't leave Santa Cruz."

"Can you move in on Sunday?" Audrey was eager to finalize the arrangement and get back to work.

"That would be totally righteous."

Audrey stuffed a chuckle, glancing at Claire. The woman wasn't joking—an authentic Santa Cruz homie.

They signed a contract and made plans for Claire to meet the kids on Friday. Claire would sleep on an extra twin bed in Lillie's room. She would move in on Sunday, in time to help put the kids to bed.

The next day, Audrey arranged for a property manager to rent out the condo. She began packing and rented a storage unit for her furniture. She would finish emptying the condo when she had established a routine with the kids and Claire.

CHAPTER SEVEN

Small birds rustled in rose bushes as Audrey and Luke walked to the school's records and registration office. Redwoods and firs cast morning shadows across the school's sports field. A red-shouldered hawk glided across the clear sky.

Inside, Meredith, an administrator, guided them through the forms the school needed to authorize Audrey's involvement as guardian. They withdrew the boys from the after-school care program, since Claire would pick them up.

When they were done, Meredith walked them to the door. "Don't worry about explaining anything. An email about your situation went out yesterday."

An email? No secrets here! Audrey bit her lip.

They stepped outside, almost bumping into a man walking up the ramp. He was tan, a one-with-nature poster child, with sun-bleached, messy hair and complicated hazel eyes that took meaningful gazing to new levels. The effect was other-worldly and to some women, Audrey guessed (but not her), very attractive.

"Luke!" His smile revealed glossy teeth and a dimple in his left cheek. He side-stepped around them. "Are you looking for someone?"

"Audrey, Swift is the school band teacher." Luke turned

to Swift. "My sister, Audrey, will be my kids' guardian for a while."

"Audrey, good to meet you!" Swift's look was warm and open. He turned to Luke. "Hope everything's OK, man. Is Easton playing oboe still?"

Luke looked down. "Not since his mom left."

"Sorry. Sounds tough." Swift's raised eyebrows and gentle tone invited conversation.

Audrey wanted to interrogate Luke about his bills and call the condo property manager. She turned and walked down the ramp. "Nice to meet you," she called over her shoulder.

Luke followed her. She heard the mobile unit door click shut behind Swift.

"Swift's a nice guy." Luke caught up with her.

"I'm sure he's great. Sorry, Luke, I didn't have time for the love fest."

"Welcome to my world."

"Would that email have gone to all the teachers?"

"It's a small town. Teachers probably knew before they read it. Swift might not. He stays out of the loop."

"He didn't seem to know." Audrey sighed and added small-town gossip to her list of new challenges.

~

The next day, Audrey nudged Luke's kitchen door open, her arms full of essentials from the condo. "Need help packing?"

"No." Luke came from his bedroom. "They take everything when you check in."

She set her bags on the kitchen table. "Let's put your stuff in boxes and store it in the shed."

"That's what I said earlier." They went to Luke's bedroom. Luke began tossing clothes onto the bed.

Audrey labeled boxes. "I've arranged for Tesla to install my wall connector. They'll be here this weekend."

"You can always use the sedan."

"I know." She didn't mention her reservations about Luke's decrepit car.

They stored Luke's things, cleaned the cabin, and tidied the yard. Luke removed the paperwork and mugs from his desk. Audrey put her clothes in Luke's emptied dresser and set her high-powered blender on the kitchen counter. She tidied Lillie's room and cleared a space for Claire's bed.

When they were done, Luke went for a walk around the neighborhood. Sunlight filtered through the kitchen window. The sink shone. The walls and floor were grime-free. Audrey taped a weekly schedule and chore list to the refrigerator.

She went to the living room and sat on the couch, resting her feet on the coffee table. She looked forward to getting back to work, especially to winning Meghan's case. She was behind on most of her cases, but she could catch up.

Caring for the kids would be good. They could make happy memories. She would read to them on rainy days. Run and play with them at the beach. Introduce them to classical music, take trips to the city, cheer Lillie on at gymnastics. Tears blurred her vision. *Sometimes, the worst events bring the biggest blessings.*

Luke pushed the kitchen door open. "Time to go."

~

They picked up the kids and drove to Santa Cruz. At the jail, they walked past ice plant ground cover and tall trees. The lobby door faced a sunken patio with broad cement steps. Inside, Luke spoke with an officer. The officer took his watch and wedding band, then pointed to Audrey and the kids. "Say your goodbyes."

Slowly, Luke walked to Audrey and the children. He stood before them, hands hanging listlessly, head bent low.

"I'll miss you, Dad." Easton cried and wrapped his arms around his father's waist.

Warwick joined his brother, clinging to Luke.

Lillie sobbed and pushed her way between them. "I love you, Daddy."

"I love you, too." Luke embraced his children. He knelt, his forehead damp as he looked into the kids' eyes. "Listen to Auntie Audrey and your nanny while I'm away. Promise me!"

"Yes, Dad."

Lillie sniffed still, but their crying was over. Luke stood, swaying with the frailty of dry grass. Audrey wanted to whisk him safely home.

"When can we see you?" asked Easton.

"Auntie Audrey will bring you on Saturdays and Sundays. It might be a while before the first time, but after that it will be every weekend."

"Can Bella come?" asked Warwick.

"No. I don't think she'd like it here, though."

The officer cleared his throat. "Wrap up your goodbyes, Mr. Beach."

Luke glanced at the officer, then turned back to the kids. "Do what Auntie Audrey tells you, got it?"

The kids nodded. Luke went to the officer. Towering over Luke, the man opened a door and gestured for Luke to walk ahead of him. Audrey glimpsed her twin's hands clench and unclench as he went—his trademark stress signal she'd known since childhood.

A familiar, unyielding boulder settled in her chest. Her inner world groaned and shifted under its weight, as it had when her father left. She had pushed and kicked at that boulder, trying to dislodge it from the carefree landscape of her childhood. Her mom had been gentle, offsetting as much of the weight as she could, taking Audrey to the park, buying ice cream, indulging her with cheap trinkets from the dollar store. Now, Audrey was alone.

Tears for Luke pricked her eyes, but she forced her attention onto the kids. She was here to support them, not their dad. She pushed the lobby door open. "Want to hit the beach, and then get ice cream?" She forced cheerfulness into her voice. To her astonishment, the kids lit up.

"Yes!" Lillie and Warwick squealed together.

"Awesome!" Easton jogged up the cement steps to the path and did jumping jacks at the top. "I'll be first back to the car!"

The kids raced along the path to the parking lot. Audrey gaped for a moment, then dashed to catch up. The kids climbed into the Tesla, chattering about the beach and ice cream.

~

Minutes later, she pulled onto a dirt parking lot. Across the road, a path sloped to a wide beach. The tide was low, and the waves distant. She unlocked the doors. The kids flung them open and ran towards the beach, oblivious to the road.

"Stop!" Audrey lurched out of the driver's seat. The kids ignored her. Cars swished along the road. Horrified, Audrey slammed the Tesla door and tore across the dirt, darting between parked cars.

Lillie and Warwick reached the road, Easton close behind. A minivan lurched to a halt in front of Lillie. Lillie grabbed Warwick's hand.

"Guys, be careful!" Easton stepped in front of his siblings and pushed them backwards.

Audrey grabbed Lillie and Warwick by the shoulders, spinning them around to face her. "Don't run away from me!" she shouted, terrified.

Warwick wriggled out of Audrey's grasp. "You pushed me!" He swung his fist at Easton.

"Don't hit people, Warwick!" Lillie stopped Warwick's hand, glaring self-righteously.

The minivan's dark window descended. The woman in the driver's seat frowned at Audrey. "You need to work on your discipline." The car behind the van honked. The woman rolled up her window and drove on.

Ignoring the reprimand, Audrey marched the younger two kids back to the Tesla, Easton following. "Stand there!"

She lined the kids up, alongside the Tesla. They looked up at her, pale and defiant. "Didn't you hear your dad? He told you to do what I say!"

Lillie began crying. "I didn't know what you meant! I miss Daddy!" Easton put his arm across her shoulders.

Warwick snuggled into Lillie. "You're mean!" He turned his back to Audrey and wailed.

Regret and guilt flooded Audrey. "I'm sorry." She reached out her hands, shaking, but the kids pulled back. "I was so scared you'd get hurt!" Tears welled in her own eyes now.

"We thought you were mad at us," Easton said.

Audrey shook her head.

Easton tapped Warwick's shoulder. Warwick pulled back from his sister's side and looked at Easton. "Auntie Audrey's not mean, Warwick. She was just scared."

Warwick swiped the back of his hand across his nose. "I want Dad." He started crying again, loudly this time. Lillie put her arms around him.

"It's OK, Warwick." Lillie stroked her brother's small back.

Audrey cautiously extended her arms. "Who wants a hug?" The kids ignored her offer. No one talked. Gradually, Warwick calmed down.

"We're fine, Auntie Audrey," Easton said, at last.

Still shaking, Audrey took a deep breath. "Why don't we unload the beach stuff?" She opened the Tesla's frunk. "I brought some toys for you."

Subdued, the kids stood quietly as she pulled out a tote bag that Luke had helped her pack. The weather was sunny and warm, and she distributed buckets and spades to the kids. Carrying snacks and towels, she led the children to the beach.

So much for happy memories. She'd settle for keeping them alive.

~

The beach provided more practice in preserving life. Warwick waded down a scalloped curve of sand, into the water. A retreating wave pulled him off his feet. Audrey rushed to her nephew and grabbed him by the arm. After that, she stayed with him, leaving Easton and Lillie on the sand. She wasn't worried until she looked back and didn't see them.

She half-dragged a protesting Warwick out of the water. Panicked, she searched for twenty minutes before finding Easton and Lillie climbing rocks that jutted out into the ocean.

"We always climb here, Auntie Audrey," Easton assured her.

This time, she kept her emotions under control. "Please stay where I can see you."

For a while, the kids dug in the sand and Audrey read— until she noticed Warwick was back in the water. She threw down the book and dashed after him.

"I want to swim by myself!" Warwick pulled back as she took his hand.

"You're too young." Firmly, she led him back to shore and pulled her phone from the tote. "And I need to look at my emails."

Warwick flopped down on a towel. "Can I have a snack?"

Audrey stowed the phone and gave the kids bags of chips and water bottles. For the rest of the afternoon, she didn't take her eyes off them.

~

On their way home, she picked up tacos. The kids ate in the car. They stopped for ice cream in Scotts Valley and arrived at the cabin as daylight faded. Sand, wet towels, and bits of taco with scrunched-up wrappers littered the Tesla. Audrey hurried the kids inside, hoping to get them ready for bed before Claire arrived to meet them. Cleaning the car could wait.

Claire was late. Around seven thirty, Audrey turned on the porch light and opened the kitchen door. Headlights lit up the driveway and an old car stopped under the trees. Stickers covered its rear bumper. The car door opened, and Claire stepped out.

"Running late?" Audrey didn't soften her tone.

"Great to see you!" Claire's thick, husky voice floated through the evening air. "I'm so excited to meet the kids!" She crossed the yard and approached the kitchen door.

Audrey shelved her irritation. "Please come in quickly. The moths fly in at night."

Claire stepped in, and Audrey closed the door. "Kids, come and meet our new nanny!"

Mouse clicks and explosions continued from the family computer, where Easton was playing a video game.

"I'm taking a bath!" Lillie yelled.

Warwick came from the living room and stood shyly beside Audrey, wearing his pajamas—so far, he was the only one ready for bed.

"Call your friend!" Warwick's toy phone spoke from the couch. Warwick ran back to the living room.

Claire shrugged and giggled. "I guess they're busy. Have you eaten?" She looked around the kitchen.

Audrey nodded, not feeling obligated to feed Claire. "I'll show you around while we wait." She led Claire through the cabin, explaining the layout and storage. Passing Easton in the hallway, Audrey placed a hand on his shoulder. "Easton, finish up. It's time to meet Claire."

"Have a seat, Claire." She indicated the couch in the living room and went back to the bathroom. "Lillie, hurry up." She tapped on the door.

"I'm getting out!" Water sloshed.

"Don't soak the bathmat." Audrey spoke through the closed door. Linoleum was peeling up by the bathtub.

"Where will I sleep?" Claire asked, when Audrey returned to the living room. "You mentioned a bed for me in

Lillie's room?"

Audrey stared. "I completely forgot. I apologize."

"Well, dang!" Claire grinned and shifted on the couch.

"I'll have one here by the time you move in." Audrey couldn't believe she'd forgotten.

Claire smiled and flapped her hand. "No worries."

"Kids, hurry up!" Audrey called.

Ten minutes later, everyone sat in the living room. The children were tongue-tied at first, but Claire proved the agency's recommendation, telling kid-level jokes and asking questions about their lives. Soon, the children wanted to show her their rooms.

Audrey watched as Claire exclaimed over the kids' projects, played with their toys, and admired Lillie's handstands. Later, the children snuggled with Claire on the coach. Lillie tried on some of the endless colorful bangles that hung on Claire's wrists. Warwick sat on Claire's lap, showing her his latest Lego creation. Easton leaned against her, playing on his gaming device. They were happy. The transformation far outweighed Claire's tardiness.

"OK, you guys, I gotta go." Claire gathered up her purse and a drawing Lillie had given her.

"Aw, not yet, Claire!" Lillie put her arm around Claire's shoulders.

"Can you stay and watch our movie with us?" asked Warwick.

"I have to pack." Claire untangled herself from the kids and stood. "You can keep the bangles until I come back, Lillie."

Lillie lifted her arm and watched the bangles slide down. "Are you going on a trip?"

"I'm moving in here. I'm your nanny, remember?"

The kids' faces lit up. They squealed, and Lillie danced around the room. Audrey recalled their nonplussed response when Luke had told them Audrey would care for them during his absence. They clustered around Claire as she walked to the kitchen door.

"See you on Sunday." Claire hugged Lillie, gently shook Easton's hand, then knelt and wrapped an arm around Warwick's small shoulders, giving him a squeeze.

Audrey opened the door. "Thank you, Claire. You've done a great job already."

"No prob!" Claire went down the steps and waved goodbye.

Audrey cued a kids' movie on her laptop and plugged it into the TV. The children piled cushions on the floor, ready for their weekly show. The magic of Claire's visit lasted until morning when a crash in the kitchen woke Audrey.

CHAPTER EIGHT

Audrey dashed down the hall, whacking her hip on the computer table. Warwick stood next to the kitchen counter, a shattered cereal bowl at his feet. Bella was licking up splashes of milk.

"Oh great!" Audrey pushed her hair out of her eyes. "Come here, Warwick. You need to get out of the way so I can clean that up." She stretched out her hands to him.

"I was hungry!" Warwick started walking towards her, then stopped abruptly. "Ouch!" He hopped on one foot, grabbing at the other. Audrey saw a streak of blood on the linoleum.

"You're bleeding. Stay still!" She extended her palm towards Warwick. Shattered fragments lay in his path.

Warwick saw the blood. "I'm bleeding!" He ran into the living room and sat on the floor, holding his foot and wailing.

Audrey picked him up and carried him to the couch. She knelt next to him and tried to wrest his foot out of his hands.

"No! Don't touch it!" Warwick pulled away.

Easton and Lillie ran from their rooms.

"Is he OK?" Easton asked.

"He's bleeding! Warwick's bleeding!" Lillie pushed against Audrey, crying and trying to see Warwick's injury. Easton leaned over Audrey, peering at Warwick's foot.

Audrey grabbed a Kleenex. "Kids!" she snapped. "Could

you give me some room?"

Lillie and Easton moved back a little but remained in Audrey's space.

Lillie wailed. "What should we do?"

"Let me get it clean." Audrey elbowed Lillie backwards.

Lillie leaned in again. "I want to see!"

"Lillie, please!" Audrey pushed Lillie away and yanked Warwick's foot free. Lillie flopped onto the living room floor and howled. Audrey dabbed at the cut, until Warwick pulled his foot from her grasp.

"Want me to get a band-aid?" Easton asked.

Audrey turned to Easton, gripping Warwick's foot. "That would be helpful."

Easton brought band-aids and cotton balls from the bathroom. He set them on the couch.

"Thank you." Audrey grabbed a cotton ball and pressed it against the cut. Behind her, Lillie continued crying. Audrey squeezed her eyes shut, praying for patience.

"Lillie, Warwick's fine. Would you please stop crying?" Her voice rose.

Lillie stomped to her room and slammed the door. Audrey sighed. Warwick quieted. Easton sat on the end of the couch, watching closely.

She pulled the cotton ball away. Strands of cotton stuck to Warwick's skin, but the bleeding was slowing, and the cut looked minor. "Could you get this wet, please, so I can clean it?" She handed Easton a new cotton ball. He took it to the kitchen.

"Use the bathroom sink. You're barefoot."

Easton returned with the damp cotton ball, and Audrey cleaned the cut. She pressed a Kleenex against it for a few more minutes, stopping the bleeding. "There. It's fine." She smoothed a Band-Aid into place.

"It still hurts."

"Totally normal. Just ignore it."

"You're mean!"

Ignoring her nephew's assessment, Audrey pulled a dustpan and broom from the small closet next to the kitchen door and swept up the broken pottery.

~

She floundered through the rest of the day. The kids refused to tidy their rooms and vacuum, much less tackle the additional chores Audrey had listed. Warwick went outside when she told him to put his clothes away, limping dramatically across the yard. Lillie was irritable and moody. Audrey reacted by raising her voice, immediately regretting it but unable to communicate. Easton announced he was sick of the arguing, went to his room, and closed the door.

After she got the kids to bed that night, she lay on the couch, exhausted. The cabin was a mess, the kids had done nothing she'd asked, and she was too worn out to tidy. Her only accomplishment for the day had been getting the wall connector installed for the Tesla—the technician had taken most of the afternoon doing the job. She made a mental note to charge her car each time she arrived home. Not that it mattered right now. There was no way they would be awake in time for church in the morning.

She was beginning to dream when she heard Warwick get up to use the bathroom. The toilet flushed, the boys' door clicked shut, and she fell asleep. An hour or two later, she heard one of the boys use the bathroom again. Then, she heard Warwick crying. She went to his room.

"Warwick, want me to hold your hand?"

"Go away!" He pushed at her.

"I'll just sit here until you fall asleep." She waited until his breathing grew heavy, then crawled into bed, still wearing her clothes.

Lillie had a nightmare and screamed but didn't want Audrey to stay with her. Easton walked in his sleep twice. Audrey gave up trying to sleep. She thumbed through a parenting book, yawning, but there wasn't much about nightmares and losing parents. Around three in the morning, the house was finally quiet. She fell asleep with the book across her chest and the light still on.

~

In the morning, Luke called. He told the kids he was fine and promised to call the following Friday. The kids cheered up a little when they heard their dad's voice. They didn't seem to notice what was obvious to Audrey—Luke's dark tone and tight, distracted comments. Her brother's speech had always given away his stress level. The more anxiety he felt, the quieter he grew, retreating deep into a cave of isolation Audrey could not enter.

God, please show him how to cope. After Luke's call, she pointed the kids to their rooms and told them to clean up. "I'll get you donuts when you've put your clothes away and vacuumed your rooms. Claire's moving in tonight."

"Donuts!" Lillie grabbed Warwick's hands and pulled him in a circle around her.

"Stop it!" Warwick broke free and ran to the living room.

Audrey directed him to his room. "No donuts until you've cleaned." She hated to resort to bribes.

The children threw their clothes into their dressers and vacuumed just the very middle of their rooms. Audrey decided that was good enough.

She found a bed online for Claire in the Forest Lakes community of Felton. It was only one hundred dollars. She arranged for Claire to watch the kids while she picked up the bed that afternoon.

The GPS took her down Highway 9 to a contemporary home far back in Forest Lakes—a sprawling community of cabins perched along narrow mountain roads that wound through the forest. She pulled up the steep driveway and got out of the Tesla.

A second-story deck fronted the property, and sunlight filtered through the redwoods that towered around it. Wood stairs led up to the deck and front door. A petite woman in her twenties darted out, letting the screen door slam behind her. She looked strong and energetic, as if she would enjoy an afternoon swing through the redwoods the way normal people enjoy walks. "Here for the bed?" She leaned over the deck rail.

"Correct. I'm Audrey."

"I'm Dominique. Come on up!" The woman smiled with her whole face as Audrey ascended the steps to the deck.

The spacious home was stunning inside. Audrey wondered what Dominique did for a living. The property must be worth upwards of eight hundred thousand dollars.

"This is my parents' house, but I live with them still." Dominique followed Audrey's gaze at the high-end kitchen appliances.

"Got it." Audrey was annoyed that the woman read her so accurately. "And the bed is where?"

"Down here." Dominique zipped down a set of stairs off the living room, Audrey hurrying to keep up.

Their guest room was messy. Boxes of yarn and crafts, clothing, games, and books were on the floor. Dominique shoved them to the side and pulled a pile of winter coats off the bed. "My parents are selling my childhood bed. Do you think that's a hint?"

Audrey glanced at the bed. "A hint about what?" She handed Dominique the cash payment.

"I was joking." Dominique tucked the cash into her pocket. "My mom's always telling me to move out and get on with my life."

"Oh." Audrey was confused. She hadn't lived with her mom since high school.

Dominique casually lifted the thick mattress off the frame and leveraged it towards the door. "Want to grab the other end? We'll put it in the truck." Her bright, brown eyes, beneath carefully plucked eyebrows, peeked over the top of the mattress. She was friendliness personified. Audrey stiffened.

They carried the mattress out a downstairs slider and put

it in a pickup. After they had put the frame and slats in beside it, Dominique ran back for her purse and keys. "My parents are out, or they'd help us." She returned to Audrey in the driveway. "Your cabin is in Ben Lomond?"

"Off Love Creek Road." Audrey gave Dominique the address.

Dominique hopped into the truck. "I'll help you unload and set up the bed."

"Thank you." Audrey got into the Tesla. Closing the driver door, she sighed, hoping the woman's help didn't come with a side of on-demand friendship. In her new life, drama was out of the question.

~

The kids ran to meet them, followed by Claire. When Dominique jumped out of the pickup, Lillie squealed. "Coach Minnie!" She ran to greet her.

Dominique hugged Lillie. "Lillie! Great to see you! I'm Lillie's gymnastics coach," she explained, as Audrey joined them. "Lillie's one of my troopers."

Dominique would be a feature in regular life, then. Audrey smiled, for Lillie's sake. "What a coincidence! I'm Lillie's aunt. My brother's away for a while, so I'm taking care of the kids."

Dominique's smile faded as understanding lit her eyes. Clearly, she had heard about Luke's sentence. She changed the subject, asking Lillie what she thought of the new bed.

"Is it yours?" Lillie hung on Dominique's arm.

"It was when I was your age. I have a big bed now."

Thankful for the coach's sensitivity, Audrey introduced Dominique to Claire. "You'll be seeing a lot of each other. Claire will take the kids where they need to be, while I work."

She was looking forward to that.

~

She woke early on Monday morning. Beginning Tuesday, her departure time would be five thirty, before the kids woke up. Today, she planned to go with Claire to drop the kids at school, so she could meet their teachers and see the school and arrangements.

She listened to the quiet, wondering why she didn't hear Claire. She had told the nanny they would need breakfast by seven. She went to the kitchen. A dirty pan from last night's dinner sat on the stove, and the counters needed wiping. Audrey put the pan in the sink and set out a frying pan. She peeled strips of bacon from a package.

In the hallway, Lillie and Claire's door squeaked open. Claire joined Audrey in the kitchen. "Good morning!" Claire yawned. She wore stretchy yoga pants and an oversized t-shirt. "Got any coffee?"

Audrey bristled. "If you want to make it. I thought you were going to handle the kids' breakfast." She pointed to the schedule on the fridge door. "Did you sleep through your alarm?"

"Sorry! I totally forgot to set my alarm. I'll get things ready. I'm just gonna get dressed." Claire rushed back to Lillie's room and closed the door.

"Could you get the kids up?"

Claire poked her head back out the bedroom door. "Sure!" She closed the door and Audrey heard her talking to Lillie. "Time to get up, Lillie. It's a new week!"

Audrey left the bacon for Claire to finish and got ready for work. When she returned, Lillie and Easton were dressed and eating. Claire bustled around the stove, grabbing sips from a large mug of coffee as she worked. She had dressed for childcare action, wearing jeans and a t-shirt. Her hair was loosely secured in a messy bun. The usual jewelry was absent.

Warwick wandered into the kitchen, still in his pajamas. Claire set a plate of bacon and fried eggs at his place. "Here you go, buddy." She tapped his back lightly as he sat down.

Warwick stared at his plate. Easton looked at him. "Warwick, you need to eat fast. We're going soon."

"Eat up, little guy." Claire stroked his hair.

Warwick picked at his bacon. Lillie went into the living room for her backpack. She loaded up books and binders from the computer stand.

"Lillie, clear your place, please." Audrey glanced at the table as she hurried to find her purse. Her niece scowled but took her plate to the sink.

"Did you have nightmares again?" Audrey asked. "I didn't hear you scream last night."

Lillie glared at Audrey and stomped away to her room without answering.

"Great job embarrassing her." Easton spoke quietly as he grabbed a piece of toast from the plate Claire had set on the table. Claire ignored the conversation and kept working. Lillie returned and stuffed her gymnastics clothes into her backpack.

"Sorry, Lillie. I didn't mean to upset you."

Now Lillie rolled her eyes and went to find her shoes. Warwick left his breakfast and went to the hallway computer desk. He opened a video game. Slumped in the chair, he ignored the activity around him and stared at the screen, his small hand resting on the mouse.

"Warwick, get dressed!" Audrey's stress was rising.

"I'm almost done."

"You don't have time for that."

He ignored her.

Frustrated, Audrey gently took his hand off the mouse and tugged at him. "Come on!"

He pulled away and grabbed the mouse again. "You're not the boss! Dad's the boss."

Audrey folded her arms sternly and looked down at her nephew. "Dad's not here, and he told you to do what I say."

Easton passed them on the way to his room. "Warwick, you can play games later. Want me to get your backpack ready while you put your clothes on?"

"Ok." Warwick slipped off the chair and followed his

brother.

Audrey sighed and fetched her briefcase from the living room. She put her laptop in the protective sleeve and loaded up her gym clothes. She hadn't worked out for days.

~

Claire took the kids to school in Luke's sedan. Audrey followed them in the Tesla, opening the windows. The beach mess stunk from the back seat.

Ahead of the turnoff to Ben Lomond Elementary School, a line of cars crawled along Rose Avenue and turned onto the sloping driveway. Audrey drummed the steering wheel, inching towards the school building. At last, she and Claire parked and convened with the kids at the school's front doors.

"I don't know why you have to be here. We know where to go." Easton shifted his heavy backpack.

"I want to see where you are, and Claire needs to know what's going on, too."

"Audrey! Happy Monday!" Dominique grinned. She slammed her car's door and power-walked towards them. Watermelon-slice earrings dangled from her ears.

Lillie jumped. "Coach Minnie!"

"Hi, Lillie!" Dominique hugged Lillie.

The door behind them opened and Swift walked out, carrying a trombone case. "Oh, hey!" He paused and looked at Audrey. "Do you need to talk to the staff?"

"I'm fine."

"If you need anything, let me or Dominique know."

"Swift, have you met Audrey?" Dominique asked. "She's Luke Beach's sister. So, she's Easton's auntie."

"Yeah, we've met." Swift turned to Easton and lifted his hand for a high five. "How's it going, my man? Are you coming back to band?"

Easton exchanged the high five, then looked down. "Don't have time."

Swift frowned. "Come to my office any time. Maybe I

can help you figure out a practice schedule."

Easton glanced at Swift and nodded.

"Swift, this is Claire." Dominique gestured to the nanny. "She's their nanny. I met everybody yesterday when Audrey bought my childhood bed."

Swift shook Claire's hand warmly.

"Hi, Swift." Claire's gaze lingered on Swift's Greek-god face, her lips slightly parted in a soft smile. Inwardly, Audrey rolled her eyes.

Swift nudged Dominique. "How's the gym carpool working out?"

"Thanks soooo much for reminding me!" Dominique rolled her eyes, sarcastically. "It's chaos." She sighed, dramatically, but grinned.

"Sounds like a challenge you can handle." Swift handed her a small packet of M&Ms.

Dominique slipped the packet into her purse and turned to Audrey. "Swift and I have a standing agreement. I whine, he gives me M&Ms." She and Swift shared a look and laughed again.

Audrey fidgeted. "Kids, you should get in there." She squeezed Lilie's shoulder.

Easton and Lillie dashed into the building, joining their friends. Warwick sighed and trudged in behind them, bent under the load of his backpack. Audrey hurried to the Tesla. Dr. Taylor's deposition was in two days. She meant to be prepared.

CHAPTER NINE

Audrey reviewed medical records, interrogatories, and Dr. McKenzie's reports. She worked late, and the kids were asleep when she arrived home. The next day, she outlined her plan for the deposition, with detailed questions to tease out an admission of error. Later, she Facetimed with Meghan. "Did you or your mom try to talk to the doctor about the dosing error?"

"My mom called him at the clinic."

"What did he say?"

"He was sorry it happened, but he said it was a software error. He wouldn't admit it might have been his fault."

"Did your mom try to get him to admit it?"

"I don't think so. She just asked him how it happened."

"What was Dr. Taylor like when he treated you at the clinic, on your regular visits?" Audrey wanted to get a more complete picture of the man's personality.

"He was nice. He didn't take my mom very seriously."

"What do you mean?"

"She would ask about health treatments—supplements and stuff. He just changed the subject, like she hadn't even said anything."

"That's rude." Doctors who cared didn't ignore patients' questions.

"Right? My mom's not a doctor, but she isn't stupid. And she only wants to help."

The conversation fueled Audrey's determination to hold the doctor accountable. She drove home itching for the next day's battle. She arrived at the cabin late. A partially eaten meatloaf and green beans waited on the stove. Claire was talking softly in the boys' room. Audrey set down her briefcase and went to the bedrooms to say goodnight.

In Lillie's room, a nightlight glowed. Lillie lay still, and her steady breathing told Audrey she was asleep. Quietly, Audrey closed the door and went to the boys' room. Easton was reading a chapter book in bed. His backpack sat on the floor by the closet, and for the first time Audrey could remember, the floor was cleared of clothes.

Easton looked at her briefly. "'Night, Auntie Audrey!"

"Goodnight, Easton."

Claire perched on the edge of Warwick's bed. "Look, Warwick! Auntie Audrey's home."

"Hi!" Warwick's hair was damp. Claire must have given him a bath before bedtime.

"Hi, Warwick." Audrey looked at Claire. "How did it go today?"

"Great! I saw Lillie's gymnastics practice. Have you been to the gym?"

"Not yet."

"She's good! It was so fun watching the kids swooping around those high bars. They're amazing." She looked at Warwick and stroked his hair. "Warwick isn't feeling well. The kid I watched before got like this when he was catching a cold. I gave Warwick ginger tea."

Warwick pulled Claire's hand to his chest. His face was pale and dark smudges lay under his eyes.

"Why don't you say goodnight to Auntie Audrey now?" Claire leaned close.

"Goodnight, Auntie Audrey." His voice was almost a whisper.

Audrey crossed the room. Hesitantly, she bent and squeezed his shoulder. "Goodnight, Warwick. I hope you feel better by tomorrow." She smelled his freshly washed hair and the tiniest, sweet exhale. "Your breath smells sweet."

"That's because he's the sweetest boy." Claire tucked the covers over Warwick's shoulders. "Goodnight, Warwick! You'll be fine tomorrow, I bet. I'll help you get ready for school, ok?"

"'K."

Claire giggled again. "Goodnight, Warwick and Easton. My new boys! I'm so excited!"

~

In the morning, Audrey walked into the expansive lobby of Elizabeth Weaver's office tower. The heavy glass door swung shut behind her.

Dr. McKenzie stood by the sweeping staircase. With him was a tall man she assumed was Dr. Taylor, and Elizabeth Warren, Dr. Taylor's lawyer. The required court reporter stood nearby, carrying her small steno machine.

"Audrey, great to see you!" Dr. McKenzie waved. He wore a finely tailored wool suit. Beside the entry, the receptionist glanced in the direction of his rich-timbred voice.

"Dr. McKenzie, thanks for coming out." Audrey's practical, rubber-soled clogs squeaked as she crossed the tiled floor and joined the group. She shook Dr. McKenzie's hand and turned to Dr. Taylor and Elizabeth. "I guess you've met my client's expert witness, Dr. Harrison McKenzie."

Elizabeth Weaver nodded. "Audrey, this is Dr. Taylor. And I'm Elizabeth Weaver."

They shook hands. Dr. Taylor nodded briefly at Audrey, no smile softening the lofty battlement of his face. Audrey couldn't help feeling defensive under the disdainful glance of his steady blue eyes.

"Lead on!" Dr. McKenzie gestured grandly, smiling at Elizabeth, eyebrows raised congenially.

Elizabeth smiled stiffly. "Elevator's this way." On the

third floor, she opened the door to a conference room and motioned to leather chairs arranged around a vast, marble-topped table.

Dr. Taylor sat across from Audrey, with the animation of a boulder. Dr. McKenzie sat next to Audrey. He took a notepad and pen from his pocket, sighing deeply. Audrey saw him write the date and "Taylor Depo." across the top. He underlined the note and set his pen down firmly, then crossed his arms and looked at Dr. Taylor.

Dr. Taylor ignored him, his face unreadable. Elizabeth joined Dr. Taylor. The court reporter sat by a corner window, set up her white machine, and waited.

Elizabeth explained the rules and procedures. "The plaintiff's attorney, Audrey Beach, will now examine the witness." She rested her papers on the table and tugged her red jacket close around her shoulders.

"Dr. Taylor, how long have you worked as an endocrinologist?" Audrey put on her warmest smile, hoping to disarm the doctor.

"Six years." He spoke abruptly, giving no hint of emotion.

"Did you earn your doctorate earlier than most?"

"I was thirty."

"Please describe how you treated Meghan Patel on April fourteenth of this year."

The doctor gave a brief rundown of Meghan's treatment. He folded his arms. "When I became an endocrinologist, I didn't plan on badly designed software and pointless lawsuits."

Elizabeth glared at her client. "Dr. Taylor, please answer the questions directly, as I recommended."

The court reporter tapped away. Dr. McKenzie cleared his throat loudly and jotted down notes.

"How often are you called into the emergency department?" Audrey asked.

"Rarely."

"Why? Almost eight million people live in the Bay Area. Many diabetic emergencies must occur every day."

"Emergency departments have hospitalists trained in endocrinology. I like to hear from California Oaks' hospitalist if a new pediatric patient comes in. I also require a call if my patients are in the ER."

"Why would your patients go to the emergency room instead of contacting you?"

"Because they have an emergency." He rested his forearms on the table and clasped his hands. "Isn't that obvious?"

Elizabeth frowned. Dr. McKenzie sighed again.

"Do you go to the ER, if one of your patients is there?"

"Always."

"Why do you go in, if the hospitalist is there?"

"My staff tells me it's overkill."

"Interesting word choice."

Dr. McKenzie chuckled. Elizabeth pursed her lips. Dr. Taylor ignored the humorous jab.

"Have you taken the training on NewDay's software?"

"Of course."

"Could your input to the medical records software on your end, at the clinic, confuse the hospitalist? Is that why you go to the ER?"

"I am scrupulous. I go in to ensure the best care."

"Yet my client was injured under your care at the ER."

The man stayed silent. He was a hard read—face blank, eyes cold.

"Is it fair to say a good endocrinologist's care includes thorough competency on any software?" Her phone pinged. She silenced it and shoved it into her purse.

Dr. Taylor paused and looked closely at Audrey. "Every situation is different. Complicating the best care is badly designed software, which could have killed a patient in this case. You should pursue that angle, instead of wasting my time and yours."

"Right." Dr. McKenzie rolled his eyes and scribbled something on his pad.

"Stick to the question!" Elizabeth commanded.

Dr. Taylor's scolding was a line too far. "Why don't we review the basics, for my benefit? Dr. Taylor, please describe the symptoms of type 1 diabetes in a new patient, which in your opinion would precipitate a visit to the ER."

Dr. Taylor nodded and rattled off the symptoms in a quick monotone. "Extreme thirst, unexplained weight loss, frequent urination, irritability. Sweet-smelling breathe indicating the presence of ketones followed by unresponsiveness in advanced cases—"

Adrenaline flooded Audrey. "Sweet-smelling breath?"

He unclasped his hands and glanced at Elizabeth. "Yes, along with extreme thirst, weight loss, irritability, frequent urination, general fatigue—"

Audrey's scalp prickled. Warwick used the bathroom several times a night. She remembered his demands for water throughout the day. The weight loss Easton had commented on at dinner. His tiredness and pale skin. And his sweet breath the night before. "What happens after these symptoms show up?"

"It depends on how many and to what degree the symptoms present." Dr. Taylor looked at Audrey, the stern planes of his face serious. "Sweet breath is a major concern, as it indicates the presence of ketones, suggesting blood glucose has built to a dangerous level. Coma and death can follow within hours."

Elizabeth cleared her throat. "I don't know that we need to spend any more time on symptoms."

But Audrey was already on her feet. "I have to go. This deposition is adjourned."

McKenzie tossed his pen onto the table and rested his forehead on his fingertips.

Dr. Taylor stood, gripping the back of his chair. "Is someone you know showing these symptoms? Can I help?"

"I wouldn't trust you with my dog!" Frantically, Audrey tapped her phone.

Claire had texted her. "Looks like we're going to be late to school, sorry. Warwick won't get up."

"Jesus!" she prayed, in a half-scream. She shoved her laptop into her briefcase, grabbed her purse, and bolted from the room.

CHAPTER TEN

Audrey prayed non-stop as she sped through the streets and tore along the onramp to Highway 280. The Tesla's milometer flicked rapidly as she hurried south towards the intersection to Santa Cruz County. On Highway 17, she called Claire.

"Hey!"

"Claire, what do you mean Warwick won't get up? Is he talking to you?"

"Don't worry. My other kid was slow in the morning, too. I just texted so you'd know we're going to be late to school."

"Is he up?"

"Still in bed. I tried bribing him with donuts." She laughed and told Lillie to get her backpack ready.

Audrey's scalp crawled and a shiver spread over her shoulder blades. She stuffed her fear and forced herself to think. "Claire, listen to me carefully."

"Listening."

"I think Warwick may be seriously ill. I want you to call 911 and get an ambulance."

"Really? An ambulance? Are you sure?"

"Yes, do it!" Audrey was losing patience. "I'm on my way. When the paramedics arrive, tell them he may have type 1 diabetes."

"My mom and my uncle have diabetes. They use

cinnamon to keep their blood sugar in range. Would you like me to—"

"Call 911!" Audrey screamed. She ended the call. The traffic was light on Highway 17. Audrey pushed the Tesla to its limits, thankful for its fierce grip on the road as she guided it around the steep curves. She charged through Scotts Valley, cursing the stop lights, darted along narrow Highway 9, and pulled into Luke's driveway. An ambulance, lights flashing and doors open, waited near the cabin. She ran inside and dashed to Warwick's room, ignoring Claire, who sat in the living room with Easton and Lillie.

"Is he going to die?" Lillie's voice sounded frantic behind Audrey. She had followed her aunt. Audrey turned. Easton had joined his sister. They clung together, looking at her, eyes fearful. Claire stood behind them, her brow creased with worry.

"I promise you, he won't."

An enormous gurney and three paramedics crowded the bedroom. Audrey squeezed past the gurney and pressed in beside the female paramedic who knelt at Warwick's side. She gasped. Her nephew's face was ashen, his cheeks sunken, his eyes half-closed. He had looked tired the night before, but now he looked desperately ill. "Hello, Warwick," she managed to stutter.

Warwick's eyes rolled up to meet Audrey's, then dropped back to the paramedic's. "I don't feel well."

"We're going to take you to the hospital, so they can make you better."

The paramedic looked at Audrey. "Ma'am, we need you to step aside, please. We're going to transfer Warwick to the ambulance."

"Did Claire tell you I think he has type 1 diabetes?" Audrey prodded.

"Yes, but we don't carry insulin. We need to get him to the ER."

"You should keep insulin in the—"

A storm transformed the woman's face. "Ma'am, step aside!" Her voice was a thunderclap—and something inside Audrey fell, defenseless and relieved. She put her hands on Easton and Lillie's shoulders and guided them out of the room.

~

The paramedics placed Warwick carefully on the gurney and wheeled him out to the ambulance, lifting the bed slightly over the threshold to avoid jostling him. They loaded the gurney, and a paramedic leapt in beside it. Audrey ran to the back of the vehicle and watched the paramedic connect a bag of fluids to an IV that hung from the ceiling. The other workers jumped into the front cabin and started up the engine.

"Warwick, we'll follow you in the car." Audrey went to the driver's window. "I'll meet Warwick at the Emergency Room at Dominican Hospital."

The driver nodded. The paramedic in the rear of the ambulance swung the doors shut. The driver eased out of the driveway and started the vehicle's alarm system to clear the road.

Audrey watched the ambulance leave down the road, yowling, its lights flashing. She turned to Easton and Lillie. "Get in the back of the Tesla, please." The two children quickly obeyed, their defiant attitudes gone.

She dashed to the cabin, where Claire watched from the kitchen. "Claire, you've done a wonderful job. Thanks for calling the ambulance. I don't know how this will play out. I'm sorry, but I can't promise to keep you on."

Claire nodded and touched Audrey's arm. "No worries. I'm here if you need me." Spontaneously, she grabbed Audrey in a bear hug. "You've got this, Auntie!"

Audrey ran to the Tesla. She pulled out of the driveway and followed the ambulance. Siren wailing, the vehicle pushed through traffic along the narrow valley artery that was Highway 9. Cars pulled to the side, squeezing close to embankments and giant trees. Audrey pressed in close, insisting on passing the sidelined cars. The ambulance eased through and continued its frenetic flight.

Easton and Lillie sat in the back seat. No one spoke.

~

Audrey lurched the Tesla to a stop in Dominican Hospital's Emergency Room parking lot. She leapt out, dinging the Tesla's door on the next car's mirror, and ran into the ER lobby. Easton and Lillie followed closely.

A receptionist approached them. "Are you Audrey Beach?"

"Yes!"

Quickly, the woman handed Audrey a visitor's lanyard and pointed her to a pink door with a tall, narrow window. "They're waiting for you."

Audrey pushed the pink door open and hurried to the information area. "I'm Audrey Beach. My nephew's here."

A technician led them past a few curtained rooms along a short corridor. At the last room, the technician held aside the curtain that shielded Warwick's bed. Warwick lay on the bed, hooked up to an IV and a heart monitor. He turned when Audrey entered the room, eyes half-shut.

An elderly African-American doctor stood beside his bed. "I'm Dr. Bennet. We want to give Warwick a subcutaneous injection of insulin to start bringing his glucose down. Could you sign to give permission, please?" He handed a clipboard to Audrey.

Audrey signed a form, and a nurse injected a clear liquid into Warwick's abdomen. She patted Warwick's shoulder and left the room.

Dr. Bennet glanced at the room's computer. "Warwick is in a state called ketoacidosis, which needs immediate treatment. With your permission, we'll rush him to California Oaks Hospital. They have a pediatric ICU and access to leading endocrinologists. An ambulance is ready to take him."

"Of course."

Dr. Bennet stepped to the doorway. "We're ready to go!"

A team of healthcare professionals gathered around Warwick's bed. They transferred his IV fluids to a portable stand, checked his vitals, and put him onto a gurney. Audrey pulled Easton and Lillie close while they worked. The staff wheeled Warwick out of the room.

Audrey hesitated, then rushed after them. She touched the cold railing of the gurney. "Warwick! I love you."

Warwick's eyelids fluttered open, and he looked at her. The gurney moved on.

Lillie ran after the gurney, then stopped in the corridor. "'Bye, Warwick! Don't be scared!" The team wheeled the gurney down the hall and out the door. Lillie spun to Audrey, threw her arms around her, and wailed.

~

Dr. Bennet gestured to the guest chair. "Before you go, I should update you."

Audrey squeezed Lillie's shoulders. "Stand with Easton." Lillie wiped her eyes and pulled Easton's arm over her shoulders. Audrey perched on the chair, gripping her hands together.

Dr. Bennet leaned back against the counter and folded his arms. "Warwick has elevated levels of glucose and ketones. That suggests his pancreas isn't producing insulin. If this is true, the diagnosis will be type 1 diabetes.

"Insulin is a hormone that unlocks the body's cells to glucose. If there's no insulin, glucose from food can't get into his cells. The glucose saturates his blood—kind of like sand in a river." He waved his fingers to imitate the motion of a river.

"Is it curable?" Audrey's research on Meghan's case had already answered the question, but perhaps there was some new development she didn't know about.

"Not yet. But the endocrine teams in the Bay Area are second to none. Warwick should receive the best care."

"Is he going to be ok?" Easton's voice trembled.

The doctor looked at the children. "He will be fine. He will have to give himself injections of insulin for the rest of his life, and he'll have to take extra good care of himself. But can you guess how many people in America have type 1 diabetes?"

"How many?" Easton's brow furrowed.

"About one and a half million." The doctor smiled. "You probably already know someone with the disease and just didn't realize it! They live happy, productive lives."

Lillie wiped her nose with her sleeve. "I don't know anyone with it." Her tears began again, this time quietly.

Audrey stared at the floor. The thought of Warwick saddled with a lifelong disease stunned her. Suddenly, she realized she needed to tell Luke, and the jail didn't permit phone calls to inmates. She would have to wait for his call on Friday. She ran her fingers over her hair and sighed.

"Do you have any more questions for me?" asked Dr. Bennet.

"No," she said, quickly. "Thanks for your explanation, Dr. Bennet. The kids and I should go."

"I'll be in touch to see how Warwick is doing. I know this is difficult news, but I want to reiterate that Warwick is in the best hands."

"Thank you."

Dazed, Audrey took the kids back to the Tesla.

CHAPTER ELEVEN

After Dr. McKenzie left the conference room, Eric turned to Elizabeth. "What happens now?"

"I'll let you know, Dr. Taylor. I've never seen this. We'll reschedule, certainly." She wrestled her jacket across her shoulders and moved towards the door. Eric followed.

Elizabeth breathed quickly as they descended the stairs and crossed the foyer. "It's actually a good thing, now that I think about it. Audrey's behavior is a serious strike against the plaintiff."

It didn't look like a good thing for Audrey Beach.

They went outside and stood on the sidewalk, beside Eric's SUV. Elizabeth shouldered her purse and settled her briefcase in the crook of her arm. "The case will be delayed. That's more time for the plaintiff to decide to settle."

"Thanks, Elizabeth. I'm sure the case will unfold as it should."

"It will, but we need to stay ahead of things and not let our guard down."

Staying ahead of legal issues was not on his agenda. "Sounds good."

"I'll be in touch." Elizabeth walked back down the sidewalk. Eric pushed the key fob button to unlock his SUV. The temporary reprieve was a relief, but Eric wondered what was happening with Audrey Beach. He prayed for the situation as he eased onto the busy downtown street and drove to the clinic.

~

The practice bustled with patients and staff. Glad to be out of the legal gloom, Eric picked up the rhythms of work. He updated a teen's insulin doses to reflect changes in his hormones. He advised the parents of a ten-year old girl to switch her over to a better glucose monitor. He explained to a family that the siblings of their child with type 1 diabetes should be tested, to determine if they, too, were at risk. At noon, he went to his office for a quick break. Nurse Jenny knocked on his door.

"Come in."

She rushed in, pulling a folded paper from the pocket of her colorful scrubs. "You have a call to the ER at California Oaks. A four-year old boy is coming in from Santa Cruz."

"Please have the admin reschedule my patients." Eric grabbed his key fob and hurried outside. His heart raced with the adrenaline that followed a call from the hospital. He pulled out of the clinic parking lot and merged with traffic.

This couldn't be about Audrey Beach's situation—could it?

~

Tensely, Audrey navigated Highway 17. Ahead, the ambulance flashed—garish and urgent below the stately redwoods. She pursed her lips, staring at the ambulance as she descended from the Summit.

Dr. Taylor's words haunted her: "Sweet-smelling breath… followed by unresponsiveness in advanced cases…" She remembered Warwick's sunken eyes and sallow skin as he lay on the hospital bed. What would she tell Luke? Her research on the Patel case had taught her a lot. But as the disease shattered her world, she struggled to understand it. Lifelong. Forever. No over, no recovery. And Warwick was so young.

She passed Lexington Reservoir, dark and rippling under the clouded sky. The textured cityscape of Silicon Valley appeared briefly between the hills as she descended the final curves into Los Gatos. At California Oaks, she parked, hurried Lilly and Easton inside, and found the receptionist. "My nephew, Warwick Beach, is in the ER."

"Follow the signs." The woman pointed, then looked at her screen. "Room 232."

Audrey rushed down the hallway, past rooms with patients and family members. Sounds of low voices, rattling equipment, and squeaky footsteps permeated the place. Warwick had just arrived. In a room, technicians and a nurse were setting up his monitors and refilling his saline IV bag.

Audrey rushed into the room. "I'm Warwick's aunt and caregiver. These are his siblings."

The nurse glanced over her shoulder and smiled. "We've been expecting you. Have a seat while we get Warwick hooked up. Kids, you'll need to wait in the children's area." She pointed to a central space set up with bean bag chairs, toys, and a TV playing a children's movie. It was conveniently located so parents in patients' rooms could keep an eye on their other children.

Lillie and Easton settled into the bean bag chairs. They examined some books, then tossed them aside. Lillie looked back at Audrey and waved. Tense, Audrey waved, then sat in a guest chair and focused on Warwick.

The technicians finished their work and left. The nurse fastened a small blood-pressure cuff around Warwick's arm and pressed a button on a machine. The cuff swelled. Warwick was slightly flushed, and still listless. Audrey went to his side. "How are you feeling, Warwick?"

"I still don't feel good."

Tentatively, she stroked his forehead, her back to the door. Warwick didn't resist. "The doctor will be here soon. This hospital has excellent endocrinologists, and your prognosis is very positive. I understand you'll stabilize soon."

"What's an encrollygist?"

Footsteps approached the door.

"Hi, Dr. Taylor!" said the nurse. "This is Warwick, the patient from Santa Cruz."

Audrey froze.

CHAPTER TWELVE

Eric stopped in mid-stride and stared. It was her. Same short, unflattering haircut, same nondescript business clothes, masking her slim form in heavy folds.

He glanced at the bed. The patient was conscious but presented the familiar washed-out pallor of ketoacidosis. "Hi." He shot the greeting over his shoulder as he hurried to the computer, glimpsing her stiff nod and severe frown. He pulled up Dr. Bennet's report, aware that Audrey was watching him closely. This was her son, after all.

Crouched on the exam stool, he read silently, shoulders tight, feet pressed hard against the floor. The nurse stood by the counter, waiting to assist. He glanced at the nurse. "Has his blood sugar been checked since Dominican?"

"Not yet."

He grabbed a glucose meter from a tray and addressed Warwick. "Warwick, I'm Dr. Taylor. I'm going to prick your finger to get some blood out."

Warwick moaned. "Will it make me better?"

"No." He ripped open a small packet. "Finger, please."

"You'll be better soon, Warwick." She delivered her first words like bullets.

Ignoring Audrey, he grabbed Warwick's hand, swiped his fingertip with an alcohol swab, and clicked a lancet against his skin. The blood droplet emerged, and he touched it with the meter's test strip. Seconds later, the device gave its reading. "Six hundred twenty-two," he announced. It was a gut punch. He glanced at the nurse. "What was it at Dominican?"

"Urine sample presented above seven hundred."

He stood and checked Warwick's IV line. "Set up the syringe pump with a fast-acting dose of 0.1 units an hour, please. And let's put a CGM on him."

The nurse pulled boxes from the supply cabinet and connected tubing from Warwick's IV stand to a rectangular syringe pump. She set the device up. Slowly, the carriage pressed on the plunger flange, delivering insulin. She cleaned a small patch of skin on Warwick's abdomen, placed the sensor housing against it, and pushed a button, injecting the sensor.

Eric turned to Audrey. "A CGM is a continuous glucose monitor. It sends the glucose level in Warwick's interstitial fluids to our computer."

"Who watches the computer?" Her eyes were narrow.

"We all do." Abruptly, he turned back to the computer.

"How does that gadget read his levels through his skin?" Audrey asked the nurse.

"It doesn't. I just injected a little catheter. The part you see is the housing."

Warwick moaned again. "I'm thirsty."

Eric turned to the nurse. "Could you get him some water, please?"

~

"Sure." She left the room.

He turned back to Audrey. She was leaning forward on the chair, legs crossed, her forehead creased, her skinny fingers twisting together. He realized she probably was anxious, like any parent—not angry. He breathed deep, one hand fiercely gripping the edge of the exam stool. Warwick wasn't close to safe yet. "We need to admit your son to the pediatric ICU until he's stabilized."

"I'm his aunt."

He stared, mouth open. "Are… are his parents coming?"

"Uh, no. I…" She flushed and looked away, then met his eyes squarely. "Warwick's mom left my brother. We don't know where she is. My brother is in jail. I'm Warwick's caregiver—his and his siblings'."

"Ah!" Eric spun to the computer screen, blinking hard. The information stunned him. She was caring for three children, alone? With her brother in jail? He scrolled aimlessly, then faced her again. "That's commendable. Warwick is lucky you're here." It was the least he could say.

"I'm not exactly the godsend he needs. It is what it is."

He couldn't suppress a smile. "It's like that for most of us, right?"

She nodded and flushed a little. An awkward smile crossed her face.

Now that Warwick was onboarded, Eric should give her some space. He went to the exam table and crouched beside her nephew. The boy looked at him, dully.

"Warwick, we'll take you to another room soon. Tell us if your head hurts, or you feel dizzy, or any other changes. Got it?" He spoke slowly. The instructions were crucial.

"OK."

Eric stood. "Warwick's diagnosis is type 1 diabetes. Stay strong, Auntie."

She nodded; her face pinched again. He left her to cry in privacy.

~

Audrey called Easton and Lillie from the children's area. They followed Warwick's gurney to the PICU. The technicians wheeled Warwick into a room that included a caregiver cot and a separate bathroom with a shower.

"You can drive home and collect some overnight supplies if you like," suggested a nurse.

"I'm fine. We can sleep in our clothes." There was no one else to wait with Warwick.

"Warwick can get some rest here. Make yourself and the

kids comfortable."

Easton and Lillie stood by the far side of Warwick's bed. Audrey sat on the caregiver cot. She sighed and ran her hands over her hair.

"How are you doing?" The nurse looked at her kindly.

"Pretty stressed." *To say the least.*

"That's normal with a new diagnosis, but Warwick is in the best hands. Dr. Taylor would never brag, but parents of type 1 kids rave about him. He truly cares. He's also a genius with the disease." She glanced at Audrey as she tidied the room. Audrey tipped her head. This was a side of Dr. Taylor she had not discovered.

"Will your other kids be going home with a family member?" the nurse asked. "They can't stay past seven tonight."

"Their nanny will pick them up."

"Are you hungry? There's a café on the first floor." The nurse indicated a sign beside the door.

"I'll take them when we've had a rest."

The nurse and technicians dimmed the lights and closed the curtains across the frosted window. They pulled the door to and left the room. Their voices faded as they moved on to other areas of the unit.

The PICU was quieter than the Emergency Room. Warwick closed his eyes. The monitors beeped intermittently above his bed. Shoes squeaked in the hallway as a worker passed.

To Audrey's surprise, Easton and Lillie came to the cot and curled up beside her. She hesitated, then gingerly put her arms around them, like the mother hen in her favorite childhood book. Their breathing became slow and regular as they drifted to sleep.

She gazed down at Lillie's messy hair, strewn across Audrey's legs. She could still trace tears on the girl's cheeks. Easton's rumpled clothes were dirty, and his socks didn't match. He stirred, let out a little moan, and pressed closer to

Audrey's side. Reflexively, she bent and drew them closer with a squeeze of her arms. She closed her eyes and leaned her head against the window behind her.

~

After ensuring that Warwick was set up in the PICU, Eric handed his care over to the hospitalist for the afternoon. He drove to a diner close to the hospital, parked, and walked heavily to the door. Inside, a waitress handed him a menu.

"Want your usual?" She held pen and notepad ready.

"Thanks, Sandy." He smiled and returned the menu, unopened. She had been bringing him meatloaf since his first call to the hospital.

"Coming up, doc!" Sandy went to the kitchen, smoothing her grey hair into place, and handed the order over the pass-through.

Eric rubbed his eyes and sat quietly until she returned with a glass of iced tea.

"I added your sugar, Dr. Taylor." She moved on to other customers.

He unwrapped the straw she had handed him. Slouched on the seat, he scrolled through his emails until Sandy brought his plate.

"Long day at the hospital?"

"Yep." He inhaled the sharp, comforting scent. The diner was always a welcome retreat.

She tipped her head. "Get some rest, OK? You look tired."

He nodded and unfolded his napkin. "How's your husband?"

She frowned. "Resting a lot. He had an appointment last week."

"That's good. I keep him in my prayers."

"Thank you." She left.

Eric leaned on his elbows, listening to the standard fifties music as he ate. The music was another reason he always chose the diner. When he was finished, he wiped his fingers and set his credit card on the check tray. He left Sandy a generous tip. Her husband's illness was a grief no one should carry.

91

CHAPTER THIRTEEN

Audrey woke up groggy. Room-darkening blinds blocked the daylight, and the hallway window curtains were closed. Nurses and technicians had checked on Warwick throughout the night. In the dim light, Audrey discerned his small, hunched form. His blanket moved with his breathing.

She read a text from Claire. "Kids are fine. I'm taking them to school. Keep in touch!"

The night before, Claire had picked up the kids and brought a few essentials. Audrey went into the bathroom and brushed her teeth. She took a hot shower, then dressed in the same clothes she'd worn to Dr. Taylor's deposition.

A strip of light appeared under the bathroom door, and a motor whirred as the morning shift nurse raised the head of Warwick's bed. "Good morning, young man!"

Quickly, Audrey put her toiletries into a bag and opened the bathroom door. Steam drifted around her into the hospital room, where the nurse was adding a bag of fluids to Warwick's IV stand. Dr. Taylor walked in, giving Audrey a brief nod on his way to Warwick's side. Audrey felt her stomach tighten defensively. Despite the nurse's glowing testimonial, Audrey planned to replace Dr. Taylor as soon as possible. Personal interactions with her client's defendant were a conflict of interest. She focused her attention on her nephew.

"How are you, Warwick?" Dr. Taylor's forehead

wrinkled.

"I feel like I could play a bit. My arms and legs don't ache anymore. I'm hungry."

A twist of joy unfurled inside Audrey. Warwick sounded so much better.

"We'll bring you breakfast soon." Dr. Taylor turned to Audrey. "Are you ready for an update?"

Audrey raised her chin, trying to ignore the water still dripping from her hair onto the linoleum around her bare feet. "Yes." She sat on the cot, straightening her back. The nurse tossed a few used supplies into the hazardous materials bin and left.

Dr. Taylor pushed an exam stool to the end of the cot and sat. "Warwick's blood glucose has descended to 237 milligrams per deciliter. Below 300 puts him in Phase 2 of our treatment plan." He gestured to Warwick's IV pole. "We've added glucose to his fluids, to prevent a low sugar. He's almost better."

"Thank God!" The joy softened to relief, and Audrey took a deep breath. Her shoulders relaxed, and despite her best efforts, tears escaped her eyes.

The doctor waited as she wiped her eyes. "His ketoacidosis will resolve quickly. I anticipate you can take him home this evening. First, though, you need a lot of information. Unfortunately, Warwick's type 1 diabetes goes home with you." He sat quietly, not moving as he spoke.

"Right." She straightened, swiping at her damp hair.

"Sandra is a Diabetes Educator. She'll train you. You'll leave with everything you need. Plus, you can call the Pediatric Diabetes Hotline any time."

"What time do we check out?"

"You should plan on being here until around ten this evening." He returned to Warwick's bed. "Let's check your tummy." The doctor pressed the diaphragm of his stethoscope against Warwick's belly. "Sounds clear. Want to listen?" He held the diaphragm up so Warwick could see.

Warwick nodded, and Dr. Taylor transferred the earpieces to Warwick's small ears and put the diaphragm on his belly. Warwick scrunched his eyebrows in concentration. "It sounds like thunder!"

Dr. Taylor smiled. "You better eat your breakfast!"

Audrey studied his face, fascinated. The harsh, demanding edge was gone from his voice. Friendliness replaced his cold demeanor. Clearly, his bedside manner was better when the situation wasn't urgent. He turned to Audrey. She looked at Warwick, embarrassed the doctor had caught her staring.

"Do you have any questions?"

"No." Audrey was flustered. Warwick was out of danger. The sooner Dr. Taylor left, the better.

But as he exited the room, Dr. Taylor glanced at her, his head tipped to one side, his eyes soft. A gentle smile warmed his face, and he was gone.

~

Late that afternoon, Audrey watched Warwick sleep. His color had normalized. He looked healthier than she'd seen him in weeks. They could leave at ten, as Dr. Taylor had predicted.

A fat binder lay open next to her. Sandra had explained its sections, teaching her the details of Warwick's care. She'd introduced lists of innovative medical devices, articles on chronic grief, explanations of insurance issues, and information about medical studies.

Audrey slapped the heavy volume shut and lay down, exhausted. The team at the hospital was great, but she would be on her own soon. Responsibility for Warwick's survival terrified her.

She swiped her phone open and scanned her emails. Clients needed her attention, but Warwick's condition consumed her. She tossed the phone aside and rubbed her eyes, weighing her options.

Claire was too inexperienced to care for Warwick—and

medical care went beyond her contract. If Audrey quit the law firm to care for Warwick, she was back to Plan A: Part-time work, plus a very strict budget. Luke's mortgage would take a big chunk of her monthly savings withdrawals. She bit her lip. *God, please save my career!*

Her phone rang, and Alex Tate's name popped up. She had texted him, explaining that she had a family emergency and couldn't come in for a couple days. "Alex, hi."

"Audrey! You expect to be in tomorrow? Everything OK?"

"My nephew was diagnosed with type 1 diabetes."

"Sorry to hear that. When will you be in?"

"I need a couple more days. Turns out caring for a child with type 1 diabetes is complicated."

"How's that going to impact your case load?"

"I don't know yet." She felt her heart rate increase.

"Well, honey, you need to figure that out."

Anger pushed her to her feet. "Actually, Alex, I just did. My nephew is more important than climbing your ladder. I'm stepping away from the firm starting today."

"You can't just 'step away.' You need to do the responsible thing and come in to hand over your cases."

"Don't worry. I'll talk with Patrick next week."

"Audrey, I want two weeks' notice, and—"

"Goodbye, *honey*." She hung up and paced the room, stunned by her own decisiveness. Briefly, she considered calling Tate back and offering to come in the next day, figure out a solution, keep her career going somehow. But she knew she'd regret it.

She went to the window and looked down at Silicon Valley's shining buildings and swarming highways. Behind her Warwick slept on, small and fragile in the rumpled sheets.

"Speak up for those who cannot speak for themselves, for the rights of all who are destitute." The verse that had inspired her career flashed through her thoughts.

When she signed up for law, she could never have anticipated this.

A dove glided to a tree in the hospital patio. It balanced on a leafy branch and looked around with quick movements of its head. Audrey walked to Warwick's side and stroked his cheek with the back of her fingers.

CHAPTER FOURTEEN

After her fiery exchange with Tate, Audrey called Claire. She thanked the nanny, and regretfully let her go. "I'm so sorry. I'll write you a great reference."

"No worries, Audrey. Want me to watch the kids until you bring Warwick home this evening?"

"Bless your heart."

Late that night, Audrey pulled into the driveway. When she parked under the redwood grove, the new moon cast no light from the black sky. Her phone battery had died. She huffed, grabbing her purse. Couldn't this nature-obsessed county manage a streetlamp? She fumbled in the trunk for the backpack of supplies the hospital had provided.

Claire was packed and ready to go. She had even stripped the extra bed in Lillie's room. "Hope all goes well, Audrey!" She hugged the kids goodbye and went out to her car. Audrey heard the vehicle's engine fade. Quietness replaced the sound.

~

The curtains were open. Dirty dishes were piled on the counter. The ambulance gurney had scuffed the kitchen floor. Audrey went through the cabin, closing the blinds and curtains. Easton and Lillie sat with Warwick on the couch. When she was done, Audrey joined them and sat in the armchair, giving them time to reconnect before bedtime.

"Are you feeling better, Warwick?" Easton put his arm

over Warwick's shoulders.

"Uh, yeah." Warwick spoke as if Easton should know. "I have insulin, ya know!"

"What's insulin?" Lillie asked.

Warwick shrugged. "Dunno."

"What does it taste like?"

Warwick raised his arms and twisted his hands above his head, wiggling. "I don't EAT it. I poke it into my skin with a neeeeeeeedle. Peew!" He jabbed at his stomach.

Audrey yawned, her adrenaline long gone. The kids could skip baths—going to school a little grubby wouldn't hurt them. She went to Luke's bedroom and put on her sheepskin slippers, relishing their softness. There was no time to change. She had to get the kids to bed, and Warwick needed his long-acting insulin.

She returned to the living room. "Bedtime. Let's do your insulin, Warwick."

Warwick ignored Audrey. "The doctor took blood out of my finger. He used a machine."

"Can we see?" Lillie asked.

"Maybe." Warwick tapped his chin with his finger. "Want me to ask him?"

"Kids, let's go!" Audrey went to the kitchen and pulled out the heavy care binder. "Let's do your shot, Warwick." She opened the binder and calculated Warwick's daily dose.

But Warwick ran to his room and slammed the door, crying. When Audrey tried the doorknob, she found he'd locked it. "Warwick, let's getter done, now."

"Leave me alone!"

Easton went to the door and talked his brother out of isolation. The kids joined Audrey in the kitchen. They gaped, riveted, as she prepared a syringe and slipped the needle into Warwick's skin. She pressed the flange, delivering Warwick's dose into the fatty layer beneath his skin.

"I can't *even!*" Lillie whispered, sounding like a teenager.

After his shot, Warwick ran to the computer and pressed the on switch.

"Bedtime!" Sternly, Audrey set her hands on his shoulders and guided him towards his room. He shrugged her off and ran into the living room.

Easton sighed. "Warwick, we have to go to bed. Come with me, OK?" He pulled Warwick off the floor and led him to their room.

The kids fell asleep well after midnight. Audrey closed their doors and tiptoed to her room. The black night was silent, and her sleep was restless. She still hadn't adjusted to the quiet.

~

Her alarm melody woke her at two thirty. Sandra had instructed her to check on Warwick at night, to verify his doses. She swiped the alarm off, squinting at the bright display.

The cabin was quiet. She crept to the boys' room, where Warwick's meter lay beside his bed. She loaded a test strip, gently grasped Warwick's hand, and dabbed an alcohol swab on his finger. When she applied a drop of blood, the meter read 192 ml/dl. Warwick slept on.

She went to the kitchen, calculated Warwick's dose, and loaded insulin into a fresh syringe. She returned to the boys' room. "Warwick," she whispered, "you need a little insulin."

Warwick sighed and rolled onto his side. "Where's Daddy?" He sobbed a little and slept again.

She cleaned his skin and injected the dose. He cried again, then breathed quietly. Audrey went back to her room and set her alarm for four thirty. As the fog of sleep drifted over her, she saw Dr. Taylor walk beside Warwick's gurney, one hand resting on the side rail. He looked at her nephew tenderly. Concern animated his demeanor, as he rushed to order the insulin and check his data.

She jolted awake. An image of Meghan, wobbling and stumbling out of her stork stand, shattered the dream. She recalled the doctor's defensiveness. *"I didn't plan on badly designed software and pointless lawsuits."*

Kindness and competence were great, but humility was just as important.

~

They were late for school. Warwick was tired. He fought Audrey when she checked his blood sugar and tried to give him insulin. She had to wrestle him into her lap and restrain his hands.

Easton and Lillie got themselves ready, even packing their own lunches. Audrey dropped them at the school entrance and took Warwick to meet the school nurse. After they set up his care plan, she walked him to his classroom. The kids were sitting on the floor, listening to their teacher read. They stared at Warwick as he put his backpack in a cubby.

"Hi, Warwick!" the teacher said. "Are you feeling better?"

Warwick nodded. "Anyone want to see my blood?"

The kids knelt up and leaned towards Warwick.

"Where?"

"Can I see?"

"I'll show you at lunchtime." Warwick knelt and looked at the teacher. "What are we reading?"

Proud of Warwick's confidence, Audrey hurried to the Tesla and sped home. It was time to find a new endocrinologist.

~

She loaded the dishwasher, wiped the table, and changed into sweats. As she dialed the department of health services, she made a mental note to buy new clothes. Her work outfits were impractical, and she refused to live in sweats.

She enrolled herself and the kids on state healthcare, glad to learn that Warwick's hospital visit would be covered retroactively. Next, she looked up endocrinologists. Only one was available in Santa Cruz County through the state program. A search for reviews revealed that doctor didn't specialize in pediatric diabetes.

She switched to Santa Clara County and filtered the search to show pediatric endocrinologists on the government plan. She found around thirty. She selected the diabetes specialists and then those with excellent reviews, reducing the list to two doctors. One was not accepting new patients. The other was Dr. Taylor.

Quickly, she looked at those with less favorable reviews. That only sent her back to Dr. Taylor. She rested her forehead on her fingertips, frowning. There had to be a way around this. She searched several more times, using different filters. But the results were unchanged, and Warwick had to have the best care. Dr. Taylor stood out as that option.

She called the clinic. "I need to schedule a follow-up appointment for my nephew. He was diagnosed this week."

"Sure!" The receptionist's tone was warm. "Let's schedule his checkups, too. He'll need to see the endocrinologist quarterly."

"Yes."

They scheduled Warwick's check-in visits for the winter and spring quarters.

"Going forward, you'll want to secure Warwick's appointments early. Dr. Taylor's clinic is always busy. He's well respected."

"Mm-hm."

~

Audrey needed to tell Meghan she could no longer represent her and offer Patrick as a substitute. She stared out the kitchen window, frustrated. She had meant to secure a speedy justice for Meghan. Now, the kid would have to wait on Patrick's busy schedule.

The communication deserved an in-person visit. Audrey just had time before picking up Warwick, so she changed back into a work outfit, poured some coffee into a travel mug, and drove to the Patels'.

Meghan was brushing a black horse tied to a fencepost when she arrived. The teen waved.

"You're back to the horses!" Audrey closed the Tesla door.

"Just groundwork. My mom checks on me." Meghan tossed the wood-backed brush into a box and patted the animal's glossy neck. She joined Audrey on the path to the front porch. Her balance seemed perfect, her strides steady. "Mom! Audrey's here."

They climbed the steps to the porch, Meghan grasping the banister. Beverly came out, the screen door slamming behind her. She held a rag smeared with colors, and Audrey saw a white smudge on her cheek. Whisps of hair escaped her messy bun. "Is everything OK?"

"It will be. Can we sit and chat?"

Beverly gestured to a wicker chair. Meghan joined her mom on their porch swing. The swing creaked faintly and swung. Beyond the path, the horse snorted and dropped its head, grazing.

Audrey sat down. "I have to drop the case."

Beverly twisted the oily rag.

Meghan leaned forward, frowning. "Why?"

"Just listen, honey." Beverly put her hand on Meghan's leg, calming her daughter.

Audrey drew a deep breath. "A lot has happened since my last visit. Warwick, my nephew, was diagnosed with type 1 diabetes last week."

Meghan gasped. "That's terrible!"

"Is he OK?" Beverly asked.

"Yes, and we're learning to manage it. But also, Luke was caught embezzling from Cabrillo. He's in jail for a year. I'm the kids' caregiver."

Meghan's mouth fell open.

"I'm so sorry!" Beverly stared at Audrey. She crossed her legs, uncrossed them again, and rubbed her palms on her plump thighs. "Your nice brother—in jail?"

Audrey nodded.

"Why can't you still do my case?" asked Meghan.

Beverly turned to Meghan. "She's got her hands full."

"I'm sorry this impacts you, Meghan." Audrey paused and watched Meghan's face. The teen nodded. "I have to be there for the kids. They've lost a lot. First their mom left, then their dad goes to jail, and now Warwick gets diagnosed."

Meghan threw up her hands, then rested them in her lap and sighed, head drooping. "Yeah, I get it. Nothing you can do. It's just frustrating, I guess."

Audrey's stomach clenched as a tear slipped down Meghan's cheek.

"What about the case?" asked Beverly.

"Well, that's the good news. Another attorney at the firm, Patrick, is taking my caseload. With your consent, I will turn the case over to him."

"Can he expedite it?" asked Beverly.

"Unfortunately, no. But the case is strong. Dr. Taylor made an avoidable mistake. The discovery is a wrap, and the depositions are done—except the doctor's. Warwick's diagnosis interrupted that. Patrick will likely negotiate a settlement. It won't cost you more—and Patrick has a great track record."

"Since you recommend Patrick, we'll go with him," said Beverly. "Gosh, what a lot for you to take on. You're a hero, Audrey!"

Audrey looked at the trees, uncomfortable with the praise. "Honestly, I'm way out of my depth."

Meghan wiped her cheek and looked up. "Diabetes is a pain. But Warwick just needs your support." She stared away at the horse for a few moments. "Come to think of it, my mom's support made my diagnosis way easier."

Beverly gaped at Meghan. "Thanks for that, honey!"

"You didn't know?"

"Of course, I knew. I just didn't think you did!"

They all laughed.

"Meghan's right. The dosing and medical care are critical, but the important thing is to be there for Warwick. You don't have to be perfect, either. You'll get the hang of things."

Audrey stood. "Thanks."

"Thank you for coming over to tell us, Audrey." Beverly followed Audrey to the porch steps. "We'll be praying for you and your family."

"Let me know if you need any medical advice. I'm a pro." Meghan waved, one eyebrow raised, cynically.

CHAPTER FIFTEEN

"Can we have a snack, Auntie Audrey?" Easton dropped his school backpack on the kitchen floor.

"Go play, while I make it." Audrey paused as she reached for a bag of chips. Now was a good time to set a healthy precedent. She gave Warwick insulin and took a bag of greens from the fridge. In her high-powered blender, she made her favorite smoothie—bananas, dates, and greens, with unsweetened almond milk. "Snack time. Auntie Audrey's special smoothie!"

The kids ran to the kitchen, and she handed out mugs of the drink. Warwick gagged and ran to his room.

Lillie scowled at the green sludge. "Can't you even make snacks?" She stalked out and slammed her bedroom door.

Only Easton tried the concoction. "It's OK." He set down his mug and went to play a video game.

Audrey gave Warwick a cookie to use up his insulin and lay on Luke's bed, wondering how they would survive the year. Lillie was crying. Wearily, Audrey got up and knocked on her niece's door. "What's wrong?"

"I miss Dad." More sobbing.

"He'll be back in a year. I know it feels like a long time when you're a kid, but—"

"That's *forever!*" Lillie wailed.

Audrey waited until she was quiet. "Lillie, think. You're eight. That makes a year one eighth of your life. But trust me, when you're thirty-two, like me, it doesn't seem that long."

The door opened. Lillie looked up at Audrey, her eyes red, her blond hair messy. "Auntie Audrey, you don't know much about kids, do you?"

"Nope." Audrey leaned against the doorjamb and hung her head, rubbing her eyes. She looked at Lillie, not knowing what to say.

One corner of Lillie's mouth twitched upwards. She snorted, and the lifted corner spread to a wide grin. Her amusement tickled Audrey, and suddenly they both doubled over, laughing uncontrollably. Audrey staggered to Lillie's bed and curled up, howling. Lillie joined her. Soon, Easton and Warwick came into the room.

"What's so funny?" Easton asked.

Audrey gasped and blurted, between giggles, "I don't know what I'm doing!" She shrieked.

Easton and Warwick climbed onto Claire's old bed, and then, they were all laughing—although Audrey was pretty sure Warwick didn't know why. They calmed down, finally, and Audrey looked at the children. "Since I don't know about kids, how about you tell me?"

"Okay." Lillie spun in a circle. "What do you want to know?"

"What works for snacks?"

"Dad gives us cookies!" Warwick jumped.

"No, he doesn't." Easton stood. "He gives us fruit and cheese or toast and maybe crackers."

"And chips!" Lillie did a handstand and flopped over into an arch.

"He says we have to eat fruit. Warwick always wants cookies."

Audrey nodded. "I'm going to find a better smoothie recipe—one you'll like. With chocolate. How does that sound?"

"That sounds yummy!" Lillie rubbed her belly.

Warwick started playing with a stuffed animal. Audrey went back to the kitchen and browsed her phone. She found a recipe with hidden veggies, cocoa powder, and fruit. She gave Warwick more insulin and ten minutes later called the kids. "Come and try this frosted shake." She handed out glasses filled with the creamy, mahogany mixture. The children didn't know she had snuck in spinach and carrots, or that fruit alone sweetened the drink. They sipped, then looked at each other.

"Yum!" Easton downed his smoothie and smacked his lips.

Lillie and Warwick watched Easton. They finished their smoothies, too. Congratulating herself, Audrey didn't mention the veggies. She glanced at the kitchen clock. "It's time for Daddy to call!"

~

Warwick wiggled, squished his cheeks, and ran into the living room. "Daddy, Daddy, Daddy!"

They gathered on the couch. Audrey's phone rang, and she slid the green button across the screen. "Luke?"

"Hey."

"We're all here. I'm putting you on speaker."

"Hi, Daddy!" Lillie leaned on Audrey's lap, speaking into the phone. Easton and Warwick squeezed close.

"Hi, Dad," said Easton.

"How are you all doing?" Luke spoke in a monotone, without energy. Audrey sensed he was still depressed—perhaps, he was worse now.

"I have type 1 diabetes." Warwick blew out his cheeks and wiggled, bumping Audrey.

The hair on Audrey's arms stood up. She'd planned to break the news gently. So much for that!

"What do you mean? Audrey, what's he talking about?" Luke's voice was tight and fast.

"Oh, Lukey!" Audrey's throat closed and she shut her eyes tightly. Tears escaped her lids.

"Audrey? Are you there?"

She managed a squeak.

Easton glanced at Audrey and leaned over the phone. "Dad, you know how Warwick was losing weight and thirsty, and tired a lot?"

"Yeah?"

"Well, the nanny couldn't get him out of bed, so Auntie Audrey came home from work and he went to the hospital. He has to take insulin now before he eats."

"I can take blood out of my finger!" Cheerfully, Warwick poked his bloated cheeks with his fingers, making a puffing noise.

Silence.

Audrey swiped away her tears. "Luke, sorry, I'm a bit emotional." Her voice shook. "Warwick was in the PICU last week. I realized he had type 1 diabetes while I was deposing the endocrinologist in Meghan Patel's med mal suit. He had all the symptoms the guy was describing. He was in the hospital until late last night."

Luke sighed.

"Luke, Warwick will be fine. He has good care, they trained me, and he will live a normal life. Mostly."

"Oh, boy!"

Audrey could barely hear him. "I had to let the nanny go. It's just me and the kids now."

"I'm kind of glad about that."

"Why, Dad?" asked Lillie.

"Audrey is family."

"Yeah. I'm glad, too." Easton swished his feet on the carpet.

Audrey was surprised. She thought the kids preferred Claire's fun energy to her own cluelessness. "We just had a good laugh at my incompetence. I guess if we can find the humor in it, we'll survive."

"What about your career?" asked Luke.

"I left Tate Personal Injury."

"For good?"

"For good. Luke, in the hospital, I realized no one can give Warwick the care and attention he needs like a family member. My career can wait."

"You'll do great." Very slightly, Luke's voice brightened. "Like when we were kids, and you took that beat-up doll everywhere."

Audrey laughed. "Mom still has that doll!"

"Daddy, do you like it in jail?" Lillie curled her fingers around her chin and kicked her feet.

"It's fine. My bed's comfy and the food is OK. I might get a job." He spoke quickly, and Audrey guessed he had prepared for that question.

"Do you play games, Daddy?" Warwick asked.

"Um, hmm." Audrey knew her brother's head was tipped, his finger on his chin, as he pondered the answer. "No games." His laugh sounded forced, but Audrey took hope in his effort.

"I miss you, Dad," said Easton.

"I miss you, too. Be good for Auntie Audrey. Do what she says."

The kids agreed.

"Time for me to go."

"We're going to church on Sunday. Couldn't make it last week. I'll put funds in your commissary account tomorrow. You'll be able to call weekly. We're planning our first visit, too."

"OK, 'bye." Luke hung up.

Lillie put her arm around Audrey's neck. "I love you, Auntie Audrey."

"Yep. You're not just a machine that walks around the house taking care of us." Easton leaned against Audrey.

Audrey forced her fears aside. "I'm not?" She nudged her nephew, playfully.

"You're Auntie Audrey!" Warwick hopped off the couch and ran into the kitchen. "I'm going to play in the yard."

"Fine, homework can wait." Audrey gave them the evening off. Easton and Lillie followed Warwick outside, and Audrey started dinner.

~

She poured boiled potatoes into a colander and watched Warwick from the kitchen window. With insulin, he was a different child—running after Lillie on her scooter, throwing rocks into the creek.

Sandra had cautioned that Warwick would struggle to adjust, and Audrey anticipated more outbursts, especially given his parents' absence. But her nephew's revived energy thrilled her. She called the kids for dinner, checked Warwick's blood sugar, and drew insulin into a clean syringe. This time, he did not resist his shot.

"How did it go at lunch time?" She slid the needle into his skin.

Warwick winced dramatically, then glanced at his siblings, who were watching. "It went cur-a-zee!"

"What do you mean?" She tossed the syringe into a hazmat box.

"Nurse Mattie gave me insulin. The other kids were saying, 'Whoa, heeelp, yoooouch!'" He accompanied his screeches with wild gestures.

"Did you ask Nurse Mattie to give you your shot in private?"

"I didn't care. She gave it to me in the ate-it-yum room."

Lillie giggled. "It's called the atrium, Warwick!"

Warwick rolled his eyes. "Actually, I know that, Lillie." He closed one eye and pointed his elbow to the ceiling. "It's called a *joke*."

Easton put plates on the table.

Warwick grabbed a plate and looked at Audrey. "I'm ready for my potatoes." He threw back his head, bending and straightening his knees, then lifted his plate. "Pile 'em on, Aunt!"

Audrey stuffed her amusement. "We have to wait for

your insulin to work. Put your school stuff away, please."

Warwick sighed, put down his plate, and lugged his backpack to his room. Easton took a plate to the stove, where Lillie was helping herself to green beans. Audrey put her hand on Lillie's arm.

"Wait for Warwick." Audrey meant to set a precedent. Waiting would help Warwick feel less alone with his disease.

"Bleh!" said Easton, but they both put down their plates.

Sandra had told Audrey that when a child is diagnosed with type 1 diabetes, the whole family gets it. She wasn't kidding.

CHAPTER SIXTEEN

Audrey stood outside the gleaming office tower that housed Tate Personal Injury. She held an empty box under her arm. Inhaling deeply, she swung the tall door open and went in. The lofty glass ceiling swooped in a peak above her.

She crossed the marble-floored foyer, with its stately plants and svelte reception furniture, and stepped into the brass-trimmed elevator. The car ascended, whirring and dinging softly. Below the glass walls, the foyer shrank.

Early in her career, the building had riveted her imagination. She had emailed her dad, describing its grand proportions and polished corridors, along with her wins. She gave up when he didn't reply.

The car stopped at the sixth floor. Across from her was the door to Tate Personal Injury. She walked in—back straight, chin lifted. Suzanne waved as Audrey passed her desk. She had set some dried gourds and a small, plastic turkey on the reception counter, in honor of Thanksgiving. The décor reminded Audrey that she wouldn't have time—or family—to plan a proper celebration for the kids.

Patrick waved from his desk. Tate ignored her. In her office, she took down her bar certificate and law degree. She put them, with her CDs, photos, and Irish sweater, into the box. She emptied the desk drawers, adding their contents and her coffee maker to the box. There was nothing else to do.

The plant and furniture belonged to Tate.

Patrick knocked on her door, and she welcomed him. He sat comfortably in the guest chair.

Audrey sat across from him. "So, did Tate tell you what's going on?"

"Yes, and I'm so sorry. He said you'll hand over your cases today, assuming your clients want my help. Nanny didn't work out, huh?"

"When you throw in a disease, family is best for the kid."

He nodded empathetically and pushed his brown hair neatly aside on his forehead. "Are you planning to get back into law? I can give you a reference if you need it."

Her throat tightened. "I will, when this is over."

For the next few hours, she introduced Patrick to her caseload, glad she had kept an organized system. Her documents were clearly labeled and easy to understand.

She presented Meghan's case last, for emphasis. If she couldn't finish the case herself, she could at least push for justice. She placed the files squarely in front of Patrick. "I know these people personally. A doctor messed up the plaintiff's insulin dose. She could have died, and I don't want him unpunished."

Patrick nodded. "Agreed."

"The case is almost finished. After the doctor's deposition, you can talk settlement."

Patrick promised to keep Meghan's case, even after Tate hired Audrey's replacement. "I'll do my best on this."

"Any chance you can prioritize it, Patrick?"

"I'll put it as close to the top as I can." He paused, then added gently, "I probably can't get to the deposition until summer."

She would have to accept that.

He stood and walked to the door. "I'm sorry things didn't work out for you. Happy Thanksgiving!"

"You, too, Patrick."

~

She texted Tate: "I'm free."

Tate rapped on the door and hurried in. "Got everything handed over to Patrick?" He straightened his silk tie over an expensive dress shirt. Audrey deduced today was a court day.

"He's informed. You have nothing to worry about."

"Well, you did your best here. Good luck with your future pursuits."

"Can I tap you for a reference in the future?" She had nothing to lose by asking.

"Sure! I can't say I will overlook how suddenly you left, though." He returned to his office, leaving her door ajar.

Audrey rolled her eyes and chuckled. The man would never see past his own agenda. So be it. Picking up the box, she left her office.

In the reception area, Suzanne put a caller on hold. "Audrey, sorry to see you go. Everything ok?"

"I had a family emergency." Briefly, Audrey explained.

"You've made the right decision." Suzanne leaned over the reception counter and beckoned Audrey close. Her coiffed grey hair brushed Audrey's cheek, and Audrey smelled her cheap perfume. She lowered her voice. "Tate is a fool to not work with you on this. He doesn't value family. I happen to know he divorced and ditched two wives, and he never sees his kids."

They heard Tate's door open. Suzanne stepped back, glancing over her shoulder.

"Thanks, Suzanne," Audrey bluffed, as Tate walked to Suzanne's desk. "It's been great to work with you, too. Enjoy your grandkids and have a great Thanksgiving!"

She went to the door, glancing back as she opened it. Tate's back was to her, and he pointed to a document on Suzanne's desk. Suzanne met Audrey's eye over Tate's shoulder. She winked and smiled.

Audrey waved and closed the door.

~

Her next stop was the condo. She drove onto the sleek black pavement of the parking lot and eased the Tesla into her spot. Today—Monday—she meant to grab a few essentials. The kids would be out of school on Thursday and Friday, for Thanksgiving break. She planned to finish moving out the following week, so the property manager could clean and find a tenant.

She walked the shady, perfectly groomed paths, past blooming flowers and thick-leaved bushes. She'd been thrilled to purchase the condo. She'd saved the down payment, living on as little as possible. Renting it out had never entered her mind.

A mother sat by the pool. Her two kids splashed and squealed in the water. An elderly gentleman walked his small dog across the neatly trimmed lawn. Inside, the condo was quiet and chilly. She stuffed the items she needed into a couple of bags. The fridge was almost empty. She tossed a few leftover take-out meals into the trash and set the garbage bag by the door.

Pausing, she went back to the kitchen and opened a cabinet. Her chipped dishes and cups stood perfectly arranged, serving no one. In the bedroom, her shirts and pants hung, organized by color and item, in the small closet. She touched their stiff fabrics, then gazed at her professional shoes—all perfect for work, but useless for her new lifestyle.

She took her flute from the closet shelf and rifled through her sheet music. Setting a sheet on her music stand, she played a few measures from Korsakov's "Flight of the Bumblebee." It was a challenging piece, but she had been mastering it. She hadn't practiced for a couple weeks now, and the notes came clumsily. She set her flute down. If anyone took music lessons, it would be Easton.

She started for the door, then dashed back to her room and stuffed her flute and a few slim books of music into her tote purse. If she couldn't continue her lessons, she could at least practice.

CHAPTER SEVENTEEN

Thanksgiving Day dawned clear and sunny. It was nice to lie in bed, instead of getting the kids ready for school. Warwick was making engine noises in his room. The other kids were quiet still.

Audrey hadn't made plans for the holiday. She sat up and read her Bible, then went back to sleep. When she woke again, Easton was on the computer playing a video game. Lillie and Warwick were talking in Lillie's room.

"Warwick, do you know what a Biles is?"

"Nope! I don't."

"It's what Simone Biles did in the Olympics. Want me to show you?"

"Yep!"

Was Lillie about to try the celebrated gymnast's move? Audrey got up, worried that her niece might break her neck. She went to Lillie's room. Lillie was opening a video on the kids' shared laptop.

Audrey crouched beside her. "Mind if I join you?"

Lillie shrugged and tapped the play arrow. Audrey sat cross-legged next to her niece. Showing an interest in Lillie's sport might build a connection.

The video showed Simone Biles tear across the floor, feet pounding. Her bulging thighs thrust her high in the air. She flipped and flipped, sailing down to a firm landing, then twisted joyfully at the edge of the mat, arms extended. Her red, white, and blue Olympics uniform twinkled.

"She's amazing." Audrey hadn't seen the video before.

Lillie looked up at Audrey. Tears shone in her eyes. "I want to do that."

"Keep practicing!" Audrey patted Lillie's back and stood.

In the kitchen, Audrey rinsed the coffee carafe and put grounds in a fresh filter. Last Thanksgiving, Nancy had been home. Audrey and Luke's mom had flown out, too, and they'd all celebrated together. Now it was up to Audrey. Even her mom couldn't make it.

She put away a few pans and lids she'd washed the night before. Bella shuffled in and lapped at her water. Audrey gently pushed her aside and refilled her dish. Halfway through loading the dishes, she remembered Warwick's blood glucose. She dashed back to Lillie's room and had Warwick check. Reassured, she returned to the kitchen.

She grabbed a cup of coffee and sat at the table, indulging self-pity. Heaviness settled in her chest. It wasn't fair the kids had no family to celebrate with. Or that she was alone, trying to create a sense of family.

She slapped her hand on the table. *Knock it off, Audrey!* Self-pity had played no role in her success as a lawyer. It would sabotage her job as substitute parent. She forced herself to think. Preparing and sharing a traditional meal alone might be depressing. It was time for a new take on the holiday.

She opened hiking and weather apps on her phone. The skies were cloudless, and the temperatures would be moderate. She wiped the kitchen counters and found sandwich ingredients in the fridge. When the kids came into the kitchen, she was dressed in hiking clothes. A backpack filled with sandwiches and drinks waited by the door.

"What are we doing for Thanksgiving?" asked Easton.

Lillie and Warwick put down cereal bowls and looked at Audrey.

"What's Thanksgiving?" asked Warwick.

"You don't remember?" Lillie's voice trembled. "It's where we get together with family and eat turkey. And this year we can't because Mom left and Dad's in jail." She went into the living room, crying. Warwick joined her. Easton sighed and stomped to his room.

Audrey held up a hand. "Wait, kids!"

Quietly, Lillie and Warwick returned.

"We're going on a surprise trip."

Lillie grabbed Audrey's arm and hopped.

Warwick jumped around the kitchen. "We're going on a surprise!"

Easton came back from his room. "Are we going to the beach?"

"That's for me to know, and you to find out," Audrey teased. "First, you have to get dressed."

In a few minutes, the kids jumped into the Tesla, and Audrey stored the backpack with some blankets in the frunk. Half-eaten snacks, empty water bottles, and discarded jackets and socks littered the Tesla. But Audrey was learning to let the mess go.

She drove down Highway 9 and took a right onto 1 North. They sped past the last homes, eucalyptus groves, and restaurants of Santa Cruz. Open fields bordered the ocean to their left. Beyond the fields, the ocean sparkled to the horizon, dazzling blue. Sloping up, far away to the right, more fields ended at the dark redwood forest that covered the Santa Cruz Mountains.

Audrey pulled in at the historic Wilder Ranch State Park. The Tesla's tires crunched onto the dirt parking lot and stopped. The kids piled out, chattering and excited.

"What is this place?" Easton gazed at lavender fields nearby.

"It's Wilder Ranch. Come on!" Audrey slung the backpack over her shoulder and strode towards the path that led to bluffs above the ocean. The kids scampered after her.

For the rest of the day, Audrey let the kids explore the historic ranch. Along the bluffs trail, pelicans flew in stately lines beside them. Foamy waves crashed over rocks near the shore, leaving a glistening wash of water over their brown surfaces. Seagulls and terns swooped above the waves. The kids raced across the turf beside the trail, panting and gasping as they paused on wide stretches of dirt that overlooked the ocean. They climbed down paths to small beaches encircled by cliff walls.

Once, a pod of dolphins flicked in and out of the waves, leaping across the water in shiny arcs. The children squealed with excitement. Far offshore, a whale shot sprays of white from the water. Its sleek, black form rose up and crashed down again amid white foam.

After the bluffs trail, Audrey let the kids peek through the windows of the old farmhouse and outbuildings, lifting Warwick so he could see inside. She led them along the dirt road that tunneled under Highway 1, to fields and pastures beyond. They hiked up the fields and stopped to rest in the shadows of the redwood forest. There, she gave them the sandwiches and watched them gaze down at the farmlands and ocean. *Thank you, Lord!* This was a Thanksgiving they would remember fondly.

Finally, she led them back to the Tesla. The kids jumped into the car, talking excitedly about their day.

As they drove through Santa Cruz, Easton turned to Lillie and held up his hand. "I'm Flip the Dinosaur!" He formed his fingers into a point and jerking his hand up and down.

Lillie giggled. She mirrored Easton's hand motions. "I'm Benny the Dinosaur!"

Soon, Warwick joined in. The kids laughed and continued the game. Their pretend dinosaurs went to the beach and found a frisbee.

Audrey's skin tingled. Her muscles were pleasantly tired. It was almost better than Legally Fit.

~

The next week, during school hours, she packed up her condo and hired a couple college students to move her furniture to a storage unit. Her gym bag and workout clothes joined the furniture—her abandoned fitness goals seemed trivial now. By Friday, the condo was ready for the property manager.

"Moving?" The elderly gentleman paused with his dog, as she carried the last box to the Tesla.

Audrey smiled. "Just for the next year. I'm taking care of my brother's kids."

"Best of luck." He walked away, his dog sniffing the grass.

It was the first time Audrey had spoken to him. When she closed the Tesla door and drove out of the parking lot, no one else noticed she was gone.

~

She parked at the mall, and an hour later carried bags stuffed with new clothes to the Tesla. It was high time to dress like a mom—a stylish one. She'd been a substitute mom for three weeks now, and she was sure her sweats embarrassed the kids. They deserved a caregiver who at least looked competent.

When she got home, she spread the clothes across the bed and gazed at them. "Welcome to your new identity, Audrey." She ran her hand through her hair, a thousand daddy issues demanding attention.

She started with easy pieces—a simple t-shirt that tied at the waist, ripped jeans, tan ankle boots. In the bathroom, she played with her new makeup, then swung the bedroom door closed and looked into the cracked mirror behind it, to get the overall effect.

Her skin glowed against the coral t-shirt. Her hair had grown to chin-length, and its whisps around her face softened the line of her square jaw and enlarged her eyes. Her legs looked graceful and slim in the jeans and boots.

"My Mom Competence Wardrobe." Naming her clothes put some needed emotional distance between her and her new look. She stood tall and rotated before the mirror, recalling the well-off moms she'd observed around town and at Luke's small church—those she presumed had it all together.

She looked the part. Now, she just had to play it.

~

Nancy's boots thumped the frozen ground, stinging her feet, as she ran past the field in front of her grandparents' Indiana farmhouse. Her down parka scraped against her ears, clashing with the honks of a flock of geese overhead. Duchess, her grandparents' golden retriever, pulled joyfully at her leash.

Laughing, Nancy yanked the dog's leash and slowed to a walk. Her breath came in harsh gusts. The cold air chilled her nose and cheeks. "Good job, Duchess!"

The dog glanced back, grinning widely, then sniffed the path ahead. Nancy walked the driveway to the farmhouse, catching her breath. Beside her, black cows grazed. Tall oaks and hickory trees crowded the east side of the driveway. The rising sun lit their top branches and trunks to pale yellow. Light from the kitchen window beamed across the dusky yard, illuminating chokeberry bushes to brilliant reds. Nancy's grandmother washed dishes behind the kitchen window.

Nancy pushed the front door open, and Duchess lunged in ahead of her. "Hi Grandma! Me and Duchess had a wonderful walk."

"Have some coffee, dear." Her silver-haired grandmother handed her a mug and pointed to the coffee maker.

Nancy sat at the table, sipping her coffee, and considered her plans. After her trip to Iceland, she had traveled around Europe. In London, Jasmine had abandoned her and returned to California, refusing to stay in the hotel Nancy picked.

She went to the fridge and splashed cream into her coffee. "Got any sugar?"

Her grandma handed her the sugar bowl and turned back to the stove.

Nancy stirred her coffee and sat at the round oak table. She had enjoyed working as a bartender in London. She'd made new friends, experienced English culture, and attending New Age spiritual meetings. What adventures awaited her here?

She'd come because she wanted to explore her farming roots. Her grandparents had agreed she could live with them, in exchange for a reasonable rent. She had arrived the previous November night. Today, she would begin her job search.

Her grandmother opened the oven and flipped the bacon. Homey scents of baking muffins and crisp bacon filled the room.

"Smells so good!" Nancy closed her eyes and tilted her head back, her dark blond eyelashes grazing her cheeks. Her grandmother's cat twisted against her legs. She giggled and stroked its arched back.

CHAPTER EIGHTEEN

Dr. McKenzie wheeled his suitcase to the front door and lifted a garment bag from a hat stand. It was five-thirty in the morning. His son, Nolan, was asleep.

"Olivia, time to say goodbye!" He tapped his foot, impatiently.

His wife was finishing the breakfast dishes. She came from the kitchen, carrying a dish towel. She wore a jade satin bathrobe with a black border. Her dark, thick hair was pinned up. She was almost as tall as her husband and supposed to be slender—but she'd gained weight lately, he thought. He'd bring that up when he returned. "Did you pack my cufflinks?" She'd probably forgotten something. She always did.

"Yes."

He glanced at his watch. He'd have to buy whatever she'd missed. He must remember to deduct that from her allowance. "Good, sweetheart. I'll be back Friday." He leaned towards her. She touched her lips briefly to his, stepped back, and looked down.

Draping the garment bag over his arm, he lifted her chin, forcing her to look at him. Every little movement she made smacked of rebellion—it really was disgusting. He spoke softly. "Do not speak to anyone while I'm away. Stay home, except when necessary for Nolan. If you try to leave, I'll know." He squeezed her jaw hard. Firmness was the only way with this woman.

She nodded, but he doubted her sincerity. He would just have to watch her carefully, as always. He turned and opened the door, then glanced back. Olivia's robe had fallen open slightly, revealing welts and bruises on her thighs. "Keep those bruises covered, honey. If you didn't cheat on me, you wouldn't have them."

"Harrison, I've never even—"

"Shut up!" *Liar!* He swung his suitcase over the threshold and slammed the door.

~

Nancy stepped into Jones Coffee Shop from the cold Linton street. Rich aromas of brewing roasts mingled with the sweet scent of baked goods.

"Nancy! Come through here." The manager, an overweight woman in her forties, gestured to a gap in the counter.

"Morning, Janice!" Putting on her biggest smile, Nancy took her place beside the cash register. She'd dressed modestly, with a plaid shirt and jeans.

"Put this on." Janice handed her an apron.

Nancy knotted the apron strings behind her back. "Want me to learn the cash register? I used one in London."

"Sure! Watch me, then you can take the next order." Janice served an elderly couple, talking Nancy through the steps.

The doorbell jangled and a tall man strode in. Nancy glanced at him, then allowed herself a longer look. He assessed the menu like a king, his hands thrust deep into the pockets of his long wool coat. He was well built. His eyes invited trust.

Nancy turned the microwave's dial, warming the elderly wife's croissant. The new customer approached the counter. He met Nancy's eyes for a long second, sending quivers through her belly. He smiled, then looked back at the menu.

"I'll take a shot of espresso, a couple hard-boiled eggs,

and one of those yummy croissants, like the one you just sold." He flashed another quick smile at Nancy, with briefly raised eyebrows.

Nancy's torso warmed. Her cheeks burned. She took another plate from the stack and reached for the display case.

"Use these, honey." Janice handed the tongs to Nancy.

"Oops!" She giggled and glanced at the stranger. "This is my first day. In fact, you're my first customer." She'd never felt this awkward bartending.

"Well, I'm honored." The man dipped his head and smiled, and Nancy's heart thudded. He took a step back, returned his hands to his pockets, and waited politely.

She swiped at her forehead. *Phew!*

Janice wiped the back counter. "Would you like the croissant heated, sir?"

"Please—warm it! I'm not used to Indiana weather." Cheerfully, he blew on his hands and rubbed them together.

After Nancy had set the heated croissant on the counter, Janice guided her through the payment process. Nancy began tapping in the order, struggling to focus on the items.

Janice turned to the customer. "Are you from a sunshine state?"

"Arizona. It was 70 degrees when I left yesterday." He chuckled softly.

"Totally different than Indiana!" Nancy giggled, feeling stupid and not caring. She stared at the screen, confused.

"What brings you to Linton?" Janice pointed to the "Eggs" entry. Nancy entered two eggs.

"I'm a medical expert witness in a personal injury suit. Wish there were no such suits, but someone has to help the victims." He cleared his throat humbly and looked at the floor.

A legal expert! Nancy about swooned. "Are you a doctor?" She tipped her head. Quite involuntarily, her eyelids fluttered.

"Endocrinologist." Dr. McKenzie handed her a credit

card. "I treat diabetes, thyroid, and so on."

"Wow!" Nancy ran the card through the magnetic strip reader and handed it back to Dr. McKenzie. Her fingers brushed his, sending a zap up her arm.

"Nancy, put the good doctor's eggs in a little bowl, please." Janice gestured to the dishes. "Then you can watch me make an espresso. Thanks for your patience." She looked at Dr. McKenzie.

"No problem!" He strolled to the shop's brick wall and studied local art pieces hung from a wire. Tiny price tags dangled from their frames.

Nancy set the eggs on the counter. Janice tamped coffee grounds into the espresso machine's steel filter and clicked the machine into action. Soon, a thin, fragrant stream hissed into a cup, which Nancy set out with the eggs and croissant.

"Doctor, your order's ready!" called Janice.

Dr. McKenzie picked up the cup. He looked at Nancy through the rising steam. "This coffee smells as good as anything I'd find in Arizona." Nancy's stomach flip-flopped.

He carried his order to a table and draped his coat over a chair. After eating his breakfast and reading emails on a tablet, he left.

For the rest of the day, Nancy tried to focus. She forgot the tongs twice when taking food from the display case. She gave a customer the wrong change, even though the register displayed the correct amount. She even broke a plate. It was fun connecting with the customers, though, and she noticed Janice's approving glance as she got people laughing at the counter.

"Good start, Nancy. You'll catch on." Janice switched the Open sign to Closed. Nancy helped her sweep the floor and clean the machines.

CHAPTER NINETEEN

Eric stared at Nurse Jenny. "Audrey Beach has an appointment for her nephew?"

"In ten minutes. Is there a problem?"

He gripped the arms of his chair. Why was Beach bringing Warwick to see him? The situation was awkward enough! Was she trying to gather more evidence against him?

"It's the kid I treated at the PICU earlier this month. Beach is his aunt and caregiver. She's also an attorney—suing me." He hadn't mentioned the lawsuit to his nurse—or to anyone.

Jenny's eyes grew round. "Oh, gosh! Dr. Taylor, I had no idea you were being sued. Why didn't you tell me?"

He was afraid of this. Taking a deep breath, he settled deeper in his chair, trying to reassure himself. "It'll be fine. It's about that dosing error with Meghan Patel. They should be suing NewDay. I'll win." Not reassured, he rotated a pen through his fingers. Jenny nodded but looked away, raising an eyebrow. That didn't help.

"Isn't it a conflict of interest to bring her nephew to me?"

"I don't know! I'm a nurse, not an attorney."

He walked to the window and rubbed his chin stubble. He'd forgotten to shave that morning. "Can you reschedule him with Fisk?" Maybe he could avoid the whole thing.

"Dr. Taylor, I can't do that! You know it, too."

He could count on Jenny not holding back her ire. He returned to his seat, massaging the back of his neck. "I'll see him."

"Of course, you will." The nurse checked her watch and rose to go.

"Wait! Do you have any advice?" Ire aside, experience had taught him to value her input.

"David and I encourage each other to trust God in everything. Maybe He has a lesson for you." She went to the door. "I've got work to do, Dr. Taylor."

~

Audrey led Warwick across the parking lot to the clinic, a travel mug in one hand. Lillie and Easton lagged behind, carrying backpacks full of schoolwork. Lillie was angry. Audrey had tried to reach Dominique, but the busy coach hadn't answered. In the end, Audrey had texted that Lillie would not be at practice.

"Coach Minnie says I have to go every day," Lillie had yelled. "You have to take me, Auntie Audrey!"

"Sorry, I just can't, Lillie."

Inside, Audrey told the receptionist they were there for Warwick's appointment. Lillie sat and pouted.

"Fill out these forms, please." The receptionist handed Audrey a clipboard. When Audrey sat down, Lillie turned away.

Warwick ran to a big aquarium at the end of the room. Easton followed him and watched the fish flick through a vertical stream of bubbles. Lillie joined her brothers, glancing angrily at Audrey as she went. Soon, she was chatting with Easton and pointing at the blue-green, underwater world.

Audrey handed the completed forms to the receptionist. She returned to her seat, glad for the Mom Competency Wardrobe. Her dark green t-shirt and casual jewelry buoyed her confidence.

"Warwick?" A red-haired nurse looked through the side

door.

"That's us. I'm Audrey."

"I'm Nurse Jenny." The woman gestured for them to follow her. She checked Warwick's height and weight and led them to a small exam room. "Here's where you'll see Dr. Taylor. Have a seat, Audrey. Up here, please, young man!" She patted the thin, crinkly paper on the exam table. Warwick climbed up.

Audrey sat. Soon, Easton and Lillie were giggling, bracing their outside legs as they jostled each other on the other chair. Lillie's stormy mood was gone.

Nurse Jenny entered Warwick's information on the computer, then left. Warwick played with his transformer toy. Easton and Lillie fidgeted on their chair. The clock above the small sink ticked.

After a quick tap, the door opened, and Dr. Taylor stepped in. "Good morning." He glanced at Audrey. "Everyone's here, huh?" He washed his hands, sat on the exam stool, and scrolled through Warwick's information. "How are you feeling, Warwick?"

"Pretty good. Want to check my blood again?" Warwick held out his finger.

"Later." Dr. Taylor looked at Audrey. "Do you have his meter?"

She took the meter from her purse. The doctor inserted its USB connector to a port on the computer. He sat straight and folded his arms, watching the screen.

"Warwick's been doing a great job." Audrey hoped the doctor would cheer Warwick on. "He always knows where his supplies are."

"Good." Dr. Taylor swiveled the screen, so Audrey and the kids could see it. He pointed to a chart. "Your blood sugar is trending high after dinner, Warwick, so we're going to adjust your evening insulin-to-carb ratio."

Audrey peered at a swarm of data dots above the graph's timeline. Easton jumped up from the chair and went to examine the screen.

"Easton, move! I can't see," complained Lillie.

"Easton, sit down." Audrey pulled on his t-shirt. Easton returned to his seat.

Dr. Taylor entered Warwick's new doses into the software. "Let's check your injection sites, Warwick."

Warwick lifted his t-shirt, and the doctor inspected his skin for infection. Easton leaned past Lillie to get a good view. Lillie elbowed her brother.

"Looks good." Dr. Taylor returned to the computer. "An insulin pump would make dosing easier and help control his levels. I can prescribe it if you're willing to come in for training and weekly check-ins."

"What do you think, Warwick?" Audrey asked. "Do you want an insulin pump? Meghan has one."

"Um, who's Meghan?" Warwick tipped his head.

Audrey's heart raced. "A friend." *Idiot!* Things were awkward enough.

Dr. Taylor ignored the gaff. "Warwick, you'd wear the pump on your arm or your tummy, like a little packet, and it would deliver your insulin all the time so you wouldn't need injections."

Warwick tipped his head. "Does it hurt?"

"Not much. First, you get a little poke in your skin, like your injections. Then, it stays there for a few days, until you need a new one."

"It sounds helpful." Audrey pursed her lips. "Warwick, why don't we try it? We can always stop using it if you don't like it."

Warwick shrugged his little shoulders. "OK." He leaned towards his siblings and lifted the transformer toy over his head. "I'm getting a Iiiiiinsulin puuuuuump!"

"Good on ya, Cap'n!" Lillie gave Warwick a double high five, then swung her hands sideways, bumping Audrey's travel mug. Coffee splashed onto Audrey's shirt.

"Oops, sorry, Madaaaam-mooooselle." She spoke in a

high, chirpy voice. Audrey saw Dr. Taylor's mouth tip up for an instant. Her face heated.

"We'll schedule a training session for next week." Dr. Taylor stood. "Now Jenny will go over your daily care." He reached to shake Audrey's hand. "Good work, Auntie. Warwick is right on track."

~

The doctor's voice sounded from down the hall. "Jenny, could you check in on Warwick, please? Review their treatment protocols and remind them about our resources. They're getting an insulin pump, so she'll need a release form."

"Super!" Jenny replied. Her voice quieted. "That wasn't so bad, see?"

Lillie said loudly, "What wasn't so bad, Auntie Audrey? What did she mean?"

Silence followed. Audrey rested her forehead on her palm and squeezed her eyes shut.

Nurse Jenny returned. "Here's a release form for the pump. Let's talk about uploading your data from your meter."

They discussed Warwick's care for a few minutes.

"Now let's talk about something fun." Jenny handed the meter back to Audrey. "There's a camp just for kids with type 1 diabetes."

Warwick squealed and jumped off the exam table.

"It's called Camp Strong n' Free." Nurse Jenny ruffled Warwick's hair. "Kids play games, make new friends, go swimming—lots of fun! I think they even have a horse-riding program this year."

Audrey realized this was the camp Meghan had mentioned. She mentally kicked herself for not thinking of it for Warwick.

Warwick bounced back onto the table. "Can I go?" He wiggled, looking at Audrey.

"Maybe. When is it?"

Jenny pointed to a wall calendar. "In April. They try to match it with spring break. They have a summer session, too, but spring camp would be a good introduction."

"Looks great."

"I'll email you the link and you can look it up. The deadline to register is January 15th, so you have time to think about it." She paused, thoughtfully, and added, "Scholarships are available."

"Anything else?" Audrey asked. The woman's correct assumption about the scholarships irritated her.

"Just sign this release form, for the pump educators." Jenny handed Audrey a form. "We're done for today, unless you have any questions."

Audrey signed the form and asked to speak with Dr. Taylor. Stained shirt aside, she had to make sure he knew she was no longer on the case.

"Of course!" Jenny smiled. "Keep up the good work. We're always on call if you need help." She went to get the doctor.

~

Dr. Taylor came in. Audrey looked at him squarely. "I have stepped away from Tate Personal Injury, including the med-mal case for Meghan Patel. You'll be hearing from another attorney—Patrick Rogers."

He shifted his weight and rubbed the back of his neck. His eyes flicked to the coffee stain, then back to her face. He glanced around the room. "Um, sure, no problem. What have you done with the case? Sorry, I don't understand."

"I'm no longer representing Meghan Patel. Have you heard from Patrick Rogers? He's another attorney with Tate Personal Injury."

"I haven't met Patrick. Is he a lawyer friend of yours?"

"Patrick was my coworker before I stepped away from Tate Personal Injury." She forced herself to deliver a clear message. "I turned all my cases over to him, and Meghan Patel's was one of them. You'll be hearing from him." She wished she could bolt.

"You quit?!" Dr. Taylor exclaimed. His mouth hung open for a second. He grabbed at the door handle and cleared his throat. "I haven't heard from anyone named Patrick. But it's good to know where you stand." He stopped talking and stared at her.

"I quit to take care of Warwick and his siblings. It had nothing to do with where I stand. I represent my clients because I care about their outcomes—especially Meghan's." She might as well be absolutely clear.

His neck reddened. "Right, gotcha!" He reached back and opened the door.

Sweat dampened the back of her shirt. "Kids, pack your things. It's time to go."

A piece of Warwick's transformer toy clattered to the floor. Audrey lunged for it, forcing Dr. Taylor to step back and bump against the door.

"Sorry!" She glanced at the doctor as she returned the piece to Warwick. "Warwick, put that away. Easton and Lillie, pack your devices."

Lillie stood up. "Easton, Auntie Audrey says to pack your things," she said in a sing-song voice.

Easton rolled his eyes and stood. Somehow, Audrey got the kids down the hall. Dr. Taylor followed—Audrey acutely aware of her shirt's damp back.

The doctor reached past her and pushed open the door to the reception room. "Thanks for trusting Warwick's care to us." He squeezed towards the wall, awkwardly, allowing her and the kids to pass.

"Thanks, Dr. Taylor." She dipped her head and moved quickly into the reception room, breathing deeply as the door swung closed behind her. The Competency Wardrobe was not doing its job today.

~

In the breakroom, Eric poured himself a cup of strong black coffee. He took a deep breath, leaned against the counter, and sipped the steaming liquid.

Nurse Jenny came in. She tossed the packaging from some office supplies she'd unpacked. "Taking a break?" She opened the fridge.

"Yeah."

She grabbed a can of flavored water and popped it open. "Audrey seems nice."

"She told me she quit at the law firm."

"Wow! Did she say why?"

He sighed and stared at the spotless linoleum floor, remembering how gently Audrey had guided those active kids down the hall. "To care for the kids—Warwick, especially."

"I was right—she's very nice." Jenny settled into a chair. "Does that mean the lawsuit goes away?"

"No. Another attorney is taking the case."

Jenny nodded. She sat quietly, drinking the water.

His mind drifted to the determined lift of Audrey's sculpted chin. "It's admirable she made a choice like that."

"Very. Warwick is a lucky boy. I don't know the situation with his parents, but to have a relative who steps up like that is amazing, really."

Eric sipped his coffee, then set it on the counter. "She told me she was the kids' caregiver when I treated Warwick at the hospital. Not my place to share the circumstances, but I will say I was impressed. Warwick's diagnosis prompted her further to quit her career. She's a good person." Why had his voice risen with that statement? He felt Jenny studying the side of his face.

"Attractive, too," she ventured. "And about your age."

Her implication jerked him back to reality. He dumped the rest of his coffee into the sink and set the cup in the dishwasher. "Please don't take that on-ramp. She believes I should get what's coming for the Meghan Patel case." He sighed and rested the heels of his hands on the counter, staring at the floor again.

"All doctors get sued. Learn from it and move on."

"Audrey Beach doesn't get it. Medical records software is notoriously glitchy. Someone in Washington needs to investigate and hold the developers responsible." Why did it matter so much what Audrey thought?

Jenny shrugged and finished her drink. "OK." She left to clean the exam room.

Eric blew out a strong breath and clenched his fists. He pushed away from the counter and went to his office.

CHAPTER TWENTY

The receptionist gave Audrey the paperwork showing Warwick's data and new doses. Audrey and the kids walked to the Tesla, Audrey enjoying the fall breeze that cooled her skin. She eased the vehicle out of the parking lot. For a while, they traveled in silence. Lexington Reservoir glimmered, dark and rippling, as she drove up Highway 17. Clouds were gathering, treetops swaying. She was glad the awkward conversation was behind her. Now, the case could not interfere with Warwick's care.

"Auntie Audrey, can I go to camp?" Warwick's feet gently bumped the back of her seat.

"I'm not sure, Warwick. We'll try." She needed to check the budget.

"Nurse Jenny said there's scholarships," commented Warwick, quietly.

Audrey was surprised he knew what a scholarship was.

"I wanna go. Is there a scholarship for me, Auntie Audrey?"

"I'll check. I want you to go, too, Warwick. Let's do our best, OK?"

"OK."

The Tesla rushed through the rising wind. A few raindrops lightly touched the windshield. Audrey tapped the wipers on and glanced at Warwick in the rear-view mirror. Her nephew's expression was flat. He stared at his hands, which were folded in his lap.

"You're going to camp, Warwick. I'll figure it out."

"Yay! I'm going to camp!" His face broke into a big smile, and he bounced in his booster seat.

Lillie hugged Warwick's neck. "You're going to camp, Cap'n!"

Audrey knew the cost would be a stretch. If they needed a scholarship, she would just have to ask.

In the passenger seat, Easton turned to Warwick. "It'll be fun for you, Warwick. Camps are good for your mental health."

"How did you know that, Easton?" asked Audrey.

He shrugged. "I've heard people talk about it."

~

The cabin was chilly. Audrey put the heat on and changed into sweats, tossing the stained Competence shirt into the laundry. The kids went to their rooms.

"Put warm clothes on!" Audrey called.

She heated coffee in the microwave and took it, with her phone, to the living room. Lillie sprawled on the living room floor with her laptop. She snuggled with Bella and opened a game.

Audrey sat in an armchair. "Lillie, don't you have schoolwork?"

"I'm taking a break. Then I'll practice gymnastics outside."

Audrey walked to the slider. Tree branches tossed in the wind, and dark spots showed on the dirt. "It's starting to rain."

She returned to the armchair and checked her phone. Dominique had left two voice messages and a text.

"Audrey, please call when you get a chance. I know there's been a lot of change, but Lillie needs to keep up her practices." Audrey heard children's voice, echoes, and pounding feet in the background.

Dominique's text and second message were similar.

Audrey sighed and glanced at the clock. She needed to make dinner. She went to the kitchen and opened the fridge. At least Warwick's appointments were only quarterly. She slapped her forehead, remembering that the insulin pump would require weekly visits. How would she manage that, on top of picking up the boys from school and accommodating Lillie's practice? Her phone rang, and she recognized Dominique's number.

"Is Lillie OK?"

"I had to take the kids to a doctor appointment for Warwick. We couldn't fit practice in."

"I know it's complicated with your nephew's illness but try getting in the carpool. Lillie needs to be at practice consistently."

Audrey stuffed a pang of defensiveness. Dominique had no idea what Audrey was up against. "I'll try."

"Please do. See you tomorrow." Dominique hung up.

~

Outside, the wind picked up. It howled around the cabin. Darkness filled the windows. Audrey closed the blinds and pulled some cooked rice out of the fridge. It was already six o'clock. She took a package of frozen chicken from the freezer.

Warwick came into the kitchen. "My blood sugar's high."

"How high?" She set the frozen chicken in a bowl in the sink and added warm water. In half an hour, she would pry apart the frozen pieces and get them into the oven.

Warwick handed her his meter. The small screen showed 278 mg/dL.

"Did you eat something?"

"I had a cookie while you were on the phone."

"You need to ask for insulin before you eat anything." Audrey massaged her eyes.

"You were busy, and I was really hungry."

Audrey crouched in front of Warwick and gently grasped

his arms. "Warwick, you can always interrupt me about your type 1 diabetes. Just touch my arm, like this." She took his hand and tapped it against her forearm. "Say, 'Auntie Audrey, I need help with my diabetes.' I'll stop and help you."

"OK."

She went to the utility cart in the corner of the kitchen, where she kept Warwick's supplies and the binder from California Oaks. She flipped the binder's heavy bulk to the section about dosing and daily life and found Warwick's evening insulin-to-carb ratio. She grabbed a clean syringe from his supplies and took his vial of insulin from the fridge door.

As she was filling the syringe, she remembered Dr. Taylor had adjusted Warwick's evening doses. She set the supplies down and pulled the paperwork out of her tote. She made a mental note to update the doses in the binder after the kids went to bed, then adjusted her calculations and filled the syringe with the new dose of insulin. She replaced the vial in the fridge door. "Come here, buddy. Ready?"

Warwick nodded.

She injected the insulin and put the used syringe into the hazard materials box on the cart. "We'll check your level again in forty minutes. Drink this." She handed him a full glass of water, hoping his blood sugar would be in range in time for dinner. She never knew. There were so many wild cards.

As she tried to pry apart the chicken pieces, a cracking, whooshing sound filled the air, followed by a deafening thud. The ground shook. The power went out, leaving the cabin completely dark. Lillie screamed and ran into the kitchen.

CHAPTER TWENTY-ONE

Startled, Audrey dropped the frozen chicken pieces, splashing water onto her sweats. She fumbled for a kitchen towel.

Stark light illuminated the hallway, and Easton carried a flashlight into the kitchen. He put his arm around Lillie. "Want me to see what happened?"

"Let's go together." Audrey found the kids' coats and they went outside. The wind tossed her hair. She pulled Warwick close, worrying about falling branches.

The huge oak near the driveway entrance had fallen. Its massive limbs almost filled the front yard. Leaves and twigs littered the ground. The tree had barely missed the cars and shed. Broken branches hung from drooping power lines, and the nearest utility pole leaned over the road.

Audrey put her hands on her head and squeezed her eyes shut, stifling a scream of rage. How long would it take the power company to restore service? She turned and stomped back to the cabin. The kids followed her.

"What about dinner?" Warwick asked, as they took off their coats.

Audrey didn't have an answer. The tree was blocking the driveway, so they couldn't eat out. Easton pulled battery powered lanterns from the hall closet, and Audrey set one up in each room, thankful that Luke had prepared for power outages. They must be frequent in the winter.

"Dad makes peanut butter sandwiches sometimes," Lillie offered.

Audrey taped the fridge door closed and made the sandwiches. The kids did their homework as they ate, excited about the change in routine.

"Maybe we won't have school tomorrow." The lantern cast harsh light across Easton's face.

Audrey wiped a smudge of peanut butter off the table. "You have to go to school."

~

The power company arrived around midnight. For hours, workers shouted, and chainsaws roared. Just before dawn, light flooded every room. Audrey rushed to turn out lights and urged the kids to try to sleep. The cabin was finally quiet as morning light outlined the colorless bulk of furniture and toys.

Almost asleep, Audrey heard scratching in the ceiling. A swift scampering followed, then thumping behind the bathroom wall. Her skin prickled.

When sunshine filtered through the redwoods, she sat in the kitchen, bleary eyed, still wearing sweats, sipping fresh coffee. Warwick's blood sugar was a stable 110 mg/dL. She gave him insulin and set out cereal.

Lillie was slow to get ready. By the time they got into the Tesla, the kids' classes were beginning. Fastening her seatbelt, Audrey stared at the Tesla's blank screen.

"Why aren't we going?" Lillie asked.

"Battery's dead. We'll take Daddy's car." Audrey forced her voice to remain calm.

After searching for twenty minutes, she found the keys. She sped to the campus, thanking God Luke's old car still ran, and walked the kids to the school building. They dashed off to their classrooms, and Audrey turned to leave.

"Audrey!" Dominique sprang out of the building, smiling a greeting. Today's earrings were short cascades of silver feathers.

Audrey forced a smile, embarrassed by her uncombed hair and grubby clothes.

"We're having a quick meeting for gym club parents at two forty-five, at the gym."

"Got it."

As she drove back, Audrey raked her hand through her hair, planning the day. Easton and Warwick would have to sit and wait during the meeting. She charged the Tesla. Inside, she went to Lillie's room and sat on her niece's bed. Lillie had taped pictures of famous gymnasts to her walls. Ribbons and a trophy sat on the shelf next to her closet.

Audrey had read that hobbies and extracurricular activities were important stabilizers for children. Lillie's sport was second to Warwick's life-threatening disease, but she would try to accommodate it.

~

She took a long nap and hurried to Dominique's meeting, picking up the kids on the way. The gym was in a boxy, single-story building at the back of a weedy parking lot. Inside, the huge room smelled faintly of cleaning agents and microwaved spaghetti. A little breeze came through the high, narrow windows and stirred Audrey's hair.

Well-organized equipment filled the gym. A tumbling track ran along one wall. Knotted ropes dangled from the high ceiling. Bright mats covered the floor. A set of bleachers by the door provided a viewing area for parents. Nearby was a small office, enclosed by windows and short walls.

"Sit up now and do some homework." Audrey pointed to the bleachers.

"I'm hungry!" Warwick complained.

Audrey had forgotten to bring a snack. "You'll only have to wait a few minutes," she promised.

Easton climbed onto the bleachers and pulled a workbook from his backpack. Warwick jumped from one bench to another.

On the gym floor, Dominique talked with a sporty couple. The dad wore a baseball cap. The mom—taller than her husband—wore an athleisure dress. Groups of parents stood chatting by the bleachers. Audrey wished she'd shortened her nap and changed. She smoothed her hair.

Lillie ran to a circle of kids sitting on the gym mats. She settled next to a dark-haired girl, who beamed at her. Soon, they were giggling together.

A well-dressed woman with perfect makeup turned to Audrey. "Is your daughter new? I don't think we've met."

"I'm Lillie Beach's aunt. I'm looking after the kids for my brother."

"Lillie's my daughter's best friend! See? They're palling around." She extended her hand. "I'm Miriam."

"Audrey." Audrey shook the woman's hand.

Another woman interrupted them. "Are you Lillie's aunt? How's Luke? Are the kids missing him? It must be so hard!" She scrunched her well-groomed eyebrows into a concerned knot and shifted her expensive leather tote on her shoulder.

"How did you know about Luke?" Audrey was astonished.

"We're a close group. Coach Dominique told us about it the week before he went in." She gave Audrey's arm a gentle squeeze. "We're praying for you and the kids."

"Thanks." Audrey turned away and exhaled slowly. Luke was right about small-town gossip.

Dominique blew a whistle and jogged over to the group. "Let's get started."

The parents gathered around her.

"I want to update you on the team's progress and make arrangements for upcoming meets." Dominique's friendly gaze moved among the parents. "Thank you for getting your kids to practices and encouraging them at home. It truly makes a difference." Her eyes met Audrey's briefly.

As Dominique continued, Audrey stood straighter,

staggered by the demands on her schedule and budget. The club attended two meets a month, most of them far away and all weekend long, requiring hotel reservations and dining out. Added to that were the costs of uniforms, transportation, and meet fees. Signups for the required carpool were online.

Audrey glanced at Lillie as Dominique talked. Her niece was leaning over her friend's shoulder and watching a video. How had Luke accommodated this, as a single parent with a full-time job? What did Easton and Warwick do while Lillie was at meets? How would Audrey pay for it all?

Dominique concluded and gave the parents printouts of the schedule. The parents left the gym, and Audrey started gathering the boys.

"Audrey, do you have a minute?" Dominique smiled widely, eyebrows raised.

Audrey waited while the coach put papers in the office and approached her.

"Please prioritize Lillie's practices. She's doing great, and her dad wants her to succeed, even though it can be a logistical challenge."

Audrey frowned. Did Dominique understand how challenging this was? She met Dominique's eyes. "I'm doing the best I can, but we are still adjusting to Warwick's disease. And I have to find a part-time job soon."

"I get it."

Audrey was certain she didn't.

"Lillie could compete at top levels." The sparkle in Dominique's eyes dimmed to a low burn. "Please make every effort, Audrey. She's worth it."

"I know that," Audrey snapped.

"Of course!" Dominique laughed, companionably. "See you after practice."

"Before you go, I understand you told the families about my brother's jail sentence?"

"I had to." Dominique voice was level. "We communicate here."

"Not with me, you didn't!"

Dominique straightened. "Audrey, things happened fast, and the parents would have asked anyway. It's best to keep things in the open."

"And I'm irrelevant?"

Dominique stared at her. "Listen, I apologize for offending you. I have to coach the kids." She strode to the gym floor, blowing a couple of sharp trills on her whistle.

Audrey left the building and got her nephews into the car. Shutting down her anger, she perused the schedule. The next meet was on an upcoming Saturday, at a facility in the North Bay. Suddenly, she remembered Luke's jail visits were on weekends. She slapped the paperwork onto the passenger seat and put the Tesla in reverse. *Forget it!* She would have to set limits on the coach's sky-high expectations.

~

After giving the kids dinner, she reread Luke's document about the kids' care. "Lillie gym practice daily 3-5:30 at Felton gym. Carpool there, I pick her up." She scanned the page and noticed a footnote for the first time: "Meets too hard since Nancy left. Lillie only doing two meets. December 8 and the one April 13. Coach, Lillie, me already discussed."

Poor Lillie! Even as Audrey's stress dissipated, she wondered if Nancy had a clue what her daughter had lost. Anyway, it was a relief that Luke had already told Lillie she couldn't go to all her meets. Apparently, Lillie had accepted it. She'd never complained.

Audrey took a deep breath. Two meets would be manageable. The meets Luke had chosen were within driving distance and only a day long, so no hotel reservation was necessary. She wished Dominique had mentioned the arrangement—but she probably assumed Audrey knew.

Signing up for the carpool was easy. Madelyn's parents had requested a ride to the December meet for their daughter, noting they would be late to the gym. Audrey committed to pick Madelyn up from the family's Ben Lomond home.

She smiled as she entered her contact information. She had read that knowing the kids' friends was an important way to engage with their world. It felt good to do the right thing for Lillie. She set the gymnastics papers on the coffee table, checked her chore list on the refrigerator, and called Easton. It was his turn to help with the dishes.

CHAPTER TWENTY-TWO

"**When are we** going to see Dad?" Easton asked, the next morning.

Lillie and Warwick looked up from their plates of scrambled eggs.

"This weekend. They approved his visitor list yesterday."

Warwick squealed and Easton whooped. Lillie hugged her brothers. Three weeks had passed since their last call with Luke. Audrey had called the jail daily, anxious to learn when they could establish weekly calls and in-person visits.

"What's a visitor list?" asked Lillie.

"Dad had to give the people our names. Then, they do some office work, and then they have a list of visitors."

Easton rolled his eyes. "It shouldn't take this long. Dad's been in jail for almost a month."

After she dropped the kids at school, she called the jail and learned they were cleared for weekly calls. They could visit Luke any time on Saturdays and Sundays, starting immediately. She scheduled two visits and wrote a list of things to tell Luke.

~

Even Bella was excited on Saturday morning. She shuffled around the kitchen, yelping and jumping on her stiff little legs. The kids were too giddy to eat. Audrey put Warwick's insulin in a cooler and packed snacks. She hoped

Luke's mood had improved since their phone call.

At the jail, an officer swung open the same door Luke had walked through. "This way."

Audrey followed the children along a harshly lit corridor, past doors with small, darkened windows. The kids jumped and skipped, their shoes squeaking on the linoleum. The officer opened a double door, and they entered a gym-sized room with a high ceiling. At one end, two officers watched vigilantly. Long tables stood in parallel lines.

Orange-clad inmates sat with family members or friends at some of the tables. A girl wearing skinny jeans crossed the room and sat opposite an inmate. Tattoos colored his thick biceps. A middle-aged couple sat across from another inmate, speaking earnestly. The young man leaned back, listening. Other groups chatted quietly. Once in a while, laughter rang harshly. A raised voice or two brought looks from the officers. The door on the opposite wall opened. Luke walked in, escorted by an officer.

"Daddy!" called Lillie.

The officer shushed Lillie. "No talking until you're at the table, miss."

~

Luke slouched, like a hollowed-out boulder that waves had worn almost through. The orange suit hung on his slim frame, wrinkled and garish. He scanned the room, saw the children, and waved.

His escort walked him to a table. Luke pulled out a chair and spread his hands with a sad smile, inviting Audrey and the kids to join him. They sat across from Luke, and the officers left them. They had been instructed not to hug, but they could touch across the table. Luke squeezed the kids' shoulders and held their hands. His beard was a thick stubble. Heavy smudges underscored his bright eyes. He didn't seem to be sleeping well.

"Dad, I miss you," said Easton.

"I miss you guys, too."

"Shall I tell you about Warwick's hospital visit?" Audrey asked.

He nodded. Audrey summarized the long hours. "The doctor who treated Warwick is the one I was suing for Meghan. He'll be Warwick's doctor going forward." Luke might have resented her hiding that information.

Luke frowned. "Is he any good?"

"He's well-respected and parents rave about him."

"OK."

Warwick set his meter on the table. "This thing tells what my blood sugar is. Want to see me take blood out of my finger?"

Despite the sad atmosphere, they all chuckled.

"Sure." Luke's gaze swung down to the meter.

Warwick demonstrated the process, Audrey intercepting him with an alcohol swab. The meter showed 110 mg/dL.

"What does that mean?" Luke spoke as if the words were boulders he had to pull from a pit.

Warwick shrugged. "I dunno."

Audrey nudged him. "Yes, you do!"

Warwick tilted his head and tapped his chin with his finger. "Oh yes!" He raised his finger and smiled. "It means I have a bit of sugar in my blood, but it's nothing to worry about."

"Bingo, Capt'n!" Lillie punched her fist into the air, although Audrey knew she didn't understand.

"Want to tell Dad how you counted carbs for breakfast?" Audrey touched Warwick's back.

Her nephew flicked his fingers, pretending to count. "A thousand carbs for my French toast and eight million for the syrup. I only ate two bites, so that's minus all the carbs except one…"

Audrey ruffled his hair. "Silly guy!"

As she summarized Warwick's insulin doses and shots, Luke nodded occasionally. She wondered how much was registering. The downturn of his mouth suggested a consuming grief.

"Easton is a great brother. He sat in the bleachers with Warwick while I was at a gymnastics meeting."

"Good."

"Next weekend's my meet." Lillie clasped her hands under her chin.

"Oh."

"I can keep my arms straight for my kip now!"

"Good."

Lillie reached across the table to her dad. He took her hands and pressed them briefly against his chest.

"Easton, how's school?" More boulder words.

Easton shrugged. "Haven't had time to practice oboe."

"Hm." Luke leaned on the table and stared at his hands. Audrey wanted to scream at him to engage. She folded her arms and looked away, stuffing her frustration.

"Did you notice Auntie Audrey's new clothes, Dad?" Lilly asked.

"I'm dressing like I know what I'm doing." Audrey smiled at Luke. She had given the Competency Wardrobe another try, with tan carpenter pants, a white t-shirt, and a pink bomber jacket. "You never knew I could have been a model, huh?"

"I did." Luke managed a half-smile. He took a deep breath and rested his head on his hands, staring down at the table.

"How about we pray?" suggested Easton.

"Please," said Luke.

They held hands around the table. Luke spoke slowly, like a rock climber seeking footholds. "God, thank You for Auntie Audrey taking good care of the kids. Thank you for Warwick's insulin, for Lillie's straight arms on her kip, and for Easton being a great brother. Amen."

Lillie prayed. "Dear Lord, thank you for my dad. I'm very glad I have a dad like him. Amen."

"Jesus, thank you for Auntie Audrey telling me Daddy

isn't bad." Warwick's eyes were squeezed shut, his hands pressed together on the table.

Audrey stared at him, astonished. So, her words had made an impact, the night they told the kids about Luke's sentencing. She closed her eyes, willing away tears. "Dear Lord, please help us all to do our schoolwork and our chores. Help Daddy remember to make his bed in the morning." The kids giggled and a slight smile crossed Luke's tired face. "And thank You for helping us. In Christ's name, Amen." She glanced at the clock above the officers' table. It was almost time to go. "Luke, I read on the website there's a Bible study for inmates."

"Hm."

"Whatever you can do to get busy would be good." She glanced at her list. "Also, the money's in your commissary account. You can call weekly and buy toiletries. Looks like you could use some." She grinned, teasing.

The faint smile flickered again, and Luke nodded. They stood as the officers approached.

"When will you call, Dad?" asked Easton.

"Friday at six thirty."

"Dad's going to call every week. And we're coming tomorrow afternoon for another visit," Audrey reminded the kids.

"'Bye," said Luke.

Audrey and the kids watched him walk away with the officer. The door swung shut behind him.

~

Sunday's visit was no better. Luke's gestures were strained, his eyes distant. His face hung sorrowfully, like a grey, blank sheet pinned over a window. The kids tried to tell him about their friends, the movie they'd watched, their hopes for summer break. But Luke stayed in his black hole, sending out occasional glimmers of interest, barely present. They prayed again, and again Audrey pressed him about the Bible study.

Afterwards, she took the kids to a park, hoping to mitigate the stress their dad's bleak mood had inflicted. Easton and Lillie played for a while, then fought, leaving Lillie in tears and Easton sullen. Audrey attributed Warwick's irritability to a high glucose level. She gave him a corrective dose of insulin and took the kids home.

After dinner, the kids cheered up, chattering about their visits with Luke as if they had been at a party. Their edited memories persisted all week, and Audrey worried that they were in denial. During their Friday phone call, with prompting from Audrey, Luke promised to pray for Lillie's meet the next day.

CHAPTER TWENTY-THREE

The wind swept grey morning clouds across the Silicon Valley sky. Due to an emergency at the hospital, the clinic had rescheduled Warwick's first pump-training appointment, and it coincided with Lillie's meet. The clinic was a forty-minute drive from the gym.

"I can't watch you compete, Lillie." Audrey drove the final curves of Highway 17.

"I'll be fine. Maybe Coach Minnie will take a picture."

The traffic was light, and they parked at the sports complex early. Lillie leaped out of the Tesla. Audrey had to grab the back of her warmup jacket to stop her from sprinting away.

Lillie hopped and spun. "Hurry up, Easton!"

Inside the sprawling white building, peppy music played. Parents crowded the enormous bleachers. Dozens of kids gathered in groups and chatted. Their sparkly leotards represented several regional teams.

In a far corner, by a wall of bleachers, Lillie's friends gathered around Coach Minnie. Lillie glanced at Audrey, then ran to join them. Audrey and the boys followed.

Swift sat far up in the bleachers, reading a book. He waved at Audrey and the kids. Audrey nodded and smiled, wondering if he and Dominique were dating.

Dominique ended her team pep talk and went to meet Audrey. "How are you doing, Warwick?"

Warwick ignored the coach, staring at the gym equipment and gymnasts.

Dominique laughed, then turned to Audrey. "Where's Madelyn?"

Audrey was confused. "Who?"

"I saw you signed up for the carpool." Dominique's smile faded. "Weren't you supposed to bring Madelyn?"

"I forgot." Audrey recalled the sign-up sheet. "Have you contacted her parents?"

Dominique stood straighter. "I have not. I assumed you were bringing her."

"You don't have a contingency plan?" Dominique should, since she claimed to understand Audrey's situation.

"I don't do the parents' job!" Dominique looked up at Audrey. The flash in her eyes made her feelings plain. "Get on the phone, Audrey. Go pick her up if necessary. Madelyn better be here in time for warm-ups!"

"That's not going to happen." Audrey was astonished. "I'll barely make it to Warwick's appointment."

Swift looked down from the bleachers, eyebrows scrunched.

"Get that kid here." Dominique spun and headed back to her team.

"Come on, Easton and Warwick." Audrey didn't have time for drama.

"Don't you have to get Madelyn?" asked Easton.

"I can't. They'll figure it out."

Easton sighed. He slouched to the door, ahead of Audrey. His downward gaze reminded Audrey of herself, when her dad had yelled at a grocery clerk. She bit her lip.

As they reached the door, the sporty couple from the parent meeting walked in, with two girls—one of them Madelyn. Athleisurewear Mom saw Audrey. "Did you forget about the carpool?"

"I got distracted. Did you bring Madelyn?"

"Yes. Miriam called us. She couldn't reach you." The

woman frowned.

"Mom, can we go join the team now?" Her daughter pulled on her hand.

"Go ahead, Hailey."

The two girls ran to join their team. When Dominique saw them, she glanced across the gym at Audrey, then continued instructing the kids.

"Glad you made it. I have to get my nephew to a doctor appointment." Audrey took Warwick's hand and followed Easton outside, feeling more discombobulated than when she'd arrived. It didn't help that she'd noticed stains on her Competency outfit again.

~

She tossed her purse into the back seat. The boys got in, and she paused, tipping her face towards the grey sky. She closed her eyes and shook her hair in the wind, savoring the brief solitude.

Warwick had woken with high blood sugar. The fight with Dominique had increased her stress. She did not look forward to receiving more help from her prior defendant.

She got in the car. "How are you doing, Easton?"

Easton ignored her, playing with a gaming device. She pursed her lips, entered Dr. Taylor's clinic into her phone, and drove to the clinic.

~

"There you are!" Nurse Jenny ruffled Warwick's hair. "Come this way."

She led them to a conference room, where two women waited, a laptop and supplies on the table before them.

"I'm Leia," said the younger woman. "This is my boss, Theresa."

Audrey shook their hands and sat with Warwick. Easton took his gaming device to the far end of the table. The door opened behind Audrey, and Dr. Taylor joined them.

The educators introduced Audrey and Warwick to the pump and continuous glucose monitor. Dr. Taylor listened, interjecting clarifications. Two hours passed, and the educators said goodbye and left.

"Now we'll set up the pump with saline, so you can practice at home." Dr. Taylor stood and went to the door. "We'll also start up the glucose monitor."

Audrey followed him to an exam room, holding Warwick's hand. Easton followed her, still playing on his device. Jenny went to get saline. In the room, Warwick climbed onto the exam table. Dr. Taylor opened his chart on the computer. Easton's device emitted blasts and beeps. Warwick swung his legs and kicked the base of the table rhythmically.

Dr. Taylor rotated the exam stool to face Audrey. "So."

Audrey raised her eyebrows, anticipating words. But he sat silent, a light flush coloring his cheeks. Eventually, he wiped his forehead and asked how their week had been.

"We saw my dad." Warwick stopped kicking the table.

"Really?" Dr. Taylor reddened.

"He's in the Santa Cruz jail, so we'll be seeing him every weekend." Audrey was anxious to put the topic to rest.

"Sorry, I didn't mean to pry." Sweat beaded on the doctor's forehead.

Audrey flapped a hand. "No worries."

The doctor turned back to the computer and scrolled through Warwick's information. Denim scraped denim as he crossed his legs. Audrey sat straight and prayed for Jenny's return.

~

The nurse bustled in, and Audrey felt her shoulders relax. Jenny beamed at Warwick. "Now we can start!"

"Audrey, you should input Warwick's doses." Dr. Taylor stood and offered her the exam stool. Audrey caught a whiff of aftershave as she stepped past him and sat.

She programmed Warwick's doses into the controller, Dr. Taylor watching the screen from behind her. His closeness was comforting. Audrey dismissed the feeling, forcing herself to focus. Warwick's life could depend on her knowledge.

"Where's your niece this morning?" Jenny asked.

"At a gymnastics meet." Audrey studied the controller's screen, checking her work.

Dr. Taylor turned to Warwick. "Lie on your back, please, Warwick. We'll put the pump on your tummy." He cleaned Warwick's skin, then handed the little device to Audrey. "Go ahead, Auntie."

Audrey set the device on Warwick's cleaned skin. "This good, Warwick?"

Warwick nodded.

Dr. Taylor stood next to Audrey, pointing at the controller screen. "Push that button to inject the cannula."

She tapped the button. The device clicked. "Did you feel it, Warwick?"

"Hmm. It stung a bit."

Audrey's eyes stung, too. She turned, trying to hide, and felt a hand on her arm.

"It's a tough adjustment," Nurse Jenny said, gently. "Take your time."

Audrey nodded, her throat tight.

Dr. Taylor cleared his throat. "Now for your glucose monitor, Warwick. Do you want it on your arm or your leg?"

"My arm, approximately."

Everyone chuckled. Dr. Taylor clicked the device into the fleshy back of Warwick's upper arm. The monitor came with an app. Soon, Audrey saw Warwick's blood sugar level on her phone. The device would update every ten minutes.

Dr. Taylor powered down the computer. "That's it for today. Time to pick up your sister, Warwick."

"Can I see the app?" Warwick asked Audrey.

Audrey passed him her phone. "Don't change anything." She watched him closely.

"He won't," said Easton. "He's smart."

"What a nice brother." Jenny smiled at Easton as she

tossed packaging into the trash. Warwick nodded and slid off the table. "Are you going to catch the end of Lillie's meet?"

Dr. Taylor opened the door and gestured for them to exit.

"Lillie has probably already competed." Audrey went into the hallway. The kids followed.

"That's too bad." Jenny led her and the kids into the reception area, Dr. Taylor following. "Is the team supportive for Lillie?"

Audrey paused. She was still annoyed at Dominique for making such a fuss about the carpool. "I, uh…. Yes, I think so."

"The coach yelled at her this morning. She forgot to pick up a kid for the carpool," Easton explained.

Audrey gasped, horrified.

"Oh gosh!" Jenny said. "That sounds stressful. Did you have to go back?"

"No." Audrey glanced at the exit door. "Some other parents got her there."

"Please accept our apologies." Dr. Taylor's gaze was direct. "We understand the impact a new diagnosis can have on other obligations. You can always let us know if you have a schedule conflict."

"Thanks." Audrey felt like crawling under a rock.

"Good work today, Warwick!" Dr. Taylor patted Warwick's shoulder.

Audrey led the boys to the exit. Jenny and Dr. Taylor returned to the hallway.

~

Impatiently, Audrey drove through the midday traffic. The boys were quiet—Warwick fell asleep, and Easton was back to his gaming device. She frowned. Dr. Taylor probably assumed that, as a lawyer, she pursued her own agenda. Now, with Easton's revelation, he had proof. She wanted to explain herself. She swiped her hair off her forehead, facing the truth: It bothered her that Dr. Taylor thought badly of her. The admission flung her out of orbit—a situation she had to fix. She couldn't function in emotional freefall. *God, please fix my perspective here!*

At a red light, a teenage girl walked the crosswalk. She wore a black miniskirt. Her hair was dyed black and fell down over her pale shoulders. She glanced at Audrey, her black-rimmed eyes radiating sadness. The light turned green, the girl walked down the sidewalk, and Audrey eased the Tesla onto the highway.

In a few short years, Lillie would be a teenager. Maybe Audrey should apologize to Dominique and the athleisurewear mom—and Madelyn's mom. It couldn't hurt, after all.

CHAPTER TWENTY-FOUR

"And she didn't even apologize!" Dominique finished telling Swift about Audrey's carpool mistake.

Swift recognized Dominique's stress signals—her pursed lips and the quick flash of her eyes away from him. "Let it go, Min. She's dealing with a lot, and it's all new to her."

The coach watched her team stretching. Lillie kept glancing towards the gymnasium doors. Dominique spun back to Swift. "Look at Lillie! She's distracted. Her dad's in jail and her aunt can't even keep a schedule."

"She'll be fine."

Dominique thumped her clipboard. "Lillie has only two meets all year, Swift. Two! A poor performance will wreck her confidence. A scholarship could be at stake."

"Are you helping?" She'd listen eventually. They'd challenged each other before, and Dominique could receive input as well as give it. It was part of why he loved her.

Dominique took a deep breath and turned back to her team. She glanced at Swift. "I need to be over there." She walked to the edge of the mat. "OK, gymnasts! Stretch deep."

Swift returned to his seat and worked on the lyrics to a song. The National Anthem played, the teams were introduced, and the meet began. He prayed for Lillie, but as the day progressed, it became clear she would not advance to Level 6. Her performance was subpar, and Dominique said it was due to the dysfunction in her family. Lillie would have to try again, in April. During a break, he went down the bleachers again.

"Lillie is so talented." Dominique's shoulders sagged in her pretty track coat. "She needs her family."

"That must be tough to watch, as a coach."

Dominique lowered her voice. "I'm furious with Audrey. She probably doesn't even know what Lillie's competing in. And that carpool fiasco! So irresponsible."

"At least the kids got here."

"Thank goodness their parents noticed Audrey's immaturity."

Swift folded his arms and looked across the gym.

"Thanks for being here, Swift. It helps to vent."

"No problem!" He laughed, then furrowed his brow. "Min, do you want some input?"

Dominique groaned. "Fire away." She faced him squarely, pulling herself straight and looking up at him. Her sideswept bangs framed her tight jaw and flared nostrils.

Swift was glad she wasn't mad at him. She was fierce. "You and Audrey are on the same team, from what I can see."

She threw her hands up. "That's ridiculous. *I* care. Audrey is just there because she has to be."

"Why does she have to?"

"There's no one else. She's a career woman, Swift. Kids are low on her list."

"Yet here she is. Apparently, whatever career she had, she gave it up for Lillie and her brothers."

"I—" Dominique's mouth snapped shut. Her dark eyes grew big, and she stared at Swift. She blew out a strong breath and ran her fingers through her bangs. "OK, I hadn't seen it that way."

"And you're right—she's in over her head. She needs a friend, Min. Maybe God has you here for that reason."

Dominique's eyes filled with tears, and the tightness fell from her posture like a heavy coat. "You're totally right. I'm not helping."

As it had a million times, his heart melted. "The way I see it, we can all be Lillie's support system. By supporting Audrey."

"How?"

"Well, for starters, I'm videoing Lillie's routines." He held up his phone. "Audrey and Luke will want to see them."

"That's a great idea! I'll tell Audrey, the minute she gets here."

"After the meet, we can invite them to eat out with the team. It's fast food today, right?" It was time to bring back the humor.

"No, Swift—no garbage!" Dominique was laughing now. "The team needs a healthy salad."

"Right on, Coach!" He fist-bumped her arm and went back up the bleachers—loving her like crazy.

~

A downpour splattered on the Tesla's glass roof as Audrey parked. She grabbed her purse.

"Is Lillie done?" Easton asked.

"Probably. Let's go find her."

They hurried across the parking lot, heads bent to the rain, and went inside. Peppy music filled the gym, and families swarmed. Audrey told the boys to stay close. She looked for the parents she had let down.

Families milled around beside the bleachers, where Audrey had left Lillie with her team. Moms gathered up snacks and team jackets, dads hoisted kids onto their backs, laughing. Madelyn and Lillie sat on the lowest bleacher. Miriam stood nearby, chatting with another mom. A grey-haired man stood beside her. Audrey waited where Miriam could see her.

Miriam laid her hand on the other mom's arm. "Congratulations on Chloe's win!" She turned to Audrey, and the other mom left to get her daughter.

Audrey straightened her spine. "Miriam, I owe you an apology. My nephew had a doctor appointment, and I forgot about the carpool." She felt her face heat up but kept her gaze steady.

Miriam smiled. "No problem! It worked out."

"Thank you for understanding."

"I'm Blake, Miriam's husband." The grey-haired man extended his hand.

"I'm Audrey, Lillie's aunt." Audrey shook his hand.

The man nodded. "Oh, right! Madelyn's always talking about Lillie."

Miriam laughed. Audrey saw the sporty couple walking towards the exit with their daughter. She said goodbye and jogged after them, leaving the boys with Lillie. She reached them at the exit. "I'm Audrey, Lillie's aunt. I apologize about the carpool. My nephew had a doctor appointment, and I was preoccupied. I'm new to parenting." Her breath came in gasps.

Sarah looked Audrey up and down, then smiled stiffly and shook her hand. "We do what we can."

"It won't happen again."

The woman's face softened. "Thank you, Audrey. I'm Sarah, and this is Bob."

Bob smiled jovially and shook Audrey's hand. The family left, and Audrey returned to the team's area.

"Hey, Audrey!" Dominique's voice rang high. She held a folded banner under her arm. Swift and the boys were picking up empty water bottles.

Audrey wound her way through the groups of excited kids and parents. She had planned her apology. "Dominique, I owe you—"

But Dominique shook her head, tapping Audrey's arm. "Audrey, let's chat over here." She set down the banner and went to an empty area between banks of bleachers. She turned to Audrey, her eyebrows tilted and her mouth straight.

"I should not have yelled at you. I know you're dealing with a lot, and anyone would be forgetful under the circumstances. I apologize."

Audrey gaped. "I should apologize. It was inconsiderate to leave Madelyn's parents in a bind. That added to your stress, too." Dominique's apology made her own easier.

Dominique's eyebrows flew up. "I didn't expect that. Consider it over."

"Didn't know lawyers could apologize, huh?" Audrey grinned.

Dominique slapped herself on the forehead. "Dope!"
They laughed.

"Also, I should have asked you before I told the gym families about Luke." Dominique's face was serious again. "I can see why that felt disrespectful."

"They needed to know. Believe me, as a lawyer I've seen the unknown create a lot more drama than the facts."

Dominique nodded. "I'm sure."

"So how did Lillie do?"

Dominique frowned. "Truthfully, she wasn't at her best."

Audrey looked at Lillie. She sat hunched over, staring at a phone with Easton. Tears pricked Audrey's eyes. "We're all struggling." Her chin quivered—and she didn't try to hide it.

"I'm here for you and the kids, Audrey. Anything I can do to help, let me know? I'm a friend."

A friend. Talking with Dominique was like sitting in a cozy living room with tattered furniture that no one worried about, and maybe a Labrador snoozing by the fire. "I…"

The coach looked at Audrey. Her hummingbird earrings hung still, below whisps of her pixie haircut.

"Yeah. I could use a friend." Audrey looked away, blinking—reeling with the sudden break of her no-female-friends rule.

"Great!" Dominique clearly had no idea how her offer of

friendship had impacted Audrey. "We get a meal with the gym families after meets. Want to sit with Swift and me?"

"I think Lillie would especially enjoy that."

~

Audrey guided the kids from the restaurant's buffet area to a large booth, where Dominique and Swift sat. They carried trays loaded with food—including veggies, at Audrey's insistence.

Lillie scooted along the curved bench to Dominique. Easton went next, and Warwick followed him. Audrey sat at the end, across from Swift, who sat on Dominique's right.

Dominique eyed Lillie's tray. "Glad you got some veggies there, Lillie. That's a lot of frozen yogurt!"

"I'm only eating this today." Lillie squirmed.

Other families gathered, chatting and laughing. Miriam and Madelyn approached, looking for seating.

"We can squeeze you guys in." Dominique's trademark lively smile invited community.

Miriam eyed the space. "Blake had an appointment, so it's just us. We don't want to squish you all…"

But Madelyn had already ducked under the table and wiggled in next to Lillie. Miriam laughed, rolled her eyes, and handed Madelyn her food. Audrey moved over, and Miriam sat beside her.

Lillie wiggled in her seat and leaned against Madelyn. "I like frozen yogurt, but I'm eating this first." She dug her fork into the salmon that steamed on her plate.

"Warwick, how's your blood sugar?" Audrey handed Warwick his meter.

Warwick zipped the cover open. "This is how I take my blood out." He looked at Swift and Dominique. "Want to see?"

"Sure!" Swift set down his fork.

Everyone watched as Warwick checked his blood sugar. Audrey injected his insulin, which she'd brought in a small cooler. Slowly, she pressed the flange. "The pump will really help with this.”

“You have to do that every time he eats?” Miriam asked.

“Yep. Now he waits ten minutes.”

“I’ll wait with him.” Swift propped his elbows on the table and folded his hands.

“Oh, you don’t need to.” Audrey didn’t want to draw attention to Warwick’s condition.

“No, we all should,” said Dominique.

Easton and Lillie groaned.

“I’m starving!” Lillie had already finished half her salmon.

“You can work on your veggies while we wait,” Audrey offered.

Lillie poked at her broccoli.

Easton pushed his plate away. “I’ll wait.”

Audrey set her phone’s timer. “What were you watching on the phone, at the gym?”

“Teacher Swift videoed Lillie,” said Easton.

Swift handed his phone to Audrey. Lillie grabbed at it. “I did horrible! You can’t see.”

“You knocked my juice!” Warwick pulled his glass away from Lillie.

Madelyn giggled. Swift and Dominique were quiet.

“You should let Auntie Audrey see,” said Easton. “She won’t mind if you messed up.”

“Of course I won’t! I wanted to be there.”

Lillie rolled her eyes and looked at Audrey. “Fine.”

Audrey tapped the play arrow and watched Lillie’s clumsy vault. More videos showed her niece’s uneven bars, floor, and balance beam routines. “Looks fine to me. I couldn’t do that.”

“I didn’t move up a level. I made lots of dumb mistakes.”

Dominique hugged Lillie. “You’ll do better in April. Put this behind you and keep practicing.”

Easton turned to Lillie. “Was it harder because Dad wasn’t there?”

Lillie stared at her plate. "Yep." She glanced at Audrey. "And Mom." Her eyes were wet.

Madelyn slung her arm around Lillie's shoulders. "Well, I was there!" She pulled her friend close and rocked her violently. "Rock-a-bye, baby!"

"You knocked my juice again!" Warwick grabbed his glass and slid it back and forth across the table. "Zip, whee!"

"Warwick, stop!" Audrey grabbed Warwick's glass. Everyone laughed, and soon Madelyn and Lillie were giggling together. Audrey returned Swift's phone. Swift showed the kids videos of cute animals, while they waited for Warwick's insulin to take effect.

Miriam turned to Audrey. "I understand how you'd forget the carpool, Audrey. You've taken on a lot here, especially with a medical diagnosis."

"I never would have guessed raising children could be more stressful than law." Audrey sighed.

"You're an attorney?" Miriam paused and looked at Audrey. "So am I!"

Audrey stared, speechless. She'd assumed Miriam was an at-home mom, unconnected with professional life. "Are you practicing?"

"Part time. I took a break until Madelyn was school age. Now I work as a corporate consultant, while Madelyn's in school. What about you?"

"I'm on hiatus until my brother gets back."

Miriam looked at the girls. "Madelyn and Lillie are such good friends. Lillie gets Madelyn out of her shell. And you saw how Madelyn just comforted Lillie."

"That surprised me. Kids are still pretty new to me."

Miriam chuckled. "Me, too!"

Audrey frowned, puzzled. "I don't understand."

"Oh, gosh! I'm out of my depth. Every stage of Madelyn's development has brought changes I didn't know how to handle. I figured out how to care for a baby, then she was crawling, and I worried about her safety—even though we'd childproofed the house. When she started walking and talking, she needed books and field trips. Then she turned five, and it was time for school. I picked up my career again—" Miriam paused, twirling Madelyn's sparkly headband in her fingers, her eyebrows low. She took a deep breath. "Sometimes I wonder if I should forget the career and homeschool her."

Madelyn was confident and happy. Miriam wore beautiful clothes, and her marriage to Blake appeared great. She didn't seem at all out of her depth.

"Now I help her navigate the Internet," Miriam continued. "And of course, gymnastics forces me to trust she can keep herself safe through all those scary moves they do." She turned to Audrey. "I've made mistakes that will probably haunt me the rest of my life. Parenting is a continual process of scrambling to find your way. When I accepted that, I began to relax."

"Huh."

Miriam laughed. "Did you think moms automatically know what they're doing?"

"Kind of, I guess."

Miriam laid her well-manicured fingers on Audrey's arm. The huge diamond on her wedding band winked under the booth's pendant light. "Let me tell you a secret, Auntie. We're all in the same boat."

~

Audrey's phone pinged. "Time to eat! Thanks for waiting with Warwick."

"Can I go to gym practice when you're at Warwick's next appointment?" Lillie took a bite of salmon.

"We'll figure it out." Audrey spoke quickly. She had not been able to figure it out yet, but she didn't want to risk Dominique's ire again.

"When's his appointment?" Dominique pushed her plate aside and leaned onto the table, all attention.

"I—don't worry. I'll make sure Lillie's there." Audrey

felt herself blushing.

"If it's during practice, I can take Lillie and Easton after school. They can wait with me until you're back."

Audrey didn't miss Swift's tender look at Dominique.

"I could take Easton," Swift offered. "I hike after school. He could join me."

Easton spun to Audrey, eyes lit. "Can I?"

"Well, alright. That would be wonderful."

They worked out the details. Dominique would take Lillie to practice after school and keep her until Audrey picked her up at Dominique's home, at six. Easton would hike with Swift. The two of them would get Mexican food before convening at Dominique's.

Lillie turned to Easton. "Yay! We're going to Coach Minnie's!"

Easton grinned and ruffled his sister's hair.

"Easton!" Lillie squirmed away.

"How long do you have these appointments?" asked Dominique.

"They're weekly for at least a couple months."

"Let's make it a standing arrangement, then," said Swift.

"I can pay you," offered Audrey.

Swift shook his head, and Dominique flapped her hand dismissively. "Nah! I love having them around. They can help with the dishes."

Relieved, Audrey watched Swift and Dominique interact. They teased and joked, at ease with each other. "Are you two dating?" she asked, as they prepared to leave. It was a bold question, but she felt comfortable asking.

"Oh, no." Dominique followed Swift out of the booth and put on her jacket. "Swift gives me moral support at meets. We're just friends."

Swift's eyebrows flicked up for an instant, as he dropped his gaze to the floor. He shoved his hands in his back pockets. Audrey studied him as she gathered her things, wondering if he agreed.

CHAPTER TWENTY-FIVE

That night, the rodents thumped and clattered behind the cabin walls. Audrey lay awake, bargaining. *God, don't let them in the living space. I'll never complain again!*

At four, she checked Warwick's blood sugar, then went back to bed. Something bumped in the closet. She threw the covers back, heart pounding. The moon had set, and the darkness was total. She switched on her lamp and crept to the closet door, listening. Scuffling sounded. She slid the door open.

Her shoes, a box of files, and her overflowing laundry basket filled the closet floor. The Competency Wardrobe hung from the clothes bar. On the shelf, she had stacked exercise gear, her flute, and a few boxes of books.

A quick movement caught her eye. She leaped backwards as a thick, bare tail disappeared between two boxes, right above her clothes. A rustle ensued, and the room was silent.

Frantic, Audrey paced the room, breathing deeply and running her hands through her hair. She had never dealt with rats. *You're stronger than this!* Anger rose above her panic. She yanked her robe off its hook and went into the kitchen, trying not to wake the kids. Her hands shook as she filled a mug with water and put it in the microwave. She grabbed a box of tea bags and tossed one onto the counter. The microwave beeped, and she took her tea into the living room.

There, she researched pest control. She wasn't going to pay a service if she could help it.

Humane Pest Mitigation's website showed a rat crouching in pink insulation and cobwebs. "Human and wildlife conflicts are common. Evict intruders compassionately, with our non-lethal traps."

"Wildlife" sounded friendlier than "rats." She could catch the wildlife, unharmed, and take it away while the kids were in school. She sipped her tea and ordered more traps than she anticipated needing, paying extra to rush them to the cabin. She slept soundly until daylight shone through the bedroom window, just in time to get everybody ready for church.

~

That afternoon, she told Luke about her plan.

"Sounds fine." He stared at the table.

He was drowning. Audrey tried and failed to keep the visit fun. Lillie was still troubled by her performance the day before.

"I'm sorry, Lillie," Luke said, when Lillie told him she hadn't advanced. That was all he seemed able to offer.

On the way home, the kids argued. Warwick cried when Audrey didn't give him a cookie.

"Your blood sugar's too high, Warwick. Let's wait, OK?"

"Hmm." His voice was shaky. In the rearview mirror, Audrey saw him tip his head and press his finger to his chin.

Lillie shoved Easton, who was riding in the passenger seat. "Your seat is squishing me. I can't move back here!"

"I'm scooting it forward. Stop bothering me!"

Lillie's complaint was ridiculous. There was plenty of room, and Lillie was tiny. Audrey drove home praying the kids could refocus and stabilize.

~

The rats ignored the humane traps. On Monday and Tuesday, she found them empty, latch doors still delicately balanced on their springs, bait untouched.

On Wednesday night, the rats thundered through the walls like a herd of horses. The kids woke up, scared.

On Thursday, she found her Competency clothes stained with rat urine. She washed them and retired the Competency Wardrobe to the shed, resigning herself to sweats. She had no idea how some moms maintained their polished appearance.

She sprayed foam into the cracks around the cabin's siding. The rats chewed through it. On Friday, she pulled the foam out and stuffed the cracks with steel wool. The rats pulled it out. She stuffed more back in, tighter this time.

Luke had no advice during their Friday phone call.

~

Dr. Taylor's clinic called with another schedule conflict, so Audrey accepted a Saturday appointment for Warwick's next pump training session. She would just have to bring Lillie and Easton along. But on Saturday, after another night of rat drama, Lillie woke with a sore throat. Despite giving her niece zinc and hot broth, Audrey saw that she needed rest. She called Dominique and asked her to babysit.

"I'd rather not risk getting sick. I could take Warwick to his appointment, though."

They arranged for Dominique to pick Warwick up, and Audrey packed her nephew's things. When Dominique's shiny bug chugged into the driveway, Warwick was ready to go.

Dominique swished into the kitchen like a bracing gust of fall wind. She wore an outfit she could have picked from the Competency Wardrobe, plus makeup. Her chunky scarf matched her deep brown eyes. Her skin looked perfect. Her cheeks were rosy from the cold.

Audrey felt unsettled as she watched the cute car zip out of the driveway. The feeling lingered as she loaded the dishwasher. It grew while she pestered Easton to clean his room, dug through the shed for Christmas decorations, and brought Lillie more broth and supplements. By ten thirty, it was thrashing her peace like a hurricane.

Lillie slept on. Easton played on the hallway computer. Audrey slumped on the couch, hugging her stained sweatshirt around her. She tried to drink some tea but set it down. Her turmoil spun and tossed, like leaves in a stiff breeze. It settled into a thought. *Will Dr. Taylor like Dominique? As in, romantic attraction?* She slapped her forehead with her palm. *You don't have time for this.* But the feeling dug its claws in.

Somehow, Dr. Taylor was becoming as problematic as the rats.

~

Eric led Audrey's friend, Dominique, to the conference room, where the pump educators waited. Nurse Jenny joined them.

Dominique sat and patted the chair next to her. Warwick climbed up. "Warwick's such a strong kid. And Audrey's an awesome fill-in mom, isn't she?" Dominique set Warwick's backpack on the floor beside his chair.

"Absolutely!" Jenny sat nearby. "Audrey's support makes a big difference."

Eric sat at the far end of the table, near a Christmas tree Jenny had set up. "Dominique, meet Leia and Theresa, Warwick's pump instructors."

Dominique reached across the table to shake their hands. "I'm Warwick's sister's gymnastics coach. Lillie is sick today, so I'm filling in for Audrey." She unwound her scarf, fanning herself. "Phew! It's warm in here!"

Eric adjusted the thermostat and resumed his seat.

"Thanks!" Dominique glanced his way, then lowered her eyes.

Theresa and Leia introduced features on the pump. An hour passed, and Warwick fidgeted. His legs dangled, and he kicked the chair.

Jenny suggested a break. "I'll get snacks. Warwick, do

—

173

you want to show Dominique how you check your blood sugar?"

Warwick took out his meter. Leia and Theresa left to find the ladies' room. Eric stood and went to Warwick's chair. The lancet clicked, and Warwick squeezed a red droplet onto his fingertip.

"Ouch!" Dominique's voice was high-pitched. "Does that hurt, Warwick?"

Warwick touched the droplet to the test strip in his meter. "I'm used to it." He bent over the meter, staring at the screen.

Eric folded his arms, ignoring Dominique's clueless comment. The meter beeped and the screen showed Warwick's level was within range.

Dominique swiveled her chair slightly. "This is a lot of work. Audrey mentioned he needs insulin at every meal."

Eric nodded, uninterested in explaining details. Jenny returned with a bowl of fruit and a plate of cookies. Leia and Theresa followed her.

"What are you going to eat, Warwick?" Eric pushed the snacks closer to Warwick.

Warwick took a cookie and an apple. He pulled a book from his backpack and showed it to Dominique. Humming, he flipped through pictures of food items, with their corresponding carb counts beneath.

"You must be good at math." Dominique giggled and shrugged her shoulders.

"I can count a bit." Warwick pointed to a picture of an apple, then the number below, and held up the book. "Twenty-five!"

Dominique nodded.

Eric leaned onto the table. "How many carbs in your cookie?"

Warwick found the cookie entry and swung the book around wildly. "One six! Ah-wheeee!"

Theresa and Leia chuckled. From the end of the table, Jenny gave him a thumbs-up.

"Now watch me add them up." Eric pulled up a calculator app on his phone and added the carbs together, holding the phone so Warwick could see. "Does that look right?"

Warwick nodded. As he closed the app, Eric glimpsed Dominique looking at his left hand. He shoved his hand into the pocket of his hoodie. "How about an injection now?"

Warwick unzipped a small cooler and took out a vial of insulin. "Are you going to give it to me?"

"I think you can do it." Eric sat in the empty chair next to Warwick. He helped him clean his skin, draw the insulin into a syringe, and slip the needle into a pinch of abdominal skin.

Dominique grimaced. "I could never do that."

How was that helpful? Eric sighed. "You could if you had to."

"'Course I could." Dominique gave Warwick a playful nudge.

Eric put his hand on Warwick's shoulder. "This week, ask Auntie Audrey to help you give yourself one shot every day. Never without her, though. Got it?"

"Yep!" Warwick saluted and squeezed his eyes shut.

Eric returned to his seat and watched, quiet, until Theresa and Leia closed their laptops, told Warwick what a brave boy he was, and said goodbye.

"Time to go, Warwick." Jenny led Dominique and Warwick to the reception area. Eric followed. He told Dominique that Leia would email the training to Audrey and pushed the reception door open.

"Thanks for helping today," Jenny said. "Please say hi to Audrey from us."

Dominique pulled a business card from her purse. "Dr. Taylor, it was so nice meeting you! Call me if you want to grab coffee sometime." She smiled and handed him the card.

Oh shoot! Eric forced an awkward smile and took the card. He turned it over and over, wondering how to politely decline. "Have a good afternoon."

Dominique took Warwick through the exit door and out to the car.

"Well!" Jenny watched the door swing shut. "Looks like someone's interested in more than coffee!"

Eric laughed briefly. "Sweet woman. Not my type." He walked down the hallway, tossing the business card into a trash can as he went. Hopefully, that was the end of it.

CHAPTER TWENTY-SIX

When Warwick arrived home, Lillie seemed better. Audrey decided to keep their visit with Luke. Driving through the valley, she asked Warwick about his appointment.

"I had a cookie."

"Did you learn anything new about the pump?" She glanced at her nephew in the rear-view mirror.

"It can wake me up with alarms."

"Did Dr. Taylor help you set the alarms?"

"Nope! You have to do that."

Audrey made a mental note to explore the alarm feature after she'd reviewed the session.

"Coach Minnie told Dr. Taylor they could get some coffee if he wanted."

The hair on Audrey's arms prickled. "What did he say?" She forced a light-hearted tone.

"Um, hmm, I don't know. He wanted more cookies, I think."

"He didn't want cookies," Lillie objected. "He's a doctor."

"Doctors like cookies, too, Lillie."

The two of them began playing their dinosaur game. Audrey stared at the road. The coach's confident smile and dancing eyes replayed in Audrey's mind. So did the glances she consistently got from men. Dominique attracted attention wherever she went. She could date any man she wanted.

Again, Audrey scolded herself. Really, who cared? The plan was to get through the coming months and then revive her career. She didn't need drama.

~

Luke cast agitated glances at the cops and other prisoners. He tapped the table restlessly.

"Go to the Bible study, Luke," Audrey urged him, as they said goodbye.

While the kids slept that night, she sat up, worrying. All afternoon, they had been whiney and irritable. Their dad's mental state was compromising their fragile stability.

She fell asleep on the couch, hoping the rats had left. But later, when she applied a droplet to a test strip and turned Warwick's glucose meter to the light, a loud clunk startled her. Quickly, she checked the meter. Warwick was in good shape for the night.

She set down the device and tiptoed to the bathroom. The children slept on. Gnawing and scratching sounds came from beneath the bathtub. She closed the bathroom door and knocked on the tub floor as loudly as she dared. The scratching stopped.

Seconds later, the noise resumed, this time closer to the faucets. She grabbed Lillie's hairbrush from the vanity and whacked the faucets. The scratching paused and continued. Stifling a roar of impatience, Audrey stomped to the kitchen.

She gazed at the fridge door, exhausted. Her eyes focused on her forgotten schedule and chore lists. She yanked them down and threw them in the trash.

~

Lillie complained of a sore throat again in the morning, so Audrey cancelled their Sunday visit with Luke—as well as the weekly church service. Perhaps it was for the best, considering Luke's mental state. On Sunday night she sat on the couch, listening for rats. Her thoughts returned to

Dominique and Dr. Taylor. She imagined them at a small table in some upscale coffee shop, Dominique's smile playful and inviting, Dr. Taylor's eyes tender and curious.

"How did you get interested in gymnastics?" Dr. Taylor asked, in his deep, doctor voice.

"I grew up flipping and jumping all over the house." Dominique giggled. "My mom had to save the furniture, so she signed me up for lessons."

They laughed intimately, then paused and gazed into each other's eyes.

Audrey slapped her knee. "It's irrelevant!" She went to the kitchen and grabbed Warwick's diabetes care binder. She might as well review.

~

The rats persisted, and on Monday she called a pest company. That evening Jake, from Dancing Pest Service, arrived in a shiny truck outfitted with a pristine toolbox.

"I'll check your foundation and perimeters." He shoved his sunglasses onto his bald head.

Audrey and the kids watched Jake squeeze through overgrown bushes against the cabin walls, kneel beside vents, and shine his giant flashlight into crevices and corners. Easton showed him the crawlspace door. He entered the space, hands first. His flashlight illuminated the dirt floor and the cabin's undergirding. Minutes later, he emerged, cobwebs clinging to his clothes.

"Any signs of rodents?" Audrey asked.

"Pawprints everywhere, rub marks on your substrates and foundation, droppings, a nest in one corner." Jake rubbed the small of his back. "They come in at night to keep warm, if they find a food source."

"How much are we talking?"

"Gimme a minute."

Audrey followed Jake to the truck, where he tapped some numbers into a calculator. The children went inside.

"You're looking at three or four months to get 'em all,"

Jake announced. "Your ballpark is $1,000 plus, for the total treatment."

"Go ahead and get started. The kids and I need some sleep." She would just have to charge the expense.

Jake's eyebrows shot up. "We can't do it today, Ma'am!" He scrolled through his tablet. "Our next availability is in March."

Audrey gasped. "March?! I need help now."

"Sorry, Ma'am. It's a busy season. Every pest service is booked out."

"I have kids here!" Her voice began to rise.

Jake gripped his truck's door handle. "Ma'am, I can't help you. I'm sorry we're fully booked…"

Audrey lost control. "Hire more people!"

Jake leapt into the driver seat and started the engine. "Goodbye, Ma'am. Sorry I couldn't help."

At a loss and breathing hard, Audrey watched the magnificent truck ease out of her driveway. It crunched over a fallen branch and turned onto Love Creek Road. The roar of its engine faded.

~

Silence fell, and Audrey went into the kitchen, wiping her eyes. "Lillie, it's your turn to feed Bella."

Lillie came from her room and opened the cabinet beneath the sink, where Audrey kept a big bag of dog food.

"A rat!" Lillie screamed and stepped back. She began crying.

Resolve flamed in Audrey—the way it did when she heard a vulnerable plaintiff's story. Boldly, she yanked the dog food from the cabinet and scooped out Bella's dinner. She scrunched the bag closed, kicked it back inside, and slammed the door. "Your days are numbered!" She yelled, hugging her niece. "Lillie, that was the only rat you're going to see."

She fed Bella and opened a browser on her phone. It was time to order more traps—and not the nice kind.

~

The traps arrived in a couple of days, and Audrey kept them baited and lethal. The first night, she trapped a rat alongside the house, close to what she figured was an entry point. She crammed the hole with steel wool and set more traps. Easton helped, and the next night they caught two rats—one in her room and one under the kitchen sink.

Easton found more access points, and they blocked them, too. The traps continued to deliver. By Friday night, the cabin was quiet.

"I can't wait to tell Dad!" Easton said, as Audrey drove the kids to their visit.

Audrey prayed that her brother would reward Easton with at least a smile. She parked and led the children inside. They seemed to have forgotten Luke's depressed mood. Lillie wanted to tell him about her improved vault. Warwick spun giddily along the corridor. Audrey sighed, her stomach tense. But the moment her brother walked into the visiting room, she saw it. Luke had changed.

~

He walked towards them, still tired and thin—but peace showed in the carefree slope of his shoulders and the relaxed lines of his face. At the table, he grasped his children's hands.

"Easton, Lillie, Warwick." His mouth tipped down at the corners, and his eyes were soft. "I want to ask your forgiveness. I was wrong to steal the money, and now you have to live without your daddy for a year. Please forgive me." His voice was low and earnest.

"Yes, Dad." Easton sniffed and looked down. A tear trickled down his cheek. Lillie and Warwick nodded and squirmed, then were quiet.

Luke looked at Audrey. "I'm sorry, sis. My decision put you in a real bind."

Audrey touched his arm, tenderly. "We all mess up. You weren't thinking clearly."

Luke shook his head and took her hands in his. "No—I have no excuse. Even though I was stressed, I didn't have to sin. Will you forgive me?"

Audrey dipped her head. "I'm not holding it against you, Luke." Why would she? Nancy was the real problem.

Luke leaned back, releasing her hands. "Thank you. All of you."

The somber mood gave way to happiness. The kids sat a little deeper in their chairs. Warwick played a finger game on the table. Lillie bugged Easton.

"How was your week?" Luke asked.

The children spilled their stories, their eyes shining. Luke responded with questions and companionable laughter, fully engaged. Audrey couldn't suppress a grin. Luke's transformation had banished the depressing atmosphere of their previous visits.

"You've changed," she said, when the kids had finished. "What happened?"

Luke tipped his head and put his finger on his chin. "Hmm. I went to the Bible study. I did some serious praying this week. When we own our choices and accept God's forgiveness, there's nothing left to beat us up. I've been sleeping like a baby."

Warmth flooded Audrey. She grasped Luke's hands. "That's wonderful!"

"Does that mean you're going to stay here longer?" asked Warwick.

"No, Warwick!" Luke rubbed Warwick's small arm. "I'll only be here as long as the judge said. It means God's with us. Do you understand?" He looked closely at each of his children. They nodded, their faces still. "I also got a job cleaning the yard and walkways outside. And I get to use the gym."

"Daddy, do you like cleaning?" Warwick asked.

"I like it a lot, Warwick. I can be in the sunshine. I can pray and think about the Bible study."

That was a godsend.

"I'll go to the Bible study weekly. I work every day, and the exercise in the gym helps me stay healthy."

"Swift offered to get Easton back into playing oboe." Audrey turned to her nephew. "You were interested, right, Easton?"

Easton shrugged. "Maybe."

"You should do it, Easton," Luke said.

Easton nodded. "OK."

~

"How are you doing, Audrey?"

"Much better. Except—" She stopped. She'd felt so alone in her battles with the rats. She had buried the feeling in activity.

"What, Auntie Audrey?" Lillie pressed close.

Audrey frowned. "The rat ordeal might have been easier with…" She couldn't finish the thought.

"A friend?" A smile played on Luke's lips.

"We were there," Easton pointed out.

"You were!" Audrey said, quickly. "And I'm thankful. But sometimes grownups need other grownups to talk to."

Luke studied Audrey. "Sis, just admit it."

"Admit what?" But she knew what he meant.

He waited. No one spoke.

"I want…"

Luke nodded. "Go on."

"Fine. I want a partner." Suddenly, the words poured in a flood. "A committed partner—one who won't leave. I want a shared understanding with a good man. A permanent best friend to share inside jokes with. Someone to sharpen and challenge—someone who'll do the same for me."

The kids looked at her, speechless.

"And a rat killer." She might as well add that.

Warwick threw his head back and punched the air. "Yeah!"

Luke raised his eyebrows. "There's a name for that."

Audrey gripped the edge of the table and exhaled strongly. "Marriage."

Luke nodded, slowly. "Called it."

CHAPTER TWENTY-SEVEN

On Christmas, the kids opened gifts Audrey had hidden. Later, they enjoyed a peaceful visit with Luke and a chilly walk by wind-tossed waves. During the following week, winter storms blew in. Heavy rain pelted the forest. It splashed over broad tan oak and madrone leaves, poured between ferns, and swelled the creek. It pounded on the cabin roof, at times a deafening roar.

From the kitchen, Audrey watched the trees sway and a flurry of leaves blow across the yard. She shivered, rubbing her arms against the chill. The kids were playing in the living room. Audrey turned up the thermostat. The wall heater flame whooshed on, and the heater ticked and clunked.

Lillie came into the kitchen. "Can we have a fire? Dad makes fires in storms."

"I've never made one." Audrey went into the living room and swung up the latch to the enamel stove. Cold ashes covered its floor. "Do we have wood somewhere?"

Warwick looked up from his Lego model. "We live in a forest."

Easton and Lillie laughed.

"I'll show you." Easton pulled papers from a basket, scrunched them into wads, and set them on the ashes. "Want to help me get wood?"

"Sure!"

Audrey followed Easton to a stack of firewood behind

the shed. Easton moved the tarp cover and threw several logs at Audrey's feet. They carried them to the stove.

"Now we need kindling." Easton brought an armful of sticks from the yard. Soon, snaps and hisses rang from the stove's belly.

They spent the afternoon playing board games, laughing, and eating popcorn. Outside, the wind gusted and howled. The sky darkened and the windows turned black, splattered with rain.

~

Between storms, Audrey took the kids to Henry Cowell State Park. They raced through the trees. The forest's cool breezes, earthy scents, and regal beauty invigorated Audrey. She wondered how she'd lived apart from nature.

Once, when the kids were asleep, she considered setting up a dating profile. She decided against it. She couldn't afford the distraction, and it was dangerous to meet up with strangers. Still, now that she'd admitted she wanted a partner, the feeling was hard to ignore.

Her thoughts turned to Dr. Taylor. Were he and Dominique dating? Warwick's weekly pump training session was postponed for the holidays, so she didn't see the doctor. She reminded herself that he would not own his error in Meghan's case. Was there any reason to think about him?

~

The Saturday after Christmas, she called the kids into the living room. "Remember how we laughed because I'm not very good at being a mom?"

The kids nodded and giggled.

"I told you to clean your rooms. You have not cleaned them since I moved in, even though Daddy told you to do what I say. Would you agree?"

"Yup." Warwick stood up on the couch and jumped to the floor.

"I've decided to make cleaning a competition." She held up her phone. "Listen to 'Flight of the Bumblebee.'" She tapped the play button.

When Warwick heard the first dynamic notes, he danced around the room.

"What's that have to do with cleaning?" Just for an instant, the hint of a teenage sneer curled Easton's lip.

"On Saturday mornings, when you hear this piece, clean your rooms. Put your clothes away. Put your school papers in your desks. Clear up your toys. I'll play more music, too. If you're still cleaning up after the music, you get another chore."

The kids were quiet, pondering this arrangement.

"The first one to finish picks our Saturday movie."

Lillie jumped off the couch and flipped onto her hands. "OK, Cap'n!" She arched into a walkover and stood again.

"Sounds good," said Easton. "When are you going to start the music?"

"Right now!" Audrey turned up the volume and tapped play. The kids raced to begin cleaning.

That afternoon at the jail, she told Luke about her strategy. He gave her a high-five. "I never would have thought of that, Sis!"

~

Audrey barely heard her phone ring that evening. Easton was playing his oboe for the first time in months. She closed Easton's bedroom door and went into the living room.

"Audrey, it's Dominique. Swift and I are going to the lighted boat parade on New Year's Eve. Would you and the kids like to join us?"

"What's that?"

"The Santa Cruz Yacht Club puts it on every year. All kinds of boats, all lit up—they're gorgeous. The kids will love it."

Audrey quickly agreed. Seeing the boats would be fun for both her and the kids. They arranged to meet in the harbor parking lot. Audrey looked up the event and saw pictures of brilliantly lit vessels under a dark sky. She called the kids, and they peered at the website, fascinated.

"Can we go on the boats, Auntie Audrey?" Warwick asked.

"I don't think so, but it'll be a lot of fun watching!"

~

Bundled in warm coats, Audrey and the kids watched the Santa Cruz Harbor from an overlooking path. Dominique poured hot chocolate into cups. Swift stood close to Dominique and handed the kids bendable glowsticks.

Below, sailboats bobbed in their slips. Lights shone from their windows and outlined their sails. Up and down the harbor drifted little skiffs, fishing boats, and dazzling yachts, their bright reflections dancing on the dark water. An announcer introduced each entrant.

Lillie wore her glowstick like a halo and pointed to a slender boat sitting low in the water. A large red ball sat on the boat's bow. Two golden antlers hung from its mast. "What's that one?"

Easton stared at the boat. "It's Rudolph!"

"I saw that one when I was a kid!" Dominique bounced on her toes, the thick waves of her hair brushing her fake-fur trimmed hood. Swift smiled at her.

A kayak glided past, supporting a green arch that formed a neck and ended in a slim, reptilian head. Two more kayaks carried more green arches, and a final one carried a matching tail that rose from the water.

"It's the Lock Ness guy!" Easton yelled.

"'Monster,' Easton." Lillie corrected him.

A stately catamaran drifted into sight. It boasted sleek curves and dark, narrow windows in its white hulls. Nets of blinking white lights hung over its sides. White and gold lights encircled its tall mast and flowed gracefully in strands to the deck rails.

"It looks like a spaceship," Easton said.

A dark figure stood in the open-sided helm station, behind a large wheel. His hands rested lightly on a throttle.

He glanced at the shore, and Audrey thought he looked right at her.

"Boat 34, *Sweet Escape*, sailed by The Taylor Clinic," called the emcee. "Providing optimal care for endocrine disorders all over the Bay Area!"

Audrey gasped. Dominique shrieked, her gloved hands at her mouth.

"Auntie Audrey! It's Dr. Taylor!" Warwick and his siblings tugged at Audrey's coat.

Audrey studied the pilot. It was too dark to discern his face, and the boat was too distant. But she recognized Dr. Taylor's rigid posture.

"Is that Warwick's doctor?" Swift asked.

"Yes!" Dominique stared at the catamaran. "Audrey, did you know they were coming?"

"I had no idea."

"Nurse Jenny!" Lillie pointed to a shorter figure on the catamaran's bow, waving glowsticks at the crowd.

Audrey glimpsed a third, slight figure behind the boat's salon. She wondered if he was Dr. Taylor's partner.

Dominique waved her arms above her head. "Dr. Taylor!"

Audrey winced, glad the boat was too distant for the doctor to hear. The catamaran continued down the harbor like a maritime courtroom, judging Audrey's insecurities.

~

The last boat returned to its slip, and the crowds dispersed. Families went to nearby seafood restaurants, or joined the stream of traffic that clogged the exit. Audrey and the kids walked towards the parking lot. Dominique and Swift followed, chatting and laughing. To their right, boats swayed in their slips, many still lighted.

Rounding a corner, they saw the catamaran. It loomed like a cruise ship in its u-shaped port. As they approached, Nurse Jenny exited the boat's pier. "Hi! What a great surprise!" She hugged the kids.

"Did you like the parade?"

"It was real nice," said Audrey.

Easton ran to the catamaran and touched its sleek, white side.

"We saw you on the boat!" Warwick said.

"Like my halo?" Lillie pointed to her glowstick, which still emitted a faint yellow light.

"Cool! Mine slipped a bit." Jenny giggled and wiggled the fading glowsticks she had looped around her neck.

Swift and Dominique arrived.

"Dominique, so nice to see you! Is this a friend of yours?"

They made their introductions.

"Good to see you, Jenny." Audrey edged away, anxious to leave. She didn't want a chance encounter with the doctor—or a front-row view of Dominique attracting his attention.

"Can we see your boat?" Warwick stood close to Audrey, twisting his fingers together.

Jenny glanced at Audrey. "I'll ask, but it's not my boat."

Dominique squealed. "We'd love to see it!"

Audrey's belly flipflopped and her shoulders tensed. "We don't really have time," she began, but Jenny was already texting.

"I was just on my way to meet my husband. I'll have him come to the boat." Jenny grabbed Warwick's arm, stopping him from climbing onto the boat, and turned. "Dr. Taylor! Look who I found."

The doctor walked through a sliding door from the boat's interior. He was winding a string of lights over his arm. When he saw Audrey and the kids, Audrey glimpsed a quick stiffening in his posture. He paused, then smiled broadly at Audrey. "Hi!"

"Hi," Audrey said. The kids clustered around her, suddenly shy.

CHAPTER TWENTY-EIGHT

Eric hadn't imagined it—he'd seen Audrey watch him from the path, as he'd guided the vessel down the harbor. For a moment, his mind was blank.

Audrey's friend was speaking. "What a gorgeous boat you have!"

He pulled himself together. "It's my partner's." Dr. Fisk was getting dinner with his wife.

Audrey looked up at him, one arm gently resting across her niece's shoulders. Her dark hair had grown out. It spilled, winsomely messy, around her neck, touching the furry collar of her red jacket. She looked endearingly uncomfortable with the situation. Her cheeks were flushed. Her eyes, big behind thick lashes, darted awkwardly to Jenny beside her, then back to him.

Jenny squeezed past Audrey and stood by the short set of steps at the back of the boat. "The kids want to see the boat, Dr. Taylor." She nodded slightly, looking at him closely.

What was he thinking? "Absolutely!" He tossed the lights onto a bench and descended the steps. "Come on up!"

Audrey and her friends moved towards the boat.

"I hope we're not inconveniencing you," Audrey said.

Heck, no! "'Course not." He pointed Easton to the helm station. "See the steering wheel?"

Easton sprang past him and ran up the steps. He passed the cockpit's built-in table and leaped up to the helm. There, he climbed onto the bench and rested his hands on the wheel.

Eric turned to the younger children. "You two, wait for us there." He indicated the cockpit table. Lillie and Warwick raced up and flung themselves onto the bench. Lillie looped the strand of lights over her neck. Warwick yanked the back of the bench, discovering its adjustment capacity. It fell towards him. He rammed it backwards. It stopped. He laughed and did it again.

"Warwick, stop!" Audrey's face was red.

"It's fine." The last thing Eric wanted was for her to feel embarrassed. "Dr. Fisk's grandkids do it all the time."

She nodded, lips tight, and took his outstretched hand. Her hand was small and cold in his. She released his hand at the earliest possible moment, moved quickly past him, and joined the children in the cockpit.

When Eric turned back to the pier, Audrey's friend, Dominique, was waiting. Her eyes shone as he helped her up the steps. Swift and Jenny followed, and they gathered in the cockpit.

"Wow! Thank you, Dr. Taylor!" Dominique's extraversion put him at ease. Swift, he noticed, was looking away, down the harbor. Audrey sat next to Lillie, bolt upright on the built-in bench, her slim legs crossed.

He realized the group needed direction. "Want to see the controls?"

"Yes!" Audrey's niece said. Warwick jumped up and pulled on Audrey's arm.

"That's the helm station." Eric pointed to the wheel. "You drive from there. It's very dangerous." He lowered his brow for dramatic effect.

Easton grinned. Dominique laughed loudly. Swift looked down the harbor again. Warwick and Lillie rushed up to the helm, shoving each other for room.

Eric squeezed past them to the narrow deck on the boat's right side. He pointed to the large winches next to the wheel, with their thick ropes. "These knobs let you control the sails.

Look up."

The kids gaped at the window in the helm's roof. Twinkling lights still outlined the towering sail mast above—Eric hadn't finished striking the decorations. Audrey watched from the step at the bottom of the helm station, Dominique and Swift behind her.

"Dr. Taylor, why don't you give them a tour? I'll wait here for David." Nurse Jenny returned to the cockpit table and sat, reading her phone.

"Good idea! Audrey, come on up!" Again, he extended his hand, and again, she released it as soon as she could. But perhaps she relaxed a little now. He explained the boat's controls, then stepped out of the way so they could walk along the narrow deck that passed the salon, to the front of the boat. Audrey stayed close behind the children, and he followed, watching in case someone lost their footing.

"No running!" Audrey's steps looked firm and confident.

Looking over her head, he saw the older two kids reach the front of the boat. Audrey gripped Warwick's hand as she joined them. Dominique stepped past Eric and sat on the small seat that extended over the water.

"Yikes!" She squealed, pretending to fall back. Swift grabbed at her arm, and she giggled. "Gotcha!" Swift laughed, but when he saw Dominique glance at Eric, his smile faded.

The older children stepped onto the bow trampoline and bounced on their toes.

"Don't jump on that!" Audrey's voice was tense. The kids ignored her. Lillie did the splits in the air. Warwick pulled out of Audrey's grip and joined his siblings. Easton grabbed Warwick's hand. Soon, they were bouncing as high as they could.

"Kids, stop!" Audrey grabbed at Lillie, but she squirmed aside.

Eric wished he knew how to put Audrey at ease. "Who

wants to go on the salon roof?" That got the kids' attention. He helped them onto the salon roof and showed them how to hold onto the mast for balance. The children gazed down the harbor.

"See the lighthouse?" He pointed towards the structure, then directed their attention to the black expanse of open ocean. A small tug moved his coat. He looked down.

"Can you lift me up? I wanna see." Warwick gazed up at him through a drape of curly bangs.

He scooped the boy up. For an instant, Warwick laid his head on his shoulder. He glanced down, wondering if Audrey approved, and caught her gazing at him, her eyes wet. Quickly, she looked away.

When the kids started jumping on the salon roof, he helped them down. "Now let's see inside!"

In the salon, Warwick opened and closed all the kitchen drawers and cabinets. In one of the hulls, Lillie climbed onto a bed, messing up the comforter. Easton scolded his siblings, and Audrey moved to straighten up the bed. Dominique and Swift returned to the kitchen and the kids raced after them.

"I'm so sorry!" In the small hull, Audrey struggled to smooth the comforter back into place.

"I'll get it." Gently, Eric gestured for her to give him room, and she stepped aside. He shook the comforter over the bed. "Don't worry, Audrey. Dr. Fisk's grandchildren get into everything."

"Ok." She eyed the steps to the kitchen.

He faced her, longing to reassure her.

~

The hull rocked gently beneath Audrey's feet. The comforter Dr. Taylor had put back into place showed pictures of yachts and little white clouds. Neat curtains covered the porthole. A small shelf hung by the bed, holding a copy of *Moby Dick* and a Bible.

"Audrey, it's fine. Really. I know how kids are." Dr. Taylor tipped his head, his eyes soft.

She remembered Luke waiting for her the same way, while she frantically packed for school. *"Audrey, relax. I already made your lunch."*

She sighed, her shoulders relaxing. "I appreciate that, Dr. Taylor. Guess I still don't feel like the kids' godsend."

He chuckled and gestured to the steps. "They're happy, so you're doing something right. Come on, meet Jenny's husband."

She followed him back to the cockpit, where Jenny and her husband chatted with the others. David was a stout man with a thick beard whose loud laugh and extraverted personality got everyone laughing. Audrey squeezed onto the bench next to Dominique and Swift. Dr. Taylor pulled up a deck chair. The kids sat on the floor, playing their dinosaur game.

"Anyone want dessert?" A small man in his sixties stepped onto the boat, carrying a pastry box. Audrey recognized Dr. Taylor's partner, Dr. Fisk, whom she had seen in the clinic.

Mrs. Fisk followed him. "Jenny texted us. We brought cherry pie."

Dr. Taylor introduced them and brought plates and forks from the salon. Soon, everyone was enjoying pie and comparing notes about the boat parade.

"So, how'd you hear about Dr. Taylor?" Dr. Fisk asked, as the conversation quieted.

"I—" Audrey stopped, flushed.

"I diagnosed Warwick at California Oaks," Dr. Taylor said. He winked at Audrey and smiled. The conversation moved on.

"We should get going," Audrey said. The harbor parking lot was almost empty, and it was past the kids' bedtime.

They said goodbye to Jenny and David. Audrey led the kids onto the pier, and Swift and Dominique followed. Dr. Taylor accompanied them to the path.

"Dr. Taylor, it was great to see you again!" Dominique

gushed.

"You, too. Have a nice evening."

There was an awkward pause.

"Let's get clam chowder, Dominique." Swift jerked his head toward the restaurants by the harbor.

Dominique hesitated. Poor Swift! It was hard for Audrey not to shove her friend down the path. At last, to Audrey's relief, she grinned at Swift. "Sounds yummy. Happy New Year, everyone!" Swift touched the small of Dominique's back, ushering her along the path.

Audrey tapped the Tesla app on her phone. "Thanks for showing the kids around, Dr. Taylor."

Dr. Taylor's face was serious. "Did you enjoy the tour?"

"It was great. I'd never been on a catamaran."

"Was this your first time on a boat?"

"No. My dad used to take me and my brother sailing on the Gulf of Mexico."

"So, you know your way around boats!"

"I did. When Dad left, that was it for my sailing career."

"Sorry."

She shrugged.

"Can I walk you to your car?"

"Sure!"

Easton, Lillie, and Warwick ran ahead. Dr. Taylor strolled beside her, and they chatted like old friends. Again, Audrey remembered Luke. They had walked to school like this, laughing and talking.

She let the kids into the car and pulled Warwick's meter from her purse. "I should check Warwick's blood sugar." The doctor waited as she took the measurement. "One hundred and seven. Perfect." She returned the device to her purse.

"Remember, exercise can lower his blood sugar. You might keep his glucose tabs handy."

She nodded.

"Thanks for letting me walk you to your car." He stepped

back as she opened her door.

She sat and lowered the driver window. "Kids, thank Dr. Taylor."

"Thanks, Doc!" Lillie squealed, saluting and wiggling in her seat.

Easton and Warwick chimed in. "Thank you!"

Dr. Taylor stooped to view the kids. "Have a good night." He smiled and straightened.

Audrey closed the window and drove to the exit. As she reached the gate, she glimpsed Dr. Taylor in her rear-view mirror, walking back to the *Sweet Escape*.

CHAPTER TWENTY-NINE

"**What do you** think of Dr. Taylor?" Dominique pulled her scarf close around her neck. It was a cold Saturday in January, and Audrey and Dominique were taking a walk along Love Creek Road. Ahead, Warwick and Lillie climbed embankments and splashed through puddles. Easton was at the cabin, practicing oboe.

"He's competent." Audrey had noticed Dominique's interest in the doctor, during their tour of the catamaran.

"I hope so!" Dominique laughed. "Is he married?"

"Single. I know a lot about him, actually. A client was suing him before I quit law."

"And he's Warwick's doctor? That must be awkward!"

"It was." Audrey kicked a pebble into a muddy puddle. "I realized Warwick had type 1 diabetes during Dr. Taylor's deposition. When I got to the Emergency Room, guess who showed up to treat Warwick?"

Dominique stopped walking and stared at Audrey, gloved hand over her mouth.

"I didn't trust him, but he saved my nephew. He's a good doctor." Audrey paused. "It's weird, though."

"What is?"

"I believe he cares about the kids. He feels like a friend since that night we saw the catamaran. But he's never owned the mistake that could have killed my client. It's a sticking point, ya'll."

They returned to the cabin, listening to the mellow notes of Easton's oboe. Audrey had asked Swift to replace an outlet in the kitchen. When they went inside, Swift was packing his tools. "Outlet's good." He winked at Dominique and zipped up his bag.

The oboe playing stopped, and Easton joined them. He looked at Swift. "Did that sound OK?"

"Fantastic!" Swift grinned and gave Easton a thumbs up. Easton had accepted Swift's offer of encouragement with the instrument. Inspired, Audrey had made and kept a commitment to play her flute daily, too.

~

Days later, Audrey stared at an email from Alex Tate.

"Due to the firm's performance this year, I regret that you will not receive an annual bonus."

She slapped her phone onto the kitchen table. She'd been counting on the bonus. She should have counted on Alex's vindictiveness, too.

After the new year, she'd taken work as a cashier at the local market—a two-minute drive from the school. She worked until one o'clock, then picked up the kids. Today, she wasn't needed. The added income helped, but the kids ate a lot and the old cabin needed repairs. Three of her credit cards had balances.

She opened her laptop and studied her budget. About a thousand dollars more per month would help. She sighed, folded the laptop, and stared out the window. Maybe a walk would give her some perspective. She pulled on her coat, stomped down the steps, and strode briskly down Love Creek Road. Morning frost still sparkled on the roofs.

The exercise cleared her mind, and she returned to the yard refreshed. Approaching the cabin, she paused and looked at the Tesla. The sun peeked through clouds and gleamed on the car's aerodynamic roof. Audrey walked to the vehicle and placed her hand on its smooth, white frunk, remembering the day she'd driven it home.

She'd sold her old Toyota and dipped deep into savings to make a hefty down payment. Driving off the lot, she'd felt like a true professional. At last, years into her career, her car matched her career goals. *I should sell it.*

She dashed inside and threw open her laptop. Ads for similar vehicles showed prices of up to $40,000. The money would both eliminate her loan payments and beef up her savings.

Heart pounding, she hammered out a description of the vehicle. When the confirmation button appeared, tears blurred her vision. She went to the window and looked at Luke's old sedan, covered in dirt and leaves. Wiping her cheeks, she returned to her laptop and clicked the confirmation button. Used Teslas were in demand. Her dream career car was as good as gone.

~

"Let's learn about problem solving for a high blood glucose." At Warwick's pump training appointment, Theresa opened her laptop. Audrey tried to pay attention.

"What's the first thing you do when you think your blood sugar is high, Warwick?" Leia smiled at Warwick.

Warwick shrugged. He rested his arms on the table and played with his fingers. "Drink water?"

Audrey knew he was bluffing, but she didn't correct him. Diabetes was hard enough.

"Do you use any of your supplies when you think you're high?" prodded Theresa, gently.

Warwick raised his index finger. "Check my blood sugar with my meter." He spoke in a sing-song voice, then rested his head on his arms and swung his feet under the table.

"Good job, Warwick!" Nurse Jenny gave him a thumbs-up.

Audrey had trouble focusing. Her decision to sell the Tesla was a relief, but it scared her, too. She remembered her mom's beaten-up, blue hatchback—she'd driven it for years, unable to afford a replacement. Audrey had been determined never to end up in that situation.

"Audrey?" Jenny asked.

Audrey snapped to attention, looking at Jenny. "Sorry, what?"

Jenny smiled. "What do you think would help Warwick manage a high blood sugar?"

Audrey forced her mind back to the conversation. "Setting an alarm on his pump to remind him to check his levels."

"Shall we set some alarms now, Warwick?" Dr. Taylor stood and walked to Warwick's chair.

"OK."

They input some alarms. They had replaced the saline with insulin two weeks prior, and the continuous glucose monitor tracked and projected Warwick's levels. Audrey had already noticed the reduced stress. The alarms would help further.

Break time came, and Jenny took Warwick to use the bathroom.

"Can I get you a coffee or some water?" Dr. Taylor pushed his chair under the table, looking at Audrey.

"Water would be great."

The doctor brought water bottles from the break room and gave her one. He set the rest in the middle of the conference table. Snacks were omitted since it was close to dinnertime.

Audrey was thirsty. She'd been so distracted that she had forgotten to drink. Leia and Theresa sipped water and went over some of their training materials, murmuring together. Warwick and Jenny returned, and Warwick climbed into his chair next to Audrey. He took a water bottle.

"We're selling the Tesla." He slurped his water.

Dr. Taylor glanced at Audrey. "Really?"

"I listed it today."

"She needs the money to pay bills." Warwick slapped the water bottle onto the table.

Kids! Audrey blushed. "He's just being silly."

"How much are you asking?"

"Forty thousand. It has low mileage."

Leia called them back to attention, and they finished the training session.

"Next week will be your last meeting." Theresa settled her laptop into a bag. "You can always call us if you need help."

Nurse Jenny went to sort supplies and tidy the exam rooms. Dr. Taylor walked with Audrey and Warwick to the reception area. He held the door open and followed them into the empty reception area. "Good job, Warwick!"

Warwick nodded. Audrey could see he was tired.

The doctor turned to Audrey. "Can I test drive your Tesla? I've been considering a new car."

"Of course!" What a surprise! They scheduled the test drive for ten the next morning. The kids had play dates scheduled with their friends, so Audrey wouldn't need to find a babysitter. She turned to leave. "Thanks, Dr. Taylor."

Dr. Taylor nodded. Evening light slanted through the lobby, sending shadows across the lean symmetry of his face and the edges of a gentle smile.

Audrey walked with Warwick to the Tesla. She fastened her nephew's seatbelt over his booster chair and went to the driver's side. She glanced at the clinic as she opened the door.

Dr. Taylor was leaving, backpack in hand, walking briskly towards a tan SUV. The vehicle didn't look like it needed replacing. He saw her and waved.

Audrey waved, slid into the driver's seat, and guided the Tesla out of the parking lot. She pulled her hairband loose, freeing her hair from its ponytail. "Warwick, want to listen to some flute music?"

"Um, yes. I do!"

They followed the curves of Highway 17, listening to Celtic flutes and violins.

"Auntie Audrey?"

"Hm?"

"I'll miss the Tesla."

"Me, too."

"I hope Dr. Taylor buys it."

"So do I, Warwick. That would help me feel peaceful about it."

"Yeah. Dr. Taylor's nice, isn't he?"

"Yes, he is."

Stubborn and arrogant. But kind.

CHAPTER THIRTY

Audrey gave the kids breakfast, but she was too anxious to eat. She dropped the children at their friends' houses and returned to the cabin. There, she made a piece of toast, which she fed to Bella.

She changed into dark jeans and a burgundy sweater and warmed a few waves into her hair. Her hair reached her shoulders now. She turned sideways and looked at her reflection. Minimalist silver jewelry completed her look. She had retrieved some of her Competency Wardrobe from the shed, and at last, she felt comfortable in feminine "mommy" outfits.

In the living room, Bella stretched on her bed and snored. A splattering of rain pounded the roof. Wind whistled around the cabin. Audrey went to the kitchen and sat at the table. She squeezed her hands together.

It was just business. A car sale, for heaven's sake. There was no need to stress out.

She breathed deeply, closed her eyes, and wrang her hands. It was nine fifty. Dr. Taylor would arrive in ten minutes.

~

Eric woke early. He showered, dressed, and ate a scant breakfast. Then, he carefully brushed his teeth. He peered at his angular face, swiping his fingers across his clean-shaven jaw. He went to his closet and wrapped a camelhair scarf around his neck. Returning to the mirror, he unwrapped it and draped it loosely across his shoulders. Tilting his head, he pulled on the scarf and smiled, then winced and smiled again—his first smile was way too fake. He turned sideways, studied his reflection, and pushed up the sleeves of his Henley. He put on his rugged Chelsea boots, shoved a black jacket under his arm, and went out to the SUV.

He sat behind the wheel, staring at the ignition, remembering his reflection. Ugh! The scarf looked stupid. He dashed back inside and replaced the camelhair scarf with a dark grey one. He checked the mirror again, turning from side to side. Much better.

Thick clouds shrouded the Santa Cruz mountains, but the sun shone cheerfully over Mountain View and the neighboring towns. Eric's SUV spun along Silicon Valley's wide highways, towards Santa Cruz County.

He glanced at the clock. It was eight fifty-five. He took a deep breath and gripped the steering wheel. He would arrive at Audrey's cabin in about an hour.

~

The rain had stopped. Audrey heard tires swish over soggy leaves and wet dirt. She dashed to the bathroom and checked her makeup. Should she open the door, or pretend she hadn't heard the car? A knock startled her. She went to the door and paused, then yanked it open. "Good morning, Dr. Taylor!"

The doctor put out his hand, leaning towards her, one foot on the lowest step. "Good morning, Audrey."

She reached to shake his hand, which felt weird after meeting so many times. "Have you driven a Tesla?" She took her purse from the old chair. She stepped outside and locked the door.

"Never. I was hoping you could demonstrate if you don't mind?"

They crossed the yard. It was cold and cloudy, and more rain was forecast. Audrey had cleaned the Tesla. A million raindrops sparkled on its surface.

"It's a little different, but you get used to it." She tapped the app and the doors unlocked. The rearview mirror swung out as they approached.

Dr. Taylor paused, surprised. "Huh!"

"It sensed me coming." Audrey lifted her phone for him to see. They got in. "I should point out a few things. The kids have left their mark." She showed him a few stains and a scratch on the dashboard.

"Oh, that's fine. I know it's not new."

Audrey nodded.

"Did you wait in line, to order it?"

Audrey laughed. "I admit it! I waited several hours outside a dealership—along with a few hundred other people." Suddenly, her nerves quieted, and they were good friends again.

"Was it worth it?"

"Oh, yeah!" She glanced at him. "But what do you expect me to say? I plan to sell it."

He chuckled. "Good point!"

She backed in a wide arc, eased onto Love Creek Road, and took Highway 9. The San Lorenzo Valley's narrow roads required slow, careful driving.

"Is there somewhere I can test its speed?"

"We could take Graham Hill Road to the coast. On Highway 1 you could speed up. I'll drive to Felton, and we can switch seats there."

They chatted about the car's features until they reached Felton. Audrey parked at the quaint Covered Bridge Park. Tall trees bordered the park's sweeping lawn. A playground sat at the edge of the park, and in one corner, the historic covered bridge spanned the San Lorenzo River. "I take the kids here sometimes."

"You're a good auntie." He grinned and opened the passenger door. In front of the car, they dodged each other awkwardly.

"Sorry!" Audrey laughed.

"Excuse me!" Dr. Taylor spoke at the same time.

Dr. Taylor took the driver's seat and tapped an icon on the screen. "Let's see if I remember what I learned online." He peered at the screen, eyebrows lowered, and adjusted the mirrors and steering wheel. Satisfied, he leaned back and sat for a moment, staring at the dashboard. "Um… How do I start it?"

Audrey smiled. "It's on. Just depress the brake and reverse."

"Ah! Got it!" His face colored a little. He guided the car back onto Graham Hill Road and up the curve out of Felton. "Beautiful area. I like the way the car handles."

Audrey wasn't used to riding as passenger, and she enjoyed the view. They passed the expansive horse club, with its wide meadow. A couple of riders trotted their horses around the club's huge arena.

"How are the kids?" Dr. Taylor asked, as they glided between eucalyptus trees to the outskirts of Santa Cruz.

"Looking forward to seeing their dad this afternoon."

"Sorry, I didn't mean to pry."

"It's fine! I appreciate you asking."

He glanced at her. "Do I take this exit?"

She nodded. "Go right on Highway 1, out the west side of Santa Cruz."

They went through the business district to the open country. Beyond fields, the ocean was a dark grey strip under bulging clouds. On their right were the meadows Audrey and the kids had hiked on Thanksgiving. The green expanse sloped up, ending at the redwood forest. Sweeps of light rain hit the windshield as the car picked up speed. For a while, they traveled in silence.

"Where should I turn around?" The doctor slowed at a curve.

"Wilder Ranch is coming up on the left."

They turned at the ranch and headed back.

"How do you like this area?" Dr. Taylor asked.

Audrey shrugged. "I loved UC Santa Cruz. Country life is another thing—but it's growing on me."

"Had any power outages?"

She told him about the fallen tree and the power company's all-night chainsaw party. "And then I heard rats!"

"Oh, boy! And…?"

She detailed the rat saga, which seemed funny now. Their giggles grew to gusts of laughter. Audrey again recalled her abiding connection with Luke. When they arrived back in Ben Lomond, the clouds were clearing.

"It's a great car." Dr. Taylor pulled into the driveway. "I'll check the exterior and make you an offer."

They got out, and the doctor walked around the car. Audrey pointed out the ding in the driver's door. "I did that running into the ER."

Dr. Taylor waved a hand. "Adds character."

"I've had no regrets purchasing this car." Audrey watched the doctor finish his inspection. "If you need a few minutes, I can go inside."

"Not necessary." Dr. Taylor pulled a paper from his inner pocket and handed it to Audrey. "I have the cashier's check."

Audrey glanced at the check. The doctor had written it for forty-four thousand dollars.

She tried to return the paper. "I was only asking forty thousand!"

"I researched it. Forty-four is a fair price."

"I… thanks! But I wasn't asking this much." She didn't know what to say.

"But that's my offer, nonetheless." He folded his arms, his head lifted. The sun broke through the clouds and shone on his dark hair.

"Well, thanks! Very much." She put the check in her pocket.

"Thank you, Audrey." He dipped his head. "Shall we

complete the paperwork?"

They went into the kitchen and sat at the table. Bella waddled out of the living room and sniffed at Dr. Taylor's boots.

"Sorry!" Audrey set her back on her dog bed, hoping Dr. Taylor had forgotten her parting comment at the deposition.

"No problem." He read through the forms, signing where needed. "I had dogs growing up."

The last form completed, Dr. Taylor stood and slid his chair into place. "Audrey, thank you again for the car. I'm very pleased with it."

"You're welcome." She went to open the door.

He took his jacket from the back of his chair and gripped it tightly.

"Audrey—" He paused.

Audrey looked at him.

"I respect you. A lot." He paused, blushing deeply, then hurried on. "I admire your selflessness, taking on your brother's kids, sacrificing for them. I was wondering—" He stopped, dashing his hand across his forehead. "Could I take you to dinner sometime?" He looked at her, head low, hair darkened by the rain.

Audrey's mouth fell open. "I'd like that!"

Dr. Taylor beamed. "Really?"

She flushed. "Well, yeah! I would." This was awkward. Sweat dripped down her back. But she felt giddy, too.

"Please don't think I paid a good price for the car just to get you to go out with me." He put on his jacket.

"An attorney always wonders," she teased.

"When would be good for you? And by the way, please call me Eric."

"I'll have to arrange a babysitter. Can I let you know?"

"Absolutely. And if you have to change plans last minute, don't worry. I know with kids anything can happen."

Her heart melted. They walked out to the yard. Audrey looked at the doctor's SUV, parked next to the Tesla. "Did you want to pick up the Tesla later?"

He stared at the vehicles, then looked at Audrey with wide eyes. "I didn't plan that far ahead!"

They laughed.

"Would you like me to drive it to your place?" Audrey offered. "I can get a rideshare home."

"No—I wouldn't dream of it. I'll drive the Tesla home tonight and come back in a rideshare for the SUV tomorrow, if that's alright with you?"

"I may not be here, but any time is fine." She had scheduled another visit with Luke in the afternoon.

"Goodbye, Audrey. And thanks for agreeing to go to dinner with me."

"I'm looking forward to it." She handed him the key card and watched him drive the Tesla away.

~

Eric drove to Santa Cruz and parked at the harbor, electricity still zipping through his limbs. She'd agreed to go to dinner! Audrey Beach! He couldn't believe it. He stepped out of the Tesla and looked down at his feet. Yes—he was standing on the ground. He wouldn't have been surprised to see clouds below.

He walked—or was it floating?—to a slip, where a trim, white sailboat bobbed on the water. Late sunshine peeked through the clearing clouds and danced on the water, setting the boat's sides to a brilliant gleam. A man walked from the parking lot and joined him by the boat. "I'm Jared. Are you here for the Flying Scot?"

"Yes—Dr. Taylor."

They shook hands and the man gestured to the pier. "Let's take her for a sail. You'll see why they're so popular. Fun and safe."

"That's important. I hope to share it with someone very special."

CHAPTER THIRTY-ONE

The sedan's tattered wipers smeared the windshield as Audrey waited at the stoplight. The light changed, and the car coughed through the intersection. She parked outside the market, early for work.

Her date with Dr. Taylor was scheduled for Saturday—the day after Warwick's final pump training appointment, and a week after the doctor had purchased the Tesla. After the kids' visit with Luke, Easton would have time to practice oboe. Then, the children would visit their friends while she and Dr. Taylor—*Eric*—went out.

She stopped the engine and took a deep breath, resting her elbows on the steering wheel and her forehead on her palms.

Maybe she should cancel the date.

She had to admit she was warming up to him. He was a better man than she'd believed. Kind, caring, and honest. And they were friends—a great foundation. That he was an expert, thriving in his gifting, was attractive. But thoughts of Meghan's injury dampened her enthusiasm. The man had never owned his mistake. It was impossible to overlook.

Maybe he has owned it. Why should he tell me? I'm not suing him anymore, after all.

She hoped he had. Anyway, it was just dinner. She would give him a chance. She grabbed her coat and went into the market.

~

The candlelight cast a golden glow over the table. Eric leaned on his elbows, hands open by his plate, looking at Audrey. Listening. No judgment or aloofness shadowed the keen honesty of his gaze. Audrey felt heard. Valued.

He poured her a glass of water. "Are you a coffee or tea person?"

"Both. Whatever it takes to jumpstart my brain."

They laughed. Outside, seagulls hovered and glided, buffeted by a stiff wind. The sun was low over the ocean, dim and shrouded by a thick layer of clouds. The restaurant was on the Santa Cruz Wharf. Behind them, waves crashed onto the beach. Rocky cliffs, lit to bronze, shored up West Cliff Drive.

"How about you? Coffee, or tea?"

"Coffee. Dark roast, black—nothing fancy." He smiled and shrugged. Audrey couldn't help noticing the strong contours of his shoulders beneath the neat sweep of his sweater.

The waitress set down bowls of steaming clam chowder and a basket of warm bread. Eric held the basket out to Audrey. She tore off a slice and buttered it.

The restaurant was quiet. Soft jazz music played, dishes clinked, the diners' voices murmured, with occasional laughter. Setting the slice onto her bread plate, she looked up to see Eric waiting. "Do you say grace?"

"Always." He took her hand, pressing the palm of her hand with unhesitating confidence. She relaxed in the comfort of their friendship.

Eric closed his eyes. "Dear Father, thank you for this chance to get to know each other, and for this fine meal. Please bless it to our health. Amen."

Audrey laid her napkin across her lap. "Do you get a lot of pushback about your faith in the medical community?"

The doctor poured water into Audrey's glass, then his own. "Not a lot. I probably could be more open about it."

"I know what you mean." Silicon Valley wasn't exactly the Bible belt.

Eric was good at keeping the conversation going. They chatted about boats, shared their college experiences, and described churches they'd attended. At last, they finished a dense, buttery brownie, and the conversation slowed.

Audrey set her napkin down. "That was a wonderful meal!"

The same gentle smile he'd given her in the PICU warmed his face. He paid the tab, and they walked out to the Tesla. The wharf was crowded. Families explored the shops and restaurants. From the piers below, seals barked for scraps of fish. It was dark, and the Santa Cruz Beach Boardwalk's roller coasters and rides shone with lights, reflecting in the ocean.

The wind picked up. Eric helped Audrey with her wrap, lifting the fabric and straightening it into place. The security of his presence was as comforting as the wrap. "Warm enough?"

"Yes, it's wool."

Eric opened the door for her. He drove deftly through Santa Cruz towards Graham Hill Road, honoring Audrey's schedule. She needed to pick up the kids at eight. They ascended the hill, leaving Santa Cruz behind. Storm clouds blacked out the stars, and a smattering of rain hit the windshield.

"I bought a sailboat. A Flying Scott. Maybe someday you'd like to go on the bay?"

"That sounds fun!"

She was loving the friendship, but Meghan's situation was a thorn in her peace. Her back tightened, and she clenched her hands in her lap. Partly warmed, partly frozen still, she had to know the truth before throwing another fiber of trust to the flames of possibility. "So, I guess you settled Meghan's case by now, probably?" Her voice sounded harsh and incongruent with the evening's mood.

Eric gulped and stared ahead. His hands were quiet on the steering wheel, and for a few moments he was silent. "Well, no, actually..."

"I thought a thorough exploration of the software would shed some light on what happened?"

"I can't honestly say what went wrong." He looked ahead. "Medical records software is universally problematic."

Audrey's heart pounded. He hadn't even bothered to find his mistake, much less settled the case. She looked out her window. Poor Meghan was still waiting. The more Audrey thought, the angrier she felt.

Large drops of rain spit on the windshield. Treetops swayed and tossed in the wind. She waited, but Eric remained silent until the Tesla's headlights lit up the sign announcing Ben Lomond.

"Dr. Taylor, to be honest it's disappointing you haven't settled. I get that medical records software is a pain, but as a doctor, you were responsible to ensure her care. If you knew the software was problematic, shouldn't you have double checked everything?"

He flicked the indicator on and turned right onto Love Creek Road. "I did double check. I always ensure my patients' safety."

"Clearly you didn't ensure Meghan's!" Audrey's voice rose. "If you really care, apologize and settle the case. Otherwise, why should anyone believe your faith extends beyond your money and reputation?" She turned again to look out the window, and added, softly, "You doctors should try living with your patients' condition for a day or two!"

Dr. Taylor eased into the driveway. The rain pounded the car now, a deafening roar on the glass roof. The wind roared through the giant trees above them, sending down redwood needles and twigs.

"I'll walk you to your door." He got out and went around the car. A blast of wind rushed across the yard as he opened the passenger door.

Heads bent, they hurried to the kitchen door. Audrey shoved it open and flicked on the kitchen light. She stepped inside and turned to face the doctor.

His face was serious, his eyebrows pressed down. The corners of his mouth drooped, and the wind whipped his hair out of its neatly ordered style. "Audrey, thank you for coming to dinner with me. I won't keep you waiting. Good night." He dipped his head briefly, turned, and jogged back to the Tesla, hunched against the battering rain and wind.

Audrey closed the door. She yanked off her wrap and hurled it onto the kitchen floor. The cabin was chilly, and she distracted herself by lighting a fire. She scrunched old magazine pages into wads, and balanced kindling on top. "Stupid man!" Tears escaped her eyes as she set a match to the papers. The flames sped along the edges and flared into a warm crackle. She set a log on the lit kindling and closed the stove door. The fire roared to life, heating the living room.

She remembered something her mom had said, years ago. *"It's hard to change when someone condemns you."*

Wiping her eyes, she slumped onto the sofa. It was almost time to pick up the kids. Thankful they could not hear her, she sobbed alone.

~

The rain sloshed onto the windshield faster than the Tesla's wipers could move it. Eric drove slowly along Highway 9 to Felton, then over to Scotts Valley and onto Highway 17. Giant redwoods and firs swayed dangerously in the wind. Accidents slowed the traffic—vehicles skidded across the road's slick surface, their drivers too confident for the mountain highway's treacherous twists.

The Tesla crawled over the mountain. A million broken, red and white reflections shone on the windshield. Eric squinted against the light. His eyes were dry and tired.

At Lexington Reservoir, the traffic stopped. A collision

required tow trucks. Eric sat in silence, his shoulders sagging. The traffic crept forward, and he pressed the accelerator. The Tesla moved through rain and wind, taking him back to Silicon Valley and his work.

CHAPTER THIRTY-TWO

Early pink blossoms fluttered on the petite trees of California Oaks Hospital's parking lot. Wispy clouds drifted high in the blue sky. It was February. Spring came early to Silicon Valley. Eric parked the Tesla and jogged into the Emergency Room. He'd been called in to treat one of his patients, a ten-year-old boy, with a stomach bug.

Eric was tired. The nights since his date with Audrey had been mostly sleepless. He hurried inside and opened the NewDay electronic records. The intake nurse had already downloaded the patient's blood glucose meter and insulin pump data. The boy was throwing up and needed hydration.

Quickly, Eric clicked through the screens. The software stopped at the pump data screen. "Field entry required," demanded the screen, in red letters. The field in question required a carb count to match an insulin dose.

He entered the appropriate amount of carbs and ordered an IV drip of background insulin, an NPO, and a continuous glucose monitor to track the child's progress. The final verification checklist popped up, and Eric clicked through the checkboxes hastily, then prepared to complete the order.

The hospitalist paused as he passed the computer station. He was a new doctor, not experienced, but meticulous. "Did you complete the verification checklist?"

Eric hovered the mouse over the Submit Order button. "Of course."

"I usually doublecheck it."

Eric frowned and glanced at the man. "Uh-huh."

"Dr. Taylor, it's a subtle interface. If you don't use it every day, it's easy—"

"It's fine." Eric didn't appreciate being countered by a junior colleague. He knew what he was doing.

The hospitalist turned and faced him squarely. "Dr. Taylor, I hate to be a pain, but the patient's safety could depend on you doublechecking that list."

Impatiently, Eric clicked out of the final screen and reopened the checklist. The software listed the patient's doses and insulin-to-carb ratios, alongside check boxes that he had already filled in. He paused as the mouse reached the end.

"Verify carbs and insulin." The corresponding box was checked.

"That's for any carbs and insulin the patient has on board," the hospitalist said. "It's a little confusing. It doesn't refer to the insulin-to-carb ratios in the preceding lines."

Eric stared at the line. He clicked back to the intake screen and viewed the patient's meter data. Again, he viewed the insulin dose taken to cover a meal, along with the carbs he had entered to use up the insulin.

His heart began pounding. Ignoring the hospitalist, he rushed to the room where the boy lay, with his parents sitting nearby. "Did Benjamin eat anything before you arrived?"

"No. We gave him insulin to cover lunch, but he couldn't eat it. He was too nauseous." Benjamin's mom looked exhausted.

"Thank you." Eric returned to the computer.

The hospitalist waited, arms folded. "Everything OK?"

Eric leaned over the keyboard, looking at the screen closely. He replaced the carbohydrate count with a zero. Slowly, he rechecked the child's entire order, ensured the software had calculated the unused insulin into its doses, and clicked the Submit button. He turned to face his colleague.

"Thank you for pointing that out. I apologize for being abrupt."

"Like I said, it's subtle."

~

Eric turned the child's care over to the hospitalist and drove to the clinic. He greeted the receptionist curtly, then fled to his office and flipped the blinds shut. There, he stood with head bent and eyes shut, pressing his fist against his forehead.

Idiot! He sat heavily at his desk and snatched up the photograph of his brother. His hands shook as he gently traced the image with his forefinger. "Michael."

Waking his computer with a quick swish of the mouse, he leaned close to the screen and scrolled through the malpractice suit documents. There it was—the folder labeled "Sent by Audrey Beach."

A screenshot showed the NewDay training software, with its detailed instructions for entering notes and orders in the ER version. Another screenshot directed doctors to complete the verification list. Each field was followed by a paragraph that explained the field's use.

The field to verify the patient's intake of insulin and carbohydrates followed the fields for the patient's insulin-to-carb ratios. Although it was easy to mistake the field for a repeat of the insulin-to-carb ratios, the training clearly spelled out that it was, in fact, for inputting the patient's current status.

But Eric had not paid attention to the training. He'd rushed through it, confident he had grasped the concepts, sure he would manage just fine. Just as he'd rushed through the screens at the hospital.

He jumped to his feet, crossed the room, and leaned onto the windowsill, breathing heavily. Long, complicated shadows from gnarled old trees stretched across the parking lot.

Audrey Beach was right. His error, not a software glitch, had almost killed Meghan Patel.

CHAPTER THIRTY-THREE

Perched on a hay bale in the cold barn loft, Nancy pressed her phone to her ear. "Babe, I miss you!" She'd made an effort during the past weeks, and Dr. McKenzie was almost hers. She pulled her down coat close.

"I know, Sweetie." McKenzie sighed. "How's your job?"

"I was let go." She squeezed her eyes shut. A tear slide down her cheek. She pulled a bottle of nail polish from her pocket and shook it fiercely.

"Oh, Sweetie! That was a dumb move on your boss's part."

"Thank you." She sniffed and opened the nail polish.

"Let the tears flow. I'm here."

Nancy's grandfather came into the barn. Nancy froze, holding her breath. If her grandparents found out about McKenzie—a married man, it turned out—they'd make her leave. Life was so unfair.

Her grandfather took a bucket to the feed room. She heard the tinny rattle of grain falling from a scoop. He went to a stall, poured the grain into an old mare's feed container, and left.

"Janice griped because I was late. I couldn't help it!" She sobbed, stroking the thick, sparkly polish onto her nails.

"You deserve better."

She smiled. He was getting it. "My grandparents say I

have to find somewhere else to live if I can't pay the rent."

"How cruel."

"Harrison, can you come see me? I need your strong arms around me." Feeling comforted, she recapped the polish and held up her fingers, assessing her nails.

"Of course, darling! Will you be OK until the weekend?"

"I think so." Nancy sniffed.

"I'd be there in a heartbeat if I could, little Nancy."

That was the response she wanted. "I know."

"I love you, Nancy."

"I'm so glad you listen to me." She checked the barn below, then sobbed again.

"I'm here." His voice oozed compassion and longing.

"I feel better now that I heard you. I should go. They'll wonder where I went."

"Goodbye, love."

Life was improving. She climbed down from the hayloft, stuffed her angst, and walked briskly to the kitchen. "Hi Grandma! I was just looking for a new job—or another place to live, if needed. Shall I make the coffee?"

~

Days later, Dr. McKenzie stood in a quiet hotel corridor, Nancy nestled beneath his arm. He put the key card against the receiver and opened the door to his suite. He wheeled his luggage into the closet. Nancy wandered to the window and gazed out at the snowy fields.

"Come here, love." He shrugged off his heavy coat and sat on the couch. She rejoined him.

After a while, he took her for an early dinner. Nancy told him she had led her grandparents to believe she had a job interview and would be gone all afternoon.

"It's lovely to see you, Nancy." Dr. McKenzie lifted his wineglass to his lips. He meant it. She was stunning—and much sweeter than Olivia. "I've missed you."

"I think about you all the time." She twirled a lock of her long, blond hair around her slim finger, gazing into his eyes.

"Let's talk about what you're going to do."

Nancy leaned forward on her elbows. "Please! I need some direction."

"I have an idea."

"What is it? Tell me!"

"Well, you're a smart, beautiful girl." He ran his finger around the rim of his glass, prolonging his attraction to her in endless circles.

"Thank you, doctor! I'm glad you think so." She giggled, blushing.

He nodded. "I need a part-time receptionist in my endocrinology practice, in Phoenix. And Olivia could use help around the house and taking Nolan here and there. We have an apartment above the garage, which you could stay in free, since you're… connected to me." He leaned back and raised his eyebrows.

Nancy closed her eyes and breathed deep. Tears escaped her eyes. Dr. McKenzie reached across the table and took her hand. "Darling, I love to help you. And this way, we can see each other all the time."

"That's what I was thinking. Once a month is really hard for me."

"Me, too." Her nearness would be pleasant.

Nancy looked at the table, then raised her eyes. "Harrison, have you told your wife yet?"

Dr. McKenzie straightened. It didn't seem right to reveal Olivia's faults to sweet Nancy. "Ah, that." He kissed her fingers delicately. "I hate to hurt her. But she seems to know that what we had is long gone. I'll tell her I'm leaving when I find a decent divorce lawyer."

"Thank you, darling."

"Anything for you."

"Harrison…" She hesitated.

"What, love?"

"I've been thinking about my kids."

"Ah. The wounded bird seeks wholeness." Her

irresistible hair tumbled around her shoulders and down her arms.

She smiled. Impulsively, she pulled her phone from her purse. "Can I show you some pictures?"

"If you're sure you're ready?"

"I'm ready." She opened the camera app on her phone and turned it to Dr. McKenzie. "This is my oldest, Easton."

"What a handsome kid!"

"Warwick loves ice cream. And Lillie likes gymnastics."

Dr. McKenzie looked closely at the photos. *Three kids! What a hassle.* "They're adorable, just like their mom."

She nodded and opened another picture. "Here's the whole family. That's me and my ex next to the Christmas tree. And that's Audrey, my sister-in-law, on the couch reading to Lillie. Easton and Warwick are by the sliding door." She pointed to the boys playing with new light sabers.

A jolt went through him. Was that Audrey Beach? He looked closer—it was. Interesting. Nancy looked up at him. Quickly, he smiled. "Lovely family."

"I'll text you these." Deftly, she tapped her phone screen several times. "There!"

Dr. McKenzie scrolled through the photos, noting the connection between Nancy and Audrey for future reference.

Nancy grasped his hand. "Can I tell you something?"

"Go ahead, Nancy. I'm listening."

She hung her head and stared at the table, wrestling with the admission. "I feel guilty not being there for my kids." She looked up. "But I just can't be a good mom."

He softened his eyes and squeezed her hand. "I love you. You can be a great mom. Someday, you should get them back."

Nancy stared at him, breathing quick and shallow. "You think?"

"Of course! You're a loving, beautiful woman. You have the right to raise your kids. I'll text you some legal websites to get you started."

Her eyes were big, her lips parted. She looked like a kid about to ride a rollercoaster.

"And—" he set down his phone, weighing his words.

"What?" She grabbed his hands.

"Well, I love you so much, I find myself longing to meet them and become part of their lives." For now, that was true.

Nancy gaped. "Wow! I hadn't dared to dream about that. Then all our kids could grow up together!"

"Exactly!" He tipped his head and smiled, enjoying her rapt attention.

~

The following Saturday, late afternoon, McKenzie moved Nancy into the garage apartment, opposite the house. Nancy, he told Olivia, was his new receptionist, scheduled to work in the practice each morning, from nine to twelve. Afternoons, she could cook and clean.

"I hope you're grateful, Olivia. Now you can relax, while Nancy does your work. She can take Nolan to swim team practices, too—and anywhere he needs to go."

"Thank you, Harrison." Her smile looked forced. Of course, it did. She could always think of something to complain about. Never mind that he worked day and night to provide.

He turned and took her car key fob off its hook by the door. "Come to think of it, you don't even need a car key anymore." That should keep her in line.

The apartment was stuffy from the day's heat. While Nancy unpacked, McKenzie opened the three dormer windows that overlooked the parking area. Cool night air wafted in. An owl trilled its soft, repetitive notes from a nearby tree. Two of the windows were in the living room. The third was in the bedroom, and he paused as Nancy followed him there.

"Will you be making the bed, darling?" He grinned, mischievously and flipped off the light, leaving them in moonlight. "It's a housecleaner's job, you know."

Nancy giggled deliciously. "Sir, it's already made."

"Not for long."

He opened his arms. Nancy looked out the window. Lights shone in the main home's windows. "Don't you need to get back, so Olivia doesn't wonder where you are?" She nestled into his embrace, soft as an island breeze.

"Don't worry." He kissed her fruit-scented hair. "I don't think she cares."

Several hours later, he woke in the darkened bedroom. Nancy lay beside him, close and warm. He pressed the light on his wristwatch and swore quietly. It was twelve forty-five.

Nancy stirred and saw his watch. "Oh my gosh! You've slept way too long. I'm sorry!"

McKenzie scowled for an instant, then softened his gaze. It was too soon to discover Nancy's flaws. "Not your fault, darling."

Nancy turned over. Within moments, she slept again. McKenzie got up and dressed. He pulled the covers over Nancy, let himself out, and went back to the family home.

CHAPTER THIRTY-FOUR

Nancy quickly grasped the rhythms of her new situation. Harrison left the apartment around ten most nights, leaving her to enjoy her new place. She was excited for the future, too. Harrison promised her what she'd always wanted—beyond her dreams, really. She couldn't wait until they were married, and they got her kids back.

She was due in the clinic at nine, Monday through Friday, and she was never late. She drove Olivia's luxury sedan past sprawling homes, timeless on sunbaked yards dotted with palm trees, cacti, and low-growing shade trees.

She parked in the Phoenix medical office complex that housed McKenzie's practice. She picked up sweet, creamy coffees for herself and dark roasts for McKenzie at a shop down the street. Swinging a Givenchy bag over her shoulder, she walked through the practice door at eight fifty-five each morning.

That allowed time for a quick visit with McKenzie in his office. After that, she sat at the reception desk between two fake fiscus trees and welcomed in patients. At noon, she returned to the house, put the car keys in her room, and provided whatever cleaning help Olivia required. Late afternoons, she took Nolan to his swim team practices.

Nights, after McKenzie left her apartment, Nancy's phone glowed in the dark bedroom beneath her quick fingers. She updated her spending on a bank app and checked the transfers from Dr. McKenzie's credit union. She visited high-end clothing websites, jewelry stores, and fun home décor websites.

The whole thing ran like clockwork. Three weeks in, Nancy was back to loving her life and full of hope for the future.

~

Late one afternoon, she sat on a bleacher at the swim center, while Nolan practiced with the swim team. Parents chatted around her. She took a selfie, showing her pretty new sunhat with the blue Arizona sky behind her. The pool water danced and shone. Kids swam along the lanes.

"I don't think we've met." A woman hiked up the bleachers and sat next to Nancy. She held out her hand. "I'm Sondra."

The woman, like most in the McKenzie's circles, was well dressed and immaculately made up. She wore a flowing dress and stringy sandals with gold embroidery.

"I'm Nancy—Nolan McKenzie's nanny." Nancy shook the woman's hand.

"Dr. McKenzie's son? Dr. McKenzie used to be my daughter's endocrinologist."

"He's a great doctor!" Nancy tucked her phone into the Givenchy purse.

Sondra raised her eyebrows. "At Catelyn's last appointment, I smelled alcohol on Dr. McKenzie's breath. That day, he increased her doses so much, even I could tell it was a mistake. I hate to think what might have happened."

Nancy stared at Sondra, her lips parted. "Whoa!"

Sondra opened her purse. "I also suspect he abuses his wife." She withdrew a business card and handed it to Nancy, rising to leave. "Let me know if you need anything."

Nancy shifted on the bleacher, uncomfortably, as Sondra descended the bleachers.

A woman in front of Nancy turned around. "I couldn't help overhearing that. I should add that Sondra doesn't lie. I know her well."

Nancy went to collect Nolan. She hurried the boy, anxious to be alone.

~

The next morning, she floated into the practice, carrying the usual gourmet coffees for herself and Dr. McKenzie. She'd dismissed Sondra's comment. The woman must have been lying. Or she was jealous. McKenzie was a great catch.

She set her purse on the reception desk and went into the doctor's office.

"Good morning, darling!" McKenzie pushed his chair back from his desk and extended his arm.

Nancy slipped around the desk, handed him his coffee, and perched on his lap. "Good morning, love." She ran her fingers through his hair.

"Mmm!" He sipped his coffee, rubbing her shoulders with his free hand.

"Like this brew?" She snuggled against his chest.

"Especially the blond part." He sniffed her neck.

She giggled, then stood, letting her fingers slip slowly through his. "See you tonight?"

"Of course, Sweetie!" McKenzie winked, watched her depart, and turned to his computer screen.

It was a busy morning. Nancy scheduled appointments, welcomed patients with her dazzling smile, and quickly navigated the software system Dr. McKenzie had introduced her to the day before. At noon, she stood and stretched, yawning, and set her name badge in the desk drawer. The office closed for lunch for the next hour. Ronnie, the afternoon receptionist, would arrive at one o'clock.

Halfway down the street, Nancy remembered her purse. She groaned and walked back to the clinic. Opening the door, she paused. A woman's voice drifted from Dr. McKenzie's office.

Nancy tiptoed inside, carefully closing the door behind her. The clinic was empty. Dr. McKenzie's door was slightly ajar. She crept to the reception desk, silently lifted her purse from the floor, and edged to the doctor's door.

Impatiently, she shoved her hair behind her ear and leaned close. Dr. McKenzie was murmuring. Nancy held still.

"…How about this weekend, darling? Your husband's out of town, right?"

Nancy's eyes widened, and her mouth fell open. Gripping her purse tightly, she tiptoed out of the clinic, then bolted for the car. On the way home, she bought a bottle of whiskey. She told Olivia she wasn't feeling well and hurried to the apartment.

The whiskey was soon half gone, and Nancy lay on the couch, one arm over her eyes. She'd kicked her shoes off and cried. That evening, she told McKenzie she had a headache.

~

When dawn softened the sky, the whiskey bottle sat, three-quarters empty, on the coffee table. Nancy lay on the couch, still dressed in her work outfit and shielding her swollen eyes with a cushion. Her head throbbed.

The early sun warmed her arm. She rubbed her eyes, then held still and pressed her brows down, listening. Something was moving the gravel below the open dormer window.

Scrunch, scrunch.

Soft footsteps sounded from the driveway. The McKenzie home's motion-activated porch light flared, sending harsh white onto Nancy's ceiling.

Nancy sat up, holding her breath, and went to the edge of the window. Hidden behind the curtain, she looked down.

Olivia stood in the middle of the driveway, dressed in a nightie. Weird. Why was she trying to avoid McKenzie's attention? Nancy tipped her head, watching.

A light went on inside the house—the master suite—and Olivia darted back to the patio gate, yanked it open, and disappeared behind the house. More lights in the house went on.

The sun rose fully, lighting the scene. Olivia reappeared from the backyard, carrying her phone. She looked around, frantically. Slammed doors thudded within the house. Olivia crept past the front door and crouched behind thick bushes in front of Nolan's window, to the right of the home's entrance. Nancy saw her slim hand reach up and tap the window. The curtains parted, and Nolan's pale, worried face looked out. Now that was concerning. Moments later, the curtains fell back into place. Nolan's room remained dark.

The front door opened. Dr. McKenzie stood on the threshold and spoke, calmly. "Olivia! Get back here now, and I might be lenient."

Nancy narrowed her eyes. Sondra hadn't lied.

McKenzie stepped out and walked the driveway, looking carefully. He passed by Olivia's hiding spot, walked the length of the garage, and went to the hillside that bordered the far end of the property. He started up the dirt slope, peering behind bushes.

"Daddy? Why are you out here?"

Quickly, Nancy looked at the front door. Nolan stepped outside, small and quivering.

"Shut up and get back to bed!" McKenzie commanded.

Nancy's nostrils flared. Anger clenched her stomach.

Nolan began crying but did not move. McKenzie headed down the hill, towards the boy. Nolan ran for Olivia's hiding spot.

Olivia stood. "Nolan! *Tetradactyl!*"

McKenzie saw Olivia. He screamed vile names, then ran towards her.

Nancy's jaw clenched, along with her fists.

Nolan darted across the driveway towards the car. Olivia tore after her son, meeting him in the driveway. She grabbed his hand and pulled him with her. Behind them, McKenzie's heavy feet pounded the gravel.

Nancy ground her teeth, furious. She may not be a great mom, but she knew abuse when she saw it.

~

Olivia extended her hand towards the car, Nancy's keyring glimmering in her fingers. Nancy spun. Her keys weren't on the kitchen table, where she usually left them. She must have dropped them on the stairs.

The car flashed and blipped as the locks flipped open. Nancy had parked sloppily, at an angle to the garage. The vehicle's front faced the dirt slope. Olivia yanked open the driver's door, half-threw Nolan inside, and leapt in after him.

As McKenzie reached the car, Nancy heard the door locks click shut. Behind the windshield, Nolan's face was pinched with fear. McKenzie pounded on the windows and roof, screaming obscenities. But the engine roared, and the car sped backwards, spitting up gravel. McKenzie jumped aside as Olivia turned the car and hurtled towards the exit. He stood by the garage, fists clenched, roaring profanities as the car glided away, its engine fading.

Nancy opened the apartment door and walked down the stairs. "Harrison, what's going on?" Her voice was quiet, her eyebrows raised.

"You must have given Olivia your keys!" McKenzie snarled, turning to Nancy.

Nancy stared at McKenzie, head tipped. "No, actually. I *must have* dropped them." She imitated McKenzie's "must have" in low tones.

"Then you lost them, you idiot! Why weren't you more careful?"

Idiot? Rage shook Nancy's entire being. "Maybe because I didn't realize she wanted to get away from you." She stepped towards him.

McKenzie stared at her.

She narrowed her eyes and stared back. He was like maggots in an expensive steak. "Maybe I thought you really did want to give her a break by hiring me."

McKenzie took a step back.

She raised her voice. "Maybe I didn't know she was a

house prisoner. Maybe I didn't realize you were a first-class jerk—"

"Now, Nancy." McKenzie held up a hand. "I realize you're upset."

"—who would have the nerve to insult me."

"Nancy, I didn't mean to insult you."

She flew at him. "How dare you call me an idiot!"

McKenzie turned, ran to the house, and slammed the door. Nancy pounded on the wood, screaming. Getting no response, she went back to the apartment and stomped up the steps. "I know you cheated on me! I know you treat your patients while you're drunk! I'm not stupid!"

Shaking, she ordered a rideshare and packed her things. Within an hour, the vehicle pulled up at the garage. The driver helped her load her boxes and suitcase into the trunk. She got into the back seat and slammed the door. The vehicle sped towards the driveway exit. Nancy turned in the seat and gestured obscenely towards the house, hoping McKenzie was watching.

When she calmed down, she realized he could have killed her.

CHAPTER THIRTY-FIVE

"Do you think he's cute?" Meghan leaned close to Audrey. The second day of Camp Strong 'n Free was almost over. They climbed onto the arena bleachers, joining parents and kids. Warwick was riding a pony that circled the camp wrangler, on a lunge line. The pony's hooves thumped the dirt. Beaming, Warwick waved at Audrey.

"Warwick's adorable."

Meghan giggled. "You know who I mean."

Audrey frowned, faking confusion. "The pony?"

Meghan shoved her and giggled again.

"Oh! The guy in the middle?" Audrey whispered.

"Yeah—*Carson.*"

The wrangler was lanky and tall. As he followed the pony's movement, Audrey saw his clear, green eyes, focused on Warwick. His smile was wide and friendly beneath his Stetson hat. His jaw was square and strong.

She nudged Meghan. "He's attractive."

"Sh!" Meghan looked down, quickly.

Carson glanced at Meghan, smiling. A dimple showed in his cheek.

Audrey chuckled.

"We talked last night while I helped him put up the horses. He's from Texas. And get this—" Meghan grabbed Audrey's arm and leaned close. "He's got type 1 diabetes, too!"

"That's great! Wait—no it isn't."

They both giggled, and the wrangler glanced their way again. "Ready to trot, Warwick?" He spoke loudly enough for Meghan to hear, in a Southern accent.

"I'm hanging on!" Warwick grabbed the saddle horn.

"Push your heels down and hold onto the horn, right like you're doing." Carson clicked and swished the lunge whip along the ground. The little paint picked up a trot. Warwick bounced in the saddle.

"Heels down," repeated the wrangler.

Audrey watched as Warwick stopped bouncing and began moving with the pony.

"I got it!"

Carson nodded.

"Great job, Warwick!" Meghan called.

After the pony trotted a few more circles, Carson brought it to a halt and guided Warwick through his dismount. "Who's next?"

A small girl walked to the pony, giving Warwick a shy high-five on his way out. Meghan walked with Audrey and Warwick to the parking lot. Her face had filled out. Her cheeks were rosy, her eyes lively.

"You've made a wonderful recovery," said Audrey. Meghan had regained her balance and functional abilities. The only reminder of her brain injury was occasional forgetfulness and difficulty recalling words.

"I can ride again at the end of the month."

"Did you see me trot?" Warwick hopped beside Audrey, hanging onto her arm.

"You rode like a cowboy." Audrey squeezed his shoulder.

Audrey and Warwick got in the car. Meghan bent, looking at Warwick in the back seat. "Dr. Taylor will be here tomorrow, Warwick. He's the doctor on call. And on Friday, he'll give a talk. He's really funny."

Audrey blinked. "I didn't realize he'd be here."

"He always helps at the camp." Meghan turned to leave. "I gotta put the horses up—and talk with you-know-who." She walked back up the driveway.

Audrey checked Warwick's blood sugar and handed him a chocolate smoothie, hiding a smile. The children still didn't know about the hidden veggies in their favorite treat. She drove towards Ben Lomond. Shadows of leaves and flashes of sunlight alternated across the windshield.

It made sense that the doctor would be at the camp. But why was Meghan such a fan now? She frowned, strategizing a way to avoid him. Perhaps Dominique or Swift could pick Warwick up tomorrow. She would have to be there for the talk on Friday, though, to support her nephew.

She picked up Easton from a friend's. "Don't forget to practice oboe tonight."

"I always do!" Easton flipped open his thermos and drank his smoothie.

At the gym, Dominique was putting equipment away while parents collected their children. Lillie ran to Audrey.

"Lillie nailed her handspring today!" Dominique commented on Lillie's improvements often now.

"Good work, Lillie!" Audrey turned to Dominique. "Any chance you could pick Warwick up from camp tomorrow, please?"

"I can't get away from my camp. Is something wrong?"

Audrey took a deep breath. "Dr. Taylor will be there. I don't want to run into him."

"Why not?" Dominique straightened and furrowed her brow.

"He… We went on a date a while back. It didn't end well."

"A date? You're kidding!"

"Nope. Even lawyers go on dates."

Dominique tapped Audrey's arm sympathetically. "I didn't mean it that way. I'm sorry it didn't work out."

"He never owned his mistake with my client. I couldn't

get past that.”

“Got it. Try asking Swift to pick up Warwick.”

~

As Eric walked towards the campgrounds parking lot, a fit man with shoulder-length hair and water sandals came out of the barn with Warwick. His face looked familiar. Wondering why he was with Audrey's nephew, Eric lengthened his stride and joined them.

“Hi Warwick! How's the horseback riding?”

“Good.” Warwick tipped his head and tapped his chin with his forefinger, squinting up at Eric. Eric had worn jeans and a cowboy hat, to fit the camp theme. “Hmm. You're a cowboy?”

“Just dressed for camp.” He looked at Swift. “I'm Warwick's endocrinologist. Did we meet?”

The man reached out his hand. “Swift. You showed Dominique and me around your partner's boat on New Year's Eve.”

“Oh, right!” Eric shook his hand. “And you're taking Warwick home today?”

Swift nodded, pulling a paper from his pocket and turning it towards Eric. “Audrey couldn't make it this afternoon.”

Eric read the form, which listed Swift as a contact. He nodded. “That's kind of you.”

They continued to the parking lot. Eric paused at the entrance. Swift would see Audrey soon. Perhaps he would take a message. “Before you go, how's Audrey?”

“She's doing great. I help her with repairs around the cabin once in a while, and she and Dominique hang out.”

“Ah!” What else could he ask, without giving himself away? “So, she's keeping busy?” *Useless, Taylor!*

“Probably, I guess.” Swift's head was tipped, his eyes looking intently at Eric. “Want me to tell her you said hi?”

Eric felt his face warm. “I would like that. Thank you.”

Swift turned to Warwick and pointed to a dusty Jeep

parked under the trees. "See my Jeep? Get in the passenger seat and check out the dashboard. I'll be right there."

Warwick's eyes widened. He ran to the Jeep and climbed in.

Swift looked at Eric, his mouth straight, his eyes gentle. "Are you interested in Audrey?"

Eric rocked back, taken off guard. "I took her to dinner in January." He paused and took a deep breath. "It didn't end well. Pretty sure I put her off for good."

"Ouch!"

They were in personal territory now, so he continued. "I want to try again. But the issue we discussed might have been a deal breaker."

"Why don't you ask her?"

Eric watched a deer step through branches beside the parking lot. He turned back to Swift. "She was right." He was relieved to admit it out loud.

Swift winced. "Sounds brutal."

"It was—it is." Eric took his keys out of his pocket, remembering how, on the catamaran, Swift's smile had faded when Dominique looked at Eric. "I noticed you and Dominique seem compatible."

Swift laughed. "I notice that a lot."

"We're in the same boat, then!"

This time they both laughed.

"Why don't you ask her out?" Eric asked.

"I don't want to risk the friendship. Pretty sure she isn't interested."

"You don't know until you try."

"Maybe I will." Swift gave Eric a thumbs-up. "Here's to our happy futures!"

Eric dipped his head. "Here's to the beautiful women who evade us." As he drove home, the painful knot of Audrey's rejection loosened a little.

~

"I saw Dr. Taylor." Swift turned as he stepped out of

Audrey's door, after dropping Warwick at home. "He said hi."

"Thanks." Audrey was checking Warwick's sugar levels with a device.

"I guess you'll be picking Warwick up for the rest of the week?"

"Yeah. Thanks for helping me out, Swift." She glanced up and smiled.

Swift left the Beach cabin and drove to the gym. Dominique was getting into her car. She paused, her dainty fingers clutching the top of the car's open door, her nails polished a rosy pink. She tipped her head and smiled, with the adorableness and vulnerability of a lost kitten.

Swift swung out of the driver's seat and strode across the parking lot, hoping he looked more confident than he felt. "I was driving by. Want to get coffee?"

Dominique glanced at her watch. "Sure! What's the occasion?"

"Nothing." He gestured to his Jeep. "I'll drop you back here."

Dominique locked her car, and Swift opened the Jeep's passenger door. She hopped in, comfortably. She had ridden often in the Jeep.

~

In a Ben Lomond coffee shop, he pulled out a chair for Dominique and set paper cups of steaming coffee onto the table. Dominique hung her hoodie over the back of her chair. The square neckline of her t-shirt framed the fitness-trim of her shoulders. She was born for sports.

Swift rested his elbows on the table and leaned forward. "How's camp?"

"Great! Lot of new kids. My regulars are showing them the ropes. Literally!" Her lips curved in a playful smile. "Today we did rope climbing."

Swift laughed. He picked up his cup and swirled the dark liquid. "You're great with those kids, Min."

"Thanks." She looked out the window. At the hardware store, a woman hefted bags of garden dirt into the trunk of her sedan. Her eyes returned to him. She clasped her warm cup in her elegantly sculpted hands. "Swift, is something wrong? We never just go to coffee."

"I, um–" Swift paused and shifted in his seat. "I just thought you're always on the go, and you might need a break." *Right! Coward.* He could have kicked himself for chickening out.

"That's sweet, Swift. Maybe my mom's right. She says I do too much." She sipped her coffee. "Needs more cream."

Swift shoved the ceramic box at the end of the table towards her. He took a packet of sugar and turned it over and over in his hands. "I saw Dr. Taylor today."

Dominique glanced up, her well-kept eyebrows arched. "Where?" She opened a little creamer and poured a white stream into her cup.

"At Warwick's diabetes camp when I picked him up. Turns out the doctor…" he smelled his coffee, then set it down.

"The doctor what?"

"Oh, never mind, it's not important."

Dominique punched his arm, playfully. Her dark eyes sparkled. "You can't do that!"

Swift laughed and pulled his arm back, sloshing coffee onto the table. He loved her playful side. "Fine. He went on a date with Audrey a while back."

"Oh, I knew that."

Swift threw up his hands in mock exasperation. "I can never tell you anything new! Do you have spies everywhere?"

Dominique threw her head back and laughed. "She told me she didn't respect him, so I was pretty surprised she even went. I guess you know the date was a mess because of his mistake with her client." She grabbed a napkin and wiped up the coffee spill.

"What mistake?"

"Medical malpractice, Swift." She tapped her head and raised her hand. "She's an attorney. She was suing Dr. Taylor before she quit to take care of Luke's kids. His dosing mistake could have killed her client."

Swift leaned back in his chair and stared at Dominique. He blew out a slow breath. "Wow! No wonder their date was brutal."

Dominique nodded, her dainty earrings jiggling. "Audrey told me he's a good doctor, but she didn't like that he never owned that mistake. I'm surprised she dated him."

"For what it's worth, he said she was right. Anyway, what about you? What do you think of Dr. Taylor?" Swift put down his cup and leaned forward in his chair. He curled his toes, dreading her answer.

Dominique smiled, sadly, and gazed at her coffee. "I admit, I liked him when I took Warwick to his appointment, when Lillie was sick." She looked at Swift. "He's cute, and he's a doctor so I was awestruck, I guess. And you may have noticed I was crushing on him when he showed us around the catamaran."

Ouch! Swift rubbed his chin. "Yeah, I did pick up on that."

"But when Audrey told me he wouldn't admit his mistake, I lost interest, right then." She sipped her coffee, then set the cup down. "I have to make dinner. Could we go now?"

"Sure!" Swift cleared their things and carried Dominique's unfinished coffee. Light streamed onto Dominique as they walked back to the Jeep. It warmed the curves of her face to bronze and gilded the outline of her dark hair. Swift opened the passenger door. She grasped the grab bar and pulled herself gracefully, athletically, into the seat.

Swift sighed and walked to the driver's seat.

~

On the final afternoon of the camp, Audrey took

Warwick to the conference hall. Rustic and spacious, the hall teemed with children and their families. Country music generated an upbeat mood. Sunlight slanted between redwoods and firs and into the hall, through huge windows, lighting up the worn red carpet and glowing on the polished wood floor.

"There's my horse teacher!" Warwick ran to Carson and Meghan, who stood near the low stage at the front of the room. Audrey followed.

"Hi, Audrey!" Meghan's turquoise sweater matched her lively eyes. Her curls dodged the constraints of a beaded headband.

"Ms. Beach." Carson held out his hand, politely.

Audrey shook the boy's hand. "Kids got the hang of riding horses?"

"Some did, Ma'am. Warwick took to it."

"He loped today," said Meghan. "Were you scared, Warwick?"

"Um, I guess not. Nope." Warwick furrowed his brow, then raised a finger.

Meghan laughed. "I don't see many kids pick up riding that quickly." She gazed away.

Gently, Carson touched her arm. "He should take lessons, huh?"

Meghan started slightly, then smiled at the wrangler. "Thanks, Carson." She turned to Audrey. "There's a good barn that provides kids' lessons in Felton."

Warwick spun to Audrey. "Can I?"

"Maybe." Audrey turned to Carson. "Are you heading back to Texas?"

"Nah. I put in for a position at a ranch in Gilroy. Figured I'd stay around." He glanced at Meghan, who blushed.

The music faded. A voice asked attendees to take a seat. Plenty of chairs were empty near the back, and Audrey started moving away. But when Meghan invited her and Warwick to join them, Warwick's feet left the ground. They sat in front of the podium.

The camp director summarized the week and played a slide show, reviewing fun moments. During the open mic session, kids shared how the camp had given them friends, as well as confidence with their disease. A few times, Audrey wiped away tears. Then, the director introduced Dr. Taylor.

"Dr. Eric Taylor has been published in leading medical journals in the field of endocrinology. He is known as the Bay Area's pediatric endocrinologist who cares. This year, Dr. Taylor will share how to control your blood glucose levels at school. Please welcome Dr. Taylor!"

Applause thundered as the doctor walked to the front.

"Thanks." He rested his hands on the podium, smiling warmly. Momentarily, he caught Audrey's eye, stiffened for an instant, then smiled at her and continued his gaze around the room. "Every year, I look forward to seeing you brave kids. I'm proud of you. Your parents, too. It isn't easy getting up at all hours to check a child's blood sugar. You worry constantly. You make midnight trips to the pharmacy. There's a place in your fridge door just for insulin and juice."

The parents chuckled knowingly.

"Now, let's talk about school and your best friend, type 1 diabetes."

He was a captivating speaker. Throughout the presentation, the audience paid close attention. There was plenty of laughter, and a few tears.

Audrey remembered Dr. Taylor's kindness to Warwick, their tour of Dr. Fisk's boat, and the concern that prompted him to purchase her Tesla. Despite his refusal to accept responsibility for Meghan's experience, she believed his concern for patients was authentic.

She was surprised that Meghan laughed along with the presentation, as if her injury had never happened. Silently, Audrey reviewed the girl's medical challenges.

Dr. Taylor finished to a standing ovation. Audrey stood,

too—remaining seated would have been ridiculous. The clapping stopped, and people lined up to chat with the doctor.

She took Warwick's hand and they walked to a table in the back, laden with fruit, water bottles, and cookies. Warwick slipped away to play with friends. She should say hello to the doctor, Audrey knew, but her anger flared. The man was quite a hypocrite.

Suddenly, he was at her side. "Audrey! How are you?" He was slightly flushed.

"Hi!" She turned to face him.

"Did Warwick enjoy the camp?"

"He did—especially the horse program."

"The camp gives the kids a lot of confidence."

Meghan and Carson joined them, and they chatted about plans for the upcoming summer camp, until a woman pulled Meghan and Carson aside. "My daughter wants riding lessons. Can you recommend somewhere?"

Dr. Taylor turned to Audrey. "I hope I can see you again." He folded his note papers into halves, and halves again.

Audrey hadn't expected that. "Dr. Taylor, thanks for asking. I'd rather not."

Dr. Taylor nodded seriously, his gaze direct and steady. "That's understandable. Thank you for letting me ask, Audrey."

She watched him walk out the door. Meghan rejoined her. The mom was still peppering Carson with questions.

"Meghan, I'm curious. You seemed happy to see Dr. Taylor. What's going on?"

Meghan tipped her head to the side and pressed her eyebrows together. "Didn't I tell you? Dr. Taylor settled. I got everything I asked for."

Audrey reeled inside. "Did Patrick tell you why?"

Meghan laughed. "Is there something unusual about it?"

It was easy to forget that Meghan was so young. "I

expected him to settle eventually, but not without a fight. Last I knew, he was adamant that his error was all about the software."

"I guess he changed his mind. My mom and I felt good about how the whole thing ended. He sent a nice email, too."

"Is it OK to ask what he wrote?" She hoped to gain some insight into the doctor's motives.

Meghan tapped through her apps and handed her phone to Audrey. "Read this."

Audrey read:

Dear Meghan and Mr. and Mrs. Patel:

After thinking through your case, I've decided to settle, giving you everything you rightly request. My insurance company and lawyer will work out the details.

I owe you an apology—although apologies aren't enough in situations like yours. A wise friend gave me some perspective. Had I been more careful, the dosing error would never have happened.

I hope you can forgive me.

Best regards,

Eric Taylor

Audrey stared at Meghan, her thoughts flying. She spun to the door. Dr. Taylor had left several minutes ago. She returned Meghan's phone. "Could you keep an eye on Warwick, please?"

Meghan nodded. Questions showed in her eyes, but Audrey dashed out the door. She walked briskly towards the sloping path to the parking lot. She ran to the top of the slope, just in time to see the Tesla pulling out of the driveway. "Dr. Taylor!" She waved her arms, but it was too late. The vehicle eased around a bend, sending up a cloud of dust as it disappeared.

~

Part of Audrey wanted to walk into the dust cloud and wrap it around her—carry it with her and hide for the rest of her life. She gazed at the empty driveway. If she'd known about Dr. Taylor's confession, she wouldn't have been so cold. What a judgmental assumption she'd made! She rubbed away tears with the heels of her hands.

Behind her, the happy crowd of families and camp staff emerged from the conference room. It was time to take Warwick and pick up Lillie from her gymnastics camp.

She walked back up the path. Nurse Jenny passed her, on her way to the parking lot. She paused and looked closely at Audrey, then smiled kindly and continued when Audrey waved and walked briskly past. Meghan and Warwick chatted as they approached Audrey. She forced a smile and went to meet them.

~

Two things were true: She had every right to turn him down. And her second rejection was another gut punch. Eric needed to decompress, to refocus—to remember that no matter what anyone else decided, he could always choose God's call on his life.

Running might help. He stopped at his house, changed, and drove to Fremont Older Open Space Preserve. A late spring rain pelted the car, and water drops fell from the heavy oak branches that hung over the empty parking lot. He got out, stretched, and took a steep trail into the green hills.

The rain drenched the park's oaks and wide meadows. Eric ran along a lofty ridge, high above Silicon Valley, leaning into a cold wind. He timed his breathing with his strides—in for two foot strikes, out for two. Rainwater splashed up from the dirt trail. Ahead, a buck saw him approach and leapt for cover.

He reached a vista point and slowed to a walk, breathing hard. He followed the trail to the edge of the mountain ridge and leaned onto the curved fence. Rain dripped from his hair. Straightening, he gazed over the cityscape. Clouds roiled over the grey jumble of Bay Area cities. Across the valley, shadowy streaks of rain slanted over the greening foothills. Distant lightening flashed.

He finished his run, descending through the trees past tech billionaires' mansions on the hillsides. Shivering, he drove home and grabbed his Bible from the coffee table. For a good half hour, he browsed the psalms, echoing their words in a whisper. "Hear my cry… ever-present help… I trust in You… I have set the Lord always before me… I will not be shaken…" Steadied again, he texted his weekly update to his parents and stretched out on the sofa.

It was amazing how owning his pride had changed his outlook. Given him peace.

Reconciled him to God.

CHAPTER THIRTY-SIX

Audrey woke from a restless night, her sleep torn by doubts and regrets. Her head throbbed, but there was no time to indulge her angst about Dr. Taylor. Lillie's second, and last, meet of the year was today.

She got up and took a pain reliever. At least she had plenty of time, before seeing Dr. Taylor again. Warwick's quarterly appointment was a month away. She went in the kitchen and made breakfast, determined to be emotionally present for Lillie.

~

Music blared in the crowded Santa Cruz gymnasium. Audrey sat tensely in the bleachers, fighting her fears for Lillie and trying to pray. Her niece stood at the beginning of the vault runway.

Warwick put down his book and grasped his knees. "I'm going to watch."

Suddenly, Lillie tore along the blue strip with a ferocity that sent chills down Audrey's back. She leaped onto the springboard and sailed into a quick handstand on the vault. She flipped in a tight, straight line, and landed firmly, finishing with a snappy salute.

Audrey shrieked.

"Good job!" Easton yelled.

Dominique lifted Lillie and spun her around, the team cheering around them. Swift grinned as he congratulated her.

Throughout the day, joy displaced Audrey's fears. Lillie swung powerfully between the uneven bars. She sailed through her floor routine and flicked precisely over the balance beam. She helped carry her team to victory, and Audrey wiped away tears as her niece strode to the first-place podium, smiling joyfully.

After the awards ceremony, Audrey hugged her niece. Dominique joined them.

"I'm so proud of you, Lillie!" Audrey said. "Dominique, thank you for coaching Lillie."

"I knew she had it in her." Dominique grinned.

Lillie hugged Audrey's waist, and she looked up. Her hair ribbon hung loose over her ear. "Auntie Audrey, I knew you were watching, and Coach Minnie and Swift. That's why I won."

~

Her spirits lifted, Audrey took the kids to meet the team at The Pizza Place in downtown. Swift poured water for everyone. He and Dominique peeled slices of pizza, steaming hot, from circular trays, and passed around loaded plates. The kids chatted and giggled, exuberant from their win. Parents discussed their summer plans.

Swift was quiet. Quick glances at Dominique replaced his relaxed manner. Audrey decided to investigate. "Dominique, your support made a big difference to Lillie."

"You're doing a great job, too, Audrey."

"I couldn't have done it without you and Swift." Audrey noted Swift's soft expression as he looked at Dominique.

"Minnie's always there for the kids," Swift bragged.

"Lillie will advance to Level 6 now." Dominique's eyes shone.

Audrey nodded. "Do you know what she told me?"

Dominique tilted her head. Swift leaned close.

"She knew you both were watching her, and that helped her win. You make a great team." Audrey tried to gauge Swift's reaction to this blatant hint.

Swift looked at Dominique. "Min, can I talk to you over coffee after this?"

Dominique gently put her hand on Swift's forearm, her brown eyes serious. "Sure! But Swift, I have to make an announcement."

Swift looked at her, his eyebrows pressed together. Dominique stood and waved her hands. "Hey, gymnastics families! I have a few words to share with you, before we're done." The families quieted and Dominique tucked a strand of hair behind her ear. "We had a great meet. Congratulations, everybody!" She looked from face to face. "Over summer, there will be several gym club camps, as well as regular practices."

Some girls gave each other high fives.

"And, I have a change coming up that you need to know about."

The parents leaned forward.

"Working with kids and teaching gymnastics makes my heart sing. Because of that, I've decided to pursue a master's degree in kinesiology. I'll be relocating to Florida in June, after the school year ends, and so, sadly, I'll also be stepping down as coach."

Groans and sighs burst from the group. A few of the girls cried.

"I'm sorry to give you the news at the end of such a great day," Dominique continued, "but I wanted to tell you in person. I assure you that gymnastics club will continue. I have a few great candidates I'm looking at to replace me. I promise, I won't leave you hanging."

Lillie was crying, but when she looked at Audrey, she managed a smile.

"Coach Minnie, we're sorry to see you go, but thank you for all you've done for our kids," one of the moms said. Other parents chimed in their agreement.

"And we wish you all the best," said a dad. "Here's to Coach Minnie!"

He began clapping. Soon, the entire group was on their feet, applauding Dominique's contributions to their children's lives. Dominique blushed and bowed her head. The families lined up and shared their private thanks before leaving. There were many hugs and tears.

The last family gone, Audrey stepped up to Dominique. The coach wiped tears from her cheeks and blew her nose. "Wow! That was harder than I expected."

"Dominique, I'm sorry you're leaving. But it's great you're pursuing your dream."

Swift had stood quietly behind Dominique throughout the goodbyes. His face looked tired, and his mouth drooped. He pushed his and Dominique's chairs under the table, then stepped aside so Dominique could go first to the exit door. He followed her slowly.

Audrey and the kids said goodbye and walked to the car. As Audrey closed her door, she looked back. Swift was draping his jacket over Dominique's shoulders. Dominique looked at him and said something, then laughed. Swift nodded, not smiling, and they walked towards a nearby coffee shop.

~

The coffee shop was crowded, but a small table in the back corner was free. Swift set two coffee cups down and pulled out a chair for Dominique.

"Thanks." She pulled his jacket from her shoulders and handed it to him, then sat as he pushed the chair in for her.

"Dominique, I'm proud of you. I always thought you had a great career coming." Swift sat across from her and set the jacket across his lap. He twisted one of its buttons.

"Aw, thank you! You're my biggest fan!"

"Yep."

"So, what are you doing this summer?"

"The usual. Running music camps. I might hike in the Sierras. Trip to LA to visit my dad."

"You don't seem thrilled. Are you hiking with the same

group you went with last summer?"

"Nah, going solo. They were partiers." He didn't add that he only wanted Dominique with him.

She leaned back in her chair. "I understand."

No, she didn't. Not yet. "Hey, I'm curious why you didn't find a degree program in California?"

She laughed and tapped her forehead. "Stupid me! I didn't think to tell you. My parents are moving to Florida. They can't afford to retire here. I can't afford to live here on my own, on a gym coach's salary. You know how it is."

"Yeah. It's why I like my cabin." He chuckled. His inexpensive cabin was off the grid, far above Boulder Creek.

"I'm going to live with my parents until I finish the program. Florida's cheaper, and I can still have the ocean nearby."

Swift nodded. "So, tell me about the program. What school are you going to?"

Dominique told him about the master's program in Florida, her parents' new home, and the beauty of the Florida coast, which she couldn't wait to explore. The topic exhausted, she paused and finished her coffee.

"Min, I wonder—" He stopped and leaned forward in his chair. His heart raced, but he wasn't going to miss this chance.

"What, Swift?"

He took a deep breath. "Is there any chance we can be more than friends?" He paused, flushed, then plunged on. "I admire you a lot, Dominique. You're so loving to the kids, so passionate about their success. You look out for your parents. You're sweet, kind, and beautiful, and you mean everything to me." Spontaneously, he reached across the table and grasped her hand. "I don't want to live without you by my side."

Dominique looked at him through wide eyes. "Wow!" Gently, she withdrew her hand. She lifted her empty cup to her lips, then set it down. She looked around the room, coughed, and looked back at Swift. Finally, she said, "Swift, I really love you as a friend. I'm honored you would ask me that. I've just never considered it."

Swift laughed, awkwardly. "Oh, don't worry, Minnie. It was just a thought." Inside him, the warm light of hope he'd carried all day burst into a thousand fragments and fell at his feet, leaving him cold, plunging him into darkness.

"Oh, I know, no worries!" Dominique's face turned red. "Stuff like that comes up between friends a lot, I'm sure."

"Course it does." He couldn't smile.

"Well, I better get going." Dominique stood quickly and pushed her chair under the table. They left the coffee shop. Outside, Swift offered his coat against the cold.

"I'm fine, thanks for offering that, Swift." She touched his arm lightly for an instant. They parted ways and walked to their cars.

Swift drove to the harbor. He walked the moonlit beach until dawn outlined the mountains and lit the water to a dim grey.

CHAPTER THIRTY-SEVEN

The next afternoon, Audrey took the kids to the jail. Luke was fit and tan from his outside work, and his face radiated confidence. He joined them at the table. "How's it going?"

"My team won first place!" Lillie raised her arms, triumphantly.

Luke leaned across the table and rubbed Lillie's shoulder. "That's great! How did your floor routine go?"

Lillie described her accomplishments, with her brothers chiming in and Audrey interrupting to clarify.

"She basically carried her team to the first-place podium," Audrey finished. They told Luke about Warwick's camp and their upcoming summer activities. Easton described Swift's encouragement to resume oboe.

"I like Swift." Luke leaned back in his chair. "And I'm proud of you all. How about you, Audrey? Anything new?"

"Church was good this morning. And I got promoted to shift manager. I'll take the first week of summer off, so the kids and I can do some fun things, before summer camps start. I've been playing my flute." There was nothing to say about Dr. Taylor. She had never mentioned their failed date to Luke.

"She went out with Warwick's doctor a while back," Easton offered.

Audrey's face heated up. "Easton, that was ages ago. It

doesn't matter."

"I think Dad should know. He's your brother."

Audrey frowned but gave Easton a side hug. "I guess you're right." Her nephew was ten, going on thirty.

Luke nodded. "We should be here for each other. Why didn't you tell me?"

"Embarrassed, I guess."

"No need, Sis. 'Fess up." He smiled kindly.

It still amazed Audrey that Luke could carry her pain, despite his circumstances. "Dr. Taylor bought the Tesla. He overpaid me. I don't think he needed it, but Warwick let it slip that we were struggling financially."

"You had to sell your Tesla? I'm sorry!"

The kids whipped around to look at Luke, then back to Audrey, riveted.

"Tate didn't give me a year-end bonus." She paused. She hadn't planned to mention her financial strain. But Luke just nodded, encouraging her to speak.

"After he bought the car, he asked me to dinner. He said he respected that I paused my career to care for the kids. I didn't see anything heroic in it, but whatever."

"Anyone would admire your choice—or should."

"I agreed to go. I hoped he'd owned his mistake with Meghan." Audrey paused, her throat suddenly tight.

Luke nodded. Meghan's injury had horrified him. "Go on."

"He treats Warwick well. The parents all love him. He's compassionate. But I was pretty harsh." She related the conversation that ended their date.

"I'm glad you were honest."

Audrey looked at him, surprised. "Really? It didn't do any good."

"If it didn't, that's on him. So why would you care?"

"Fair point. But I could have shown some grace. I want grace, after all."

Luke shrugged his assent.

"Anyway, he asked me out again on Friday, at Warwick's camp. I told him no. Then, Meghan told me he'd settled. Voluntarily. He even wrote an apology, and she let me read it."

Luke's eyebrows flew up. "Wow! So he did listen."

"I went to talk to him, but he'd already left. To be honest, owning his error removed the obstacle I'd had to getting to know him." She swiped at a tear.

Lillie put her slender arm around Audrey. "It'll be ok, Auntie Audrey."

"Dr. Taylor should have owned his mistake long before," said Luke. "You mustn't feel bad about speaking your mind, Audrey. I thought you knew that—you're a lawyer!"

"I meant to keep the lawyer out of my personal life. He must think I'm a jerk. Can't blame him."

Luke squeezed her hands. "Audrey, it's not so bad. Sure, you could have been kinder. But Dr. Taylor owned his mistake, so God used you." He extended his hands to the family. "Why don't we pray?"

They joined hands.

Easton began. "Dear Lord, we all know that Auntie Audrey needs to get married. She is a strong auntie, but she just doesn't look right by herself."

Audrey snorted. She saw Luke suppress a smile.

"Lord, we ask that You would work this out in Your timing," Luke prayed. "Please help Auntie Audrey trust You and feel your peace. And thank You for providing the money. In Christ's Name, amen."

"Amen!" agreed Warwick, loudly enough to get a glance from the attending officers.

"Daddy, I'm glad we can talk to you," said Lillie.

"So am I," said Luke. "Audrey, please don't hide stuff. We need to stick together."

Audrey nodded. "Alright."

Luke sat straighter in his chair as an officer approached their table. "OK, guys, our time's up. Keep your eyes on the

Lord, Audrey. He'll get us through."

It was easy to believe Luke. His difficulties gave his words credibility. They said goodbye, and Luke followed the officer to the exit door.

The relaxed, slouchy walk Audrey remembered from their childhood had replaced Luke's exhausted demeanor. It hurt to see him in jail, but his growing faith amazed her, and his new-found peace was contagious. He turned at the door and smiled. She waved and walked with the kids to the parking lot.

~

After the kids were in bed, Audrey sat in the living room, drinking tea. Her phone rang.

"Audrey? It's Dominique." The coach's voice was thick and low.

Audrey set down her tea and sat forward. "Hi! Is everything ok?"

Dominique sighed. There was a long pause. "I don't know."

"Why? What happened?"

"Swift and I went to coffee after the dinner last night. He asked me for a relationship."

"Well, that's great! I always thought you were perfect for each other. Why are you upset? Or are you happy?" Audrey thumped the chair arm, frustrated by her unhelpful words.

Dominique laughed briefly, then sniffed. "No, this isn't my happy mode. I told him no. I don't see us as a couple at all. But I'm really gonna miss him. It's not like we can hang out now."

"You should tell him you want the relationship."

"Why? I don't want it."

"Oh, right." Audrey pushed her fingers through her hair, flustered. "Maybe you should call him and see if you can continue the friendship?"

"No, that would hurt him."

"Gosh, I don't know what you should do." Audrey felt

like a Kindergartener with relationships. "I am truly sorry for your pain." Bleh! That sounded so fake.

"I guess I just needed someone to talk to. I can't tell my mom. She'd say I'm an idiot and to call him back and start the relationship. She really likes Swift."

"Well, why not? I like him, too."

"I need a man who's going somewhere, Audrey. I'm very driven. Swift just wanders from summer to summer, always the same routines, never committing to anything great." She sniffed, loudly, and her voice became tight. "It's like he doesn't care about his life. Honestly, it makes me question his commitment to follow God."

"I had no idea, but it makes sense. Have you talked to him about it?"

"He needs to change for his sake, not mine. Otherwise, how would I know it was genuine?" Dominique sighed heavily, then spoke again, her voice shaky. "These twenty-four hours have been the worst of my life."

"I bet! I always expected you and him to become a couple, sooner or later." Audrey scrunched her brow. Dominique could be so perplexing.

"Really? Why?"

"Oh, the way he looks at you. He takes care of you. He respects you. He's always there when you need him. He believes in you. Plus, he's your best friend. Just a few little things I noticed." She was a little irked by Dominique's blindness to these wonderful qualities.

"I guess I took that for granted. Now I really miss him."

"That stuff isn't enough to offset his stagnant side?"

"It's like you and Dr. Taylor, Audrey. There's that one sticking point you can't get past."

Audrey's heart twisted. "If it helps, my sticking point came unstuck, but we're still not together. I messed things up."

"Oh, shoot! What happened?"

Audrey updated Dominique about the doctor's decision

to settle the case, and her presumptive coldness on the final day of Warwick's camp.

"Ouch! I'm sorry."

"You and I are sort of in the same boat."

"Why don't you ask him out?"

"I can't risk a no. He's Warwick's doctor, remember? If he isn't interested, that would be super awkward. Of course, we've had some practice with awkward."

Dominique sighed. "Well, here's to our happy futures."

"Yep. Here's to the wonderful men who keep missing the cues."

CHAPTER THIRTY-EIGHT

California sunshine warmed the rainforest canopy, and hikers swarmed the dusty trails, staying cool below redwoods, oaks, and rangy bay trees. Fawns followed their mothers, stepping daintily over fallen trees and pausing to browse on evergreen shoots and shrubs.

"I'm sick of school!" Lillie rolled her math paper into a tube, fidgeting at the kitchen table.

Audrey couldn't blame her niece. It was late May, and she too longed for an end to the school year. She struggled to push her nephews and niece through the year's last assignments.

Lillie hurled her pencil onto the kitchen table, eraser first. It sailed in an arc, landing in the spaghetti sauce Audrey was heating for dinner. "Oooh! Look at that!"

Warwick spun in his seat, pointed at the ceiling, and tipped his head back. "Good shot, sista!"

"Lillie, stop it!" Audrey fished the pencil out of the pot and rinsed it off, while Lillie and Warwick giggled together.

"Easton, dinner!" Audrey called.

Easton came from the hallway computer, and they ate. After dinner, they went for a walk. The air was still and cool in the mountain shadows. They stopped to offer handfuls of grass to a neighbor's horses.

"That horse likes me," Warwick said.

"Of course, he does." Audrey had signed Warwick up for

weekly riding lessons, and he was catching on to his new sport. Financially, the lessons had been out of reach until her promotion at the market.

~

The following Friday, she hung up her apron and waved to the market's owner. She took the kids to the gym, where the parents had organized a going-away party for Dominique. Swift's Jeep was absent when she pulled into the gym parking lot. Audrey had not seen Swift since Dominique had told her about his request for a relationship.

Cards and gifts for Dominique sat on a table by the office. Someone had set food on a folding table in the parent area. Colorful balloons bobbed above the tables. Audrey added a plate of cut fruit to the sandwiches and cookies.

Madelyn ran to Lillie. "Coach Minnie said we can play on the equipment!"

Lillie squealed and jumped, and they ran off together. Lillie's brothers followed. Dominique had set up stations around the gym. Teenage gymnasts supervised the activities, and Audrey saw Warwick try the vault table. Easton climbed a thick rope that hung from the ceiling.

Sarah and Bob, the couple who had picked up Madelyn when Audrey forgot the carpool, greeted Audrey.

"Is Lillie going to continue with the new coach?" Sarah asked. Bob stood close beside her. He nodded a greeting.

Sarah's friendliness surprised Audrey. "Lillie is continuing. How about Hailey?"

"Hailey would never give up gymnastics. She's going to miss Dominique, but I'm glad Lillie will still be there." Sarah's tan, lined face grew serious. "Lillie is lucky you're here. I went into foster care at ten years old, and gymnastics fell by the wayside."

Audrey stared. Sarah's confidence and happy life belied her difficult past. "I... I'm sorry to hear that."

Sarah laughed. "Oh, I'm over it. Buried in therapy, years ago."

Bob put his arm around her waist. "She's been putting up with me all these years. I guess that put her past into perspective."

They laughed. Sarah invited Audrey to a summer hiking group for the kids, which some of the moms had planned. While she took Audrey's email address, Dominique blew her whistle. Everyone gathered around her.

Dominique had grown her hair out, and glossy curls brushed her shoulders and tumbled down her back. "Here we are, the end of the year. I'm so proud of each of you. You've put in a lot of work, and all of you have improved." She clapped, and the parents joined her. "Everyone, thank you for making our gym club such a great place. I'm going to miss you a lot."

One mom gave Dominique a huge bouquet of roses and a card. "This is from all of us."

Dominique opened the card and pulled out a gift certificate to the elegant Shadowbrook restaurant in Santa Cruz. The kids had written personal messages on the card. Dominique read a few and wiped away a tear.

"I'll never forget my time with you." She fanned herself with the card and glanced at the ceiling, her mouth turning down. "I better stop." Her voice was a squeak.

Everyone laughed. The mom who had presented the bouquet took over. "We've embarrassed Dominique enough. Eat up, everyone!"

The adults broke into smaller groups to chat and visit, and the kids returned to the gym equipment. When the party ended, Dominique stood by the door, sharing personal words with each family as they left. Audrey's throat tightened as she stepped closer to Dominique.

The coach turned to Audrey, her smile wide and sincere. She squeezed Audrey's hands. "I appreciate you, and I'm glad we're friends."

Audrey nodded. "Let's stay in touch."

"Absolutely."

Lillie wrapped her arms around Dominique's waist. "I'll miss you, Coach Minnie!" Her eyes welled with tears.

"I'll miss you too, Lillie." Dominique bent to embrace the girl. "Maybe you can visit me in Florida."

Lillie looked up at her coach. "I want to!"

Warwick and Easton waved awkwardly, and Audrey took the kids to the car. "OK, enough sad stuff. Let's hit the beach!"

The kids chattered and played as Audrey drove down Graham Hill Road towards Santa Cruz. Summer was finally here.

~

Small waves sloshed onto the wet beach. The sun hung low over the ocean. Warwick and Lillie dug in the sand, and Easton dragged washed-up driftwood to the ocean's edge and hurled it across the water. He'd grown. Sometimes, Audrey almost mistook him for a man.

Her phone rang as she shook out a beach towel to sit on. She didn't recognize the number. "This is Audrey." She sat on the towel and pushed her heels into the warm sand.

"Audrey, nice to hear your voice! This is Dr. McKenzie, your prior expert witness." He chuckled companionably.

She paused. Why was Dr. McKenzie calling her? "Hi!"

"Listen, I apologize for contacting you when you're no longer practicing. This is just a friendly call. I like to keep in touch with my contacts."

"No problem. I assume Patrick was in touch before Dr. Taylor settled?"

McKenzie cleared his throat. "Yes."

"Great! Thanks for being flexible."

"So, how's it going? Patrick said you had to step away from law for a time?"

"Yes, due to a family situation."

"Your win against Dr. Taylor will be good for your career. You can use that on your resume if you go back into law."

Audrey rolled her eyes. Mansplaining was a trigger, but she didn't react. "That's very encouraging, thank you."

"I have to admit, Dr. Taylor's suit was a challenge for me. I get emotionally involved in my clients' cases." He laughed, apologetically. "Especially when I feel there has been a real injustice."

"I'm just glad my client got her settlement." Audrey wanted to end this weird conversation.

"So do you anticipate getting back to law?"

"Probably." Why did he need to know?

"If you don't mind me asking, how's your family doing? Kids doing OK?"

A chill spread across her back. She was sure she'd never mentioned Luke's kids.

"I'm sorry, Dr. McKenzie. I need to get going. Have a great day." She ended the call.

~

She shook off her concerns by playing Scottish and Irish reels, popular bands, and a mix of the old classics for the kids as they drove home. The kids rode in silence, watching the trees and fields.

As they entered Ben Lomond, Easton turned to her. "I like this song!"

Audrey smiled. It wasn't a song. The haunting melody of Tchaikovsky's *Swan Lake* swelled against a background of strings and flute. "This is from a ballet. An oboe plays the main melody."

"I thought it was an oboe." Easton leaned forward, putting a hand on the dashboard.

"Do you want to learn it?"

"It sounds really hard."

"You could do it. I can get the sheet music. Maybe you could join the youth chorus at Cabrillo College, and they could perform this piece."

Audrey glanced at her nephew as she turned onto Love Creek Road. Light from the streetlamps sparkled in his eyes and a wide smile crossed his face. After dinner, Audrey enrolled him in the youth orchestra and helped him choose an audition piece. Then, they sat on the couch and listened to piece after piece for oboe, until Warwick and Lillie complained that they'd never get to watch their movie.

~

During her week off, Audrey and the kids slept late. Sometimes, the kids helped Audrey mix pancake batter or set strips of bacon onto a pan. They ate breakfast in their pajamas. The kids played, read books, or sat and chatted with her. Easton practiced for his audition.

Almost always, Warwick's blood sugar remained stable through the night. They had learned to avoid high carb dinners and eat early. Warwick benefitted from his improved sleep schedule. At his quarterly appointment with Dr. Taylor, they learned Warwick had grown an inch since his diagnosis. Dr. Taylor was pleased with his overall health.

Audrey considered telling the doctor that she knew about his apology to Meghan. But Warwick was there. Besides, Dr. Taylor had not told her about his confession.

The doctor paused as Audrey followed Warwick through the waiting room door. "Audrey, great to see you. Please don't hesitate to reach out if you need anything."

"Thank you." She found his care comforting. She felt she was over the failure of their budding relationship, and she threw herself into assuring the kids' well-being. Their week off included fun, laughter, and play—aspects of life they all needed badly.

CHAPTER THIRTY-NINE

On Friday, Audrey took the kids to Quail Hollow Ranch to meet the gymnastics families for their first summer hike. Her backpack pulled heavily on her shoulders. She'd packed the kids' smoothies.

Six moms with around fifteen children had shown up. The kids ran and played on the ranch's well-kept lawn. Nearby stood the old ranch house. Oak trees shaded the home and surrounding gardens.

Sarah had volunteered to lead. "We'll hike up to Sunset Ridge. The trail leads into the forest, behind the house here." She pointed to a eucalyptus grove at the foot of the hills that cradled the property.

They took a sandy trail through the trees. Around a corner, they overlooked the hills around Ben Lomond. The afternoon sun hit the white banks beside them. Audrey followed Lillie and Madelyn, listening.

"I was crying on the rug my mom got me." Lillie skipped sideways, looked at her friend.

"Like this?" Madelyn curled her hands under her chin and made a sobbing face, pulling her lower lip in and out. The girls giggled.

"Yeah! Just like that!" Lillie squealed, jumping.

"So, then what happened?"

"Auntie Audrey said she could help me get into my bed."

"So did she help you?"

"No!" Lillie jostled against her friend. "I put myself to bed."

"Like this?" Madelyn skipped and hopped, pretending to climb into an imaginary bed. She finished with loud snoring.

Lillie giggled and linked her arm through Madelyn's. "Yup!" She made snoring sounds, too. "Me and my brothers liked having Auntie Audrey there. We knew she was going to stay with us, so we got to sleep, even though Daddy was going to jail."

Audrey wiped her eyes, thankful she'd caught her niece's confession. Miriam joined her. They watched Lillie and Madelyn skip ahead, arm in arm.

"This is good for us, too, isn't it, Audrey?" Miriam huffed beside Audrey. "I don't get enough exercise."

"I used to lift every day. Now I get my exercise chasing the kids."

They laughed. Audrey glanced behind them. Easton and Warwick had joined some boys and were finding sticks—probably to sword fight. The trail turned, entering cool forest shade. Towhees chirped and jays squawked. Some kids found salamanders among the ferns. Audrey's heartrate increased as the trail traced a mountain ridge.

"Let's take a breather." Sarah stopped beside an overlook. Shrub-covered hills and forested mountains stretched to the horizon. A dark road threaded through fields below. After a water break, the group continued up the trail.

"How are the kids doing?" Miriam swatted at a mosquito. "Do they miss their dad?"

"Of course. But they've stabilized."

"I can see that in Lillie. She's happier than I've seen her in a long time. Maybe even since her mom left."

They neared the mountain top. A woman warned the children away from poison oak. Easton and a boy his age passed Audrey and Miriam, pointing out things they noticed along the trail. Easton's new friend had a pair of binoculars. Through its lenses, he and Easton studied the landscape below.

Ahead, Sarah paused. "This is the dwarf redwood forest. We're almost at the top."

The trail sloped up through a stand of slender, pale redwoods, each not more than twenty feet tall—diminutive versions of their giant counterparts. The little forest was quiet and still, as if the mysterious trees held their secrets close.

Audrey's heart beat hard, and her legs burned. They joined Sarah at a clearing surrounded by manzanita shrubs. Below were fields and hills, surrounding Quail Hollow Ranch. Spring warmth tinged the air. Some of the moms handed out snacks.

Gazing at the mountains, Audrey realized she was more than half-way through the year. Luke would be home in five months.

"I brought chocolate smoothies." She handed thermoses to her nephews and niece. "Drink your veggies!"

Easton turned to his friend. "My aunt brings the best snacks!"

"Our veggies?" Lillie tilted her head.

Audrey had finally slipped! Her face heated.

"Do you sneak veggies in these?" Miriam asked.

"Sort of…" Audrey floundered.

"These have veggies?" Easton's eyes widened. "What kind?"

"Just a little spinach and some carrots."

Several moms gathered around.

"How do you make that?"

"Can I have the recipe?"

"This is brilliant!"

"They look just like a treat!"

Lillie swept her empty thermos upwards, scanning her friends and their parents. "Auntie Audrey's chocolate veggie smoothies, people! Step right up!" She and Madelyn convulsed in giggles.

~

The kids flopped into the car, tired and asking for hamburgers. Audrey drove Quail Hollow's curved driveway, past the pond with its turtles and ducks, and pulled onto Quail Hollow Road. She stopped for ground beef at the market. The kids followed her, playing their goofy dinosaur game. She would just have time to make dinner, before their weekly movie. Maybe Easton should help. His cooking skills were improving. She drove up Love Creek Road and turned into the driveway.

A shiny red sedan sat in her Tesla's old parking spot. Its brake lights were on, indicating the driver was inside. Audrey stared, puzzled. She hadn't scheduled anything, and she didn't recognize the car.

The door opened, and a petite blond woman stepped out.

"Mommy!" yelled Warwick.

The kids squealed and scrambled out of the car.

CHAPTER FORTY

Audrey watched, horrified, as Nancy welcomed the children into her outspread arms. "Easton, look how tall you are! I've missed you so much. Lillie, your hair is so cute. Aw, Warwick, I love you, too, honey!" Her voice croaked on and on. The kids pressed into her, kissed her hands, pulled her arms over their shoulders—wiggling with joy and excitement.

Nancy looked up and smiled at Audrey. "Audrey! Great to see you!" She walked to Audrey and opened her arms.

The kids were watching. Stiffly, Audrey embraced her ex-sister-in-law. "Nice to see you, too, Nancy."

"I've had so many adventures!" Nancy squeezed Easton and Lillie's shoulders, looking down at them with a wide smile. "Let's go inside."

She led the kids towards the front door. Luke's front door. The door Nancy had walked out of sixteen months before, and Audrey had walked through countless times since. Audrey followed them inside.

"It's so good to see the cabin again!" Nancy spun in the kitchen, like a movie star in a chick flick. Bella trotted in, dancing stiffly on her short, arthritic legs.

"Bella!" Nancy swooped the dog into her arms. Bella licked her face wildly and wagged her little tail.

Warwick reached up and petted the dog, blissfully. "Mommy's come home, Bella!"

Audrey wanted to throw Nancy out the door and lock it behind her. "Nancy, we were about to make hamburgers for dinner. You're welcome to join us. If you want to visit the kids, we can talk about that later."

"Oh, I'm getting custody. The judges always give preference to biological parents. Didn't you get the notice of hearing?"

The kids grew quieter. Audrey shuffled through a stack of mail and found an envelope from the superior court. She looked at Nancy thoughtfully. Clearly, she had done her research. But would a judge really turn the kids over to this unstable woman?

Turning her back to Audrey, Nancy bent, resting her hands on her knees so she could look into her children's eyes. "I'm really back, kids!"

"Mom, Auntie Audrey has been taking good care of us," Easton said, quietly. "I don't want her to leave."

"Oh, honey, don't worry! You'll still get to see Auntie Audrey." The tiniest edge hardened Nancy's voice. She looked at Audrey. "Thanks for stepping in, Audrey." She turned back to the kids and giggled, impulsively.

Audrey watched loyalty demands twist the children's peace. She crossed the kitchen, placing herself in Nancy's sightline. "We're going to have dinner. See you at court, Nancy."

"Actually, I'm taking my kids out to dinner." Nancy bent and draped her arms over Easton and Lillie's shoulders. She raised her eyebrows. "I made reservations at a restaurant by the ocean!"

Warwick squealed. "Dinner at the ocean!" He ran around Nancy.

Lillie and Easton remained subdued.

"I want to stay home," protested Lillie. "I'm tired."

"It'll be fun, Lillie." Easton's mouth was downturned, but Audrey sensed he was trying to keep his younger siblings calm. She realized he had grasped the situation. She moved in front of the door. "Absolutely not. I'm their legal guardian, as you seem to know. You have not earned my trust, and you will not be taking them anywhere." She could not risk an abduction.

Nancy turned back to the kids. "Come on, guys, let's get you ready for dinner. I'll help you."

"If you take them, I'll call the cops."

Lillie began crying. "Will the police take you away, Auntie Audrey?"

"No, Lillie."

After a long pause Nancy shrugged and went to the door. Audrey stepped aside.

"Fine. I'll be back soon." Nancy turned and opened her arms for a goodbye hug. Quietly, the kids embraced their mother, then moved close to Audrey.

Nancy went outside and got into her car. Audrey told the kids to wait. She dashed down the front steps and stood by Nancy's window. "Nancy, I will fight to retain guardianship. No judge will turn them over to you unless you prove you have changed. You realize that, I hope."

"I'm their mom. I deserve to raise them. You're just their aunt." Nancy narrowed her eyes and spoke slowly. "You see, Audrey, there's the Parental Preference Rule. I can take care of my kids." She started the car and slammed it into reverse.

Audrey rolled her eyes. "Also, I'm sure you know Luke is in jail."

"Of course!" Nancy smiled, sarcastically. "That's another reason the judge will give me preference. Kids need their mom."

"No, it's another reason I will retain guardianship. They need a stable adult, Nancy, not someone who could walk out of their lives at any moment."

Nancy spun the wheels, lurched the car backwards, and turned it towards the gate. "I'm gonna raise my kids!" The red car exited the driveway.

~

Audrey returned to the cabin and opened the envelope from the court. She had read a million legal documents with indifference, but this one twisted her heart.

"Notice is given that: Nancy Beach has filed: Petition for Termination of Guardianship."

The hearing was three weeks away. Audrey sat at the table and covered her eyes, tears dampening her palms. She pulled herself together and opened the court's website. A quick read revealed that abandonment was the main reason for terminating parental rights. Audrey groaned. It would have been so easy to terminate Nancy's rights.

The child's best interest principle guided the family law court's decisions, she read. Parents who had abandoned their kids must prove they could provide a stable home. Audrey began to relax. The court would never rip the kids away from her and place them in Nancy's care. As far as Audrey knew, Nancy couldn't even keep a job.

~

Her phone rang, and the kids joined her for their dad's weekly call.

"How's it going?" Luke's voice was upbeat.

"Mommy came over!" said Warwick.

"What? Audrey?"

"Here." By now, Luke must be bracing for anything on his weekly calls.

"Dad, Mommy says she's going to take care of us," said Lillie.

Easton remained silent, his face serious.

"What's going on, Audrey?"

"She was waiting at the cabin after our hike today. Did you get a notice of hearing?"

"Not yet."

"I got mine today. She wants custody, but she won't get it. She abandoned the kids." Audrey stopped. The kids didn't need to hear that.

"I want Auntie Audrey to stay with us," said Lillie.

Easton put his hand on his sister's shoulder. "It'll be OK, Lillie."

"Let's pray," said Luke. "Lord, thank You that the kids got to see Mommy. Help them not worry about who's going to take care of them. May Your peace calm us. Amen."

The tension lightened. Warwick fetched Bella, and Lillie stretched at the counter while she listened. Easton remained focused, sitting quietly with Audrey.

"Kids, Audrey will probably take care of you until I'm home, but if Mommy steps in, you'll be fine. Mommy loves you. Trust God."

"I think we all feel better now," Audrey said.

"So do I," said Luke. They laughed.

They updated Luke on their first week of summer. Audrey described the camps she'd enrolled the kids in, so they would be cared for while she worked at the market. The kids said goodbye, and Audrey and Luke remained on the line.

"Round Three," said Luke.

"Yep. Buckle up."

CHAPTER FORTY-ONE

Each morning, Audrey dropped the kids at their camps and worked at the market. In the afternoons, she took them to the beach or let them play by the creek. She built the case for her continued guardianship at night.

Dominique, Swift, and some of the gymnastics moms provided character references. Luke helped Audrey document Nancy's negligence, using emails and texts from before she left. Audrey wrote a financial summary to prove she could provide for the kids. She retained a family lawyer—Michelle Gonzalez, Esq.—and consulted her while the kids slept.

The day of the hearing, she dressed professionally and loaded her briefcase with extra copies of her documentation. She dropped the kids at their friends' homes and drove to the courthouse.

Luke was already in the small, shabby courtroom, conspicuous in his orange jumpsuit. He sat attentively at a table, handcuffed. A middle-aged man sat with him, presumably his court-appointed attorney. He turned and smiled when Audrey entered.

Nancy sat with her attorney at a table next to Luke's. Both tables faced the judge's bench, a desk on a platform at the front.

Audrey joined Luke and his attorney. Moments later, Audrey's attorney arrived, wearing a non-nonsense outfit in shades of black and brown. She sat, giving Audrey a confidence-building wink. "We've got this." She pulled her files from a stiff briefcase.

In the gallery behind, people waited for their hearings. There was no privacy. The courtroom was open to the public and hearings were held in blocks. A door beside the bench opened, and a balding man wearing a black robe entered. Everyone stood, and the judge sat between the state and US flags behind his bench.

"Please resume your seats," he instructed. After completing the administrative matters, he turned to Nancy. "You're seeking custody of your three children. Why should I terminate the guardianship of Audrey Beach, their—" he glanced at his papers, "their aunt, and hand the children's care to you?"

Nancy and her attorney stood. Nancy raised her chin. "I'm their mother, your honor. No one can care for kids like their mom. Audrey's a career woman who has never had children. She can't care for my children the way I can."

The judge turned to Audrey. "And why should I allow you to continue guardianship?"

Audrey stood and read her statement. "Since November 2018, I have been guardian for the children in Nancy's absence. I've given them a stable home, including regular meals, a clean home, help with schoolwork, extracurricular activities, and care for their health. I'm financially able to provide for them while their father is incarcerated.

"The children have not seen their mom for sixteen months. As my exhibits show, their mom has not demonstrated the stability of a competent parent. Returning the children to her care would not be in their best interests. They are attached to me. We have a routine and healthy relationships."

The judge nodded and turned to Luke. "What is your input on Nancy resuming custody of the children?"

Luke stood, his hands held in front by the handcuffs. His

court-appointed attorney also stood, glancing at his watch. "It would not be in their best interests, your honor," Luke said, calmly. "Nancy hasn't had contact with them for sixteen months. Before she left, she was emotionally unstable."

"What do you mean?"

"I got the kids to their school and appointments on time. If I left it to Nancy, she often didn't follow through. She frequently lost her temper, even throwing a plate at me once. And her disappearance triggered behavioral issues in the kids. My sister included emails from the school about that."

The judge thumbed through the paperwork and read them silently. He looked at Audrey. "Do you agree that turning the children over to their mother's care would not be in their best interests?"

"Yes. Nancy left no information, made no effort to keep in touch, and didn't provide financial support for sixteen months. Technically, that was abandonment, and she could have had her parental rights terminated."

"Yet she's here." The judge gestured to Nancy. "Why did no one terminate her rights?"

"I had no reason to expect her back."

"Luke?" asked the judge.

Luke glanced at Nancy. "I think I hoped she would eventually step up."

"You were hoping she'd come back?"

Audrey winced. Luke's attorney whispered something to him.

"I hoped she would become a stable mom. Kids need their mom. But until Nancy has proved she can care for them properly, I don't want her resuming custody. Audrey is doing an excellent job." He sat.

The judge glanced at his paperwork. "Nancy, did you expect Audrey to take over for you while you were gone?"

"No. I didn't know my kids' father would get himself in jail."

Michelle huffed under her breath, then stood. "Your honor, if I may, please refer to Exhibit 3, the last email the children's father received from Nancy Beach, their mother." She sat.

The judge looked through his papers and read aloud a printout of Nancy's email. "'Luke, I need to work out some issues. Please don't contact me. Nancy.' Did you receive any other contact from the children's mother during the past sixteen months?" This time, he looked at Luke.

"No, your honor." Luke stood again, awkward in his chains. "I tried to contact her when I was sentenced, but I didn't hear back."

The judge frowned and looked at his papers. "How do you interpret this to equal abandonment?" He looked at Audrey.

Audrey stared at the judge. Legally, the issue was clear.

"Spell it out," murmured Michelle, standing with Audrey.

"Abandonment occurs when a parent hasn't had contact with a child for at least a year and hasn't provided any support. That describes Nancy's actions."

"There must also be evidence of intent," lectured the judge. "I don't see any evidence Nancy intended to abandon her children."

"Seriously?" Audrey asked, incredulous.

"Why don't we ask her?" The judge looked at Nancy, who was smiling slightly. "Could you tell us your reasons for leaving, please?"

"Your honor, I had no intention of abandoning my children. I love them. I left because I felt that I needed some time to work on myself. I always planned to come back a better mom."

"Have you accomplished that goal?"

"Of course! I learned to speak up for myself. I found out I can be a great mom, and I have the right to raise my kids."

"Did you miss them?"

"Every day."

"Can you provide for your children? Are you employed?"

"Yes."

"Where?"

"I'm a financial analyst at Retirement Solutions in Bonny Doon."

Audrey's jaw dropped. She glanced at Nancy, astonished. Nancy returned her look, a triumphant smile across her pretty face. Apparently, she had finally put her business degree to use.

"How long have you held that position?" the judge asked Nancy.

"Since April 24th, your honor. I arrived in California on April 22nd to get my kids back."

A shock burst along Audrey's back and arms. Nancy had been planning this since April?

The judge shuffled his papers. "I see here you make $90,000, correct?"

"Yes."

"Audrey, Exhibit 6 shows your finances. You're providing for the children partly from your savings and partly from your work at the market. How is this more stable for the children than Nancy's income of $90,000 a year?"

Michelle stood. "Your honor, may I ask the plaintiff a question?"

The judge sighed and rubbed his forehead. "Go ahead."

Michelle turned to Nancy. "What have you done to address your anger issues?"

Nancy smiled. "Just because my ex mentioned anger issues doesn't prove I had them. I am a good mom."

The judge looked at Audrey. "Let's get back to your answer."

"Objection, your honor. I brought up an important point," Michelle said.

"Objection overruled. That's not the issue we're here to

discuss," said the judge. "Audrey?" Michelle sat down, scowling.

"I'm concerned about Nancy's anger issues, your honor," said Audrey, wanting to at least make a statement. "To answer your question, I paused my career when my nephew was diagnosed with type 1 diabetes. I was making $95,000."

"I said we aren't here to discuss anger management," repeated the judge. "And I don't care what you made in the past. The children need shelter, food, and clothing now. They need proper financial support today." He emphasized the words past, now, and today as if talking to a defiant child.

"I left my high-earning career because my nephew was diagnosed with an incurable disease. His health was more important than a higher income." Audrey's voice grew louder. "I have provided them with everything they need—food, clothing, medical expenses, gymnastics lessons—everything! Their routine stabilized them from their mother's abandonment.

"Nancy must prove her ability to care for her kids. She has an anger issue. She abandoned her kids. She's not fit to parent. If I hadn't been here when Luke was sentenced, they would have ended up in foster care."

A gentle tug on her sleeve distracted her. Michelle shook her head, telling her to calm down.

"And Nancy has anger issues?" The judge smirked. "Nancy says she planned to come back. She left the kids in the care of their father. You have no proof of anger issues. All you've got is this email, a few other exhibits, and Nancy's failure to communicate.

"She took time off to make herself a better parent. She's working. She wants her kids back. I don't see any evidence that she is an unfit parent. You haven't shown me she's violent, or verbally abusive, or even neglectful." He swung his pen back and forth as he spoke.

Michelle sprang to her feet. "Abandonment is neglect,

your honor. The plaintiff literally left the kids for sixteen months. They didn't hear a thing from her in all that time. She's like a stranger to them."

"Like a stranger," the judge mused. "Audrey, were you present when she came to see the kids, in…" he looked at his notes, "late May?"

"I was."

"How did the children respond to seeing their mother?"

Audrey sighed. "They were excited. But children don't understand."

"Stick to the question. Nancy didn't anticipate her husband would be jailed. But if something happened to him, she knew you were available."

Nancy looked at Audrey, her head held high. Her eyes flashed, and the corners of her mouth twitched upwards.

"She put her wants ahead of her children's needs!"

"Why didn't you terminate her rights, then? Something must have stopped you."

"I told you. I assumed she wouldn't be back."

The judge turned to Nancy. "Is the defendant fit to care for your children?" he asked in a gentle tone, tipping his head.

Nancy's face fell, and she appeared to control her emotions with difficulty. She looked up at the judge, her expression sad. "I don't believe so, Your honor."

"If it's not too troubling, could you explain why, please?"

Audrey gripped the edges of her chair seat fiercely, disgusted by the judge's deference to Nancy's flagrant manipulation. Nancy's attorney whispered something to her.

"My ex's sister didn't notice my son's symptoms of type 1 diabetes until it was almost too late." Nancy's voice was husky. "If I had known, I would have come back right away."

Clearly, Nancy and her counsel had done their research.

Luke sighed and stood. "She should have been there in

the first place, your honor."

"I'm listening to the plaintiff," said the judge sternly. Luke's handcuffs clinked as he sat. The judge looked at Nancy. "Go on."

"Audrey can't care much about my kids. The first thing she did was hire a nanny to take over, so she could carry on with her career. She only went full time as a guardian because my son got sick."

The judge looked at Audrey. "Is that true?"

"I hired the nanny for the weekdays because I needed to keep my job. My work required me to leave the house early and get back late."

"But you're not working now, except as a grocery clerk. How have you managed that?"

"I've lived off my savings. I also sold my Tesla. You can see that in Exhibit 6."

"So, you hired the nanny to avoid full-time childcare?"

Audrey saw the traces of interest fade from the judge's expression. No doubt his docket was full, and he wanted to get on with his day. She tried anyway. "No, your honor. Exhibit 6 shows my financial planning for the year of my guardianship. I hired the nanny to ensure the kids had care, and I could provide adequately until their dad returned home."

"Why didn't you keep her?"

"Warwick was diagnosed with type 1 diabetes. I felt he needed my full-time attention. It's a serious disease."

"So even though you missed the signs, you felt you had the capacity to look after him?"

"I learned, like any caregiver must. If Nancy regains custody, she will have to learn the whole disease herself, and she's not mature enough to handle it. Type 1 diabetes requires—"

"That's enough!" The distracted murmuring in the gallery quieted at the judge's raised voice.

"Can you care for a child with type 1 diabetes?" he asked

Nancy.

"Of course, your honor. I'm a mom."

Someone in the gallery chuckled. The judge shifted in his seat, removed his glasses, and rubbed his eyes. "The court orders that sole physical custody of the three children, Easton Beach, Lillie Beach, and Warwick Beach, be returned to their mother, Nancy Beach." He shuffled his papers. "I have found the children's mother competent to care for her children. She will share joint legal custody with the children's father, Luke Beach.

"My findings are informed by the Parent Preference Rule, which grants a fit biological parent preference over any third party. Therefore, the temporary guardianship of the children provided by their aunt, Audrey Beach, is terminated immediately."

"At least let me show her how to care for Warwick!" Audrey yelled, tears coursing down her cheeks. She sat and put her hands over her face, shaking and trying to stifle her sobs.

The judge paused, and Audrey looked up. He was perusing the exhibits both parties had provided. "Nancy Beach, the mother of the above-mentioned children, will meet with Audrey Beach to go over the care of Warwick Beach for his type 1 diabetes. Nancy Beach will reside with the children at the residence located at 132 Love Creek Road in Ben Lomond."

Luke sighed.

"Your honor, my client would like to request visitation rights," said Michelle, rising. "Maintaining contact with their aunt is in the children's best interests."

"Audrey Beach may work with the children's parents, Luke Beach and Nancy Beach, to schedule weekly visitation with the three above-mentioned children. The children's visits with their father will also continue as they were for as long as he is incarcerated. You may work the details out between yourselves and file a court order." He looked in turns at Luke, Audrey, and Nancy, and set his papers aside. "The court is adjourned."

CHAPTER FORTY-TWO

Audrey moved to a rented room in Boulder Creek, to be near the kids. The landlady's kitchen clock, on the other side of her bedroom wall, ticked and chimed the hours. Most nights, she barely slept, swinging between faith and fear as she worried about Warwick's overnight blood sugar levels.

Her meeting with Nancy had partially reassured her. Nancy was immature, but not stupid. Audrey had walked her through the thick binder and explained Warwick's insulin-to-carb ratios. She was satisfied that Nancy understood the basics of her son's doses, his pump, and the timing of meals. Audrey had urged her to contact the diabetes educators at the hospital if she was stuck.

"Warwick's quarterly wellness check with his endocrinologist is scheduled for August. You should call to confirm." Audrey pressed Dr. Taylor's business card into Nancy's hand.

"Thanks, Audrey. I'm sure we'll be fine." Nancy said goodbye and closed the kitchen door, smug and self-assured.

On Saturday and Sunday afternoons, Audrey took the kids to see Luke. Warwick's blood sugar was usually within range, and Easton told Audrey that he reminded his mom to check Warwick's levels each night. After their visits with Luke, they went to the beach and then out for dinner. Nancy said they might as well; she needed the time for self-care.

Audrey updated her resume and put in applications at

some law firms, planning to resume her career. But when a request for an interview arrived, she ignored it.

She was relieved that Nancy kept the kids enrolled in the summer camps she had chosen. The kids had looked forward to the activities.

Sometimes, she drove up Love Creek Road, slowing at the cabin. The kids were usually away. Once, Audrey saw them playing outside. Lillie practiced a gymnastics flip. Warwick swung a stick at the bushes, and Easton rode a new bike around the driveway. She rolled down her window and listened.

Warwick tossed the stick aside. "Lillie, I've got more raptors than you." He raised his hands to play their dinosaur game.

"I don't play that anymore." Lillie flipped onto her hands and arched over gracefully.

The kitchen door opened. "Easton! Get in here and do the dishes."

Easton left the shiny bike on its side in the dirt and trudged to the kitchen. Audrey sobbed as she drove away.

CHAPTER FORTY-THREE

Early July's fierce sunshine pressed down on Paradise Valley in Arizona, the sun a merciless dictator. Streets sent up shimmering mirages, animals sought shade, children stayed inside and played video games.

Breaking glass clashed in the McKenzie residence. Cold water darkened the textured stonework of Dr. McKenzie's home office fireplace. Glass shards sparkled on the floor.

McKenzie slammed his laptop closed, shoved his chair away from his desk, and stood. He grabbed his phone and strode to the living room.

Wrinkled clothes, dirty plates, and liquor bottles covered the floor. A blanket hung off the couch, dragging on the floor. The TV was on, in a low tone.

Hands shaking, McKenzie grabbed a dusty remote and punched the Off button. The TV quieted, and McKenzie threw the remote on the floor. The battery cover cracked open. Scowling, McKenzie kicked the device to the wall.

He sat on the couch, hunched over his phone, and scrolled impatiently to the email he'd viewed on his laptop. "Come on, open!"

Arizona Medical Board was the sender. The subject line read "Investigative Summary." The email stated that Dr. McKenzie was under investigation for treating patients while impaired by alcohol, and for spousal abuse. It did not reveal the complainant's name.

McKenzie stood and pulled up a photo of Nancy, wearing a sunhat he'd bought her to use at the pool. He stared at the picture, his mouth turned down, his jaw tight, his eyes slits.

She was worse than Olivia. He'd realized that the day she left, when he'd peered out from behind the living room curtains at the rideshare vehicle, carrying her away. Later that day, he'd found an empty whiskey bottle on the apartment floor. Later still, he'd found his checking account empty.

Suddenly, a smile curled his lips. He scrolled through the photographs and found the picture of Nancy's family at Christmas. Nancy was with her ex. Audrey read to Lillie on the couch. Easton and Warwick played with lightsabers.

Dr. McKenzie returned to his office. He opened his laptop and searched for Audrey Beach. He researched the family, their connections, their places of work. More digging gave him a specific detail:

The Beach home, where Nancy's children lived, was on Love Creek Road in Ben Lomond.

CHAPTER FORTY-FOUR

"Lillie, put your clothes away!" Nancy stood in her daughter's doorway. She'd already told her several times, strongly. But Lillie still sat on her bed, staring at the phone Nancy had given her the week before. That phone cost a lot. Lillie was taking it for granted.

Nancy scooped a load of dirty laundry off her daughter's floor. "What part of clean don't you understand?" She stomped down the hall and threw the clothes into the washer, next to the kitchen. Briefly, she considered calling McKenzie.

She considered calling him often now. Kids were a lot of work. It would be nice to have a man around the house. Maybe Olivia had driven McKenzie crazy, and that was why he was mean. She guessed she could get past being called an idiot if he supported her—and never did it again.

She poured detergent into the machine, switched it on, and went to the bathroom. She'd gained ten pounds since coming back. Stress eating. She turned sideways, studying her figure. Not bad, even with the extra weight. Maybe she'd call him tonight.

Someone pounded on the front door. Weird.

"Open it!" she shouted, towards the kitchen. Warwick was supposed to be doing the dishes. None of the kids did what they were told. Audrey had spoiled them.

The door scraped across the floor as Warwick dragged it

open. It needed fixing.

"You must be Warwick."

Nancy stared at her reflection, astonished to hear Harrison's voice. She wasn't wearing makeup. Quickly, she tousled her hair into place and yanked on the flattering t-shirt she'd dropped on the floor the night before. She dashed to the kitchen. "Harrison!"

He ignored her. He leaned against the doorpost, hands in the pockets of his expensive shorts, sneering down at Warwick. "Your mom's in trouble."

Warwick put his finger on his chin. "Hmm." He raised his finger. "I'm going to my room."

McKenzie jerked him back. "You're not, actually." His bloodshot eyes met Nancy's, and he pulled a handgun from his jacket pocket. His thick finger curled around the trigger. "Traitor!"

A gun! She held her breath, shaking. Easton and Lillie came from their rooms and stood behind her, staring at McKenzie.

"Mommy, who's that?" Lillie began crying.

"Shut up!" McKenzie roared. Lillie started and clung to Nancy. Easton stepped in front of Lillie.

McKenzie glanced around the cabin. "Sit in there—all of you!" He waved the gun towards the living room and shoved Warwick in that direction. Nancy and the children huddled on the couch. McKenzie followed them and stopped, swaying, in the doorway. "So, Nancy, it's been a while. How've you been?"

Nancy kept her eyes down. "Put the gun away, Harrison."

"I said, how've you been?" McKenzie screamed and stepped closer. "Answer me!" He added profanities.

Nancy squeezed her eyes closed and pulled the children close. "OK." The kids whimpered.

McKenzie grabbed Nancy's chin and yanked her head up. "I got an email, *darling,* from the Arizona Medical

Board." He tightened his fingers, bruising her jaw. His voice softened, almost to a whisper. "How dare you betray me?"

Tears stung Nancy's eyes. "I don't know what you're talking about." Her voice was high-pitched and tight.

McKenzie released her jaw and slapped her, hard. The shock sent her crashing into Easton, beside her. The kids wailed. "Don't lie to me!" He glanced at the children. "Quiet!"

Nancy stood and laid her hand on the familiar bulk of his chest. His breath reeked of hard liquor. "Harrison, please, we can talk—"

He shoved her onto the couch. "Oh, no, Nancy. Not after what you've done." He gripped the gun in both hands and pointed it at her.

"Mommy, what did you do?" Lillie's voice was small and trembling.

"Nothing! McKenzie, I did nothing!" She shook, uncontrollably.

Warwick put his finger on his chin. "Hmm," he whimpered, tears coursing down his cheeks.

McKenzie grabbed Warwick's hair, raising his head. "I said no talking."

Warwick closed his eyes and clenched his fists, his small brow creased. "My blood sugar's high."

"He needs his insulin." Easton's voice was stress-bound. "His pump battery died."

McKenzie swung the gun at Easton. Easton shut his eyes, grimacing, and instinctively, Nancy pulled her son close. McKenzie turned and paced the room, his fist pressed against his forehead. He breathed hard, staring at the floor. Suddenly, he spun to face the family. "Warwick, you're coming with me."

Nancy looked up. "No!"

Warwick clung to Nancy, crying. She held him tightly.

"Get duct tape." McKenzie swung the gun to Easton again. "Don't try anything, or I'll shoot your mom."

Easton went into the kitchen and brought back a roll of tape. Sweating, McKenzie taped Nancy, Easton, and Lillie's wrists, then secured their ankles to the couch legs. Unbound, Warwick huddled close to Nancy. McKenzie tore the boy from Nancy's side, his strong hand a vice around Warwick's slender arm.

"Don't take me!"

"Stop!" Nancy screamed. Easton and Lillie cried.

Waving the gun, McKenzie walked backwards to the kitchen, dragging Warwick.

Nancy struggled against her restraints. "Let him go!"

McKenzie cursed and hoisted Warwick over his shoulder. He went out the open door and slammed it behind him. Through the kitchen window, Nancy heard her son screaming. A car door slammed, an engine roared. Tires ground over dirt. Then, all she heard was the clamor of jays, madly squawking their alarm, and her children's frantic cries.

CHAPTER FORTY-FIVE

"Audrey, it's Nancy." Nancy's voice was tight.

Audrey stared at her phone. "Everything OK?"

"Warwick was taken, about half an hour ago. I need your help," Nancy rapid-fired.

Adrenaline catapulted Audrey to her feet. "Taken? Who took him?"

Nancy's voice slowed. "A guy I was dating showed up and took Warwick. He duct-taped me and the kids. An officer's coming to take you to the Felton police office, because you're family. Sheriff Baker is picking us up. We'll meet you there. Will that work for you?"

Audrey's heart pounded. "Where's Warwick now?" She paced her bedroom, running her hand through her hair.

"Listen, I don't know. Just meet us there, please? I have to go."

"Of course!"

~

What's she done now? Audrey threw herself into the patrol car's back seat.

"Fasten your seatbelt, Ma'am." Officer Partow flipped on the siren, and the vehicle wailed as it rushed down the narrow roads to Boulder Creek. Horses, cars, and pedestrians filled the streets for Boulder Creek's annual Fourth of July Parade. Partow bleeped the siren and pushed through traffic, along Highway 9.

Audrey exhaled through pursed lips, swiping absently through her phone screens. The app icon to Warwick's continuous glucose monitor caught her eye. She opened it. The green and blue pattern swirled a welcome, then displayed the login screen, which she couldn't use. She stared at the faded options, behind the login. Parents could check their child's blood sugar levels, history, and insulin delivery—the latter, if a pump was connected to the monitor.

They could also access their child's location.

Audrey leaned forward. "Officer, my nephew is wearing a medical device that will give us his location. I can't access it, but his mom can."

The officer paged the Sheriff.

~

Nancy sat in the back of Sheriff Baker's patrol car, with the kids. The Sheriff didn't speak as he blared the siren and darted past cars along Highway 9.

A woman's voice came over the radio. "Victim's aunt says (static, static) to give the child's location."

"Repeat that, please." Baker eased the patrol car past sidelined traffic, flipped on the siren, and pushed through a red light.

"The (static) says the victim is (static) a GPS device."

"OK. I guess I need more information."

"(Static) the victim has a GPS," the officer repeated.

"How do we access it?" Baker asked, patiently.

"(Static, static) the login information."

The radio quieted. Sheriff Baker ran his hand over his thinning hair.

"I think I know what she means." Easton spoke timidly.

In the rear-view mirror, Baker's greying eyebrows lifted. "Go ahead."

"My brother has a glucose monitor. It tracks his blood sugar and his location."

"Do you know how to access it, son?"

"The app is on my mom's phone."

In the mirror, Baker's tired brown eyes swung to Nancy. "Can you open it, Ma'am?" He quieted the siren and picked up speed through thinning traffic.

Nancy yanked out her phone and swiped through cluttered screens. "I can't find it."

"I know what it looks like." Easton gently took her phone, found the app, and handed the phone back to her.

"I remember this." Nancy tapped on the login field, then squeezed her eyes shut and frowned. She'd only opened the app once.

"Mom, do you know the password?" Easton asked.

Baker slowed the car and turned in at the Sheriff's office parking lot.

"I don't." She sighed and wiped her nose with her sleeve, then rubbed her sweaty palms along her jeans.

Baker remained silent. He parked and led the family inside.

~

They crossed the receptionist's area, went into a hallway, and entered a small room with a folding table in the center. A cluttered desk was squeezed into one corner, a credenza under the window. Baker gestured to metal-frame chairs around the table. Nancy and the kids sat.

Sheriff Baker picked up the phone on the desk. He issued an Amber Alert. He ordered a shelter-in-place for San Lorenzo Valley's towns. After activating the SWAT team, which began gathering at the Live Oak Police Station in Santa Cruz, he left the room.

Another officer entered. The brass name plate pinned to his shirt read J. Rodriguez. Younger than Baker, he grabbed paper and pens from the desk and set them on the table. "For notes." He sat opposite Nancy. "Did you bring an item for the K-9 unit?"

Nancy handed a small t-shirt to Officer Rodriguez. "Unwashed." Why had she ever cared that the kids wouldn't do their laundry?

Officer Rodriguez laughed. "The riper, the better." He opened a laptop. "I'm going to ask you some questions, Ma'am."

Nancy told him all she remembered about McKenzie's profession, personal life, and history, until she was sick of thinking about the monster who had her son. At last, Rodriguez closed the laptop. "When the SWAT team takes over, this information will give them a head start. I looked up his online profiles, too."

~

Nancy swiped at her tears, too stunned to know how to comfort her children. Too worried about Warwick.

Lillie leaned towards Easton. "What's a K-9 unit?"

Easton shrugged.

"When we're trying to find someone, we use a dog." Rodriguez leaned back in his chair.

Lillie's eyes brightened. "Can I see?"

Rodriguez pulled up a photo and turned his phone towards Lillie and Easton. They stared at a muscular Belgian Malinois.

"Will that dog find my brother?" Easton asked.

"He will, or we will. Somehow, we'll find him." Rodriguez sounded confident. Nancy took a little hope.

Sheriff Baker returned. "Could I see the app for your son's medical device please, Ma'am?"

She handed the Sheriff her phone. He took the landline phone from the desk and set it on the table. He looked up the device manufacturer on a tablet and called their number. When the phone system announced the company was closed for the holiday, he hung up.

~

McKenzie swerved onto a broad overlook off Highway 9 and killed the engine of the rented SUV. He yanked Warwick out of the backseat and pulled him to the end of the parking area. Hoisting him over his shoulder, he edged around the cement barrier and scrambled down the wooded hillside, between redwoods and manzanita bushes, ferns and rocks.

Reaching the valley, he jogged north along the railroad tracks that ran from Felton to Santa Cruz, Warwick bouncing on his back. Voices sounded from the river below. McKenzie paused, listening. Sweat dripped down his face and darkened his shirt. He ran on.

Around a corner, people walked, carrying towels. McKenzie dove off the tracks and crouched low behind a rock.

"Quiet," he warned Warwick.

The people passed and McKenzie jogged on, until a tall trestle bridge loomed ahead, spanning the San Lorenzo River. Voices rose from the water below, where families played. McKenzie dodged into the undergrowth. He set Warwick down and looked around quickly.

His fingers pressed against the CGM device beneath Warwick's t-shirt. He lifted the shirt and yanked the device from Warwick's skin. He held it against a tree trunk, smashed it with the butt of his gun, and hurled it into the undergrowth.

Picking Warwick up again, he headed south from the bridge, finally crossing the river at a deserted area. He sloshed onto the opposite bank and began ascending the mountainside.

CHAPTER FORTY-SIX

Officer Partow parked at the Sheriff's office and Audrey hurried inside. He showed her into a room and left for his patrol duties. Nancy and the kids sat at a table, with a young officer and an older man Audrey guessed was the Sheriff.

She joined Nancy at the table, barely able to look at her. Whatever was going on, she had no doubt Nancy's selfishness had played a role. Easton and Lillie joined her, snuggling onto the chairs on either side of her. Nancy glanced her way, mumbled a greeting, and lowered her gaze.

"Warwick's blood sugar was high when he left, and he doesn't have his pump," Easton said, shakily.

"How does that effect our planning?" The younger officer wore a nameplate—Rodriguez.

"It could be a medical crisis." Audrey's heart thudded as she directed the kids back to their mom. Nancy covered her face and sobbed. Lillie followed her example.

"Don't worry, we're going to find him." Officer Rodriguez leaned across the table and squeezed Lillie's shoulder. "These types of situations are what we're here for."

"I realize this is difficult, Ma'am," said the Sheriff, "but we need your attention. We never know when someone might remember a detail that can help us." He rose and took a box of Kleenexes from the credenza, which he offered to

Nancy, shooting her a stern look. Nancy gulped and blew her nose. Lillie calmed down.

"Can we get the kid's doctor here?" The Sheriff—Baker, his nameplate said—sat down.

Nancy frowned. "I don't have his information."

Audrey blew out a frustrated sigh. "I've got it." She entered Dr. Taylor's number into her phone.

Officer Rodriguez handed out chilled water from a mini-refrigerator. He took a box of granola bars from the credenza and set them on the table. Easton and Lillie glanced at their mom. She nodded absently. Soon, crumbs lay across the table.

~

The white sails of Eric's Flying Scot snapped taut, propelling the boat across Monterey Bay. The winches clicked with the ropes' movements, adjusting the angle of the sails. The wind whispered, and the hull swished through the water.

Eric perched on the boat's side, leaning back. The boat exited a wide arc, and he straightened. It was a great day for sailing. Only Audrey's companionship would have made it perfect.

His phone pinged. Audrey had texted him. "Please call me. URGENT!" He had missed her call, his ring tone silenced. He went aft, pointed the boat towards the harbor, and entered Audrey's number.

Her voice was frantic. "Dr. Taylor, Warwick's been kidnapped. You should go to the Sheriff's office in Felton."

He leaned forward, heart pounding. "Are you OK?"

"Someone's kidnapped Warwick. Please hurry!"

"On my way, Audrey." He analyzed the wind, trimmed the sail, and willed the boat forward.

~

The boat cut through the water, towards the harbor. Eric guided her into her dock. The bow smacked against wood. He leapt out, whipped the boat's lines around its cleats, and dashed to the Tesla.

Santa Cruz was crowded. While he crept through traffic, he opened an app to Warwick's CGM, hoping to locate the boy. But the password was in his office, and the app denied access.

Highway 17 was more open, and he sped through Scotts Valley to Felton. At the Sheriff's Office, he parked and jogged to the door.

The receptionist leapt to his feet and yanked open an inner door. "Back there. They're waiting for you."

He stepped into a short hallway. A door opened, and an officer beckoned him into a briefing room. Inside, Audrey, Warwick's siblings, and a woman Eric didn't know sat around a table with the Sheriff. Easton and Lillie sat close to the woman, Easton half-sprawled in his chair, Lillie leaning against her. Audrey acknowledged Eric with a nod.

The Sheriff offered him a phone. "Please access Warwick Beach's GPS on his medical device."

"Already tried. I need to call my assistant." He pulled up Jenny's number.

The Sheriff removed his glasses, rubbed his eyes, and leaned back in his chair, watching Eric.

"Hi, Dr. Taylor! Happy Fourth!" Jenny's clear phone voice filled the room.

"Jenny, can you give me the password to Warwick Beach's CGM, please?"

The officer slid paper and pen across the table. Eric yanked a chair back from the table and sat, grabbing the pen.

"I'm at a parade with my husband right now. Is it urgent?"

"Very."

There was a long pause. Sounds of cars, band music, and laughter came over the phone's speaker. Eric clenched his jaw, staring at the table.

"Ready?"

"Go ahead." He scratched down the password she read

off.

"Is Warwick OK?"

"He's been kidnapped. I'll update you when I can."

"Oh my gosh! Please keep in touch."

~

"Got it! His last report was at one forty-two. He was here." Eric handed his phone to the Sheriff.

The Sheriff squinted, then tossed the phone aside, suddenly as energetic as a greyhound bursting from the starting gate. "He's at Henry Cowell Park. Get the t-shirt over there, Rodriguez."

Officer Rodriguez dashed out the door, clutching the shirt. A siren screamed, then faded, indicating his route to the park. The Sheriff grabbed a desk phone's receiver and punched in a number.

"Officer Starnes," a man answered.

"Starnes, this is Roger Baker in Felton. Kidnapping victim was in Henry Cowell Redwoods State Park at 1:42 p.m., near the Trestle Bridge. I'm ordering the park closed and searched. How's your SWAT team coming together?"

"We're leaving now."

Eric waved his hand, attracting the Sheriff's attention. "Sheriff, the CGM is supposed to send signals every ten minutes. Its last signal was over an hour ago. It's not working."

"Got it." Sheriff Baker sped through calls, spitting out terse orders to park rangers and officers, slamming down the receiver, picking it up again to reach his next subordinate.

~

Eric looked at Audrey. Her face was pale, her slim eyebrows pinched. Her clothes were wrinkled, her hair gripped into a messy ponytail.

She gestured to the woman he didn't know. "Dr. Taylor, this is Nancy, Warwick's mom."

Their mother was back? He gaped for an instant, then extended his hand. "How do you do?"

Nancy looked at him, her eyes bloodshot and tired. Her blond hair frizzed, untamed, around her face. A tattoo peeked from beneath the edge of her t-shirt's neckline. She shook his hand, showing fingernails that were bitten to the quick. Had she resumed custody of the children? If so, Audrey must have been devastated.

Sheriff Baker summoned Officer Partow from his patrol. Minutes later, Partow arrived. "Partow, you'll wait here. I'll serve as temporary incident commander at Henry Cowell, until the SWAT team arrives. Once they're set up, the SWAT will brief you all as events unfold. Dr. Taylor, do we know how the kidnapped child is doing?"

Eric cleared his throat and turned away from Nancy. "Warwick's blood sugar was 416 mg/dL at 1:42. Fortunately he wears an insulin pump, which delivers insulin automatically to reduce the glucose load."

"He's not wearing his pump," Easton said.

Eric stared at Easton, then looked again at Nancy, whose face was red. "Where is the pump?"

Nancy took the device from a tote bag and handed it to him. "The battery's dead."

"Double A battery, please," Eric requested, switching to work mode. This was no time to analyze Audrey's family dynamics.

The Sheriff fetched a battery from the reception area. Soon, the pump screen glowed. Now he could access Warwick's doses. "Sheriff, the patient's blood glucose is likely too high. Without insulin, he's in danger of ketoacidosis. How can we ensure he's treated quickly?"

"The TEMS ambulance is bringing insulin to the command center in the parking lot. The negotiator will focus on his medical condition as a bargaining device, Warwick being the kidnapper's leverage."

"How close can I get?" Eric pressed.

"That'll be up to the SWAT incident commander. You can't approach the situation until they apprehend the suspect.

When we learn his exact location, we'll establish a perimeter to contain him. Then, you might be allowed at the command center." The Sheriff stood and tossed an empty water bottle into a trash can.

This didn't look good.

"What is ketoacidosis?" Nancy spoke quietly.

"An acidic blood condition." Why didn't she know that?

"What do you think his blood sugar is now?" Her eyebrows peaked.

"I can't know. His CGM is down."

Audrey huffed, quietly.

Sheriff Baker went to the door. "I'll be in touch." He left, and soon another siren wailed through the town.

Easton turned to his mother. "Mom, ketoacidosis is serious. Warwick had it when he was diagnosed."

Nancy nodded, squeezed Easton's hand, and stared at the table. "Thanks." She whispered something, but Eric didn't catch it.

"What, Mom?" Audrey's niece pulled away from her mother, looking at her intently.

"I'm so sorry." Nancy glanced at her daughter, then looked at the others in turn, her face flushed. "I'm truly sorry."

The girl climbed onto Nancy's lap. "I love you, Mom."

Warwick's mother folded her arms around Lillie and sobbed.

CHAPTER FORTY-SEVEN

To Audrey's relief, Nancy's tears quieted. Audrey listened to Partow's radio as Sheriff Baker filled them in. The Sheriff was waiting in the Visitor Center parking lot for the SWAT team. His shelter-in-place order had shut down a living history festival at Roaring Camp. Actors and visitors filled the barn, train cars, and museum buildings at the bottom of the lawn.

The police presence was heavy, owing to the holiday. Patrol vehicles were blocking all exits from Henry Cowell Park and Roaring Camp Railroads. The park rangers were having a little trouble keeping the crowds from panic. They needed Sheriff Baker's help. "I'll be in touch." Partow's radio went quiet, and Partow returned it to his clip.

~

Audrey slipped paper and pens across the table to her niece and nephew. "Draw me a picture of the K-9." They needed a distraction.

The kids scribbled a little. Lillie tossed her pen aside and leaned on Nancy's shoulder. Fiercely, Easton slashed lines across the page, his fist tight. The radio crackled. The kids looked up.

"Partow, this is Baker. The SWAT team's here. They're setting up the Command Center in the parking lot. The K-9 has the victim's scent. Its handler is taking the K-9 to the trestle bridge, where the CGM gave its last signal. Over."

The radio went silent. Audrey wrang her hands. Dr. Taylor drummed his fingers lightly on the table.

The radio crackled again. "The K-9 found the medical device. It was destroyed. K-9 leading them to the river."

Easton looked up from his drawing, fixated on the radio.

"Ambulance and fire engine present. I'll remain at the Command Center to assist as needed. Commander Starnes will update you going forward."

~

Starnes told them the SWAT team was gathering intel, drilling docents about the park layout, and performing background checks on McKenzie. Other SWAT team members brainstormed rescue plans, including a last-resort contingency plan, "in case things go sideways," he said.

Audrey shuddered. The updates, though essential, amplified her stress. Every communication underscored the danger her nephew was in. She kept an eye on Lillie and Easton.

"My tummy hurts." Lillie stood and lay on her tummy, over her chair seat.

~

Late afternoon, they learned the K-9 had led its handlers to the top of the mountain and signaled that McKenzie and Warwick were inside the base of an Observation Deck. Audrey searched for the Deck. Images on her phone showed a rectangular structure at the top of a hill. Cement walls supported the Deck. An old staircase led up one side, brown paint peeling off its banister. A metal door provided access to the Deck's base.

Three trails converged at the Deck—one coming through a sandy habitat, another wider path, and a third, narrow trail, leading into the forest on the opposite side. Beyond the Deck, the Santa Cruz Mountains lay in dusky ridges, descending to Monterey Bay.

Audrey considered showing the pictures to the others. Realizing they could upset the kids, she put her phone down.

Easton and Lillie went to the window, jostling each other.

"Stop shoving me, Easton!"

Nancy didn't seem to notice their stress.

~

Commander Starnes radioed the briefing room. The SWAT team had established a containment perimeter, and Sheriff Baker had lifted the shelter-in-place order. The police were evacuating Henry Cowell Park and Roaring Camp.

"There's no cell reception at the Deck, but we'll send a throw phone on a robot. If he takes it, our negotiators will communicate for Warwick's release."

Partow's radio buzzed, and a new voice spoke. "I'm Negotiation Team Leader Forrest Jackson. I have a few questions to help with strategic development."

"Sure." Dr. Taylor spoke for all of them.

"Is Audrey Beach there, please?"

"Here." She leaned close to Partow's radio.

"Do you know the hostage taker, Ma'am?"

"I haven't heard his name yet."

"Dr. Harrison McKenzie. He's an endocrinologist. Is that name familiar?"

Audrey stared at the radio, looked at Nancy, turned to Dr. Taylor. The doctor looked back at her, his eyes round. Audrey's mind reeled. What was McKenzie thinking? And how did Nancy know him? The strange phone call she'd received from McKenzie replayed in her mind.

"Ma'am?" The SWAT member needed her input.

"I—yes. He was my expert witness in a med mal case. I'm a personal injury attorney."

"Wait, what?" Nancy gaped.

Audrey just nodded.

"Thanks. Nancy Beach, do you know McKenzie?"

Nancy looked away from Audrey quickly, her face red. "I was... involved with him. It's in the notes Officer

Rodriguez gave you."

Wow! Just... wow. Audrey struggled to keep her mouth shut. Now the phone call made sense.

Easton and Lillie fidgeted, looking out the window. They didn't appear to notice Nancy's statement.

"Dr. Taylor, do you have a connection with the subject?"

Now Dr. Taylor reddened. "I, um… I was the defendant in the case Audrey mentioned."

Easton turned from the window, frowning, and looked at Audrey. "What's a defendant?"

Audrey shook her head. "Later." This was a real fun party.

"We're coming to the briefing room," said Jackson. "I will try to establish a rapport with McKenzie when he has the throw phone. Supporting Negotiator Elliot will coach you on negotiating with a hostage taker."

Audrey stared at Partow's radio. "What do you mean?"

"It's unlikely you'll speak to McKenzie, but since you all know him, you might become 'accidental negotiators.'"

"Shouldn't trained negotiators handle this?" Audrey pleaded.

"Of course. But this is a volatile situation. The kidnapper didn't set this up rationally, he's emotionally charged, and anything could happen. We want you prepared."

CHAPTER FORTY-EIGHT

Lillie returned to the table, fiddling with a paperclip she'd found on the floor. "Mommy, I'm bored."

"Shh, baby." Nancy scooted a chair closer to hers. Lillie curled up and rested her head on Nancy's lap.

Easton sat down and lay his head on his arms, yawning. "I miss Warwick."

"Nancy, come with me." Audrey led Nancy to the hallway, stuffing her anger and shelving her fears about negotiating with McKenzie. Closing the door, she turned to her ex-sister-in-law. "I can ask Lillie's gym coach to watch Lillie and Easton. It's too stressful for them here. What do you think?"

Nancy nodded. "I think that's a good idea."

"I'll call her. Why don't you get them ready?" Audrey dialed Dominique's number.

As Nancy turned back to the briefing room, she paused. "Audrey?"

Audrey raised her eyebrows, listening for Dominique's voice.

"Thanks for all you've done for my kids." Nancy's eyes welled with tears.

Audrey took a step back, her anger flaring again. *God, does she even understand what she's saying?* The trauma from this event would plague the kids for life—to say nothing of the impact of Nancy's abandonment. The damage to Audrey's career was minor in comparison.

...forgiving each other... just as the Lord forgave you, so also should you.

The command was harder than Audrey had ever imagined. She stopped the call to Dominique and closed her eyes for a long moment.

Forgive...

Feeling nothing, but choosing faith, she laid aside the stony words she longed to throw and reached her hand to Nancy. The warmth she'd felt when Luke had told her about the Bible study flooded her again. Gently, she squeezed Nancy's arm. "You're welcome, Nancy."

Nancy returned to the conference room. Audrey reentered the gym coach's number and made her request.

Minutes later, Dominique arrived. "We have a new puppy!" She hugged Lillie and led them out, one arm around each child, chatting softly as they went.

~

Two men joined them in the briefing room.

"I'm Negotiator Forrest Jackson. This is Supporting Negotiator Ben Elliot." Jackson, silver-haired and in his fifties, plugged in a brown intercom box and set it on the table. He attached a cable and radio and began quietly testing a conference phone and two headsets. His movements were focused, his demeanor casual. The tension in Audrey's core relaxed a little.

"With this setup, I can hear everything going on, as well as speak with the hostage taker. I can listen in on calls and communicate with SWAT Commander Starnes, who will also hear our conversations." He put on a headset, handed one to Elliot, and pointed to the conference phone. "That phone's our line to the throw phone. I'll talk to McKenzie on it—and you will, too, if needed."

Negotiator Elliot sat at the end of the table, leaned

forward, and clasped his hands. He was a slight man with intense blue eyes and a shadow of dark stubble along his jaw. "Listen to the subject," he advised. "Hostage takers are wound tight. Validate his perspective, diffuse the tension, build trust. Otherwise, no deal."

Dr. Taylor mirrored his posture. "Can we get insulin up to the Deck? That's our immediate priority."

Elliot smiled. "Our immediate priority is to build rapport. We'll send the victim's medication on the robot, but it won't help unless McKenzie gives it to the kid. If we can drag this out, the subject's emotions will calm, and he may negotiate."

Dr. Taylor slammed down his hand, startling Audrey. "We can't drag this out. I don't know the patient's blood sugar level. He could be critical."

"Acknowledged." Elliot didn't flinch. "Our first objective will be to learn the victim's condition. Unfortunately, the subject's mental state also makes this critical. A direct assault to extract the victim comes with high risks."

Partow's radio crackled. "This is Sheriff Baker. Officer Partow, please report to Roaring Camp to assist me with evacuation."

"Copy." Partow left for his new assignment.

Elliot and Jackson walked Audrey and the others through possible scenarios. They decided to offer McKenzie a chat with Nancy if Warwick was stable. First, McKenzie must treat Warwick's blood sugar and send pictures proving he had done so. They drafted an email from Nancy to the Arizona Medical Board. They would send McKenzie a copy, if needed.

If Warwick's condition was critical, the SWAT operators would enact their contingency assault plan—despite the risks to Warwick's safety.

Audrey sighed. So much could go wrong.

"Can McKenzie administer insulin?" Negotiator Elliot asked Dr. Taylor.

"I wouldn't trust him to give an aspirin, in his current state."

"This may be all we've got."

"I understand."

Elliot finished his coaching while they waited for the throw phone to reach McKenzie. "I know you're nervous but keep respect and empathy in mind and you'll do fine."

Nancy squeezed a tissue into a tight wad. Dr. Taylor stared out the window. Audrey gripped her hands together, trying to stay calm.

~

"McKenzie took the throw phone," Commander Starnes confirmed. "Go ahead and reach out, Negotiator Jackson."

"I'll step out to make this call." Jackson pressed a button on his headset. "Minimizes distractions."

Minutes later, he returned. "I wish I had better news. McKenzie refuses to talk to anyone except the three of you. He wants to begin with you, Audrey."

I'm a lawyer, not a counselor! Audrey grabbed her hair at the roots and squeezed her eyes shut. Her specialty was talking tough and asserting dominance. The finer points of listening and empathy were not in her wheelhouse—not even close.

The conference phone rang.

CHAPTER FORTY-NINE

"Audrey, this is Dr. McKenzie."

"Dr. McKenzie." She struggled to keep her voice level. "How's it going?"

"Not great. Put Nancy on the line. You must know where she is."

Jackson shook his head, his lips forming a "No."

"Sorry, I can't help you with that."

"You'll find a way if it keeps Warwick safe."

Elliot passed a note to Audrey. *"Take a message."*

"Can I take, um, can I get… can I give her a message?" Sweat ran down Audrey's neck and spine.

"Tell her to email the Arizona Medical Board and say she lied. I want to talk to her, too."

"I'll try." Audrey paused, heart thudding. "How's Warwick?"

"He's fine." McKenzie sighed into the phone impatiently. "Get this right, Audrey. I want to keep him that way."

"Can I talk to him?"

Elliot nodded approval.

There was a long pause. "Hey, Warwick! Want to speak to your aunt?"

A clattering suggested McKenzie was handing the phone to her nephew.

"Auntie Audrey?" Warwick's voice was high and shaky.

Everyone shifted in their seats. Tears pooled in Nancy's eyes.

"The phone's on speaker," warned McKenzie.

"Warwick, are you OK?"

"My blood sugar's high." He started crying.

"Sh! Listen up." Audrey spoke sharply. "We're going to get you home safely, I promise. Meanwhile, I want you to stay calm. Understand?"

He quieted and sniffed. "OK."

"I love you, Warwick. Daddy loves you, too, and Mommy, and Easton and Lillie. Everything's going to be OK. Let's pray."

"Um, OK."

She took a deep breath. "Jesus, we are in Your loving care." Her heart rate slowed a little. "Please help us get Warwick safely home. And help Dr. McKenzie…" She paused. How did you pray for a kidnapper? "Show Dr. McKenzie that You are the way, the truth, and the life. Amen."

Again, the phone clattered loudly. "Leave religion out of this!"

The phone beeped, ending the call.

~

Stress bloated Audrey's stomach with sharp pains. Had she just blown their chance at saving Warwick? She turned to Negotiator Jackson. "What now?"

Jackson looked at Dr. Taylor. "What's your assessment of the victim's medical condition?"

"I don't know his blood sugar or ketone levels, but the fact that he carried on a coherent conversation is good."

"Can we continue negotiating? Remember the high risks associated with a tactical assault."

Dr. Taylor looked at the ceiling and wrinkled his brow. "We can try. But not for long."

Audrey gripped the edge of the table, praying for direction.

"You're up next." Elliot's steady tone was unchanged. "Speak to him like a colleague. If he senses respect, that'll diffuse some tension."

"Got it." Dr. Taylor straightened and ran his hand through his hair.

The phone rang again.

~

Purposefully, Eric pushed back from the table, hung his head, and sat quietly. *God, help me out here.* He pressed the phone's talk button, knowing the job was beyond him. Beyond anyone—except God. Peace settled in his chest, slowing his breathing. "Dr. McKenzie, how are you?"

McKenzie sighed. "Not great."

Eric closed his eyes, tuning out the people around him. "Rough day, huh?"

"Yeah."

"Why don't you tell me what's going on?"

"Well, my wife left with our son, for one thing."

"Your wife and son left. Sounds difficult."

"Lying woman accused me of abuse and got custody. Haven't seen my son since April."

The circumstances convinced Eric that McKenzie's wife had told the truth. *Lord, please protect that woman and child.*

"I don't know why I'm talking to you, though." McKenzie's voice suddenly rose. "You're the one who almost killed your patient. And here you are, lecturing me like a saint."

"I don't blame you. I'd feel the same." He wasn't lying. He was no better than McKenzie.

"What?"

"I understand, and I'd feel the same. Dr. McKenzie, can we speak as colleagues?"

"OK."

"I did some soul searching about that case. You're right. I did almost kill Meghan Patel, and I was too proud to admit it. I was a mess until I owned that."

"Huh."

"My negligence was reprehensible." Eric paused, his throat tight. "I settled the case and sent a sincere apology. Then I took some time off to face the truth: I had almost killed a patient."

"Really."

"A Christ-centered support group helped. It's for doctors who struggle with stress, depression, and guilt. I can connect you with that resource." The offer hung in silence—a dangling lifeline over an ocean of sin, awaiting the tug of an answer.

"You know, after my wife left, I loved this other woman who also left. Emptied my checking account, too."

The lifeline twisted idly. Eric cleared his throat.

McKenzie's voice grew louder again. "So, see, this isn't my fault. I was driven to it. Stupid girl didn't know a good thing when she had it. She's Warwick's mom, you know."

Nancy's hair fell over her flushed cheeks. Eric looked out the window. He tried again. "Let's wrap this up, Dr. McKenzie. You and I have a lot of good to do."

"I want my life back."

"I get it." Slowly, Eric lowered his palm to the table's smooth surface as he continued. "Dr. McKenzie, we're very concerned about Warwick. He normally wears an insulin pump, so he doesn't have a long-acting dose on board. If we send up some insulin, will you treat him?"

"Look, Taylor, no one thinks about what I'm going through. What about me?"

Eric didn't know what to say. Movement caught his eye. Elliot was gesturing circles, encouraging him to remain engaged.

"This isn't the real you, Dr. McKenzie. You and I didn't go into medicine to bring harm. Remember your calling."

"I'm doing my calling, Taylor." A gurgled sob came through the speaker. "You think this is easy?"

Eric leaned forward. "We'll get you through this—just like I got through my crisis. It's not too late. Let's get you back to doing good."

Elliot gave a thumbs-up.

"What if I give the kid insulin?"

"That would be great."

"Can I get something in return?"

"Of course! You can chat with Nancy, see about working with the Medical Board to resolve the issue."

"How are you going to get insulin up here?"

"We'll use a robot."

"What is this? Star Wars?"

Out of nowhere, everyone chuckled quietly. Jackson gestured for silence.

"Police use robots to keep everyone safe." Pausing, Eric closed his eyes again. "I want to help you, Dr. McKenzie. You don't need something terrible on your conscience."

"Send up the insulin." McKenzie hung up.

CHAPTER FIFTY

Starnes updated them. "McKenzie took the medical supplies from the robot. Dr. Taylor, you'll work with him to get the kid his medicine. He's ready to talk to you." He patched McKenzie through.

McKenzie's voice was hard and agitated again. "Warwick's blood glucose is 682. He threw up a while ago."

Eric's shoulders tightened. The stress was a thousand times higher than in the ER.

"I'm giving him a corrective dose of nine units, short-acting, and a background dose of the long-acting based on your ratios."

"Thank you." At least he was cooperating. Eric pressed the keys on Warwick's pump and verified the doses. He turned towards the phone. "Please send a picture."

"OK."

The photo McKenzie sent showed a syringe, close-up, with liquid to the black line that indicated nine units. The edges were blurry, the light dim. A second photo of a syringe followed, presumably showing the long-acting dose.

"Can I get photos of you injecting the insulins, please?"

Moments later, he examined images of the needles penetrating skin. McKenzie's thick fingers held the syringe, and his thumb pressed on the flange. Eric remembered the negotiator's advice about respect and empathy. "Good work, Dr. McKenzie. You're doing well. Please send a picture of

Warwick."

When the picture came, Eric exhaled. Warwick's eyes were open, his pupils dilated. He was still conscious. Eric showed the others. Audrey and Nancy hugged each other.

"Put Nancy on," said McKenzie.

~

Nancy took the phone. She pursed her lips, blew out a silent breath, and swiped at her hair. "McKenzie, this is Nancy."

"You know what to do." His voice changed completely—cold, distant.

"I've drafted an email to the Board. Want to see it?" She tried to keep the shaking out of her voice.

"Of course, darling."

McKenzie's thick sarcasm sent a chill across Nancy's shoulders. Why hadn't she seen what he was? She copied and texted the email they had drafted.

Dear Arizona Medical Board:

I'm writing to try to cancel a complaint I filed against Dr. Harrison McKenzie in April 2019. Dr. McKenzie is a good doctor, and I was having a bad day when I filed the complaint. I request that you dismiss my complaint.

Sincerely,

Nancy Beach

The line was quiet while McKenzie read the text. When he spoke, his voice was loud. "A bad day? What kind of exoneration is that?"

Nancy squeezed her eyes shut. "I was trying to—"

"My point, when I began this exercise, was to teach you why you shouldn't persecute a decent doctor. I'm not the criminal here, Nancy. The problem is YOU!"

"McKenzie, please listen to me! We all want what's best—"

McKenzie's voice rose to a scream. "Everything you say is making me worse! You're making me more miserable and defeated, which only fuels my stress and makes me more likely to lose control. Do you think this is easy for me?"

His words were like blows. "McKenzie, I'm sorry, I truly am! Please don't hurt my son." Nancy's heart thudded hard; her stomach clenched like iron.

Negotiator Elliot waved his hand to gain her attention, then put his finger to his lips. She looked at him and fell silent.

"Too little, too late, Nancy." The call ended, and Nancy dropped her face into her hands, weeping again.

CHAPTER FIFTY-ONE

Eric leapt to his feet. He had to reach Warwick immediately. But Negotiator Jackson raised his hand, stopping him and delaying answers to the questions that erupted from the group. He pushed a button on the radio. "Starnes, did you hear that?"

"Positive."

The phone rang again. Jackson answered.

"Put Audrey on." McKenzie sounded less agitated now. Jackson handed the phone to Audrey.

Dark smudges showed under her eyes. Her slim shoulders hunched as she leaned on the table, clutching the phone, her lips turned down. Eric ached to take the phone and carry her burden.

"Audrey, Warwick isn't looking good." McKenzie's voice was calm. Eric heard Warwick crying and saw Audrey's eyes water. "I'm going to give him another fifteen units of short-acting insulin."

"No!" Eric mouthed, gesturing across his throat.

Audrey looked at him, then back at the table, frowning. "Could you verify that's the best strategy with Dr. Taylor, please?"

"Why would I do that? He's the one who almost killed his patient." McKenzie's voice remained steady.

Eric sat down again and held out a hand, requesting the phone. Audrey handed it to him.

"Dr. McKenzie? This is Eric Taylor. I would advise against a second dose." Did he sound as stressed as he felt?

"He's pretty listless. In my professional opinion, the second dose is necessary."

"There's a risk of cerebral edema or hypoglycemia if his blood glucose descends too quickly. Please wait until we can get him to the hospital. He needs to be closely monitored—"

The call ended.

Eric bolted to the door. "We have to go!"

Negotiator Elliot stood. "How long do we have?"

"Half an hour? I can't say for sure. We can't wait."

Elliot paged Commander Starnes. "Starnes, the doctor indicates the last call presents danger to the victim's life."

"Implementing contingency plan. Please remain with the family in the briefing room."

"I need to get closer." It took all Eric's self-control not to yell.

"Do not enter the park until the subject is apprehended," Starnes repeated.

Eric clenched his fists and spun back to the table, fighting the urge to bolt.

Negotiator Jackson stood and put his hand on Eric's shoulder. "Look, waiting is the hardest part. But I trust Starnes, and the SWAT team is capable. The TEMS medical unit is there, too." He turned to Nancy, who fidgeted anxiously by the table. "They'll rescue your son, Ma'am. Let's everyone have a seat, please."

~

Tense as a highwire, Audrey waited with the others for updates.

Nancy rubbed her eyes and sighed. "I can't just sit here. Can I go outside and walk a little?"

Jackson stood. "Sure. We'll accompany you. Anyone else?"

"I'm fine." Audrey was too stressed to leave the radio.

"I'll stay here." Dr. Taylor's brow was furrowed.

The two negotiators and Nancy went outside. Through the window, Audrey saw them strolling around the parking lot. The shadows were growing long. Jackson frequently pushed the button on his radio to catch messages coming through the headset.

She stood and took a water bottle from the mini-fridge, turning to the doctor. "Water?"

"Thanks."

She handed the bottle to the doctor and took another for herself. The din of silence filled the room. Audrey massaged her neck, trying to release the migraine that had taken hold during McKenzie's conversation with Nancy.

"How are you doing, Audrey?" Dr. Taylor's face was lined with concern.

"Scared. I wish we could do something." She leaned forward and rested her head on her arms.

They sat in silence. Suddenly, Dr. Taylor slapped his water bottle onto the table and rubbed his palms on his jeans. Audrey watched him, curious.

"I've been here before."

She straightened. "At the Sheriff's office?"

"On the edge." He turned, looking at her intently. "I was in the kitchen, getting a soda. My mom was out shopping, my dad was at work."

"Go on." She knit her brows, listening.

"I heard knocking upstairs, but I figured my brother was just being demanding, and I wanted to play basketball." His eyes filled with tears. He blinked, rapidly. "He was trying to get help. We thought he had the flu. I ignored the noise and went outside.

"Later, I went upstairs. He was on the bathroom floor, unconscious. Mom and Dad rushed home and we took him to the hospital. They diagnosed him, but it was too late."

Audrey felt her face flush, yet her hands felt cold. "I'm so sorry."

"He was nine. I was fourteen."

The roar of silence returned. For a long time, they sat in its deafening waves.

CHAPTER FIFTY-TWO

Negotiator Jackson rushed inside. "The subject is apprehended. Let's go! Let's go!"

Audrey's heart pounded as they dashed out to the patrol car. Nancy was already in the back seat, Elliot in the passenger seat. Audrey and the doctor scrambled in beside Nancy. Negotiator Jackson sped to the Command Center.

Rodriguez's patrol car stood by the Visitors Center, Rodriguez standing beside it. Another patrol car waited, lights flashing, beside a massive SWAT tactical vehicle in the center of the parking lot. A muscular, bald man in uniform stood by the patrol car's rear door, hands on hips. He watched them as Negotiator Jackson parked by Rodriguez's car.

Negotiator Jackson got out. By the tactical vehicle, the SWAT member opened the patrol car's door. McKenzie, handcuffed, stepped out. A younger, heavily armed SWAT operative stepped out of the passenger's seat and joined McKenzie on his other side.

McKenzie's drooping shoulders and curved upper back hinted a bitter old age. His clothes, filthy and torn, hung on his lean frame. His untrimmed hair fell across his eyes, and a red scrape blazed through the days-old stubble on his jaw.

Negotiator Jackson approached the car. "Dr. McKenzie, I'm Negotiator Jackson. Glad to see this situation resolved without harm to anyone."

McKenzie laughed shortly. "You people need a course in communication. What a mess!"

The totality of his denial horrified Audrey.

"I'll be in touch as we go through the legal process. Have a good day, Dr. McKenzie." Jackson strolled away from the car, as unstressed as a weekend golfer.

The younger officer directed McKenzie back to his seat in the patrol car, then returned to the car's passenger seat. The other SWAT officer remained by the tactical vehicle. The car reversed and pulled away. As it left, Audrey glimpsed McKenzie, looking at Nancy through the window, his mouth downturned. His handcuffs flashed in the low sun, as he grasped at the glass.

~

Involuntarily, Audrey stepped forward as a second patrol car tore into the parking lot and lurched to a stop beside the ambulance. Nancy ran towards it. Audrey followed, Dr. Taylor beside her.

"Step back, please." The SWAT operative raised his hand. "Don't crowd them."

SWAT officers lifted Warwick from the patrol car. His head flopped on their arms, but his eyes were open. The TEMS staff lowered a gurney from the ambulance, and the SWAT officers placed Warwick onto it.

Dr. Taylor waved his hand. "I'm the patient's endocrinologist. Let me check his blood sugar, please."

The SWAT operative nodded. "Dr. Taylor, I'm Commander Starnes. Go ahead and approach the patient. The others may see him, too." He strolled to the patrol car.

Audrey followed Dr. Taylor and Nancy to the gurney. Yanking up his own shirt, the doctor pulled a blood glucose meter and test strips from a hidden belt. He swiped Warwick's finger, clicked the lancet, and waited for the meter's output.

"Two thirty-one." He stepped back and rested his hands on the gurney. His shoulders sagged, and he briefly dropped his head. "Good for now." He pulled a small packet from his pocket. "Eat these glucose tabs, Warwick." Warwick took them and chewed.

Nancy stepped close and put her hand on Warwick's forehead. "My baby! Forgive me." she repeated, tearfully. Warwick looked at her, silent.

"They need to get your son to the hospital." Negotiator Jackson directed Nancy away from the ambulance. "Would you like to accompany him, or should Dr. Taylor?"

"His doctor should be with him."

The paramedics loaded the gurney into the ambulance. Dr. Taylor climbed in beside Warwick.

Audrey moved close to the rear door. "Dr. Taylor, do you always carry an extra meter?"

"It's mine." His intense eyes turned to Warwick, and the paramedic swung the door shut. The ambulance siren blurted to a wail as the vehicle sped away along the road through the meadow, lights flashing.

CHAPTER FIFTY-THREE

Audrey stared at the retreating ambulance, stunned. Dr. Taylor had type 1 diabetes? She had never heard him complain. Except for the meter, she still wouldn't know.

Nancy got into the patrol car with Negotiator Jackson.

"Do you want a ride?" Jackson asked Audrey.

"I'll walk." She needed time alone. She strolled out of the parking lot towards the meadow driveway, planning to walk to the Sheriff's office and retrieve her car. From there, she'd go to the hospital, calling Dominique on the way to check on Easton and Lillie.

As she walked, she remembered Dr. Taylor at the deposition, dismissive at first, then anxious to know why she was panicking. Bringing her water during Warwick's pump training. Helping the kids climb onto the catamaran's salon roof. His polite conversation on their date, followed by a respectful goodbye when she'd exploded at him.

Always, he'd been fighting his own monster—his own type 1 diabetes. How many times had he dealt with a high or low blood sugar, and she'd never known?

Deer browsed the brown grasses and shrubs to her right. The evening sun lit the scene in tans and yellows. Tires swished behind her, and she moved onto the hard dirt path beside the road. Officer Rodriguez drew up in the patrol car. His window slid down.

"Sure you don't want a ride?"

It was getting late, and she rethought her walking plan. "Actually, I would, thanks!" She hurried to the passenger side and jumped in.

Officer Rodriguez was quiet, and Audrey's thoughts returned to Dr. Taylor, lingering on their disastrous date—and suddenly her condemning comment shot through her mind: *"You doctors should try living with your patients' condition for a day or two!"*

Her mouth opened in horror, and she curled forward, hugging her stomach, moaning. "Oh, God!" Oblivious to Officer Rodriguez's presence, she sobbed aloud. When she regained control, they were at the main stoplight in Felton. Suddenly self-conscious, she wiped her eyes on her sleeve. "I'm sorry! I guess everything got to me." She would process the real reason for her tears later, alone in Luke's car.

"Hey, I get it." Rodriguez handed her a tissue and eased the car forward.

Soon, Audrey was driving over Highway 17 towards California Oaks Hospital.

~

In the ICU waiting room, she took a seat.

Nancy sat nearby, hunched over. She glanced at Audrey. "Warwick's doing fine," she said, almost in a whisper.

Audrey heard shoes squeaking on the linoleum. Nurse Jenny swept into the room, carrying a clipboard, a pen tucked behind her ear. "Audrey! Great to see you."

Audrey stood and hugged Jenny. She hadn't seen the nurse since Nancy took custody. The tightness in her throat surprised her.

"Warwick is stable. Nancy probably told you already." Jenny touched Nancy's shoulder. Nancy looked at Jenny with the gratitude and trust of a rescued swimmer looking at a lifeguard.

"Dr. Taylor has him set up on the monitor." Jenny glanced at an app on her phone. "His blood sugar is 150. We're giving him glucose, since we can't know how much insulin he has on board."

Audrey sighed deeply and returned to her seat.

Jenny patted her shoulder. "It's been a long day for you, huh?" She tipped her head, her brow furrowed and her usually sparkly blue eyes serious.

"Yeah. Thank you so much, Jenny, for helping us. It was kind of you to come in."

Jenny nodded. "Of course! Dr. Taylor will be in to chat soon." She left, her shoes squeaking out her itinerary.

Dr. Taylor's footsteps approached, and Audrey fought the familiar need to vanish.

~

The doctor still wore casual sailing clothes. His face was etched with fatigue. "I'm sure Jenny told you Warwick is stable." He nodded to Nancy and grasped Audrey's hand warmly. "My partner, Dr. Fisk, is taking it from here."

He sat heavily in the chair next to Audrey. "What a day." He leaned onto his elbows and rubbed his eyes, forsaking his professional demeanor. Audrey glanced at her phone. It was after eight. She was exhausted. She hadn't eaten all day. Dr. Taylor and Nancy hadn't, either.

"Is Warwick sleeping? Maybe we should get dinner." Easton and Lillie were staying with Dominique overnight.

Dr. Taylor nodded. "He needs rest. There's a diner down the street."

"I'll stay here." Nancy rubbed her eyes.

Audrey stood. "What can we bring you, Nancy?"

Nancy frowned. "I don't know. Anything's fine."

Audrey chuckled softly. "I feel you." The new peace characterizing their interactions felt like a fresh breeze. Nancy managed a smile.

CHAPTER FIFTY-FOUR

The diner was cozy, with warm lighting from huge globe lamps suspended over the tables. The booth benches were padded in turquoise and edged with chrome. An Elvis recording played softly.

"Dr. Taylor, how are you?" The grey-haired waitress's greeting suggested the doctor frequented the diner.

"Sandy, this is Audrey."

"Well, hi, Audrey! Make yourselves at home."

Audrey and Dr. Taylor followed Sandy past an elderly couple, to a booth in the corner. Sandy handed menus to Dr. Taylor and left. Dr. Taylor gestured for Audrey to sit first. She scooted onto the soft seat. Dr. Taylor sat opposite her and handed her a menu. She stared at the menu, overwhelmed by the selection. Sandy returned, notepad ready.

"I'll take the country fried steak." Top right. Whatever.

Sandy turned to Dr. Taylor. "Do you want your usual?"

He nodded and handed her the menus. "Thanks, Sandy."

"You bet!" She took their order to the pass-through.

"I guess you know my secret, so I won't be discreet." Dr. Taylor pulled out his meter. He set a test strip in the device, clicked a lancet against his finger, and touched the red droplet to the strip.

Tears pricked Audrey's eyes. She leaned forward. "Dr. Taylor, I'm so sorry for my unkindness on our date. You did not deserve that. And Meghan told me you settled her case. I was wrong to judge you."

He laughed. "Oh, Audrey, forget it." He checked the meter, then set it aside and reached across the table to grasp her hands. "Audrey Beach, you don't realize how important you are. You're the strongest, most courageous woman I've ever known. I've respected you since the day you told me you were caring for your brother's children.

"Your words were a catalyst—if strongly delivered." He leaned back, releasing her hands and studying her, his eyes soft. He spoke quietly. "The guilt was killing me. Everyone said my brother's death wasn't my fault. The truth was, I could have saved him, but I put myself first. Facing my failure with Meghan Patel helped me confront my role in my brother's death. I'm forgiven."

"Dr. Taylor—" she began, but he took her hands again.

"Please stop calling me that. I'm Eric—a man whose selfishness killed his brother."

"Eric. I'm Audrey—a woman who can't keep the standards she sets for others."

The arpeggiated chords of an Elvis song began. The singer's haunting voice filled the diner.

Wise men say only fools rush in

But I can't help falling in love with you.

Eric leaned back and smiled. "I've always loved this song."

CHAPTER FIFTY-FIVE

The next evening, Audrey updated Luke by phone.

"I fasted and prayed all day yesterday," Luke exclaimed, rapidly. "Couldn't do anything else."

"God knew, didn't He?"

"He always knows. And He cares."

Audrey had stayed at the hospital with Eric and Nancy until Warwick was released at seven that morning. She and Eric had watched Nancy drive out of the parking lot with Warwick.

Eric walked Audrey to her car. "Warwick's in better hands now."

Audrey agreed. Nancy had learned everything she could about Warwick's condition.

Fatigue caught up with Audrey. Her last thought before falling asleep was how wonderful it was that she could bring all three children to visit Luke the next day.

~

"Audrey, come in!" Nancy yanked open the kitchen door late Saturday morning. Her face was freshly washed, and she'd braided her hair. The corners of her eyes crinkled as she greeted Audrey.

Inside, Audrey heard Warwick's electronic toy phone from the living room. *"Call your friend!"*

"Uh, Friend? This is Warwick. How's your blood sugar? Mine's normaaaaaal!" Warwick's voice ran through a series of exaggerated inflections, ending with a high-pitched squeak.

"The kitchen looks cute, Nancy!" A rustic tablecloth lay on the table. The counters were cleared, the floor was swept, and a vase of flowers stood on the windowsill.

Nancy sat at the table, gesturing for Audrey to join her. Warwick ran in and hugged Audrey. He skipped back into the living room and returned, carrying Bella. He plunked the dog in Audrey's lap and stroked her fur. "You chewed the duct tape, didn't you, Bella?"

Audrey looked at Nancy. "She did what?"

Nancy laughed. "McKenzie restrained us with duct tape. Bella chewed us free."

Audrey closed her eyes, bent over the dog, and held her close, her throat tight. Bella wiggled, and Audrey handed her to Warwick. "She should get a big steak."

Nancy laughed. "She had one."

Audrey smiled. "You're different."

"Can you feel it? I keep thinking new thoughts and doing new stuff. Like, I never cared how the kitchen looked, but I found this tablecloth in the shed. Then, I thought flowers would be awesome—and this happened!" She made a sweeping gesture to include the whole kitchen.

"Fantastic!"

Nancy leaned forward. She lowered her voice, glancing toward the living room. "I finally think I can do this mom thing. When—"

"Mommy, why did you leave?" Warwick stood in the doorway.

Kids and their questions! For the second time in that kitchen, adrenaline shot through Audrey. But Nancy got up and went to her son. Kneeling in front of him, she gently took his hands. "Warwick, I'm so sorry I left. I told myself it was necessary, so I could learn to be a better mommy. But really, I was being selfish. I didn't want to face the ways I was failing you. I put myself first, and I ended up hurting everyone." She paused and swiped away a tear.

Warwick tipped his head. "Hm."

"I thought God was mad at me. But when I told Jesus about it, I knew He loved me. He'd been waiting for me to ask for help, the whole time." Tenderly, Nancy stroked her son's curls. "I have asked Him, Warwick. And He is helping me. I won't leave again. I promise."

Warwick raised a finger. "Good, Mommy. I have to go potty." He skipped away to the bathroom.

Nancy shrugged, laughing. "Priorities!"

Audrey laughed through her tears. "That was beautiful, Nancy. I'm glad you're back."

Nancy returned to her chair. "Warwick's diabetes scares me. Can I call you sometimes, for help?"

"Absolutely."

Nancy frowned and looked at her hands, then at Audrey. "I was wrong to call you incompetent, after all you did. To just come back and kick you out. I'm sorry. I want to do better."

"It's all forgiven." Audrey paused. "Can I suggest something?"

"Go ahead—please!" Nancy's look was open and sincere.

"Maybe you could take some parenting classes at a church. There are also recovery groups you might find helpful."

Nancy nodded immediately. "I was thinking about finding classes somewhere."

An engine roared in the driveway. Warwick ran from the living room, and Nancy opened the kitchen door. "Do you know someone who drives a Jeep?"

"Swift!" Audrey joined Nancy.

"Easton's band teacher? I forgot all about him!"

"He's a friend of Dominique's." Audrey was as surprised as Nancy. They watched Swift step out and open the passenger door. Dominique hopped down—Swift supporting her waist. Easton and Lillie scrambled from the back seat.

Lillie ran to the cabin. "Mommy! We got to ride in Swift's Jeep!" She ran up the steps and grabbed Nancy's arm.

Easton strolled to the door beside Swift. Dominique walked on Swift's other side, Swift holding her hand.

"But you see, my band teacher was a total drill sergeant," Swift was saying, glancing down at Easton.

Dominique laughed with Easton. "Audrey! How are you doing?" She waved as they reached the door.

Nancy invited them in, and they went to the living room while Warwick joined his siblings to play outside. Dominique settled on the couch, next to Swift. Audrey sat in an armchair.

"Nice to see you again, Swift." Nancy handed out steaming mugs of coffee and sat in the other armchair. "Thank you for taking the kids, Dominique. It was good knowing they were cared for while we were freaking out."

"I'm so relieved everything worked out. We prayed a lot!" Dominique said.

Nancy told Swift and Dominique the details of Warwick's rescue.

"That's crazy." Swift bent forward, elbows on his knees, staring at the carpet. He grabbed Dominique's hand and held it tightly. For once, there was no hint of humor on his lips.

"I talked to Luke." Audrey shelved her curiosity about Swift and Dominique. "He felt compelled to fast and pray all day Thursday."

"God was in control the whole time. We forget that, don't we, when we're in the middle of a crisis?" said Dominique.

"I'm just learning it." Nancy's eyes filled with tears. "I hope I never forget."

Looking at Swift and Dominique, Audrey addressed the obvious. "You two are pretty cozy. What happened?"

Swift looked down at Dominique and smiled. Dominique blushed.

"Well, I—" Dominique began.

"We just—" Swift said, at the same time.

Everyone laughed.

"Why don't you tell them, Min?" Swift suggested.

Dominique closed her eyes and drew a deep breath. "When I picked up the kids from the Sheriff's Office, I was so worried. My parents were in Florida looking at homes. The only person I could think to call was Swift. I wanted him with me. I knew he'd drop everything, no hesitation." She stopped suddenly and wiped her eyes.

Swift put his arm around her shoulders. "So, she called me. I was hiking up to the Lime Kilns in Felton. I ran to the parking lot and drove to her house."

"He came right away, just like I knew he would. And he got the kids distracted and laughing. He had binoculars, and they looked for birds behind the house."

Audrey was puzzled. Had Dominique's concerns been resolved? She saw her silent question reflected in the coach's eyes.

"He's moving to Florida," Dominique gushed, "to set up a band program for at-risk youth."

"That's great!" Audrey was thrilled.

Swift dipped his head, agreeing. "I've always been interested in serving youth. Never had the courage to dive in. Dominique's announcement about Florida wrecked me." He paused, looking into Dominique's eyes for a long moment. "I did some research, and this program just fell into my lap. I applied and got an answer almost immediately. I may eventually lead the whole organization."

"Swift is the best thing that ever happened to me." Dominique snuggled next to him, lacing her fingers through his.

"I had to follow her. Couldn't help it. And it seemed like God opened the doors."

"That's awesome!" Audrey's voice came in a squeak. "I knew you belonged together."

Dominique flapped a hand. "Aw, go ahead. Say 'I told you so'!"

They all laughed, and Swift gave Dominique a fierce bear hug.

Audrey's phone buzzed, and she glanced down to see a text from Eric. "Audrey, it's a beautiful day. May I take you sailing, after your visit with Luke?"

Audrey's stomach jumped. "I'd love that," she answered.

CHAPTER FIFTY-SIX

Monterey Bay was a dark, rippling plain before Audrey. Dazzling light sparkled in a wide, white path below the sun. Eric's Flying Scot slipped through the water, away from the mountains that cradled the bay. Her bow churned up lacy white patterns as she dipped and splashed. A spray cooled Audrey's skin. The wind fluttered, tossing her hair against her neck.

Eric leaned back on the lengthwise seat and pulled a rope. The billowing sail above Audrey snapped tight into the wind, and the little boat zipped forward along a curved trajectory.

"Lean starboard, Audrey!" Eric looked at her, grinning.

She scooted closer to him, and they leaned back, watching the boat's port side dip towards the water. Soon, the boat straightened, and Eric held her steady. The vessel swished through the water. The steep, triangular sails of other sailboats tilted in the wind around them.

A flock of dark birds skimmed the ocean surface—sharp, angular silhouettes against fluid blues and greys. Beyond, people walked the beach, dogs ran. Further back stood homes and trees, and further still, the Santa Cruz Mountains.

"Have you missed sailing?" Eric asked.

"I hadn't thought about it, but I'd say I have." Audrey inhaled the sea air. "I love the ocean."

Far out in the bay, a spray of foam shot up. Audrey

looked closely. Again, a big splash, this one further left. She pointed. "Whales!"

Two humpbacks soared from the water. Their massive grey bulks arced, their flexible fins extended like clowns' arms. They twisted and crashed back into the ocean, their angular tail flukes rotating through wide up sprays.

"Humpbacks!" Eric exclaimed.

"How cool is that!" Audrey yelled.

Light clouds feathered the horizon, lit to fiery reds and oranges by the setting sun. The sea reflected the rich colors. Around the mountains, the sky darkened to navy.

"It's getting late. Want to get dinner?" Eric turned the boat towards the harbor.

"Sure!"

~

Candlelight glowed again across Eric's features. Audrey unfolded her napkin and set it on her lap. Outside, the moon had risen, casting a new, softer path across the ocean.

Eric poured water into Audrey's glass. "I thought we should rewrite this episode. Same restaurant, different ending."

They chuckled. The waiter brought the standard bowls of clam chowder and basket of warm bread.

"I memorized a verse last night." Eric passed the bread to Audrey.

Audrey raised her eyebrows. "Want to tell me?"

He smiled briefly. "'They that go down to the sea in ships, that do…'" He paused, frowning, and closed his eyes. "Hang on. I'll get it."

Audrey waited.

"'That do business in great waters; these see the works of the Lord, and His wonders in the deep.'" Eric opened his eyes. "Psalm 107."

Audrey stirred her soup, then set down her spoon. "'Wonders in the deep.' Have we ever seen those."

"The wonder is, God freed me from a lifetime of guilt

and regret."

"And I'm free from judging others and proving myself. Nothing matters more than loving God and the people around us."

"Let's pray." Eric took Audrey's hand. As before, his grasp was unhesitating and firm. But now, she returned the strength of his grip.

"Dear Lord, how could we ever thank you enough?" Eric prayed. "We asked for Warwick's safe return, and You delivered him from evil. We asked for help, and You gave us new life."

They dug into the clam chowder and warm bread, sipping cold water. Audrey was hungry. It felt good to eat in the warm light of trust.

~

Sailing and dinner didn't seem enough time together, so they walked the beach in the moonlight, hand in hand. The water sloshed and hissed against an outcropping of rocks. Eric paused. "Audrey, let's be real. I'd like to ask you something." He raised his eyebrows, questioning.

He's kneeling! Adrenaline raced through her arms and legs. A light wind ruffled his hair, moonlight shone on the serious lines of his face. He took Audrey's hand and closed his eyes, then looked up at her.

"Marry me?"

Tears slipped down her cheeks.

CHAPTER FIFTY-SEVEN

Audrey looked in the mirror and smoothed the lacy front of her mermaid-style gown. Her veil cascaded to the floor behind her. She'd had the dress taken in twice. Planning a wedding, it turned out, was about as stressful as being guardian of your brother's kids. She studied her reflection. A year ago, she'd never have believed she would be wearing a wedding dress on Christmas Eve, about to marry the doctor she was suing.

"Ready?" Dominique stepped behind her, squeezing Audrey's arms and giving a little squeal of excitement.

Audrey nodded. "One hundred percent."

Swathed in a dress of crimson satin, Dominique was the perfect Christmas Maid of Honor. A simple green wreath crowned her dark hair. The Florida sunshine had colored her face a rich tan. Nancy, Audrey's bridesmaid, wore the same as Dominique, her blond tresses flowing down her back.

Dominique crossed the plank floor of the little Roaring Camp Historic Schoolhouse and opened the door. The path to the barn—Berte Hart Hall—glistened from a late afternoon rain. Sunlight streamed through the parting clouds over the bordering forest, raising a mist from the wet lawns.

Audrey took a deep breath and stepped outside, carrying a lush bouquet of Christmas roses. Dominique and Nancy followed her. Dominique gathered up the dress's train and veil to protect them from the damp.

Two brightly lit Christmas trees framed the barn's front door. Beside the door, Dr. Fisk greeted them in a whisper. "Guests are all here."

Lillie, dressed in a dainty frock and holding a basket of red rose petals, waited beside him. Warwick clawed at his crimson bow tie, carrying a little green ring cushion in his other hand.

Lillie pulled his hand away from his neck. "Leave it alone!" she hissed.

Dominique and Nancy slipped into the barn. Audrey heard the light flourishes of a flute skip above rhythmic strings as they walked in to a Mozart quartet.

Warwick went next, carrying the ring cushion. He glanced back at Audrey and gave her a quick wink before disappearing through the doorway.

Dr. Fisk guffawed, then clapped a hand over his mouth. "Sorry!"

Lillie followed Warwick solemnly through the entrance. Audrey glimpsed her niece's hand flick petals from the basket. One settled on the threshold—a bright drop of red on the border of the damask aisle runner.

The flute music faded, and for a brief moment silence fell. Dr. Fisk took her arm and gestured towards the barn entrance. "This way, dear!"

Audrey smiled and nodded, her stomach in knots. Trembling, she stepped towards the entrance. Arpeggiated piano chords and the soft rustle of drums filled the barn.

Wise men say only fools rush in
But I can't help falling in love with you.

She walked through the doorway, Dr. Fisk a reassuring presence at her side. Twinkling lights brightened the rafters, and wrought-iron chandeliers cast a warm glow over the rustic room. Bright poinsettias lined her path to the altar. Chairs, decked out with silver Christmas bows, bordered the aisle. The guests rose to greet her.

Like a river flows surely to the sea

Darling, so it goes. Some things are meant to be.

At the end of the aisle, on a raised platform framed by an arch hung with Christmas ornaments, stood Swift, Luke, and Easton, all wearing the same charcoal-grey suits as little Warwick, who stood close to his father. On the other side, Dominique, Nancy, and Lillie watched Audrey, their eyes bright with tears. The minister, holding a Bible, tipped his head and watched her approach, smiling warmly.

Hands folded, Eric held her gaze, his blue eyes filled with tenderness and joy.

Take my hand, take my whole life, too
For I can't help falling in love with you.

~

During the reception dinner, Audrey and Eric visited each table. It took over an hour. They had guests from Audrey's college days, the gymnastics club, Eric's practice, and both their extended families. The Patels, Jenny and David, and Dr. and Mrs. Fisk shared a table near the front of the room.

"Let me see!" Meghan grabbed Audrey's left hand and gazed at her ring. She looked up at Audrey, eyes shining. "I love the square diamond!"

Audrey nodded. "I knew this was my ring the minute I saw it!" She rested her hand on the back of Meghan's chair. "Is Carson coming back for the next camp, Meghan?" Meghan and Carson had co-led the horse programs for the summer sessions of Camp Strong 'n Free.

Meghan giggled. "Absolutely. He's helping his dad on the ranch, but he'll be out in June."

Nurse Jenny sipped sparkling water from a glass. "We all thought you made a great team working on the horse program. I was hoping we'd see more of Carson."

"So were we." A light sheen glowed on Beverly's full, made-up cheeks. Meghan grinned and blushed.

Anish Patel nodded and chuckled. "Good man."

"Are you all ready for your trip, Jenny?" asked Eric.

"Just about. We got our passports a few days ago." She laughed and glanced at David. "We're super excited."

"Lifelong dream for Jenny, going to New Zealand." David swirled the juice in his glass and raised it to Jenny. "Happy wife, happy life!" They all laughed.

"Wash your hands," advised Dr. Fisk. "There's a weird virus going around."

Audrey and Eric moved to the next table, where Eric's parents and Audrey's mom sat with some extended family members. Mr. and Mrs. Taylor had flown in from Michigan, and Audrey's mom had driven from Texas in her ancient Camry.

"Eric, glad to have you as my new son." Audrey's mom rested her polished fingertips on Eric's sleeve. "Take good care of her."

"I promise." Eric straightened and looked thoughtful. "Would you like to be closer, so you can make sure I do?"

"What do you mean?"

"Audrey and I closed on a property in the mountains here. It has a granny unit in the back, and you'd be welcome to live there. We would love nothing more."

"It's really cute, Mom. Flower garden, view of the ocean. You'd love it!"

Audrey's mom's chin trembled, and her pale blue eyes grew red. "I'd be close to the grandchildren—" she broke off and pulled a tissue from the battered purse that hung over the back of her chair.

Audrey turned to Eric. "I think that's a yes."

Mrs. Taylor smiled at her son. "You've always been so considerate and generous, Eric. We're proud of you. And Audrey, we're so glad to have you join our family. What you've done here is amazing."

Audrey smiled her appreciation but wondered what Eric's mother meant. The wedding décor? The marriage?

Eric leaned close and whispered. "She means you're awesome."

Mr. Taylor leaned back and rested an arm across the back of his wife's chair, gazing at his son. He nodded, shifting his gaze to Audrey. "Welcome."

Audrey and Eric returned to the head table. They sat next to Dominique and Swift. Dominique shivered and pulled a wrap around her shoulders. "I'm not used to this weather!"

"Got spoiled in Florida, huh?" Eric started a piece of warm apple pie.

Swift laughed. "Long afternoons at the beach, snorkeling—even alligator wrestling for the adrenaline junkies!"

"So you're glad you followed Dominique?" Audrey raised an eyebrow.

Swift grinned and put his arm around Dominique's shoulders. "I'd have followed her anywhere." The grey suit fit his strong shoulders perfectly and elevated his tan face and gentle smile to movie-star heights. His neat haircut gave him a new seriousness, but the real change was the confident resolve that shone in his eyes.

Dominique snuggled her head against Swift's shoulder, twisting her engagement ring around her finger. "Glad you did."

Audrey glanced at Swift again. *Going places.*

Luke and Nancy sat across the table from Eric and Audrey, the children seated between them.

Easton leaned close to his father and shielded his mouth with his hand. "Daddy, are you coming home soon?"

Luke rested a hand on his son's shoulder. "Soon. When Mommy and I have worked through some issues."

Clouds filled the evening sky. Audrey and Eric and their guests finished eating. The dance music started, and Audrey and Eric swayed through their bride-and-groom dance. The song ended, a new one began, and guests filled the dance floor.

A storm blew in over the mountains. Rain drummed on the barn roof. Eric and Audrey walked to the barn door. Eric looped his arms around Audrey's waist, pulling her close. She leaned back against the broad strength of his chest. Behind them, the hall glowed in Christmas golds, reds, and greens. Energized by the music, their friends and family danced and laughed.

Outside, darkness gathered. The rain slanted across the lawns and the wind beat down savagely on the forest, whipping the branches.

THE END

A single mother for twenty years, Columba Booth has a passion for the healing of families. The characters in her stories struggle with destructive issues that undermine family relationships. Often, their choices make things worse. Is faith in God enough to overcome it all?

Columba is now happily married to Paul, who laughs at her jokes and enables her book addiction.

www.ingramcontent.com/pod-product-compliance
Lightning Source LLC
Chambersburg PA
CBHW071344300726